Paragon

ELEANOR ROSE
AUGUST OLIVER
CHASE ST. CLARE

Finch Benson
Publishing

Copyright © 2024 by Eleanor Rose, Chase St. Clare, and August Oliver
All rights reserved

The characters and events portrayed in this book are fictitious. Any similarity to real persons, living or dead, is coincidental and not intended by the author.

No part of this book may be reproduced, or stored in a retrieval system, or transmitted in any form or by any means, electronic, mechanical, photocopying, recording, or otherwise, without express written permission of the publisher.

Cover design by: Chase St. Clare
Publisher: Finch Benson
Printed in the United States of America

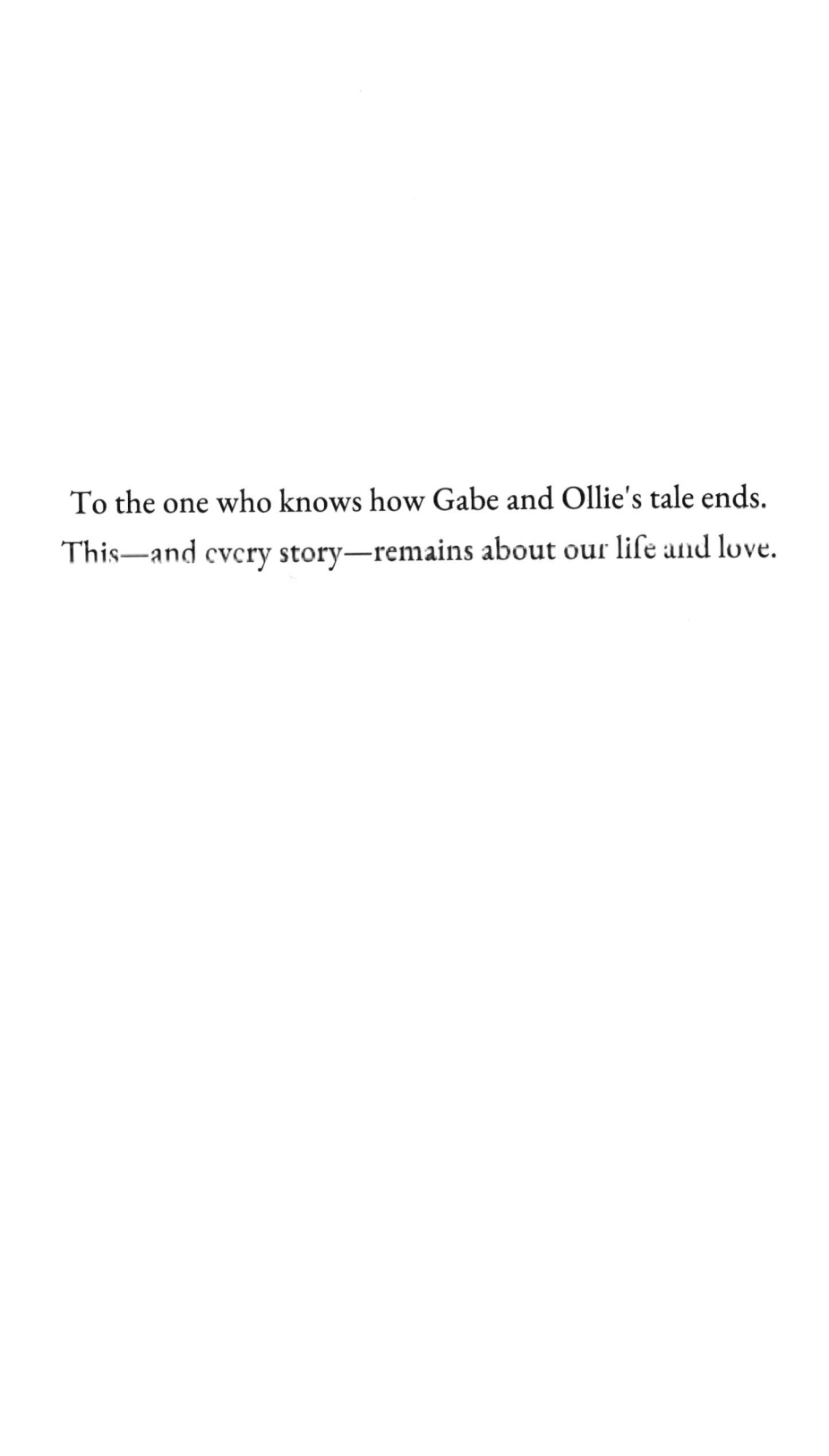

To the one who knows how Gabe and Ollie's tale ends. This—and every story—remains about our life and love.

Table of Contents

Chapter One 1

Chapter Two 16

Chapter Three 26

Chapter Four 33

Chapter Five 40

Chapter Six 46

Chapter Seven 55

Chapter Eight 69

Chapter Nine 82

Chapter Ten 95

Chapter Eleven 104

Chapter Twelve 113

Chapter Thirteen 117

Chapter Fourteen 124

Chapter Fifteen 132

Chapter Sixteen 153

Chapter Seventeen 163

Chapter Eighteen 174

Chapter Nineteen 185

Chapter Twenty 202

Chapter Twenty One 215

Chapter Twenty Two 225

Chapter Twenty Three 231

Chapter Twenty Four 236

Chapter Twenty Five..243

Chapter Twenty Six 247

Chapter Twenty Seven..252

Chapter Twenty Eight 259

Chapter Twenty Nine 264

Chapter Thirty..276

Chapter Thirty One 282

Chapter Thirty Two..287

Chapter Thirty Three...290

Chapter Thirty Four 294

Chapter Thirty Five..298

Gryfian 303

Acknowledgements 321

About the Authors 322

Hyxelon

Jouraya

PYVIERAL FALLS

ROYAL FOREST

SEFAERAN CAPITAL CITY

PRUMIUS

SCAN THE CODE IN YOUR SPOTIFY APP TO ACCESS THE OFFICIAL OLLIE AND GABE APPROVED PLAYLIST FOR:

Paragon

Chapter One
Gabriel

I had no idea how I was supposed to ever adjust to wearing clothes again after experiencing how free it was to be naked around the clock.

I sat on the teal blue sand by the shoreline, something Ollie had attributed to some kind of algae or something, and watched the milky white waves wash in and out. This year had been the best of my life, and as excited as I was to find out what being a royal would be like, I was dreading having to share *King Olympio's* attention with anyone.

"I can feel your melancholy, you know."

His voice came from behind me, though I'd felt him approaching through the bond even before he spoke. It was wild how much of what he experienced I could share, and even a year later, I still wasn't really used to it.

I shifted so he could drop down beside me, unfathomably having chosen to actually put clothes on. "Nah. You're just feeling the sand burn on my balls that I'm not sure will ever go away." I shoved him, then leaned in and kissed his freckled shoulder. We'd sat on more than a few beaches naked—did other unspeakable things on the others.

Ollie grinned and put his arm around my waist, pulling me close and pressing his nose against mine. "Are you telling me you wish we hadn't spent so much time in the sand?" His voice was a low purr, challenging, teasing, and caressing me all at the same time.

"Well..." I pulled away from him, stood, and stretched, slowly backing away. "It was pretty good." I turned to look over my shoulder for the exact distance between me and the "water" and skipped backwards a few steps. "Whenever I got bored, I'd just think of Alex Kessing—"

In a swirl of darkness, Ollie was gone, and a massive shadow demon appeared, surrounding me. His wings wrapped around us, and his smoke-like hand gripped my throat just tight enough to have me gasping for a reason *other* than a lack of oxygen.

"Bite... your... tongue." I'd seen his demon form a number of times on our adjournment, but the change in his voice never failed to send a chill down my spine. It was gravelly and unfathomably deep, like something out of a horror movie.

"I'd..." My voice wavered with a hint of fear, despite knowing this was Olympio. *My Olympio.* "I'd rather you bite it for me. Er—well, maybe not *you*, but—well, you know what I mean."

The monster's hand tightened, and then it's face turned into something that looked akin to a maniacal smile.

"You know, if I didn't know better," I said breathlessly, "I'd think scaring me takes you to bonerville, you sick fuck." I was pushing the limits, I knew, but that was part of the fun.

A guttural chuckle quickly morphed into the beautiful voice I'd come to know better than any other sound in the world as Ollie resumed his human-like form, with the shining copper hair, tanned and freckled skin, and violet eyes that matched my own, thanks to the magic of the soulmate bond.

"Perhaps," he said, grinning and pulling me closer by the hand still wrapped around my throat. "Or maybe I'm just hoping that someday I'll scare that name right out of your vocabulary."

"What name?" I asked, pressing into him with every fiber of my being. "I can't seem to remember a single one but yours."

I traced the fine lines of his collarbone with my lips, breathing him in like he was my substitute for oxygen. Even after being together twenty four hours a day for a whole year, I couldn't get enough. Sometimes I wondered if it was chemistry. Most times, I just assumed it was magic.

An unintended groan rippled out of me against the tan flesh, and I felt my cheeks sear.

Ollie's fingers softened, then trailed down the side of my neck before coming to rest on my upper arms, where he squeezed, making a small noise like a strained sigh—one I would know meant he felt the pull as much as I did.

"It's our last day. Don't you want to enjoy this beautiful place a little longer before we have to go back to our responsibilities?" he said, burying his lips in my hair, his words at odds with the way he touched me. "We can fuck and play shadow monster back in Sefaera."

But I wasn't having it. Every time he touched me, I became a live wire, and if I didn't quench the desire he'd now roused in me, I wouldn't be able to focus on anything else, anyway. "Which way back to the house—er—thing?"

He laughed and turned, pointing to the path through the trees that would lead to the place we'd been staying at for the last few weeks. "Straight through."

"'Bout the only thing straight here," I chuckled, taking off in the direction he'd indicated. This admission, something new for me to be saying aloud, was only now starting to be comfortable. It was shocking how much time I'd spent with Alex Kessinger's ding-dong in my mouth, only to turn around and loudly proclaim how "not gay" I was. But Ollie had spent this adjournment talking me through accepting who I was—without labels.

There was one night that we had been seconds from climaxing, and I had suddenly burst into tears.

"Oh, my god, Ollie. What if they're right? What if I'm going to hell for liking men?"

Olympio had stopped moving, a hell of a feat since we were propped up into a weird, sex swing type of contraption, and screwed up his face in a mix of horror and astoundment at my outburst.

"And what exactly would await you in that hell? A demon king and a world you've never seen before? Because if that's the case, I like to think you've gotten a reward rather than a punishment by finding 'hell.'"

I whimpered, my cock losing all arousal and tears emerging from my eyes like a sprinkler system had just kicked on. "But... but... Maybe I should just stick to girls, just in case."

I heard Ollie stop breathing, and, even though I couldn't see his face, I could feel the irritation in his muscles. "You are aware that I'm inside you right now, are you not?" he said, deadpanned. "I think, if you're worried about it, the damage is done."

I sniffled. "Yeah, I guess you're right. Wanna finish?"

He did not, in fact, want to finish, and we opted to go look for some wild fruit instead, exploring the land around our little shelter, which *still* took my breath away, even now, after a full year here.

When I first got to Sefaera, I was totally unprepared for the way it looked. Everything about it seemed magical, like something out of a fantasy video game. And if Sefaera was like that to the world I came from, this place, this little "pocket dimension" as Ollie called it, was Sefaera's version of fantasy.

Every color here was amplified, like being on psychedelics twenty four-seven. The blue-green of the sand, the purples, pinks, and oranges of the towering palm-like trees, even the golden color of the sky was unreal and yet *way* too real. Even after a full year of being here, I would usually wake up and just stare at the world around me in disbelief.

The sand we walked on was soft as cotton candy, even through the small rainforest that separated our lodgings from the beach. And I call it a rainforest, because as soon as we passed the treeline, every time, a heavy but soothing rain would start to come down on us, the water tingling in a pleasant way as it hit my skin.

As I passed under a branch with a colorful bird that would make a parrot look dull by comparison, it made a noise almost like a harp and flew in a circle around my head.

"Are you going to miss it?" Ollie asked, catching my eye as I smiled.

I stopped and turned around so I could look him dead on. "Why? Are *you* staying here forever?"

He grinned and walked slowly toward me, backing me up until I was pressed against a tree. "If I could, I would. But only if you did, too. I would never let you go anywhere that I couldn't follow, and even the most beautiful paradise would be nothing without you at my side."

I couldn't help but smile. "Funny," I breathed, wrapping my hand around the back of his neck and pulling him closer. "I was just about to say the same thing."

I was likely the only person in the history of ever to get away with manhandling the King of Sefaera, but waiting until we arrived back in the privacy of our shelter, especially when no one else existed in the entire world, was wearing on me.

I wanted him *now*.

I nipped at his lip, dropping my hand to be waist length to Ollie and slid it beneath his linen chiton. My arm immediately blossomed into goosebumps as I found my soulmate firm there.

"Ollie..."

His fingers closed around my wrist, and I thought he was going to pull me away, but he began to slowly guide me forward and back, stroking himself with my hand.

"Is this what you were hoping for, Gabriel?" he breathed against my mouth. "For me to be hard for you? To *need* your touch?" Suddenly, his other hand was palming my naked length as he gave an exaggerated gasp. "It seems so."

I had no idea how, but even after all this time, Ollie could pull a blush from me like a virgin. Granted, I had been before him, and I don't think I ever went crimson this much back then.

"Your Majesty..." I exhaled, springing to life in his hand.

"Your Grace," he said back before moving his lips to my jaw, then my neck... then my collarbone...

The heat of his mouth as he dropped to his knees to kiss up my thighs was so intense, I was surprised it didn't create steam as the cool rain continued to pour down on us. Finally, he reached my tip and took me slowly into his mouth, humming a noise of delight as he did.

"Ollie..." I moaned, my hands going to his sunset colored hair and gripping it tightly.

But he wasn't having that. He pulled away and grabbed my hands, then, faster than I was able to react, he removed the rope belt he wore, moved around the tree, and tied me up so that I was unable to move, completely at the mercy of the demon king.

"Is it tight enough?" he asked as he pulled the knot just a little tighter, creating an erotic ache in my wrists.

I felt my voice catch in my throat as I tried to say something witty. He could still surprise me with his prowess, making it very clear at all times that I was no fucking match.

I was born to serve the King of Sefaera, and if what he wanted was my body...

Well, I guess I could make that sacrifice.

"You had better take me to a bed to fuck me, because I'm not sure my ass can handle many more abrasive surfaces."

"Well, you should have thought of that before you teased me, Justice," he said, tugging one more time on the rope to punctuate his words. "Besides... in a few short hours, we'll be back in the palace, with all the soft mattresses you could hope for. And I'm certain Perla will attend to your ass when we get there, because I have no intention of holding back on our last opportunity to make love in paradise."

Then he was on his knees again before me, taking me deep, the way only someone with thousands of years of practice could do. His fingers trailed up my inner thigh, and I felt a slight pressure as he began to prod gently at my opening—not penetrating, just massaging, teasing the sensitive flesh there.

"Ffff..." I deflated like a kid's balloon at a party while the king of an entire world toyed with me like I was putty in his hands. Truth be told, I was. "Ollie..."

Olympio had grown fond of this game he'd thought up for himself that went a little something like this. He took me deep into his throat and breathed through his nose like a dragon. I was absolutely not allowed to thrust or pleasure myself at the expense of his mouth in any way, and all I could do was beg him for any tiny morsel of relief he would throw me. He'd been doing this for weeks, and I still hadn't decided if I liked it yet.

Today, it seemed, he had decided to combine it with his other favorite activity—making me beg to be penetrated. I was half tempted to fight against it, but I could already feel myself dripping into his mouth, and he hadn't even taken me as deep as he could yet.

At the exact same time, he pressed forward with his finger, and his lips wrapped around my base as he breached the tight ring to enter me just an inch. A slight movement on his part made me aware that he was stroking himself as he serviced me. He told me all the time that *nothing* gave him more pleasure than *my* pleasure, and I wouldn't have believed it if he didn't use every single time we fucked to prove it.

"Ollie..." I gasped. "Ollie, don't—"

He looked up at me through his lashes, somehow managing to smile even with his lips stretched wide, before he pulled back. "Why not?" he said before pressing a kiss to my inner thigh. "We have *hours* left before we go back to real life. Let me have you this way for as long as I can. We don't know when we'll have time like this again."

I pushed him back slightly with my knee, the anxiety that always seemed to come with this type of conversation threatening to steal my arousal. "But it's not gonna change *that* much, right? I mean—you're King. Doesn't whatever you say become the law?"

Olympio didn't stop teasing me, his palm surrounding the head of my cock and his thumb taking up position on my tip, making tiny circles that drew out long, dripping strings of pearly, viscous fluid. A soft exhale as he chuckled only centimeters from my length sent yet another shiver through me. "I would actually have to do my job *as* King to be able to pass laws as King. And, unfortunately, Typhir would be all too happy to use any excuse to call my rule into question. So while I fully intend to use every minute we have alone to pleasure you just like this, I'm well aware that we are about to lose our endless, uninterrupted, and paradisiacal time. So, please, Gabriel... let me enjoy just a bit longer like this, and please don't make me mention that name one more time before I absolutely have to."

"Who?" I said, a wicked idea churning in my head. "Typhir? Or perhaps you mean—"

"Don't."

"What?" I asked, grinning. "Don't say—"

In seconds I felt Olympio's hand clutching my throat like a vice as he stood, his shadowy wings flourishing out so wide they brushed several nearby trees. Then his thigh was parting my legs as he grabbed me behind one knee and hiked it up around his hip so he could press his stiffness against my cleft.

"Is that truly how you want to start forever together?" he growled, though I could see the slight smile as he played into the game, his tip running back and forth over the pucker of skin that was already throbbing for him. "With me fucking that name out of your mind one more time?"

Every hair on my body stood on end, and I panted, trying and failing to regain some sort of control.

"Yes, please."

Ollie unclipped a bottle of lubricant from his pack and sloppily coated his cock in it before thrusting deep inside me, his intent to do just what he'd promised clear as day.

With my arms tied tightly to the tree, holding me in place, he used the leverage to raise my other leg, forcing me to wrap it around him, leaving me suspended above the ground. The only things keeping me from falling were the silken rope on my wrists and Ollie's thick member driving deep into me.

"Then your wish is my command, Your Grace."

His lips were hot and hard on my skin, and as they reached the place where my shoulder met my neck, he bit down hard. The pain melded with pleasure in a way that had me screaming for him and dripping all over both of our stomachs.

Over the last year, Ollie and I had really developed a dynamic that was out of this world sexually. Like... literally. Usually anything we were doing would involve a lot of competing to see who could get the other more wound up and dying to burst. That was where I excelled. As the child of movie producers, I could really sell a plotline.

"Ol," I panted as he drove into me with purpose and passion.

"Hm?" he grunted into the crook of my neck.

"Imagine if we were at one of your nights out before me. You know—the ones where you took multiple people to bed?"

"Point, Gabriel?" He pulled back, and I watched his muscles ripple as he rhythmically stroked into me, more slow and agonizing than fast and furious.

"Imagine if—when we get back—if we brought a few girls to our room. You could watch them..." I paused to remember the exact phrasing he seemed to like. "Undo me."

He grinned in a wicked way, his fist wrapping around me to slide up and down in time with his own movements. "And, praytell, my dear soulmate, what exactly do you envision that would entail? As you well know, you would be the only one able to... partake of those particular delights. So, tell me about these women and how they would undo you." I could tell he was into the idea, his hand gripping tighter with every word, his thrusts becoming more intense.

I panicked for a moment, I hadn't really even considered details. Truth be told, I thought that would have pushed him over the edge, and we'd have a good laugh about it before a nap, then rinse and repeat until we had to leave. But he was clearly genuinely interested in this. I knew he'd missed female energy since Vassenia was... removed.

"Well, of course I'd be restrained. Much like this, in fact. Perhaps in a chair or on a bed. Their king would tell them exactly how to handle His Grace." I gyrated my hips against him as he groaned into my skin.

He drove his own hips forward and up hard, slamming me against the tree. "I think I rather enjoy that idea," he said, his fingertips digging into my skin as he held me in place, like I was made simply to pleasure His Majesty. But then he moaned, "My Gabriel... Moons and rivers, I need you."

"You have me, Olympio, my everything." My hands went to his perfect chest, and I raked my nails across his beautiful tan skin. "Take what you need. I was born for this."

"Indeed, you were," he purred, reaching around behind the tree and untying my hands. "Hold onto me. I'm not finished with you yet."

I wrapped my arms around his neck, his body cool and slick from the pouring rain, as he withdrew from me. I nearly complained until he readjusted his arms to make sure he had a good grip on me, and marched with purpose back to our lodgings.

The crystal dome was built to seem as if it sprung up out of nowhere, right at the base of a gorgeous waterfall and pool filled with colorful creatures that I supposed were something like fish.

Ollie walked right through the crystal as though it was made of air. The walls were not walls at all, rather a magical barrier that only we could enter or exit—not that it mattered, as we were completely and utterly alone here. He all but tossed me onto the massive bed in the center, which had an incredible view of the sky above.

But I didn't have long to appreciate the sight before he was on me, rolling onto his back so I was on top of him, straddling his hips.

"You know what to do," he said, gripping my thighs, his slick length arching needily against my ass.

If someone had told me that I'd spend my life fucking the most beautiful man I'd ever seen in a paradise that no one else could access, I'd have told you that one, I'm not gay, and two, what would someone like that ever want with me? But the way Ollie looked at me was like I was oxygen itself, and my body was his only means of inhaling it.

I paused only for a moment to look at him as I always did. Then I slid forward, allowing him back inside me, biting my lip at the pressure, then pleasure. I'd be returning with much stronger thighs and glutes, for sure, from a hundred million scenarios just like this one.

"You know," I breathed raggedly. "From this angle, a gorgeous girl could sit on your chest and get fucked by me."

Ollie moaned, his hips thrusting in time with my own to deepen the contact between us, his hand once more starting to stroke my own cock. "You're quite attached to this idea, aren't you?" he asked with a smirk.

"I'm attached to your attachment to it." I leaned forward and pressed a kiss to his neck. "I pay attention. I know what you li—" He began to shake against me, and I couldn't help but grin, my discovery interrupting my own thought. "Problem?" I panted. "Your Majesty?"

"Not a single one," he said, his voice strained. Sweat was glistening on his brow and chest, and his lips quivered. "Except that I'm not through with fucking you, but I think my body has other plans."

"Oh, yeah?" I bounced my hips down onto his pelvis like I was personally trying to ruin his stamina. "And what plans are those?" My own cock was throbbing, and until this moment, I'd been so engrossed in Olympio that I hadn't realized how close I was to—"Fuck!"

Spurt after spurt of hot come hit my soulmate in the chin, and I gripped his shoulders like they were the only thing holding me in place.

"Gabriel!" he cried out, his own climax following mine immediately, so that I was still coming as I felt him release inside of me. "Gabriel... *My*... Gabriel..."

The energy which had once been the soulmate bond thrummed inside us and golden, purple, shimmering light exploded out like shattered glass, raining the essence of our eternal connection down onto us as we were united. One being, two bodies.

"Ollie..." I hummed in ecstasy, laying my face against the sticky skin of his chest. "Olympio."

He reached over to a small basin beside the bed with his long arm, grabbing a damp cloth and lifting my head so he could clean my face and his torso.

"We can have a proper bath in a bit," he said softly as he ran the cloth across my cheeks and the golden scars Vassenia had left that still stood slightly out from the rest of my skin.

I nuzzled into him. "You know you don't always have to do that." I inhaled the final word, releasing its contentment in a sigh.

He laughed quietly, but didn't stop. "I'm well aware. But as I've told you a thousand times, and will tell you a thousand more, and a thousand after that, I have never loved anything in my whole, long life the way I love you, and I will take care of you and protect you, always. Until my heart no longer beats."

I leaned up and kissed him like it would be the last time, and he gripped my face with his free hand, deepening the connection. "Do we really have to go home today?" I asked as I pulled back.

I watched the flicker of pure joy in his eyes as I referred to Sefaera as "home."

"Unfortunately, yes," he said, exhaling deeply and looking up at the sky. "Not only has the kingdom been without us for a full week in Sefaeran time, but the magic that created this place is limited. It can be reopened when needed, but it will only last for one year inside. I believe the creators of this place knew how tempting it would be to escape here indefinitely."

I felt my face fall despite the effort to remain unbothered looking. "Okay..."

The rain slowed as we lay there, Ollie's chest going up and down as he breathed, lulling me into a pseudo-slumber.

When I woke a few hours later, Ollie was fully clothed in the same outfit he wore on my first day in Sefaera, watching me sleep.

"Mm... hello..." I said, reaching over and rubbing his thigh.

He took my hand and pressed each of my fingertips to his lips, closing his eyes like there was no more potent drug for him than simple contact with me. "Hello. You know, you look like some deity of ancient lore when you sleep. The kind the other gods would envy and try to destroy."

"Lucky for me I've got a god to protect me from all the rest, then." Silence weighed heavy in the air as my now waking brain recognized Olympio's expression as anticipatory. "It's time, isn't it?"

He looked a bit sad as he said, "Yes. I wanted to draw this out as long as we could, but the portal will be opening any minute, and I think the Justice arriving back in Sefaera naked would be quite the spectacle." He finally broke into another grin. "And while the kingdom would be lucky beyond measure to see that, let's save making such a scene for another time."

I sighed and stood, holding out my palm and clapping my fingers into it twice to indicate that he should hand me my clothes. There was a small part inside me that really loved that I could be so flippant to the "King of an Entire World."

But like a parent who lovingly assists a child—which, compared to Ollie, I was—Olympio grabbed an outfit he'd set aside for me and not only brought it to me, but helped me put it on. I yawned, feeling safe, happy, and wholly enveloped in love in a way I thought I'd never feel again after my parents died.

"I cannot begin to tell you what it means to me that I can feel how safe you feel with me," he said quietly with a soft chuckle.

Like magic, the warmth that he was feeling reverberated in me like waking up on Christmas morning and seeing your stocking filled. I leaned my chin up, lips pursed, silently signaling that I wanted him to kiss me. He obliged immediately, his arms wrapping tightly around me to hold me against him, as if we could merge into one person just through sheer force of will.

I breathed him in, a tiny whimper of happiness leaving me as I felt emotion overwhelm me with memories of our time here. "Forever..." I breathed.

"Longer," he said, smiling against my lips.

Something caught my eye outside the dome, and I turned my face away from him to see a sparkling, void-like mass pulsing there. "Guess that's our bus," I chuckled.

"I guess so." Ollie pulled back and took my hand. I could feel the sadness in him as he took one last look around.

Something welled up inside me and words tumbled out that I hadn't known I was capable of stringing together. "The most beautiful place in the world—in *any* world—will always be wherever you are, Ollie. We don't have to miss this place because we will have it with us every day, for as long as we're together." I tugged his hand forward, and I walked backward, leading him out of the dome and to the edge of the portal. "Until my heart no longer beats."

His face broke into a smile as he followed me. "I believe that's my line."

Chapter Two
Olympio

The hand gripping mine through the halls of the palace like it was afraid I would ever let him go, like I even could, was the sweetest sensation in the world.

It wasn't long ago that I couldn't even get Gabriel to look at me, let alone touch me. To feel the pull for him I always had and to not be able to do a damn thing when he would go off and abuse his body with drugs he got from those young Hollywood idiots, or, just as painful, when he'd choose the company of... others... over my own.

One very specific and enraging example was forced from my mind, not wanting Gabriel to know I was thinking about that pissant for even one second. But considering his stupidity had once nearly cost my soulmate his life, it seemed a valid response.

"Ollie, can't we just go to bed? That portal jumping shit is really exhausting." Gabriel dragged his feet a little, the soft leather soles scuffing slightly on the marble as he whined in an adorably sleepy way. "Plus I missed Betty."

Betty was the name he'd given his kormarrin who—besides me—seemed to be his best friend. It had taken days of convincing to leave her behind.

I smiled at him, every bit as stunning in his Sefaeran finery and crown as he was completely naked, as he had been for the majority of our adjournment. Before we'd left, he'd spent his first month as a royal slowly phasing out his human clothing, and I was surprised when he didn't even reach for his t-shirts or jeans upon our return.

"If only," I said, putting a hand on his lower back to gently guide him alongside me. "But I promised Ari we'd have dinner when we got back so she could fill me in on whatever happened while we were away."

"It was only a week," he whined. "And the palace is still standing. What could have possibly happened in that time that couldn't wait 'til morning?"

"I think it has less to do with actual politics and more to do with Ari having missed us," I said. "Or, more accurately, I think she was going to miss *you*. I was gone for sixty years in Sefaeran time when I went to get you. But, despite anything she may say to the contrary—since she is Ari, after all—I believe she's grown rather fond of you."

Gabriel's face twitched, almost smiling, though I could tell he was still committed to the "tired" act, one I'd seen him use with his parents throughout his entire childhood. They, too, had found it endearing, which was likely why he had continued to do it.

"Okay, okay," he said as we approached the doors to the grand hall, which he looked up at in slight surprise. "Dinner's in here?"

I nodded, feeling a bit of excitement bubble up inside. I tried not to let it grow too much, because I knew Gabriel would feel it already, and I wanted to keep the secret for as long as possible.

"Shall we?" I said, reaching for the door handle and pulling hard and fast.

The cacophony that greeted us on the other side was jarring after spending so long just the two of us. But Ari and I had worked this out before we left, so I'd been expecting it, especially since my sister was the one in charge.

"Happy Birthday, Gabe!" a hundred voices cried out as our faces came into view. Ari, Liro, and my mother stood at the front of the crowd with glasses of blue Sefaeran wine raised in their hands.

I felt my soulmate startle but quickly settle again as a different emotion flooded us. He flung himself against my chest, and I could feel hot, wet tears soak my chiton. "Ollie..."

He was unmistakably happy, but he was just as unmistakably wracked with melancholy, rendering the room unnaturally silent.

"Gabriel..." I crooned. "What's wrong?"

"I... I forgot... it was... my birthday," he whimpered.

My arms wrapped around him, holding him close. "I thought maybe you had. And we don't really celebrate birthdays here—just big milestone years like five hundred, a thousand, and so on. I know that, in your old world, twenty one is a big year, so I thought it made sense to make this your 'last birthday,' so to speak. And Ari would never turn down the chance to throw her favorite brother a party."

Gabriel pushed himself away from me and skidded across the space to my sister, pulling her into a wet hug. "Thank you. This is amazing."

Ari looked visibly uncomfortable at the effect, which seemed to tickle Liro as he met my eyes with humored delight. She patted my soulmate gently on the shoulder in a gesture that clearly indicated affection laced with a desire to be released.

"You can thank me by letting go," she said, her eyes gentle despite her words. "I can't have people thinking I've gone soft or anything."

Gabriel giggled and stepped backward, bowing his head slightly before wiping his nose. "Yes, Hunt Master." Then he turned to my mother and hugged her tightly.

Unlike the princess, my mother embraced him in a way that only a mother could and even kissed his forehead. "Happy Birthday, Your Grace."

Gabriel kissed her cheek and stepped back to bow. I could have exploded with pride. He was such a fast learner, and he always did things properly without losing himself. Every move he made was "Gabe-ified."

I took a few steps forward and placed my hand on his lower back, causing him to look up at me.

"Is... Is there booze?" he asked.

The entire room erupted in genuine laughter, breaking the tension. "This is Sefaera, Gabriel," I replied loudly, so that everyone was in on the joke with us. "We don't do anything without libations."

Glasses of blue wine shot into the air in a wordless toast as everyone cheered. As if he was anticipating it, Tomos rushed forward with a goblet for both me and my soulmate, his horned head bobbing with nervous excitement. "Happy birthday, Gabe," he squeaked.

"Thanks, Tomos," he chuckled, taking the glasses and handing me one. "And thank you, Your Majesty. For this incredible surprise."

Ari gave a very audible scoff, and I shot her a look that she rebutted with an expression only a younger sibling could have the nerve to give.

"You deserve it," I said, turning back to Gabriel. "And the whole kingdom agrees." I held up my wine and smiled down at him. "To His Grace, Gabriel, Justice of Sefaera!"

The entire room echoed the toast, and music began to play, a sweeping, upbeat melody.

"May I have this dance?" I said, bowing to my soulmate and extending my hand for his as Tomos took our wine glasses.

Gabriel nodded, placing his hand in mine and stepping so our bodies were touching. I shivered slightly as he nestled his face into the crook of my neck as he often did and began to lead us in a soft sway.

"This is beautiful," he breathed against my skin.

"And yet, it pales in comparison to you." My fingers flexed against his waist as I did my best to control the arousal that always came with touching him. After a full year of being able to have him whenever and wherever I wanted, the restraint I was forced into now was nearly as painful as watching him from afar back in his world.

The odd ping of recognition that always occurred when my own thoughts reached him came back at me in full force as mischief bounced along our connection.

"Gabriel..."

"All I was gonna say is how this would be ten times better if you could feel my hard cock against your stomach."

With a slight jerk, I pulled him tighter against me, subtly enough that it wouldn't be noticed by the guests. "Do you not realize how difficult it is for me to resist you at all times, without you adding fuel to the fire?" My nose rubbed a small circle against his cheek, before gliding back along his jaw so I could kiss behind his ear. "Is that what you want? For everyone to see me lose all manner of self-control and take you right here, right now, in front of our family and friends?"

I could hear him panting, and he certainly got his wish as I felt every inch of him pressing into me. "Maybe..." I could tell he was trying to maintain his teasing but was beginning to succumb to the consequences of his actions.

"Well, you'd better decide quickly," I told him. "The song is about to end, and Ari's already on her way over here."

"Fuck—"

"Your Majesty," Ari said with her signature sardonic smile. "Much as I hate to interrupt, the other guests are all eager to greet His Grace, and you and I have matters to discuss—urgently."

"Of course," I said with a nod before turning my attention back to Gabriel, grinning at him once more. "Well, Your Grace? Are you ready to mingle with your guests? Or do you need another moment?"

I relished in the nervous laugh that rumbled against my chest, and Ari looked between us, first trying to figure out the joke, then second, regretting having figured out the joke. "I'll meet you over... there. Somewhere that Gabe's erection can't hurt me."

The joy that filled me at the feeling of home and family made coming back here worth it. And having my Gabriel be at the center of it all was the perfect culmination of my efforts.

"Kiss me?" he said, looking up at me in that way he did—that special way that made me feel invincible, like I really was a god.

My lips were on his without another second wasted, and he melted into me, making the idea of letting him go seem nearly impossible. But as we broke apart, a glance at my sister over his shoulder, tapping her foot nervously, was enough to remind me that along with the feelings of home and family came responsibility and duty. I'd expected some level of upheaval in my absence, especially with Typhir as angry with me as he was, but her demeanor filled me with worry that I'd underestimated him, or worse, that some new threat had emerged in the week Sefaera had been without me.

"I love you," I said to Gabriel, pressing my lips to his head. "Enjoy this. It's all for you—the person who has brought joy and meaning to my life and to my kingdom."

"You're gonna bone me later, right?"

An unbidden laugh burst from my chest, and I allowed my hand to subtly brush against Gabriel's cock through his clothes as I stepped back, raising an eyebrow at him. "I'd tell you, but that would take away the fun of watching you squirm."

I walked away, not even glancing back to see if he'd managed to hide the evidence of my swift and firm retribution. I made a beeline for my sister, but found my path blocked by the last person I wanted to see upon my return.

"Your Majesty." Typhir's slimy, saccharine tone was an assault on my senses as much as if he'd spat poison at me, something that wouldn't have surprised me, given what a serpent he could be. "Welcome back."

"Typhir," I said with a curt nod. "I'm surprised to see you here. I didn't think you cared much for these kinds of parties."

"Oh, I don't," he sneered. "But I heard it would be the only way to speak to you upon your return."

"On the contrary," I said, plastering my face with the smile I spent millennia using to charm people, back before I met Gabriel and learned that substance mattered so much more than presentation. But the contemptuous grin was exactly what Typhir deserved. "You are more than welcome to set an appointment with me in the morning, since today is still technically the last day of my adjournment, and I intend to use this time to celebrate with my soulmate. Now if you'll excuse me, I would like to speak to my sister."

"But not about... *business*, I presume?" he asked with a single eyebrow raised in challenge, as though he had any right to pass judgment on his king.

I put a hand on his shoulder that might look friendly to anyone in attendance, but my grip was tight on his flesh. "Whether it is or isn't is up to me. You would do well to remember your place, Typhir. You may have enjoyed your reign between my father's passing and Gabriel's arrival, but I would think that the events of a few weeks ago would be fresh enough to remind you of where you now stand."

His face turned the same shade of red it had on the day I referred to. The day my oldest friend, most trusted advisor, and constant lover had been sentenced to death for attempting to murder Gabriel. Typhir's niece, Vassenia, had sent assassins after me and had beaten and stabbed Gabriel within an inch of his life. Typhir had been positively apoplectic when he was removed from the hearing for attempting to exert power he no longer had.

His molten silver eyes stared into mine, cold and calculating. He was volatile, but he was also clever and cunning. He wanted power above all else, and throwing a tantrum in the middle of a party for the most beloved member of the royal family in generations—my Gabriel—would have only hurt his goal. Not that I would have minded. Anything to knock him off his self-important pedestal.

"Certainly, Your Majesty," he said, bowing much lower than necessary before moving to the side to allow me to pass. No one could do pettiness like Typhir and his kin, especially in an attempt to divert attention away from some misdeed they committed. It was as though they believed a smaller immediate offense could overshadow a larger one.

Unfortunately for him, I was all too familiar with this tactic, having learned the art of it well from Vass over our thousands of years together. Which meant I was even more intent on reaching Ari to find out what Typhir had to hide.

Her arms were crossed by the time I reached her, her eyes narrowed at Typhir's retreating form.

"Bastard," she mumbled, shaking her head slightly.

"Yes, but why this time?" I asked quietly, leaning close so we could speak without being overheard.

She sighed and turned her eyes to mine. "He's been making moves, sowing seeds. Ones that could be deeply harmful to the throne."

"To me?" There was enough of a pause that she didn't even need to say it. "To Gabriel."

"The barriers between the worlds... something is wrong. While you were gone, a creature from Gaiada was found in the Royal Forest."

"How do you know where it was from?" I asked.

"Mother recognized it from before, from when she lived there," Ari said grimly. "And Typhir was quick to start planting seeds of doubt in people's minds that the humans might be trying to infiltrate Sefaera."

"What?" I half-scoffed, half-laughed.

"Exactly." She shook her shoulders slightly, as though the single week she'd had to deal with him had weighed her down. I could certainly understand the sentiment. Five minutes of time with Typhir was enough to make me want to abdicate so I didn't have to spend one more moment with him. "And this was after he publicly tried to bully Mother out of the Justice seat, saying it was his right, since he had taken on the duty for thousands of years since Father died."

Rage boiled inside of me. I'd learned about the type of "Justice" Typhir had been, and it was precisely because of that knowledge that I'd made it very clear that my mother, who had been Justice before my father died, would be the one to perform that duty while Gabriel was unable to.

Over her shoulder, I saw a man nearly as tall as me with silken black hair, tanned skin, and slightly curved horns atop his head make his way through the crowd. Liro, Ari's life partner, who was carrying a glass of wine for her. "Safe to assume I can guess the topic of your conversation, since you look positively murderous?"

"Is it so much to ask for an assassin to make their way into his chambers? Or for lightning to strike his bath?"

"Do you want me to go get my bow?" Liro asked under his breath. "I could make the sacrifice for the kingdom."

"Don't you dare," Ari said out of the corner of her mouth. "I'm not going to lose you because of *him*."

"Agreed," I said, though the idea was sorely tempting. "I'll deal with him. Thank you for keeping me informed."

Liro, however, looked amusingly put out by the notion of not being allowed to kill Typhir. "Can I at least take a shot at the other one?"

Ari snorted and gave an uncharacteristically cruel smile. There was obviously something I was missing.

"What other one?" I asked, looking around the room to see if I could figure out who they meant.

Ari and Liro exchanged a look as if they were silently arguing about who had to tell me. Finally, Ari deflated a bit and turned back to me.

"He's back."

"Who?" I asked, bewildered and worried.

Ari's voice was low and foreboding as she uttered a name I would have been happy to never hear again.

"Lexios."

Anxiety shot through me, and I turned, looking for him. "Is he here?"

"I saw him earlier," Liro said with a scowl. "Not sure where he ended up."

Of course, it was at that moment that I saw exactly where he'd gone, and who he was with.

The last place I ever wanted to see him   within reach of my soulmate.

Chapter Three
Gabriel

I made my way to the fountain in the center of the ballroom and held out my nearly empty goblet, allowing it to fill with the vibrant liquid, then downing it in one fell swoop. I dipped the cup again, spilling the tiniest bit on the marble floor as I brought it to my lips with haste. I loved the way it burned as it went down, sort of like a punishment for the indulgence—and Ollie had certainly spent the last three months of our adjournment teaching me about the pleasure of pain.

Speaking of Ollie, I looked over where I'd left him and found him still embroiled in a discussion with Ari. Of course, Typhir's miserable grimace wasn't too far away. I guessed I'd have to get used to him following Ollie everywhere. It was bound to happen a lot. This—as well as several other court duties—would make it increasingly difficult to find alone time, but I tried not to think about that too heavily. At least I'd have Betty to keep me company.

And suddenly it felt like I was staring down a whole life of loneliness, only accompanied by my cat. I wondered how many of them I could get before people started talking...

I turned to get more wine and accidentally bumped into someone. A tall, strong, blond someone.

"Oh, sorry, man," I said, looking up with a sheepish smile.

He stared at me, almost studying me before taking a step back and bowing. "No, no, Your Grace. The mistake was mine. I've been dying to introduce myself and have only just gotten the courage to do it."

Someone had been nervous to meet... me?

"Oh," I replied, rubbing the back of my head. "Well, there's nothing to be nervous about. I'm just... a dude. You know?"

He smiled, and I would be lying if I didn't say it was a little swoon-worthy. As much as Ollie owned me, heart, body, and soul, I was in love—not dead.

When I met his gaze straight on, I was surprised to find two almost molten silver eyes staring at me from beneath a sandy blond fringe.

"Gabe Hoffstet," I said, putting out my hand to shake his. "I... think that's still my name, anyway."

"Lexios," he replied, a friendly grin canvassing his mouth.

"How have I never seen you around before?" I asked, shifting my stance to the one I'd now been trained to offer non-royals.

"Oh," he shrugged. "My father has me running all over the countryside, getting word out to relatives about my upcoming Union. He can be a bit of a pain, my father."

At this, he reached out his hand toward my empty goblet, clearly offering to refill it. I nodded enthusiastically and handed it to him. But the glass hadn't left my fingertips when someone else's hand clasped around my wrist.

"I believe I can take care of that."

Ollie slid up beside me, wrapping an arm around my waist that was nothing if not possessive as he glared at Lexios with a look I'd only seen him give two people—one of whom didn't even live in this world, and the other of whom was—

"I see you've met Typhir's son," my soulmate said, kissing me on the cheek before nodding his head in a condescending way toward Lexios. "I heard you'd come back from your... diplomatic mission, or so your father called it."

It occurred to me this was the first time I was meeting someone whose cousin I had recently ordered to be put to death. I shuffled my feet anxiously, not knowing whether to address it or not say anything about it at all.

A squeeze from Ollie's hand against my ribs told me he thought I should stay quiet about it. And he was right. No need to stir up anger unnecessarily, even if it was to apologize.

"So, you two are... related, right?" I asked, looking back and forth between the two, remembering Ollie telling me about how he and Typhir had shared an ancestor.

Lexios nodded, an oddly curated smile morphing out of his genuine one. "Oh, yes. Olympio and I are cousins. Distant cousins, of course. His family got the crown, while my family got the good looks."

He winked at Ollie, and I felt him boil through the bond. I tried not to relish in the comedic tension between them, but it almost felt like they were fighting over my attention.

Of course, Ollie would have it every time—he was my soulmate, after all. But it felt nice to see that someone could keep *King* Olympio on his toes.

I looked up at him beside me, and the smile he directed at Lexios was so tight that it was almost a snarl. "And how fortunate for Sefaera," Ollie said. "Coricas knows that if it had ended up with you or Typhir or... anyone... in your family on the throne, Sefaera would have fallen into ruin thousands of years ago. After all, *no* amount of... 'good looks' can make up for empty heads and cruel hearts."

I felt a punch in my gut from the venom that laced each of his words. Fortunately, Typhir's skeletal fingers wrapped around Ollie's arm at just that moment, pulling him a few feet away to speak to someone.

"Yikes," I said, biting my lip in embarrassment. "You guys... uh... don't get along, do you?"

This time, Lexios did not smile. "He's always hated my family. Never once bothering to ask me personally whether I aligned with the rancor that my father holds for him."

Lexios then gestured to the outdoor balcony, the one Ollie and I had shared our first *real* kiss on, and I nodded, following him out. The night air was cool but not bracing, and the moons lit up the world below us like spotlights.

"So... a Union. Like, with someone else as life partners?" I asked him. "That's what you mean by Union, right? What's she like? Is she here?"

He shook his head with a sigh. "Truthfully, it's a politically arranged Union, but she's nice enough. My father hand-picked her."

I didn't say it out loud, but I knew what he was feeling. It was the same way I'd once felt when people kept reminding me I was *Olympio's* soulmate.

Lexios looked out over the balcony, his blond curls falling slightly into his face, and he leaned down so he could rest his chin on his hands. I felt bad for him. I couldn't imagine having Typhir for a father and also being forced into a marriage.

"Is there someone else?" I asked, knowing it was neither politically correct or correct for me as a royal to ask a question like that.

But Lexios shook his head. "Truth be told," he said, straightening and stepping closer. "I have a preference for men." He reached out his hand and gripped my bicep, squeezing ever so slightly. "But outside of the royal family, men can't procreate with men. So, I must do my duty to keep my family line going."

The way he was looking at me, paired with his softening words, made me think perhaps he had an ulterior motive for getting me out here alone. Suddenly, I didn't know what I was supposed to do, but it felt like the spot he was touching me was burning.

Immediately, a throng of footsteps rushed towards me.

"Gabe!"

I looked toward the doorway and saw not only Ollie, but Ari and Liro making their way over.

It was Ari who had called out to me, leading the other two in my direction with a look on her face like she'd never been happier in her life to see someone, which, while Ari and I were close, wasn't really like her. Liro's face was pleasant but neutral, which I had come to learn since meeting him was his equivalent of the serious expression on Ollie's face. Even if I hadn't known something was up with the other two, that would have been enough to tell me something wasn't right.

Ari threw her arms around me in a tight embrace, whispering, "Just go with it," before pulling back and taking both of my hands. "Moons and rivers, I've been looking everywhere for you. Mother has been asking me a million questions about how you enjoyed your adjournment, but I've been more than a little busy filling in *His Majesty* about the events from his absence."

She said Ollie's title with the same teasing tone she always did, but everything else about this whole interaction was... wrong. She was being way too over the top, and Liro's pose looked casual, but, having been on a few hunts with him, I recognized the tight coil of his muscles, ready to strike.

And, of course, there was the boiling, nausea-inducing rage rolling off Ollie in waves, as he no longer offered even the pretense of a smile to Lexios. He pulled me to him for a long, lingering kiss—the kind that usually ended with him grabbing me by the hand or throwing me over his shoulder to take me to bed. But this time, when he pulled back, I could see the protective fire, tinged with worry, in his violet eyes.

"Ol–"

He cut me off with another kiss, pulling my body against his briefly before ending it and looking over my head. "Oh. Lexios. You're still here." He glanced around with a pointed look. "And alone. With the Consort. With *Justice*. Without any guards. Terribly bold of you considering... recent events involving your family."

Ari's eyes hardened, even though her smile remained. Were they talking about Vassenia? Or was there more?

Lexios looked terribly uncomfortable, but stepped up to Ollie as though he had never been afraid of anything, putting one single finger in the center of his chest. "You know what the true travesty of your family ruling over mine is? The fact that the lot of you act like made up beasts in a traveling show. Dirty, no class, and absolute jokes of yourself."

I felt the visceral pulse of Ollie's fury reaching its zenith a split second before I heard the loud crack of my soulmate's knuckles impacting Lexios's jaw, sending him stumbling back to the floor.

"Ari," Ollie said, his voice eerily calm for the storm I felt raging inside of him. "Please take His Grace back inside."

"Olympio..." she replied, her voice filled with caution. "Are you certain this is what you want everyone to see?" She nodded her head toward the windows, where people had begun to take notice.

Ollie took a deep breath, then glared down at Lexios. "I don't enjoy solving problems with my fists," he said, rubbing the back of his hand. "But if you continue to move through *my* palace and *my* kingdom as if you have any kind of power that I cannot take away on a whim, perhaps you should remember what happened when your cousin crossed me. And I liked her a *lot* more than I like you."

The air went dead silent. No one looked at me, and yet I felt like I was being stared at.

I made a decision at once to step between them. "I think everyone might have had a little too much. Ollie—" I wrapped my arms around his waist and kissed his neck. "I have something I'd like to show you... in our bedroom..."

I hoped the promise of nudity would be enough to lure him away from Lexios and the rest, but right now, it was anyone's guess.

Ollie drew a shuddering breath, then looked at me, his eyes softening as they met mine. His face relaxed, the rage falling away until all that was left was the same guy who had brought me out onto this balcony at my first ball—genuine, gentle, even a little nervous.

"Yes," he said, pressing his forehead to mine. "I think I've had enough of this particular party. No offense to my sister or the monumental occasion that is your birthday." He looked at Liro and Ari. "Can you please see to it that guards escort *Lord* Lexios back to his chambers for the night? I think *my* Gabriel is right, and that *some* of us have had a little too much to drink to make intelligent choices. Perhaps he'll do better starting tomorrow."

Ari gave a small laugh that she covered up quickly with a cough, nodding to show she understood.

I was definitely missing some key info here.

Chapter Four
Olympio

I hadn't been in a fist fight since I was practically a child, and tonight marked the second time I'd punched someone hard enough to harm them specifically because of their actions in regard to Gabriel. I was no stranger to combat, but I didn't draw a weapon unless I was ready to kill.

And Lexios was *very* lucky I didn't have my sickle on me when I found him alone with my soulmate.

Gabriel's hand in mine was the only thing keeping me from going back to whatever was left of his party. His last birthday, ruined by yet another member of Typhir's horrible family.

"Ollie," Gabriel said urgently as I pulled him along behind me. "Ollie, you're hurting me."

I stopped and looked down at our hands. My skin looked like it was smoking, the shadows I had failed to keep at bay unfurling, my burgeoning demon form making my grip too rough.

I took a deep breath to return to my usual self and stepped toward Gabriel, who looked even more upset than he did when I hit Lexios—more upset than I'd seen him in a long time.

"I'm sorry," I told him, pressing my lips to his head. "I lost my temper. It won't happen again."

He nodded, and the relief I felt when he didn't pull away was enough to calm me.

"Come on," I said. Then, over his shoulder, I called, "Gryfian. Spread the word—no one enters this hallway, especially not Typhir or anyone associated with him. If my sister wants to speak to me, let her know we can talk in the morning."

My long-time guard and friend nodded and turned to give orders to the other guards, knowing that I would have no one posted outside my chambers other than him.

I pressed my palm to the golden panel on the door, unlocking it to let myself and my soulmate inside, then closed it behind us, shutting us away from the rest of the world—away from everything that, even after our bond was consummated, seemed determined to keep us apart.

I leaned my forehead on the door for a moment, then turned to face Gabriel.

He stood in the center of our chambers, looking as uncomfortable as I'd ever seen him. He'd taken off his crown and held the golden laurel in his hands, turning it over and over nervously, his eyes on the floor, but flicking up to meet mine occasionally, only to look away again.

I approached him slowly, then held out my hand for the crown, which I placed on the table before reaching out for him. Thankfully, the night's events hadn't been enough to prevent him from walking into my arms.

"Gabriel," I breathed against his hair. "*My* Gabriel..."

I held him for a while, but eventually he pulled back to look at me.

"What the hell was that all about, Ollie?" he asked.

And just like that, the spell of relief was broken, and my calm began to ebb again. My lips pressed into a thin line. "What do you mean?"

"I mean you went completely psycho back there."

My jaw dropped. Surely, he couldn't be serious. "Do you even realize the kind of danger you could have been in?"

"We were just talking," Gabriel said, crossing his arms defensively. "It would have been just as effective for you to come out and talk like a normal person instead of some fucking bully."

"Bully?" I echoed, unable to believe what he was saying. "After everything we went through, after I nearly lost you, you think me being protective of you when the cousin of your intended assassin has his hands—his filthy, unworthy hands—on you is being a *bully*?"

But he simply shook his head and turned away from me, speaking so low I almost didn't catch what he said.

"It's like Alex fucking Kessinger all over again."

"You're right," I said, gripping him by the shoulder and turning him back to face me, every atom of my being working to keep my voice steady, when all I wanted to do was scream what I'd been holding back for so long. "It *is* like Alex Kessinger all over again, but not in the way you think. You once asked me why I hated Alex, and I told you some of it, but not all of it."

Gabriel frowned, the idea of a secret still lingering between us clearly making him uneasy. "What didn't you tell me?"

I sucked in a shuddering breath. I knew there was no going back now. "The reason I acted like that tonight was that I thought you were in danger. And that is *exactly* why Kessinger pushed me over the edge that night. Do you remember that day?"

He thought for a moment, then shook his head. "Not really. I remember he gave me a really big xanny that knocked my ass out, and then I went and got drunk really fast. Then you found me."

"I don't know what a xanny is, but... whatever he gave you nearly killed you."

"What?" he said with a slight scoff and chuckle. "You're exaggerating. I was just asleep."

"No," I told him. "You weren't. That day was the third of four times the bond has turned from purple to deep red and caused me immeasurable pain. The first time was when you overdosed at a party, and I had to pull the drugs from your system. The second was when you were supposed to get on a flight with your parents. You know what happened then. The fourth was when Vass took you. That time with Kessinger, the third time? It was because whatever he gave you, combined with the liquor you were drinking, was causing your organs to shut down—something I only recognized because of the first time. I was there, in your room, and I was able to pull the drugs out of your system, taking them into myself. It was strong enough that I was out for hours, and as you know, I almost didn't make it to you before he did. I don't know if he meant to hurt you, but even if he didn't, he had proven he was a risk. I couldn't leave you alone with him again."

Gabriel went pale and walked over to the chaise, where he sat down and stared at the floor.

"Why didn't you tell me?" he asked, his voice hollow.

"Because it didn't seem important, since by that point, I was fairly certain neither of us would ever have to see him again. But I'm telling you now, because when I tell you Lexios is a threat, you need to understand how serious I am."

"But why?" Gabriel asked, turning his face toward me again. "He said you always hated him because of Typhir, but that he's not like the rest of his family."

An unhinged laugh escaped me, making Gabriel jump.

"I'm sorry," I said, holding up my hands in a gesture of calming. "But that's not true. Far from it. In fact, he, Vass, and I were inseparable for centuries."

"Like friends?"

I scowled. "Unfortunately."

"Did you guys ever...?"

"Yes," I said quickly, hating the answer, even though it was true. "But he's as much of a serpent as his father, and after one too many times of finding out he was spreading lies and rumors about me, trying to ruin my name even further than I'd already managed to do on my own—as well as about Ari and my brother—he was excommunicated from my inner circle and relegated to a low-ranking member of court. After his cousin, who I actually trusted, nearly killed you, I would think you would be a little more careful about wandering off into private with someone you barely know, especially someone related to Typhir. That family cannot be trusted."

"Okay," Gabriel said, finally standing and coming over to me to put his arms around me, just as he did outside, his touch working like a soothing balm to siphon away the rage and pain of dredging up old memories. "Okay. Look, we don't have to talk about it anymore. Why don't we have a bath and relax? I think you could really use it."

I nudged his head to the side with my nose so I could rub a few small circles on his cheek with it, before trailing behind his ear to kiss his neck. Our special kiss, one that said a million words of love without uttering a single one.

"Yes," I said, holding him tightly. "A bath sounds wonderful."

We stripped, and it was a mark of the tension the night had created that I didn't even get hard watching him move through our space entirely naked. Once in the warm water, though, he curled against my side, running his finger gently over my chest as I put my arm around his shoulders.

"So, what was it that Ari had to tell you?" he asked, clearly looking for a change in the subject, but, unfortunately, he had found one topic that would veer us right back into the same territory.

"A warning," I said with a sigh. "Apparently there have been some strange things happening, and Typhir has been using it as an excuse to try to undermine the throne. He tried to make an official challenge from the Council that would have potentially allowed him to take back over as Justice in our absence."

"Fuck no," Gabriel said, finally angry at the right person. "Over my dead, rotting body."

"Something that I will never allow to happen," I promised him.

"Good," he said. "Because I never want to see Sefaera subjected to *his* brand of Justice ever again."

"Neither do I."

He put a hand on my cheek to turn my face to him, and I looked into his perfect violet eyes, feeling his determination and love for our world through our bond. I pressed my lips to his, trying to convey just how deeply grateful I was for and to him for everything good he'd brought into my life and the lives of my people.

When we finally broke apart, Gabriel let out a trembling breath, but relaxed back into the water.

"So, what kinds of strange things happened?"

My brow furrowed as I thought about what Ari had said. "Apparently there were some... foreign beasts in the forest."

"What do you mean foreign?" he asked. I knew he loved the wilds as much as I did, and I could see and feel the concern in his words.

I barked out a quiet, dry laugh, then said, "That's the *really* odd part. They were Gaiadan."

"They were what now?" He was utterly perplexed, and it occurred to me I'd never used that word around him before.

"They were from Gaiada. The human world."

"Gaiada?" he said with a giggle. "Sounds like a Transformer or something."

"Perhaps," I said, smiling at a memory of a young Gabriel playing with toys of mechanical beings who could turn into vehicles. "But the portals to Gaiada were all destroyed after the Final War except for the ones that can be temporarily opened by those with royal blood."

"I feel like I'm missing a *lot* of info here," Gabriel said. "There used to be other portals? What war?"

With a sigh, I pulled myself from the bath and wrapped a towel around my waist before moving to the wine cabinet and pouring out a bottle into two goblets.

"If we're going to have a history lesson, we're going to need some of this."

Chapter Five
Gabriel

I thought my days of learning history were over when I left Columbia, but apparently, I was wrong. I sat, wrapped in a towel, Betty in my lap purring like she knew I was already bored before we even started and was trying to cheer me up.

"Gaiada and Sefaera used to be allies," Ollie said, pulling books off of the shelf to set in front of me. "Long ago, back when my mother was Gaiadan, people could move freely between the realms. The portals were many, and the journey wasn't as taxing as it is now."

My head felt heavy as I tried to comprehend that what he was telling me was nothing like what I'd learned in Ms. Thomas's fifth grade ancient history class. "Traveling between worlds...?"

Ollie gave me an amused, lopsided grin and ruffled my hair affectionately. "You do know how you ended up in Sefaera, don't you?"

I rolled my eyes at him, pulling the towel around me tighter. I could currently think of about five hundred things I'd have liked to do while naked at that moment, and this wasn't one of them. "In case you've forgotten," I said with as little irritation as I could manage. "I had to *buy* my way into Columbia. I am not a smart man, Olympio."

Ollie leaned in, raising his eyebrows. "You failed *chemistry*—"

"Twice."

"Yes, twice. But not history. In fact, I remember that being a favorite subject of yours in high school. But that's beside the point. You won't be tested on this, but it was highly irresponsible of me to not tell you about the connection between our worlds sooner. Now..." He opened a leather-bound book that looked like it was heavy enough to bludgeon someone to death with and pointed at a crudely drawn map of Earth—of *Gaiada*. "You can see here that there were portals all over your world. One of which was in Greece, where you know my mother was from."

He sighed and sat down beside me, gazing at the book as he rubbed his jaw, lost in thought.

"Ollie?"

He startled, almost as if he'd forgotten I was here, then smiled. He held out a hand and pulled me into his lap, pointing to the books from around me as his free hand gripped my hip, casually claiming what was rightfully his.

"Well... There was a war, of course," he said. "My mother was the root of it. She was betrothed from birth to a prince, but when my father came for her, even though her family supported her decision, the prince was offended. At least, that was the story. Many sources said that the conflict had been brewing for centuries, with humans wanting the same freedom we had to venture to Sefaera, but there had been several smaller wars by that point which had resulted in their expulsion from our world. Regardless of motive, the prince launched an attack on the main portal." He pointed to the place on the map marked "*Trojan Portal*."

"Trojan?" I said. "Like with the horse?"

Ollie looked at me in surprise. "You know about that?"

"Everyone knows about that. We learn about it in school, and there's a ton of movies about it."

He nodded, then turned back to the book. "Well, then you know what happened. The humans used deception and subterfuge to infiltrate behind the walls around the portal. Typhir was there. The way he tells it, the loss of Sefaeran life was astronomical, and the few of them who survived the ambush fled through the portal and closed it for good. Upon their return, Typhir went directly to my father. My mother, herself, consented to the order to close all the other portals."

I closed my eyes, the sound of his voice lulling me into sleepiness and submission. "Ollie, if you keep talking about this shit, I'm gonna be too tired to—" I yawned. "Be subjected to the dirty things you promised me earlier."

He tried to hide his grin, but I could feel the pulse of his delight through the bond. "I can't seem to recall what those were. Would you care to remind me, Your Grace?"

I opened one eye and looked up at him, his perfect smile trying to remain covert. Ollie always did that—tried to stay composed when he was dying to just explode with feelings.

"Why do you hide yourself like that?" I asked softly, realizing I never had before.

"Like what?" he asked, his lips pressing into my shoulder, trying to distract me.

"Like... I always hear stories about Olympio, the charismatic playboy extraordinaire and how you used to be the loudest in any room, the one who no one could take their eyes off of..." I paused, not one hundred percent sure I wanted to venture into this territory. "Vassenia once told me that everyone—*literally* everyone—wanted to sleep with you back in the day, but everything I've seen is stern Olympio, quiet Olympio..." I sighed, reaching up to touch his face. "Angry Olympio."

He covered my hand with his own and leaned into the touch.

"None of them—not a single one, not even Vass—ever really knew me," he said, his eyes not meeting mine. "So, she may have been right that everyone wanted to fuck me. I was the life of the party, after all. But I've told you before that it was empty, because *I* was empty. I was nothing but a spectacle, and I thrived in it because it was easier to put on the facade and feel wanted, even if I knew it was only because of my status. I *was* wanted, but I was hated, and because my companion was happy in that dichotomy, I allowed myself to believe I was happy, too."

Ollie pressed his forehead against my shoulder. "But then Vasileios died. And suddenly, I was actually expected to be someone, but no one liked me in the first place, and they liked me even less when I wasn't just a status symbol to add to their roster of wild adventures, but someone whose decisions affected their lives." He brushed his lips against my skin as though that light, gentle touch could fill whatever hole he'd been trying to cope with all this time.

"That man—the one everyone talks about, the one Vass was so proud to have been with—was exactly the kind of person someone like Vass *would* have been proud to be with. But that was never who I really was. I don't really enjoy being a spectacle or having people fawn over me because they want an invite to my bed. That was armor against the knowledge that I was never going to live up to my father or my brother, or even to my own expectations."

Finally, his eyes met mine again. "But I don't have to pretend with you. I don't have to be that person. With you, Gabriel... I'm safe. To just be myself. And yes, sometimes that man is quiet or stern... or angry. But all of those things are because I'm still struggling with how much I hated myself for so long."

It was a lot to take in, and it was like I was seeing Ollie for the first time. I realized the man before me was complex and tortured. "I wish I could take some of that away from you," I sighed, and I wondered how long it took someone to learn Ollie's little siphoning thing he did.

But he smiled at me and wrapped his arms more tightly around me, pulling my body closer to his. "You already do," he said. "Knowing that someone as good as you can see me for more than that empty shell I existed as for so long is enough. I love you, Gabriel. Not just because the bond said I had to, but because you fill all the emptiness I didn't even know was there with happiness and purpose."

I relaxed against him, sharing in the melancholy to the extent I could, and for a moment, it felt like we were back on our adjournment. Desire welled up inside me, but not the way it often did. I needed to lose myself within my soulmate and the universe that was ours alone.

I twisted my body and wrapped his face in my hands, pressing my mouth to his sharp as stone jaw, humming against the sweet skin there. I could have said a thousand words, but right now, the bond was humming within me so vibrantly that I could literally see the essence of it radiating off my skin. Words would be a disservice.

"Gabriel..." he breathed, his fingers flexing on my skin.

I adjusted so I was facing him, my legs on either side of his hips and my whole weight leaned into his chest. He slid one hand up my back between my shoulder blades to keep our torsos flush against each other, while his other hand wrapped around my lower back, not allowing even the space of a hair between us.

The room, previously only lit by candles, was now glowing purple that danced across the walls like reflections off water. Our kiss, slow and needy, deepened so that it was hard to tell where he ended and I began. Maybe that was the true meaning of the bond after all.

Two beings.

One soul.

His hand went to my hair, gripping it like he was trying to cling to every single inch of me, like I might float away if his fingers failed him. I could hear him softly sniffle, and I attempted to pull back and look at him.

"Ollie?"

But his hand was firm, not allowing me to lean away from him. He buried his face in the crook of my shoulder, and a shudder went through him before he finally took a deep breath and looked at me. His eyes were shining with tears, but his lips were curved in a wide, stunning smile.

"I'm alright," he said. "I just think about how close I came to ruining things, to losing you for good because I was stupid, and it makes me so much more grateful to have you now, like this."

I trailed my lips down the side of his neck, relishing in the panting noises he made, followed by his fingers tightening further into my flesh.

I wanted to drown in Olympio. To feel him take me under like a wave and tear me asunder until I was thoroughly undone. I wanted to forget everything before now and stop time in his arms.

"Take me to bed," I whispered.

And he did.

Chapter Six
Olympio

Pulling myself away from Gabriel's sleeping form, the first time I had to leave his side in over a year, was nothing short of torture. He looked positively angelic, his chestnut waves falling over his forehead and onto the pillow. His hair was longer than it was when we left. We'd had the ability to partake in magical-facilitated personal grooming on the adjournment, and while he'd allowed himself to be shaved, he had refused a haircut, saying it made him feel like a fantasy hero instead of some "trust fund brat from Manhattan." And while he was gorgeous no matter what his hair looked like, I couldn't say he was wrong.

I went to my wardrobe and pulled out the garments I always wore when facing official events. Today was my first day back, and while only a week had gone by here, I'd only had a month of being king before spending a year without a care in the world except for loving Gabriel. Now, I had to jump right back into my role as if I'd never left, and act as if the last fifteen hundred years of being at the Council's mercy hadn't affected the power dynamics between us.

With my feather-patterned pauldron, black cape, and chiton skirt held on by a gold chain, I looked at my reflection, every one of my arm, chest, and abdominal muscles on full display. This was the man who had spent centuries chasing the throne, who had gone to fetch Gabriel from Gaiada, who had failed his soulmate at every turn by being too myopic in his methods.

I wasn't that man anymore, and even just seeing the Olympio that Gabriel had asked about the night before, the charismatic but shallow party boy prince, made my stomach lurch. I tore off the pauldron and threw it back into the wardrobe, not bothering to hang it, followed by the cape and chiton. Instead, I pulled a garment from the back of the rack, one I'd never worn.

It was one of my brother's, the one he'd worn the day he first addressed the kingdom as the future king. Knee-length with golden clasps at each shoulder, holding the shining black fabric and a gold cloak in place, and a golden chain cinching the waist.

The effect was immediate and jarring. I'd always admired my brother, knowing I would never measure up to his intelligence, kindness, and easy leadership. He was the more handsome of the two of us without trying nearly as hard as I did, and the more level-headed by miles.

And yet, as I looked into the mirror, for the first time, I saw him in myself. I was no longer an insecure playboy masquerading as a prince—I was a king, confident in myself for the first time.

Because while I'd never believed in myself, a full year of being with Gabriel alone, without external pressures and criticisms, had allowed me to view myself through his eyes, as someone worthy. I was still flawed, still learning, but finally, after two and a half millennia of life, I actually believed I could do this.

I turned back to Gabriel, my heart pounding against my ribcage with the intensity of my love for him. He was the reason for all of this—not only for why I knew I was capable of ruling, but why I wanted to be a better ruler than I would have been without him.

A knock sounded on the door to our chambers, and I went to answer it. My sister stood there, a look of annoyance on her face.

"I see you finally learned to knock," I said, grinning at her. "It only took you two thousand years."

"Well, it's only been a week for me since the last time I walked in on you and Gabe doing things I'd rather not keep witnessing," Ari said, her teasing tone marred by the quiet irritation she radiated. But then she seemed to take notice of my appearance, and her eyes widened. "Oh. You look... different."

"Good different?" I asked. She was one of the only people I'd trust implicitly with something this vulnerable, since she had never once steered me wrong and had even stood by my side when the rest of the kingdom thought I was worth nothing. She'd never coddled me and had been quick to tell me when she thought I was being an idiot, but she'd never turned me away either.

And because she was never anything less than direct to the point of bluntness, I wasn't surprised when, instead of a compliment or even a gentle letdown, she said, "You actually look like you give a fuck. Well done." I smiled at her, but it was clear that she was preoccupied with what we had to do, because she went right back to the task at hand. "Ready to deal with the impending temper tantrum?"

"One moment," I said, turning away from her and walking back over to my sleeping soulmate. If I was going to face this nightmare of a meeting, I wasn't going to leave without giving Gabriel one last kiss. I had no intention of disturbing his slumber, so I bent quietly over the edge of the bed and pressed my lips gently to the top of his head. "Until tonight, my Gabriel."

It took all of my willpower to tear myself away from him, but I knew this was only the first of an eternity of days just like this—where I'd have to say goodbye to him, even for just a few hours.

Ari and I were halfway to the Council Chambers when I felt an unpleasant jolt in my chest. For a split second, I thought the bond was warning me of danger like it had on those other occasions, but then I realized it wasn't the bond that was hurting—it was Gabriel himself.

Panic that wasn't mine bubbled up in my throat, and I felt a burning, as though I was standing in a fire. Instantly, I knew what was wrong.

He was having the dream—the nightmare. The one borne of the scars he held inside, ones that, like the golden streaks on his cheek from Vassenia's poisoned blade, would never truly fade.

I froze. I could help ease his pain, but not while he slept. He needed to be awake. My instinct to turn around and run back to him was almost a compulsion, but Ari noticed I'd stopped and looked at me.

"Come on. We're already late," she said. "It's just Typhir—you know he's all wind and no waves."

She thought I was hesitating because I didn't want to face Typhir. I didn't, because his methods were infantile and a waste of my time, but that wasn't the reason for my hesitation. I could go care for Gabriel, but Typhir had already proven that he would use any excuse to undermine me and my rule. Missing a meeting where he was to be addressed for his misconduct in my absence would make me look weak.

I had to choose. In that moment, I could be either Gabriel's protector, or I could be king. Not both.

"Gryfian," I said, making one of the hardest decisions I ever had to make and turning to my trusted guard and friend. "Gabriel needs to be awakened. Now. Take his attendants and have them get him ready."

"There are no Justice hearings today," he replied, a silent question in the words.

"No, there aren't. But he doesn't know that. You can tell him that he has the day to himself once he's thoroughly roused. Do not indicate you know anything is wrong. I'll do my best to calm him once I can feel that he's awake."

Gryfian knew all about Gabriel's nighttime terrors regarding his parents' deaths, something that woke him up in a panic at least once a week. Recognizing the urgency in my order, he nodded and turned, moving swiftly.

"You sure you don't want your guard with you for this meeting?" Ari asked dryly.

"If I need him at this meeting, it will be better if he's *not* there," I said through gritted teeth, Gabriel's nightmare still wearing on me. "Because Typhir making a violent attempt on me would be a dream come true, and I don't want Gryfian to have all the fun. I'd like nothing more than for Typhir—or *anyone* associated with him—to put me in a position of having to defend myself, since I think we all know who would be the victor. Talaea knows Sefaera would be better off."

"While I agree with you wholeheartedly," she said, "it might be better to keep those kinds of conversations behind closed doors. The last thing we need is for word to get back to Typhir that the mad tyrant king is out for his blood. Trust me—one thing I learned in your absence is Typhir is much more effectively taken down by indifference than venom."

It was difficult to mirror my sister's calm demeanor, especially with Gabriel still in the throes of a panic attack I couldn't help him through. Hopefully, Gryfian would have him awake soon, and I'd be able to help him through the aftermath, even if I couldn't be there to hold him.

And hopefully, whatever I took from Gabriel wouldn't make it impossible to maintain my composure with the Council.

We entered the throne room, crossing the marble floor to the large doors that led to the Council Chambers. I paused, then looked at Ari.

"After you, *Your Majesty*," she said with a sigh.

With my fingers closing around the handle, I rolled my shoulders back. I had run out of time to prepare to face the first challenge as King since my return, and I could only hope that it was enough.

And that if it wasn't, I had to hope at least Typhir wouldn't know.

I pulled the doors open quickly, striding into the room with my head held high, my sister at my side. We had barely made it three steps in when

Typhir's slithering drawl said, "Ah... Your Majesty. We were beginning to wonder if you were coming."

I looked at the Council, the lot of them staring at me with neutral expressions except for the bastard, himself, who looked as smug as a pirpan that caught a harmot. They were seated at a long, half-moon shaped table that was raised up on one end of the long room. Across from them, a table was set up with a single chair—a power move, if I'd ever seen one, making sure that either Ari or I would have to stand.

Neither of us bothered to sit.

Ari moved to the side of the room and leaned against the wall, her arms crossed across her chest, as I took a spot in the center of the room. I was here to address Typhir's insubordination and insolence, and I wouldn't allow him to force me into a position that would make me feel like a child being reprimanded.

I mirrored Ari's posture, relaxing my stance and crossing my arms. My instinct was to come in hard, to begin dressing him down immediately, but Ari was much smarter about these kinds of things than I was. If she was in my position, she would wait for him to speak.

A long silence stretched out where Typhir and I stared each other down, the other members of the Council slowly growing restless and uncomfortable as they waited for the meeting to commence. Finally, after almost five minutes of no one saying anything, Typhir let out an exasperated sigh.

"I was under the impression, *Your Majesty*, that you had something you wished to say," he sneered.

I gave the slightest jerk of my head to one side, raising my eyebrow. "And *I* was under the impression that my subject had an apology to make."

There was something sadistically satisfying about watching Typhir's face change colors as he tried to maintain his composure in front of the rest of the Council. There was a time when, as the head of the Council, he had more power to sway their decisions, which I had to acquiesce to since I wasn't yet king. But now that I was, he needed their full unanimity in order to challenge my rule in any capacity, and a challenge did not necessarily mean that they could overrule me—only that it was a possibility, one that would be decided by the people. Which meant he had essentially been neutered in regards to his power within Sefaera.

"An... apology?" he echoed slowly, his voice gravelly with the force of control he was exerting over it.

"Indeed," I said, relishing in his indignation. "From what Her Highness, Princess Ariadne, Royal Sefaeran Master of the Hunt, and surrogate monarch in my absence had to say, you made quite a spectacle of yourself and of the Justice hearings, which you were deliberately excluded from for exactly the reason you demonstrated."

"A spectacle?" His voice was all but a shriek as several other members of the Council startled, and many looked at him warily, as though they were afraid he might explode.

If only.

"Lord Typhir, if you are only going to select two word phrases from what I say and repeat them, this is going to be a very long meeting," I said, beginning to smile innocently, though not a single person in the room could doubt my intentions. "But I suppose we could try. You may begin with, 'Your Majesty...'"

Typhir stood so quickly that his chair toppled over with an echoing clatter against the marble. I heard Ari move behind me and felt a ripple of power coming from her—a sensation I knew meant she was pulling from the shadows that ran in our blood, the darkness that was our family's ally and protector. If I turned around, I was certain to see a swirling black mass around her hands where she was forming deadly weapons made from the same shadows that surrounded me to create my demon form.

I held up a hand to motion to her to hold her position, and I heard her audibly grumble something about Gryfian not being here, which I ignored, my eyes still on Typhir.

He seemed to realize he'd lost his temper, because his chest was rising and falling heavily as he looked up and down the row of his colleagues, all of whom were staring at him. He tugged on the red embroidered collar of the robe he wore and shook himself slightly.

"Very well," he said, sounding like his tongue had swollen in an attempt to prevent him from speaking. "Your Majesty... I apologize for the events during your absence. I assure you, I will ensure that, should you take leave again, there will be no call for a meeting such as this."

Ari scoffed, and it took far more willpower than I cared to admit to not do the same. We'd both heard the words and understood the clever way he'd used them, careful that he didn't truly apologize for anything, nor did he agree to not do it again—only that he wouldn't be in trouble for it.

Luckily for him, at that moment, I felt Gabriel waking up, the panic lingering within him. I'd hoped to be out of this meeting sooner, but just then, Orella stood.

"The Council would like to beseech Your Majesty to grace us with a bit more of your time. There are many conversions to have regarding the events of your absence."

Once more, I was torn between my duty to Sefaera and my duty to Gabriel. I wanted to shift into the shadows and be by his side in seconds, but I couldn't appear like an uninvested King, not when Typhir was making such efforts to undermine me and my rule.

So, instead, I sat at the provided table, lounging backward in a show of supreme nonchalance, folding my hands in my lap. At least, that's how it would look. I carefully began to run my hand over my member, thinking of yesterday, with Gabriel tied to the tree.

It worked. It only took a few firm strokes before I recognized the familiar tension in myself that meant Gabriel was aroused, his anxiety fading just as quickly.

Good. Now I could focus.

And later, when we were both done for the day... I could finish the job.

Chapter Seven
Gabriel

Everything was burning around me. Wreckage and debris flashed before my eyes like a thousand news clips, and I was shaking as I failed to stop my feet from heading to the heart of the fiery crash. I knew what I would find there— *who* I would find there. It was the same as every time I'd had this dream before.

"Gabriel?" I heard my mom's voice whisper in my ear from behind me.

My heart exploded with adrenaline as my consciousness came back to my body, and I gripped the satin pillows for dear life as I fell from the same emotional cliff I had a million times before.

"No..." I sobbed, my entire body writhing with emotional pain that I knew only Ollie's touch would quell. But it didn't come. Instead, I was left to cry out my agony, and only when I was left with shuddering whimpers could I open my eyes to address reality.

The room was filled with warm, gentle sunlight where the balcony doors had been opened, likely by the servants, and a bath had been drawn for me. I groaned and turned over, knowing that the water would likely go cold before I felt like I had the willpower to force myself into the tub without Olympio taking me to it.

I reached up next to me, where Betty had curled up on Olympio's pillow, likely savoring the warmth when he left.

"You're missing a feather," I said to her as if she understood me. "What have you been into...?"

My fingers tingled with the numbness of an overly shot nervous system, and I nearly jumped a mile in the air when the bedroom doors opened, and I found two servants escorted in by Ollie's guard, Gryfian. He nodded at me, and I pulled the covers over my head to prolong the time before I had to be *Justice*.

"You know," I called out to him from beneath my plush fortress. "If you always accompany the people sent to force me out of bed, I'm gonna start to hate your face."

I heard him chuckle and the clanking of his weaponed belt told me that he'd relaxed his stance. "My apologies, Your Grace."

The blankets were gently pulled away, and the servants, one male, one female, stood there studying me as I lay naked, forehead soaked in sweat.

"Your Grace," the female said. "His Majesty wishes us to convey deep apologies that he had to leave early this morning, and he wishes you to know that we are at your disposal."

I rubbed my eyes to clear the remaining blur of sleep and distinctly noticed Gryfian turn away. "I'm fine. There's already breakfast over the—"

"Not like that, Your Grace," the male voiced. "It's simply that, if you wish to start your day by eliminating... that..."

I looked to where he was pointing and realized he was talking about my morning wood. What kind of fucking weirdo has a dream about their mom dying, then gets a boner?

"What? Oh... fuck. Uh, no. I mean, thank you, but no."

Gryfian emitted a not so subtle snort, and I was seriously tempted to throw something at the back of his head.

"Are you certain, Your—"

"Yep," I squeaked. "Good to go, thanks."

They looked at each other and shrugged but went to my soulmate's private guard and had him escort them out.

As Gryfian closed the door behind him, he grinned. "Have fun."

I replied with my middle finger as the thud of the doors closing shook the room slightly.

Groaning, I slid from my bed like a boneless mass of flesh and stood, stretching before trudging to the balcony where breakfast was laid out for me.

I didn't miss much about "Gaiada"—as Ollie called it—but sometimes the furniture here was... structural. Indeed, when I sat down in one of the wrought iron chairs that were flanking either side of the lavish marble structure bearing the colorful spread, I could think of nothing I'd like more than to swap it out for a La-Z-boy.

I had to stretch to reach the bit of fruit that caught my eye, and I felt my fingers sink into the oulon when I grabbed for it, leaving sticky residue all over them. I popped the fleshy orb into my mouth and was halfway through licking my fingers clean when I heard a voice behind me.

"Your Grace."

I turned so quickly, my heart shooting through my chest at a hundred miles per hour, that I nearly knocked the chair backward, leaving me—once again—wishing for the sturdiness and comfort of a nice armchair.

"Jesus, Gryf," I choked. "Why are you so quiet when you walk?"

Gryfian laughed and pushed his hair back out of his face. "Part of the job, I suppose."

I clutched my chest dramatically, and he shook his head, mirth creasing his shimmering, dark tan skin. "Well, next time just stomp through. Imagine if I'd been in here choking the chicken or some shit."

This only caused him to laugh harder before he cleared his throat and said, "Believe me when I say I've walked in on His Majesty doing much worse."

I gestured to the chair next to me, "Sit, have breakfast." I was keenly aware of Ollie's absence right now, and if I couldn't have my soulmate, I'd take his closest friend.

But he shook his head. "Thank you, Your Grace, but you have a visitor. Shall I tell him to leave?"

"Him?" I said, actually turning around in my chair now, confused thoughts scanning the list of people who I not only knew, but were casual enough to visit me here, in the royal bedchambers.

Gryfian shifted uncomfortably, his eyes going out over the balcony. "It's really not urgent..."

"Gryf, who?"

If Gryfian wasn't as absolutely effective at his position as he was, he would have vocalized the groan that was avoiding showing itself on his face. "Lord Lexios."

"Lexios?"

"Yes, Lord Lexios."

I couldn't quite ignore the excitement that flickered through me at the idea of a friend, one that was mine I'd made myself, coming to say hello. Almost like I was back at the dorms, and I was across the hall from Aiden or Kaleb.

Of course, that was before I got my bedroom in the upper classroom hallway, thanks to Alex.

I straightened up and smoothed my clothes while also trying to look casual. "No, no, invite him in."

"Your Grace," he said with just a slight hesitation. "His Majesty..."

"My room, too, Gryf," I said with a look that I hoped conveyed I understood where he was going with that statement.

Gryfian nodded and turned away, and a few seconds later, *Lord* Lexios strode onto the balcony, a giant grin on his face.

"I trust you had an attitude adjustment," I said playfully.

He chuckled, a low, earthy sound, that didn't have a hint of sarcasm in it. It was like he was a totally different person than the night before. "So, this is what the King gets to see every day, huh?"

"And Justice," I reminded him. "Let's not forget who *really* runs this place." Of course, I was joking, but he nodded earnestly.

"Absolutely."

"So, what's up? I gotta hear the history of you two from your perspective," I turned and grabbed some bread, dipping it in a jelly that tasted like butter and apricot. "Breakfast?"

Lexios sat down in the chair that was usually Ollie's and began to help himself to the bounty, lifting his feet to set them on the railing. "Thanks." He lifted a raquin to his lips and took a bite. "These are my favorites. Do you have them in your world?"

I shook my head, my stomach pooling with that feeling you get when the first buddings of a new friendship are taking root inside you. "We have apples. And oranges, grapes, peaches..."

"Peaches?" he asked, his brow wrinkling. "What's a peaches?"

"Peach," I corrected. "And it looks like... well it kind of looks like an ass." I patted my hip for reinforcement of what I was saying. "Where I'm from, people will send each other peach emojis to tell someone their booty looks fine as hell."

"Emojis?" he softly laughed. "Booty?"

God. Sometimes it was so easy to forget that this really was a wholly different world. "Nevermind." I waved my hand to dismiss the conversation, grabbing a raquin for myself. "Back to my original question. What happened between you two to make you... I dunno, archnemeses?" I giggled at the thought of the newest superhero movie, Lexios versus King Olympio.

Lexios sighed as he finished the fruit, then pushed his blond waves behind his ears. "Honestly? I was a little prick back in the day. Olympio and I were born to be thick as thieves, a built-in friendship, if you will. As you know, we're descended from the same line."

I nodded, "Yeah, he said so last night. But what actually *happened*?"

My new friend stood and leaned over the balcony, his red chiton shifting just so in the gentle Sefaeran breezes. "I fell victim to the jealousy of youth," he said as his shoulders rose and fell. It was almost like he was trying to make it as casual as possible while it clearly still embarrassed him. "I saw how many people wanted him, how many people wanted to *be* him. What young man doesn't want to feel like a god?"

I huffed, dissociation hitting me like a storm front as I tried to remember the boy who felt invisible at parties, always knowing that any attention he got was because people wanted to get close to his parents. "Yeah…" I reflected. "Something like that."

"Anyway," he turned back to face me. "I started acting like a complete asshole and spread some rumors about him, told some lies to get people to like me. Ultimately paid the price of losing my friend. A wholly appropriate punishment, if I'm honest."

I looked up at him, my hand going to my forehead to shield my eyes from the sunlight. "Sounds like you were a regular asshat."

"You've got it."

"So, is that why Gryfian was weird about letting you in?"

For the first time, he rolled his eyes. "Probably."

I reached out my leg and toed him in the knee. "Chill. As I told him—my room, too."

He smiled at me thankfully. "I'd really like to show Olympio—His Majesty—that I'm sorry, and that I'd like to at least be cordial, if not… Well, in my wildest dreams, I'd love to be friends again."

"I'll see what I can do." I reached for another piece of the jellied bread. "Thanks for stopping by."

His brow wrinkled. "Oh. Did you want me to go?"

He wanted to stay? Like... hang out?

"No!" I said almost a little too quickly. "I mean—I don't have any plans today, but that doesn't mean no one does. I just assumed you had—"

"No." He shook his head firmly. "Nothing on my agenda."

"Oh."

"Yeah."

Fucking hell, I was out of practice on how to "friendship" with anyone besides my soulmate and my kormarrin. Then, in the most awkward possible way:

"Do you want to—" I began, at the same time as he said, "So how long have you—"

"You first," he laughed.

"No, please."

Our conversation was interrupted by a clamor that was so loud it echoed through the chamber, despite clearly happening outside in the hall.

"*What?!*" Ollie's voice rang out, and rage coursed through me—*his* rage. "Move, Gryfian. Now!"

The doors slammed open, and both Lexios and I turned to look as a shadow I knew to be the love of my life shot through the room like a bullet until he was right on top of Lexios, just like he'd been on Vassenia in that tower she'd held me in.

"Get... out!" the shadow demon bellowed.

"Knock it off, Ollie," I shouted, fighting against my desire to recoil from the form I still feared and grabbing him by the shoulder.

His wing shot out, knocking me away and causing me to stumble backwards into the table, my knee colliding with the wrought iron chair, breaking the skin.

"Fuck!" I yelped, and apparently it was the magic word, because Ollie actually turned away from Lexios, the voids of his eyes shifting to the violet I adored.

"Gabriel," he gasped, his body quickly returning to the tanned skin and copper hair. He rushed to my side, running his hands over my arms and shoulders, checking me for injuries. Then, his head whipped back toward Lexios. "You've done enough. I said get out. I won't say it again."

I gripped my bleeding knee with one hand as my face burned with embarrassment. "He's my guest," I said, grabbing Ollie once more. "Don't talk to people like that."

For the first time, my soulmate turned to me with a look as tortured as I'd ever seen it, even when I told him I hated him. "Your guest?" he echoed, his voice quiet, cracking on the words.

We stared at each other in silence for a moment, his face as pained as mine was resolved.

"You know, Lexios, maybe we should just catch up later. I'd like to speak to *His Majesty* in private if you don't mind."

My new friend nodded, then bowed. "Your Majesty. Your Grace."

We stayed silent, eyes never leaving each other as Lexios exited. As soon as the door closed, I pushed Ollie gently away and got to my feet. "Guess this is why they say the first year of marriage really tests you, huh?" Olympio looked confused and moved as though he was going to try and coddle me. "Don't," I said.

"You were alone with him. Again." Ollie's tone was as much a question as it was a grievance, one that was obviously causing him pain, but after how he just acted, I was too embarrassed of him to pay much attention to his ego wound.

"Yeah," I replied, "I was. He was just explaining to me about how he used to treat you extremely unfairly and how he regretted his jealousy. But please, let's not give anyone a chance to change. It's not like anyone has ever given *you* that opportunity."

His head jerked like I'd hit him with my fist and not just my words. "Gabriel... It's different."

"Is it? I thought, as Justice, it was my job to evaluate people as they stand before me. Not to make assumptions based on past transgressions or the accusations of others." It was sharp. I had intended it to be.

"You barely know him," he argued, pleading with me. "I've known him for thousands of years. That entire family is bent on ruining mine so they can take the throne themselves, and Lexios has never, not once, shown himself to be anything other than his father's son. Even Vassenia, who I *did* trust, proved exactly how far they would go."

I let out a noise of disgust and pushed past him, going back to the bed and throwing myself down onto it. For the first time, in a long time, Ollie was really pissing me off.

There was a long stretch of silence between us. I didn't even hear Ollie move until several minutes later, when I felt his weight shift the bed.

"Explain it to me, then," he said in a strained voice, like every syllable hurt him to say. "What is it about him that you trust so readily?"

"Who said anything about trust?" I mumbled into my pillow before turning over and looking at him. "I just know... you. I want to judge for myself. He's been nothing but polite and appropriate with me since I met him yesterday, and I don't know if you've noticed, but it's not exactly like I'm having to beat people off with a stick. I have no friends. They're all too scared of *King* Olympio to come close."

"He put his hands on you." He was quiet when he said it. "And you *have* friends. Ari and the rest of the hunt all adore you. My mother likes you better than she likes me. Tomos worships the ground you walk on. Gryfian would give his life for you. And... there's me."

I sighed and collapsed backward once more. "It's not the same as making my own friends, Ollie. But fine. Forbid me from seeing him. You are my king, too, after all."

He blinked hard, like he was both confused and struck, then moved slowly to sit beside me. "I..." He cleared his throat. "Gabriel... You are as much the ruler of Sefaera as I am. But Lexios... I've known him for millennia. I won't... I won't forbid you from seeing him, because I don't want to be that kind of partner to you. I trust you. I'm only asking you to use the same judgment that makes you such a gifted Justice when discerning who would make a good friend to you—especially ones who share a bloodline with Typhir."

I turned so my back was to him. This entire interaction was so far beyond irritating me, I didn't even want to see his face. Frankly, the feeling scared me. Was this what it would be like now?

But then, he spoke from behind me, saying two words that would never fail to break through to me. "Your Grace..."

I found myself scooting away, a pout playing on my lips as I could feel the warmth that was Olympio seeping into my bones. "I don't think I have anything left to say," I mumbled.

"Well, I do," he said, his arms snaking around me as the bond echoed the embrace within me, like being held from the inside out. His lips grazed my ear as he whispered. "I'm sorry. For scaring you. For hurting you. I never want you to fear me or to be the cause of your pain. I love you, Gabriel. And... if you trust him, I won't stand in the way of your friendship. All I ask is that you really make sure you *can* trust him before you give him too much of you. I learned that lesson the hard way."

The feeling of him—god, the feeling of him. His chest against my back and the perfect way our bodies puzzled together was my happy place. There was no way I could be upset with him, even in a superficial capacity when he had me this thoroughly.

He leaned in and made a small circle on my cheek with his nose and drug it down to my neck, where he pressed several small kisses.

Fuck.

"Ollie..." I whined. "You have things to do today, you know..."

"Do I?" he said, sucking gently on my neck and pulling me even closer, so I was all but in his lap. "I can't seem to remember what they are."

"I... I... Ollie."

His hand slid beneath the fabric of my chiton and he rested it on my lower belly.

"Tell me to stop, *Your Grace*." His voice was a purr, the tips of his fingers teasing the little hairs that sat between my hip bones.

I couldn't help but squirm, which elicited a low growl from him, radiating out of his chest and rumbling through me. If I hadn't already been hard as fuck, which I was, I would be now.

"Your Majesty," I faux-complained, "If I hold you up from your schedule, the Council will start bitching about how I'm the Yoko Ono of Sefaera."

"I feel fairly certain that's a reference I should know from my time in your world," he said, "but I don't. Regardless, I wouldn't be the first king to need a way to... decompress after frustrating meetings and engagements. Imagine if we made it known just how badly we need each other all the time—if anytime I had to deal with Typhir I just came right into the Justice meetings and bent you over the throne, or brought you into the Council chambers and had you on your knees beneath the table..."

My spit suddenly clotted in my throat, and I began to choke on the visuals he was painting so clearly for me. "Fuck—" I had to sit up and bang on my chest to clear my airway. My cock, however, was unwavering.

"Is there something wrong, *my* Gabriel?" he asked. He didn't laugh, but I could *feel* him chuckling internally. "If those scenarios don't suit you, there's always the option of you decorating my lap when *I* sit on the throne. Your gorgeous cock bouncing as I rule from inside of you, making every single member of court—of the entire kingdom—envious that I get to have you, and they do not."

I turned to look at him, and I could feel my heart pounding in my ears. "You're just kidding, right?"

His eyes sparkled, his face breaking into a full grin. "Do you want me to be? Because, as king, I do believe I could enact laws to allow me to have you whenever and wherever I wish. Imagine how much more effectively I could rule if my consort could provide me with stress relief whenever I wanted."

"Oh, god..." I shuddered, and my eyes rolled at the thought of Ollie picking me up and hoisting me over his shoulder to go about his daily duties, all while I sat by to be his...

My thoughts exploded in color and light as his hand drifted lower, wrapping around my length. "No gods here, Your Grace. Just a demon and his most prized... *possession*. Because you *are* mine, Gabriel. Now and always."

"Uh-huh..." I whimpered, fully turning to straddle his hips, my lips going to his delicious mouth before I even finished. I needed him. I needed him to make good on the not-so-subtle threats. I needed...

I slid down his body and furiously pushed the fabric covering his cock aside so I could take it in my mouth, take *him* in my mouth. I needed every inch of him. This seemed like a good place to start. I groaned as the taste of him flavored my tongue, and the smell of his essence assaulted my senses with vivid lust.

"Yes," he hissed, his hands going to my hair and tangling in it, gently guiding my pace. "Exactly like that. Exactly how you would do it if I walked into your Justice hearings and exposed myself, ordering you to your knees before me. To stop no matter what the hearing was about because your mouth would be occupied until I was fully satisfied."

This was sheer ecstasy, him painting vivid pictures in my head of a dark pantomime where the king of this world forced me on display, fed me what was mine, and allowed his court to gaze upon our perfect synchronicity. The whimpers which escaped me were involuntary and sharp as every possible nerve ending alighted.

"Fuck, even my nipples are hard, Ol," I gasped, pulling back and watching in delight as the saliva connected my mouth to his base.

"Stroke yourself, then," he commanded, drawing my face back to his cock. "Pleasure yourself in front of the entire palace. Let them see how skilled you are, how easily you can bring the king to ecstasy, and that you are the *only* one who can."

He didn't have to command it, I was already there. And I made sure to position myself so that my King, my soulmate, *my* Olympio, could see it all.

It would have probably been impossible to tell from the mouthful I had, but I moaned his name over and over again as I consumed him, the scent of him making me delirious.

His hips began to buck lightly, a sign things were progressing faster than he was necessarily prepared for, but he didn't let up, urging me further down, pressing into the back of my throat and stretching my lips wide.

"Gabriel..." he groaned, no longer able to contribute to the fantasy. "*My* Gabriel..."

Without any warning, I found myself hurtling towards my own climax, and even extracting my hand from my throbbing length made no fucking difference. "Ollie—" I cried out, throwing myself up onto his chest as if somehow, some *way*, he could forbid me from exploding my release all over him. My fingers gripped his cock as I buried my face into his neck, wave after wave of my orgasm ripping through me in sharp, desperate gasps. "Ollie... Ollie... Olympio..."

It took me a moment to realize I wasn't alone. I hadn't even heard him over the sound of my own cries, but I knew he'd finished when he gently removed my hand from his member and pulled my face to his for a kiss.

"And now for a bath," he whispered before standing and lifting me in one fluid motion to carry me to the tub.

Even if I wanted to resist, my bones had all turned to jelly, and frankly, Olympio had earned my compliance.

At least for now.

Chapter Eight
Olympio

"I don't understand why my presence is required," I grumbled in an admittedly childish way. "I'm allowing them use of the grand hall. Neither of them cares for me any more than I care for them. Why can't I just have a night where my time is my own, with my soulmate?"

Gabriel grinned, reaching up to straighten my crown, which I had dropped on my head haphazardly, a visual display of my frustration at being forced to attend Lexios's pre-Union celebration.

Truthfully, as king, I could refuse any event I chose. But as Gabriel, Ari, even my mother, were all quick to remind me, appearances were nearly as important to ruling as *actually* ruling. If I allowed my own personal dislike of Typhir and his festering wound of a son to keep me away from events that were technically put on by the palace—especially after my consort and I sentenced one member of their family to death—it might look like I was a tyrant.

Sefaera hadn't seen one of those since my line split from Typhir's four generations ago, with *his* ancestor nearly causing a full-scale rebellion and coup. His sister, my great great grandmother, saw the monster he'd become and killed him herself. His children, who were young, were allowed to remain in the palace as members of court, but that half of the line was never again allowed positions of true power.

Until Typhir managed to worm his way in.

"Who says we can't do both?" Gabriel said with a voice that was clearly meant to be sultry. It was, but not in the way he intended. He was too pure to ever be truly seductive. No, his sexiness was based in the way his entire face lit up with anticipation of my reaction when he said something like that, his innate goodness like a beacon in the night. As if he was made just to bring more light to my life with every word and action.

I took his arms in my hands and leaned in to brush my lips across his cheek. "Let's only hope I have the energy to make love to you the way you deserve after kissing the asses of the scum of Sefaera all night."

A slight pout crossed Gabriel's lips. He turned his head away, and a pang of something like hurt echoed through the bond.

"What's wrong?" I asked. He hadn't rejected my touch since his first weeks here, and even that small denial of my affection was enough to send worry into every single part of me.

"Nothing..." he sighed, walking away to where a tray of drinks had been served to us before the party.

"To use a phrase from Gaiada," I said, moving closer once more and pouring a goblet of wine for each of us before he could, "bullshit. You know as well as I do that I know what you're feeling. Tell me why."

Gabriel shrugged and downed his drink much faster than someone who was unbothered would have. He slowly set it down before looking back at me. "I have a chance, one chance, to make a friend. And likely, not even for very long as it seems he goes away a lot. And in this chance to make a friend, all you can think about is some fight you two got into as kids. I guess I can't help but wonder if this is what our life together is really gonna be like. My needs falling second to the whims and grudges of *King* Olympio."

My chest felt like it was imploding, and my heartbeat pounded in my ears. The idea that Gabriel, *my* Gabriel, saw the situation that way was tantamount to a physical pain.

I gently took his goblet and pushed some of his silky waves behind his ear. "Never," I promised. "I have bad history with Lexios and his father. You know that. But... it *has* been over two thousand years. Perhaps Lexios has changed and isn't following in his father's footsteps. I won't make any promises for my own feelings, but I promise you this. I will not stand in the way, and as much as I can, I will refrain from voicing my opinions on your new friend."

Gabriel sighed. "For how long? I don't want to do this every day."

"Until—*unless*—he proves me right," I assured him, fighting the urge to retch at the idea of giving Lexios a fresh start. "I promise not to hold him accountable for the things we did in our youth. Only for things he does from this point forward."

Gabriel looked up at me through his long, dark eyelashes, and the hope I saw there was like a breath of crisp morning air. "Thanks, Ol," he said sweetly. "Now straighten that crown. We have a ball to attend."

I leaned in to press my nose to his cheek in our special kiss, then reached up to make myself more presentable. "Better, Your Grace?"

Gabriel took a step back and examined me. "I suppose it will do." Then he moved closer, pressing himself against me, and kissed me deeply in a way that never failed to take my breath away. I kissed him back greedily, then noticed his hand wandering down the front of my stomach, southward.

"Are you trying to lure me away from the party?" I asked, my lips never leaving his as my hands gripped his hips. "Because I promised to not say anything negative about your new friend. I said nothing about taking any chance I have to avoid being in his presence. Especially if that chance happens to involve you being naked."

Gabriel made a face that clearly indicated he was appalled and pulled away. "Well, now I'm definitely not gonna give you a 'good boy' blowjob. Come on!"

My soulmate was a whirlwind of golden silk and was out the door before I could fully process what he'd said. Likely, that was his intention. My cheeky Gabriel.

In a swirl of shadows, however, I cut him off only a few feet outside our door, materializing in front of him with my arms crossed and an eyebrow raised.

"You'll pay for that later," I promised him, grinning to let him know that I was both teasing and deeply serious. I saw the visible shiver of anticipation come across him, and I grabbed his hand. "Let's go."

Half an hour later, I was outside the grand hall, nodding to Gabriel's valet Tomos, a short, impish man who'd been serving my family for almost as long as I'd been alive, which was an unusually long time, even by Sefaeran standards. Gryfian was the only other member of my staff to live that long—excluding Typhir's line, who were all immortal like myself—and his extended lifespan was due to being blood-bound to the throne.

Tomos rushed to the doors, which were opened by a pair of guards, and stepped forward.

"His Royal Majesty, King Olympio, and His Grace, the Ever-wise Consort and Justice, Gabriel!"

His excited squeak as he announced our entrance brought a smile to Gabriel's face, though I was a bit annoyed when I saw that smile expand further when Lexios came into view. The woman on his arm—a girl, really, since it was clear that she was young certainly of age, but possibly younger than Gabriel—was beautiful. Sapphire blue hair cascaded like water around her shoulders and down her back, lightly coral-toned skin deepened at her cheekbones to nearly a maroon, and her eyes were entirely emerald, iris, sclera, and pupil.

That one glance was enough to tell me that she was from Jouraya, a part of Sefaera made entirely of tropical islands. All of their people looked as though they were made of the sea itself, and this woman was no different. In fact, if the color of her eyes was any indicator, she was among the nobility there and would have a lifespan that bordered on immortality without actually being immortal. It made sense why she was chosen—Typhir couldn't have his son formally United with a woman with a shortened lifespan and still hope to reap the benefits.

Gabriel and I made our way down the steps, waving regally to the crowd, stopping at a small landing halfway down.

"My dear friends and subjects," I said, avoiding the eyes of both Lexios and his father, not wanting to lose my will to be cordial. "It is my great honor to welcome you to such a momentous event. While not everyone can be blessed with a soulmate, that does not mean that love has no place in Sefaera. Lord Lexios has been lucky in finding his partner. Please, step forward."

I kept my gaze on his intended as they made their way up the stairs, stopping three steps below us, as was proper.

"I beseech you, my lady," I said with a slight bow, "introduce yourself to the rest of court, which you are, from now and henceforth, a part of."

With a perfect curtsy and a brilliant smile, she said, "Celaine, Your Majesty. It's a pleasure to be here, and to be welcomed into your court with such kindness."

As her eyes met mine, a sharp jolt in my gut nearly took my breath away. While looking nothing else alike, I was suddenly forcibly reminded of the other pair of green eyes I'd spent millennia staring into. The ones that belonged to my lover. Lexios's cousin. Gabriel's abductor and torturer.

Vassenia.

Gabriel's hand gave mine a subtle squeeze, and I felt a pang of worry from him. He wasn't even looking at me, but had managed to convey that he was here without alerting any of our guests. He had come so far in such a short time in terms of his ability to present as a royal while still being utterly Gabriel.

"Well," I said, ensuring my smile was firmly in place, "it is a pleasure to have you. And now, please enjoy the festivities. They are for you—both of you—after all."

With a flourish of my hand (and an urge to retch at being forced to be so kind of Lexios), I signaled for the music to begin to play, and the guests began to dance as first Lexios and Celaine, then Gabriel and I descended the steps to join the festivities.

"Well?" I whispered into Gabriel's ear as we walked. "How did I do?"

"Acceptable," he whispered back, satisfied. "I'm gonna go get a drink. You want something?"

"As much wine as you can fit in a single glass," I said, kissing him on the cheek and making my way to the long line of dignitaries waiting for my attention.

As he departed, I felt Gabriel give my ass a gentle, subtle squeeze, and suddenly, it seemed like everything was going to be alright. As much as it would kill me to play nice with my old rival, maybe my soulmate was right to some very small extent. I had, indeed, changed. Why couldn't Lexios do the same?

And if he wasn't Typhir's son, I might actually have been able to believe that.

After the fiftieth or so greeting, I found myself wishing heartily for the glass of wine Gabriel had promised, but he was nowhere in my line of sight, surrounded as I was by sycophants and social climbers.

"You'll have to excuse me," I said to someone who I took to perhaps be a relative of Celaine's, judging by his features. "It is a pleasure to meet you, but I am rather in need of a libation."

Moons and rivers, it was exhausting to monitor every single word, to ensure that I *sounded* like the king, as if being myself while being king wasn't enough. But fifteen hundred years of forcing myself to emulate the way my brother had presented himself had taught me to speak like he would have. I often wondered if I did, indeed, sound like him—regal and self-assured—or if I sounded like a pompous ass, or worse, like someone trying to put on a mask that would never fit.

I saw Gabriel across the party talking to Ari, but before I could make my way over to them, I encountered Lexios. Celaine stood beside him as he spoke to his father, smiling mildly, listening to the conversation but taking in her surroundings with a subtle interest.

"Ah, Your Majesty," Typhir said, summoning me over. The very idea of him demanding any of my attention, when he had no right to do so, would have been enough to make me turn and walk in the opposite direction. But with most of my court and the nobility of Jouraya watching, it would have been horrendous etiquette to do so, and I wasn't going to let Typhir, of all people, make me look bad.

"Lord Typhir," I said when I reached them with a hint of a nod in his direction. "Lord Lexios. Lady Celaine." I reached for her hand, kissing the knuckles in a gesture of welcome.

"We were just discussing the... strange occurrences during your adjournment, Your Majesty," Typhir said. "Gaiadan beasts being found in the Royal Forest."

"Strange, indeed," I agreed. "What exactly is there to discuss, though? It was a single creature, and it has been not only captured, but Liro has been taming it, himself."

"But surely you see this as a greater issue," Typhir countered. "No one had been to Gaiada in centuries, longer even, before your soulmate joined us here, and now their animals are making their way through the portals."

Fury flared within me, and to his credit, Lexios also looked a bit uncomfortable at his father's insinuation.

I stepped closer to him so that there were mere inches between us. "Are you suggesting that Gabriel is somehow, in *any* capacity, responsible for a potential portal breach?" I asked in a deadly whisper. "I would be very, *very* careful with your next words."

For once, Typhir looked like he recognized he'd overstepped. Before he could speak, however, Lexios put a hand on his father's arm, his eyes just over and above my shoulder. The shadows were forming my wings, my temper drawing forth my demon form in the middle of the grand ballroom.

"Perhaps His Majesty is right, and this isn't the venue for such conversations," he said with a half-glance in my direction. "Let's enjoy the festivities, and you can resume your political disagreements in the Council chambers tomorrow. I'm sure that Celaine would prefer not to be embroiled in this kind of discourse."

I'd nearly forgotten she was here. In less than a second, I felt the shadows withdraw, and I turned to her, her eyes once more catching me off-guard.

"My deepest apologies, my Lady," I said to her, fighting the urge to blame Typhir rather than simply smoothing things over. "Perhaps you would be willing to forgive my brutishness if I were to escort you to the dance floor?"

She glanced at Lexios as if to ask his permission, but Lexios gave me a hint of a smile and said, "If she desires, I'll happily assent."

I reached out, and Celaine put her hand in mine so that I could guide her through the throngs of bodies to the dance floor. The musicians began to play a lively tune, and I raised my hand, where Celaine quickly met my palm with her own, her emerald eyes sparking a maelstrom of thoughts and memories to converge in my mind.

It was strange. I'd been with Vassenia for two and a half thousand years, but in the twenty one years of Gabriel's life, I hadn't so much as touched a woman, with only a couple of close calls with Vass when I'd returned. Dancing with Celaine had reminded me of why I enjoyed the company of women just as much as that of men. Gabriel was graceful and lithe, but there was a softness to Celaine's movements, to the body of a woman that my soulmate could not replicate.

"So, Lady Celaine," I said, wanting to draw her attention away from the conflict before and to distract myself from thoughts of my once most trusted friend turned betrayer, "how long ago did you and Lord Lexios meet?"

Her expression gave no clues to her feelings about him or her Union. "Nearly a year ago, Your Majesty. He was on a diplomatic visit, and Lord Typhir insisted on us meeting."

"That's a rather short courtship." I shifted our positions so my free hand rested on her back and hers found my upper arm.

"I suppose," she said with the same mild tone. "But Lord Typhir and my mother decided it was for the best, and they didn't see any point in drawing things out."

Her words struck a chord. "You didn't choose Lexios, yourself?" It was a bit of a strange question from me, considering I had been bound by fate to Gabriel before I ever met him, but ours was a soulmate bond. What she was describing was a politically arranged Union.

"No," she said, "but I've known from childhood that I would likely be United to further my mother's interests. Lord Lexios is beyond her wildest dreams for a partner, and he and Lord Typhir, whatever flaws they may have, have been good to me."

The way she spoke was so matter of fact that it made my heart ache for her. It wasn't until Gabriel had come of age that I could truly comprehend what love, *real* love, felt like. But not everyone could be gifted by fate, itself, with a soulmate, and I thought back to what I had felt for Vass before I knew something more. It had been passionate and comfortable, having a best friend who you were also insatiably attracted to. Perhaps Celaine and Lexios would find that place in their Union.

The song ended, and I stepped back to bow to her as she bent in a curtsy.

"Thank you, Your Majesty," she said.

"Thank *you*, Lady Celaine," I replied. "It was a true pleasure." I meant it. She was gentle and kind, and I only hoped that her goodness wouldn't be marred by the family she was to be United with.

I had barely turned around when I ran into Ari, who looked like she was on a mission.

"Oh. Hello," I said, looking around. "Where's Gabriel?"

All my sister did was nod over my shoulder, and I knew, before she even spoke, what I would find.

Once more separated from the bustle of the party, I saw *my* Gabriel and Lexios, alone by the wine fountain. A single pulse through the bond told me Gabriel was nearly drunk, and despite Lexios intervening between Typhir and me, I still didn't trust him.

"Do you want me to follow you?" Ari asked.

"Probably best if you don't," I said with a bit of a growl. "If we keep ganging up on him, people may begin to think we're bullying Lexios."

"People?" Ari said dryly, raising a single eyebrow. "Or just Gabriel?"

"Well," I sighed, "he's the only one who matters."

"I take offense to that," she said, though the noncommittal tone let me know she was only teasing, even if she was being cautious. "I'll watch from a distance. Just in case."

"Thank you."

I made my way over to the wine fountain, and Gabriel looked at me with that heartstopping smile of his, his violet eyes, the most beautiful I'd ever seen, meeting mine.

"Hey," he said, slurring slightly.

"I was waiting for my wine, but I think you got lost," I said, pulling him to me for a kiss. I wanted to be petty and pretend Lexios wasn't there, but he *had* done a good job with diverting his father before, and

I'd promised Gabriel I'd give him a chance. I nodded at him. "Lexios. I trust the party is to your liking?"

Lexios looked at me with suspicion, then nodded. "It's wonderful. Thank you, Your Majesty. I was just talking to His Grace about his education before he came here. It sounds like an interesting place. Columbia, was it?"

Gabriel grinned, and once again, I couldn't stop the jealousy over someone else—particularly *this* someone else—making him smile like that. "Yeah, Columbia. I wasn't really there for the education though, if I'm perfectly honest." He turned and looked at me, a flicker of memory marring the smile, leaving me forced to watch it fall. "Actually, I'm not really sure why I was there. I guess..." I knew what he was thinking of. The letter I'd forged under his parents' names to get him to attend their alma mater so I could keep an eye on him after their deaths. "I guess it was to honor my parents' memory."

Lexios nodded. "Sometimes our parents do seem rather insistent that they know what's best for us, don't they?"

I could feel Gabriel retreating inside himself, and almost as if Lexios noticed too, he followed up with. "Olymp—Your Majesty, have you taken His Grace to the Pyvieral Falls yet?"

I placed my hand on the small of Gabriel's back, hoping to provide him a sliver of reassurance and comfort. "We haven't had the opportunity," I admitted. The Pyvieral Falls were a wonder of Sefaera, only an hour long lymere ride from the palace. But we hadn't had the time before the adjournment, and it had only been days since our return. "I'm sure we can find the time soon, though. I'm certain Gabriel would love them."

"Mm," my soulmate commented, still not quite present.

"I'd be happy to accompany you," Lexios continued. "For safety."

For the first time that night, he fully met my eyes, and I his. The very idea that Lexios would be needed for safety, when he'd once been a traitor of a friend, was enough to make me either laugh or lash out in rage. But there was a sincerity there that I hadn't expected. Perhaps Gabriel was right.

"That is a kind offer, and one I will certainly keep in mind." I pulled Gabriel closer against me. He wasn't panicking—I would have felt it. He was truly *absent*. "Gabriel..." I breathed into his ear. "Do you need to retire?"

He looked up at me, and I could see how distant he was. He had this way of transitioning to an almost childlike state when he was emotionally shot, and I knew that if I kept him here, it was only a matter of time before the exhaustion turned into irritability.

"I want to stay. It's Lex's party."

I looked to Lexios. Now would be a perfect test of whether he could be a good friend to Gabriel. Would he insist on my soulmate staying? Or would he recognize that Gabriel was struggling and give him what he needed?

Typhir's son smiled and put a hand on Gabriel's shoulder. "You look exhausted. Plus, I really should be attending to my intended. Get some rest. Perhaps the four of us can share a meal later this week."

He looked up at me, almost as if he was looking for approval. I nodded, not wanting to give him praise for doing the bare minimum—I'd learned the hard way what that was. But he did do the right thing, and I was willing to give him that.

"Come on," I said, moving my hand from his waist to his hand and lacing our fingers together. "Let's go. And... Lexios..." I turned my attention back to my once friend. "Congratulations. Enjoy the party."

He nodded to me as my soulmate allowed me to steer him away.

Ari caught my eye as we navigated through the crowd, and, in true Ariadne fashion, she began to move her way between the revelers, greeting people in a way that allowed Gabriel and me to slip out unnoticed.

Once out in the hallway, I scooped him into my arms as he buried his face in my chest. "I'm right here," I promised.

Gryfian followed us as we made our way back through the palace until we finally arrived at our quarters. Gabriel had dozed off as I carried him, the wine and the emotional stress taking its toll. I had Gryfian open the door for us, and I took Gabriel straight to bed.

As I laid him there, watching him sleep, I sent a pulse of calm to comfort him through the bond, and I watched as his brow unfurrowed. I pushed his hair back from his face so I could see him properly.

"I can never make up for the mistakes I made," I whispered, knowing he couldn't hear me, but that he would feel the sentiment, even in sleep. "For the lies I told or the ways I manipulated you. I wish I could regret them more than I do, because each of those mistakes still led you here, to me. But loving you the way I do, I know that I cannot stand to see you in pain because of my actions. And I will spend the rest of eternity trying to prove to you that I am better than who I was before you showed me who I could be. Until my heart no longer beats."

Chapter Nine
Gabriel

It was my first time back acting as Justice since the adjournment, and I was weirdly nervous about it. The last judgment I'd made was on Vassenia's life, and the thought of what had befallen her after my sentencing had haunted more than one of my nightmares.

Ollie was gone from the bed when I woke up, as usual now, and I ached for the times when I never woke up alone. I knew that we had eternity together, but somehow, I'd never felt as distant as I did when his side of the bed was cold.

I was complacent, if not dissociated, while the servants dressed me, and I wasn't even really conscious of my actions again until Tomos nudged me to quit slouching before he announced my name to enter the Justice hall.

"His Grace, Justice Gabriel," he called out.

I walked in, feeling queasy as I tried to figure out where I was supposed to look while I moved.

I sat on the throne that waited for me, one that was starkly different than the pair we sat on at dinners and events, which were golden and had black satin seating. No, this was cold, hard obsidian, and there was no cushioning to allow me to sink into it. Maybe that was the idea—no relaxing while there were lives to weigh on.

The first person who approached was shackled, and for a moment my heart began to pound. I wasn't sure I was ready to dole out more death sentences. Thankfully, this man was under arrest for drunk and disorderly conduct—something that, under Typhir, would have carried a five year sentence in the palace jail.

I couldn't help but laugh as the guard escorting him reminded me of the common punishment. "You can't be serious," I scoffed. "If being a drunken mess was punishable by prison where I'm from, I'd have been there—well I'd have been there a long time."

"Your Grace..."

I turned at the sound of the slimiest voice I was regretfully becoming familiar with as Typhir slid out from the back of the room. Of course, he would be here. Imagine missing a chance to catch me slacking.

"Lord Typhir," I addressed. I opened my mouth to continue, but he interrupted me.

"Your Grace. Justice... This man does not possess the money that it would take to cover the fines for his conduct. The disruption itself carries only a one-year sentence, however, his inability to pay his fines is what makes for the bulk of his sentence."

I looked down at the man with confusion, and he in turn, looked at the marble floor. "So, what you're saying," I slowly iterated. "Is that this man would, under your reign, be imprisoned for being... poor?"

I watched as the man's face went more scarlet than the chiton Typhir wore, and whispers broke out among those in attendance.

"Your Grace..."

"Lord Typhir, I believe your own son has been seen at several events over the last week engaging in drunken fistfights with the King, if I'm not mistaken. Should Lord Lexios also be forced to serve time?"

The crowd positively erupted with alarm at that point, and Typhir looked like he was about five heartbeats away from a stroke.

It was only then that I noticed, way off to the back, a second red chiton belonging to a handsome man with blond hair.

Fuck.

Thankfully, he appeared to be covering his mouth to hide his own amusement, but I wanted to sink into the floor. I had just used my new friend as a threat against his father.

"I think I'd like to dismiss this case," I said quickly, indicating that the guards should release the man. "Next time you partake, my friend, be sure to do it far, far away from Lord Typhir. Maybe a different time zone if possible."

The man looked confused but grateful, and Typhir left in a rageful cyclone of red robes and clicking shoes.

From across the hall, Lexios and I exchanged awkward silent acknowledgements, then he followed his father out of the hearings. I was helpless to do anything to find out how much I'd offended him but made a mental note to make it up to him.

By the time the hearings ended, it was well past lunch, which, of course, was the time Ollie and I had planned to see each other. And it was so far past, that I had barely stepped out of the hall when Liro swept by, grabbing me by the elbow and dragging me outside for my knife fighting lessons.

"You want me to fight you wearing this?" I whined, gesturing down to my ceremonial garments. "My fucking nut sack is gonna get stabbed."

"Guess it's a good thing I brought you something to change into then," he retorted. "Wouldn't want to damage the royal punching bag."

"Exact—hey, wait a minute."

Liro never failed to make me laugh, even as flustered as I was, and by the time we got out to the fighting pit, I was walking on my own willingly.

The sand beneath my feet was warm, and I was instantly transported back to our adjournment. I breathed in deeply, willing myself to be there with Ollie. But instead, I felt—and heard—a pile of leather drop at my feet, and I looked down to see battle gear.

"Dress," Liro commanded.

"What—here?"

"Yes, here," he chuckled. "I'll turn around, if it offends the lady's sensibilities."

I picked up one of the leather boots and threw it at him. "You're my least favorite brother-in-law."

With a quick look over my shoulder to be sure no one else was nearby, I stripped down out of my ceremonial clothing and began to adorn the fighting leathers.

"No peeking," I called out.

"That would be a lot easier to do, if you weren't bent over like that."

It hit me like a frying pan to the face that the voice behind me wasn't Liro. No, this was much deeper, much softer. I panicked and realized a second too late that my garments were tangled around my knees, causing me to fall over, face first into the sand.

"Of course," Ollie drawled as he moved to crouch beside me, "I generally prefer you in this position when we *don't* have an audience." Suddenly his lips were at my ear, his words a hushed whisper. "Unless you were trying to tease me with a reality of the... conversation... we had the other night."

"I have no idea what you just said, but given the first part, I suddenly feel compelled to smack you on your sister's behalf," Liro said, the playful smile evident in his voice.

"In front of what audience?" I asked. "Liro?"

Ollie and I both looked over at Liro who now looked even more uncomfortable.

"See, now I feel like I should hit you both—just for me."

I giggled, falling back onto the sand, fully accepting the nakedness of my situation. No pun intended. "Sorry, Liro, you're gonna miss one hell of a show, though."

"Somehow, I think I will live," he replied, turning away once more.

I gazed up at Ollie, his eyes looking incredibly tired for it being so early in the afternoon. They'd been like that since we'd returned, and I was beginning to worry about whether he was okay during these meetings he disappeared to every day.

But his smile... It was the same smile he always had for me, and he stood, holding out his hand to help me to my feet.

"Liro," he said, his eyes never leaving mine, "why don't you and Ari enjoy an afternoon off together. My meetings have concluded for the day, and I could use a bit of weapons training, myself."

I looked from Liro to Ollie, checking to be sure I was understanding correctly. "Really?" I asked.

"Really." Ollie grinned, and Liro gave an overly exaggerated bow. It was only then that I noticed Ollie had actually come dressed in his own leathers, and I realized that he (and maybe Liro, too) had planned this all along. "Unless you don't want to."

I narrowed my eyes. "If you wanted to kill me, there are a lot easier ways to do it."

But my soulmate's smile only widened. "I prefer little deaths over one big one. Several a night if I can manage it."

"Moons and fucking rivers..." Liro groaned, then turned to walk back inside.

I sighed deeply, reaching out for Ollie's hand. "I pissed Typhir off again. He, *of course*, was lurking around my hearings."

He pulled me to my feet, and his expression soured for a moment. "That sounds like his own damn fault. He isn't supposed to be doing that. You'd think he'd been reminded enough times, but clearly he's as thick as the rest of his—" Ollie paused, and I knew what he'd been about to say, but he held the words back. "I'll take care of it. I'll have guards prevent him from bothering you again."

I crossed my arms over my chest. "Lexios was there, too. I made a comparison between him and the prisoner they brought before me, and Typhir shut right up. I'm just hoping I didn't make Lex mad in the process."

Ollie's upper lip curled slightly when I said "Lex," but he held his tongue about it. "Well, if you did, that would only prove how like his father he is." He took a deep breath and put a hand on my waist, pulling me closer to him. "For your sake... I hope you're right. There are few times when I would like to be wrong. This is one of them."

I stepped back slightly to gather the leathers still at my feet and quickly donned them. The last thing I needed was for someone else to walk up on me with my clothes around my ankles and my ass hanging out. "So," I said slowly, turning back to face him.

"So..." he echoed, pulling his sickle out of his belt and twirling it with a flourish. "I hope you'll take it easy on me. I'm more than a little out of practice."

Was he serious?

"Ol," I snorted. "There is no way I'm gonna best you here. You have to take it easy on *me*." I withdrew my pair of obsidian knives from my hip harness, turning them over between my fingers and flipping one in the air before pointing it at him. "How does this immortality work again? Is it like *Lord of the Rings* immortality or *Underworld* immortality?"

He laughed in that rich, full way that only seemed to happen when we were outside of the places where he had to be "King Olympio," then said, "I'm not sure I understand the reference, but I can, of course, answer whatever questions you like. And for the record, I've seen you go up against Ari. Don't discount your abilities."

I squared up my shoulders in the way Ari had taught me and began to circle him. "Well," I cleared my throat. "I guess what I want to know is how many times you can cut me in half before it's night-night for good?"

I saw his shoulders relax, and I took that as an opportunity to lock my foot around his knee, pulling his leg out from under him. He hit the ground with a loud grunt, clearly caught off-guard, then quickly rolled to the side and flipped to his feet.

"That was good," he said, running a hand through his hair. "If you can catch your enemy in that moment where they believe they've already won, that's when you can turn the tide."

"Thanks, Yoda," I laughed. Ollie was grinning, but I could already see the wheels turning in his head. "So, what are the stakes here? We don't exactly have dishes to do."

He raised an eyebrow at me. "Stakes? As in, a bet?"

"Yeah," I replied. "A bet. If I kick your ass you have to do something, and if you make me eat dirt, I have to do something. Surely that's not a Gaiadan concept."

His face broke into a smile at my use of Sefaeran terms—distracted in the best way possible. "Well done," he began. "You—"

I took the opportunity for a forward roll, into another leg swipe, then a thrust of my blade which almost made contact.

But Ollie dodged out of the way, turning quickly and bringing his sickle up alongside my face, missing by less than an inch before he backed away, circling me.

"Normally, I would say that taking cheap shots while your opponent is distracted is dishonorable," he said, not even breaking a sweat. "But given the events since you came to Sefaera, I think that's a tactic that could serve you well. I accept your challenge. Care to define the terms a little better?"

My muscles already ached, and I walked backward from him slowly as he casually approached me. "I dunno," I coughed, an attempt to cover up catching my breath. "What about... loser has to spend an afternoon doing an activity of the winner's choice? That seems like a good bet."

Ollie stopped in his pursuit and stared at me. I could tell from the flat look he was giving me that he knew what I had in mind.

"Would you care to clarify, or should I just assume you mean spending time with... certain people I won't speak ill of, rather than spending time with my soulmate without a stitch of clothing on?"

"You can pick your prize, I will pick mine. Do we have a deal?" I dodged behind a wooden pillar, spinning and coming out the other side to grin at him, our chests nearly touching.

He stared at me hard, like he was trying to decide if it was worth it. Before I could react, he wrapped his hand around my waist and pulled me to him for a deep, lingering kiss. Then he shifted into the shadows and was halfway across the courtyard.

"Deal," he called out. "Now... show me what you can do."

I quickly back flipped away from him, my overly long hair getting in my eyes. By the time I shook my head to clear them, I felt a pair of hands on my back, giving me a gentle shove. Ollie had moved by shadow again, but when I turned around, he was solid as I was.

"No more shadows," he said, raising his hands in a show of surrender. "Just you and me."

"Good, you prick," I laughed. "Some of us can't turn into fart gas." I hauled off and flung one of my knives at him, which he dodged of course, leaving it to stick in the wooden column beside him.

"I've smelled what occurs when you fall asleep before me, and I have to lift the blankets. I think you shouldn't discount that as an ability of yours." He dove forward into a somersault beneath my arm, coming up behind me again, but this time I was ready. I struck forward with my right hand, and Ollie brought his up to meet mine, diverting the strike away from his face.

"Don't worry," I laughed. "Your face is the second best thing about you. I'm not gonna slice your eyebrows off or anything." I swung my arm forward like I was gonna low blow him, and he crunched to protect his genitals.

"Careful with that," he said, though his smile told me he knew I would never really hurt him. "I can't exactly grow another one." He swung hard with his sickle, but I parried him, and he ended up taking a dive onto the ground. He scrambled onto all fours like some kind of cat and faced me with his sickle held out in front of him.

"It's really not looking good for you, my King," I said, trying and failing to cover the fact that I was wheezing. "You know... if I was you, I'd just—" I grabbed the wrist that bore the sickle and mimicked his typical facial expression with great exaggeration. "*Sleep.* Easy Win. Ol?"

My soulmate's face went slack, and his eyes unfocused, then closed only an instant before he collapsed onto the well-trimmed grass beside the pit, his sickle falling from his grip.

"Ollie? *Olympia?*" I dropped my remaining knife and went to my knees beside him, pulling him into my lap and taking his face in my hands. "Baby?" I shook him, hoping the heat or something had gotten to him, as unlikely as I knew it sounded. "Ollie, wake up."

He gave a sleepy little grumble, and his eyes flickered open, taking longer than usual to find mine.

"Gabriel...?" he said. "What... What happened? What was that?"

I pulled a water flask from the nearby grass and opened it, pressing it to his lips. "No idea. One second we were fighting, and then I made a joke about you using your bond telepathy on me to make me sleep, and then you were on the ground."

He sat up, taking a sip of the canteen and watching me like he was studying me. "You said, 'Sleep.' You used the bond to make me sleep. I didn't know you could use it that way, too."

Me? Use magic?

"I didn't... At least, I don't think I did," I touched his face once more. "Stand."

I could feel the resistance in my mind as Ollie fought against the command, followed by a release as he allowed himself to obey. He rose to his feet, looking at me with a mix of bewilderment and pride.

"I'll be having a word with my mother about not telling me this worked two ways..." he said in a would-be disgruntled tone, if he weren't beaming at me.

I couldn't help but look at my own hand as if my fingers would be giving off an ET glow or something. I jammed one into his neck, giggling. "Kiss me."

"You never need a command for that," he said, pressing his lips to mine.

I shoved him back, suddenly consumed with the idea that I could make him do anything just by wanting it. "Yeah, but... did it work?" He grabbed for me again, and I dodged his grasp, gripping his wrist once more. "Say 'I forgive Lexios.'"

There was a firm resistance this time, as though it had only worked before because he'd been caught off-guard or because he'd let me. In fact, this time, I felt the familiar urge from him, his lips never moving, even as I felt his irritation coursing along the bond.

"Maybe another time," he said, his expression mild. Maybe I was hoping for too much, too soon. At least he wasn't saying shitty things about him anymore.

I stumbled backward, suddenly feeling distant, like I had done something wrong and bad. "Ollie..." I turned away and ran to gather my knife from the wooden pillar, biting my lip to hold in tears that I knew he would feel whether he saw them or not. "I'm gonna go for a quick run," I choked out, my voice breaking. "I'll meet you back at the palace."

"Gabriel, wait," Ollie said quickly, catching my wrist and turning me back to face him, his eye pools of violet worry as he pulled my body against his. "Don't just walk away. You're panicking. Why?"

"I did something wrong." I was trembling. Fuck, why was I trembling? "We were having fun, and I ruined it."

There was a sound almost like a cross between a sigh and a laugh as my soulmate began to run his hands over my back, soothing away the bad feelings. "You didn't ruin anything, my Gabriel. I'm still trying to get my head around Lexios being worth my time, and that has nothing to do with you. I wasn't angry with you, nor disappointed, nor annoyed. You did nothing wrong. If a time comes when I feel he's earned it, I will forgive him. But I'm just not there yet. Can you understand that?"

I nodded, collapsing into him face first like it was possible for me to sink inside him and live there. "I'm sorry," I sighed softly.

"You have nothing to be sorry for," he said, tilting my chin up to look at him so I could see him smiling at me. "Well... other than cheating to win, which I believe means you forfeit, therefore making me the winner."

I could never get over how safe I felt in his arms. Safer than I'd ever felt anywhere before. "Fine," I sniffled against his chest happily. "What is your prize?"

His lips met the top of my head, and he held me even tighter. "I have it right here."

I pulled him on top of me as I fell backward into the grass, kissing him deeply and gripping his neck with my fingertips in a way that made it clear what I hoped his prize would be. "Is that right?" I tilted my head to the side, exposing my neck for him to consume.

He didn't disappoint, his body shifting so that our legs were entwined as his lips found my pulse, kissing gently at first, before parting to allow my skin to make contact with his tongue.

"Let me take you to our room," he growled against my skin. "I need you. Now."

I quickly stuffed my hands down the front of his leathers. "Why wait so long? Have me right the fuck here." I kissed him desperately, the feeling of his reassurance as powerful as any aphrodisiac.

He hardened beneath my fingers, and his hips bucked against me, his tongue making circles around mine as his hands pulled my legs to the outside of his.

"If you insist," he said, reaching between us to loosen the lacing on my pants.

"Fuck," I whimpered against his chest. "You know just how I like it, don't you, big boy?"

"Damn right, I do," he said roughly. "You and your cock are fairly easy to read. You're already dripping for me—I can tell."

"All, all yours," I moaned as I felt his fingers slide inside my pants and down toward my hole. "You're already dreaming of your sticky, wet, come dripping out—"

"For the love of all that has ever been holy, please do not finish that sentence, Gabe."

A distinctly female voice broke through the pleasure haze, and I jumped, letting out an audible squeak as my startled jerk forced Olympio to poke me rather uncomfortably with his previously gentle fingers.

"Ariadne... what the fuck?" he said, withdrawing from my pants and looking at his sister. "Do you have some kind of magical ability to know when Gabriel and I are about to fuck each other? Someone had better be dying."

I looked up to see Ari roll her eyes from across the courtyard as she continued to approach, despite the situation. Her face showed none of the usual veiled amusement she would usually display when she walked in on us. I knew something was wrong before she even opened her mouth.

"Well, you should finish quickly or save it," she said. "Because we need you. Both of you. We have a problem."

Chapter Ten
Olympio

We followed Ari back inside the palace, where the rest of the hunt—Liro, Keevan, Dom, and Mayria—had gathered in the war room. Despite the somber looks on their faces, they all greeted Gabriel with enthusiasm, having had him accompany them on hunts prior to our adjournment.

I made to close the door behind me, but a hand stopped it with inches to spare.

"I saw there was a meeting occurring and thought a representative of the Council would be appreciated, Your Majesty," Typhir said, sliding into the room as though he'd been invited.

"That's not your decision, Typhir," I said, annoyed once again at his insistence upon himself where he wasn't wanted or needed—as if he ever was.

"No, it isn't," he said in that weaselly tone that indicated he knew something I didn't. "But it's in the bylaws that all matters of state may be observed by the Council—for posterity, of course."

My hand clenched into a fist, but Gabriel's gentle touch on my wrist, followed by a wave of calm, told me that my soulmate had utilized his newfound ability once again to relieve me.

"Fine," I snapped. "But you will be a *silent* participant." I turned my back on him to face the hunt again. "What's going on?"

Ari looked at Typhir with an expression that was nothing short of distrusting, but, like me, chose to pretend he wasn't present. "There's been... another attack."

"Attack?" I repeated. "What do you mean?" I looked at each member of the hunt, none of them showing signs of an injury.

Ari sighed and leaned forward, placing her hands on the table. "Another beast from... somewhere else. It took down a griffin."

"A griffin?" Gabriel echoed. "Like... a lion bird thing?"

"You know about griffins?" Liro asked in surprise. "I thought those were native to here."

"They are," I said. "But back when the portals were open, people would use them as flying mounts when traversing the realms. None exist in Gaiada now, but they are part of the mythology of Gabriel's former world." I turned to Gabriel. "But they are extremely hard to kill—they're apex predators. How was it felled?" I asked Ari.

"Looks like some kind of bite, serpent maybe. Venomous," she said, clarifying.

"But they're immune to all known venoms," Liro said, keeping Gabriel informed, knowing he didn't possess the same knowledge we did. "Which is why we think it's something from somewhere else."

Typhir made a noise behind me, and it took all of my willpower to just ignore him and keep my attention on the matter at hand. I wasn't about to let him interject any more of his opinions about the world Gabriel came from, not with Gabriel in the room.

"What is it you're needing from me?" I asked my sister.

"Actually..." she said slowly. "It's not you. We need Gabe."

"Me?" Gabriel was stunned. "What can *I* do?"

"You can help us to find and identify whatever it is, assuming it's from your world," Liro said, putting a hand on Gabriel's shoulder. "If it isn't from your world, we'll know we have something much bigger going on."

"And if it is, we'll know that Gaiada needs to be monitored carefully."

As he spoke, I turned to Typhir, fury making my eyes burn with rage. "I said you were to remain silent."

"Apologies, Your Majesty. I'm merely saying what you seem to be unwilling to because you have a blind spot where your consort is concerned, even in matters that could be the end of our entire world at the hands of *his*," he said, a slimy smile appearing on his face.

Gabriel looked at me in confusion and concern, and I reached for his hand.

"Don't pay him any attention," I said. "No one thinks you have anything to do with this. No one of importance, anyway."

"We should get a move on," Ari interrupted in an obvious attempt to break up the tension. "Before the creature has time to get too far from where its victim was killed. The longer we wait, the less likely we are to find it."

"At least we're already dressed for the occasion," Gabriel said, leaning his head on my shoulder before shaking himself and standing upright. "Let's go, I guess."

"I will meet you at the stables," Typhir said, sweeping from the room before I could tell him he wasn't going to be coming.

"Why does he think he needs to be involved in everything?" I grumbled.

"Because he has no real power, and he knows it," Ari said. "But you getting upset gives him some form of power. Just don't. If he insists on tagging along, ignore him."

"Easier said than done," I said. But Ari shot me a look, and I nodded. "Maybe if we go quickly we can leave before he gets there."

But as luck would have it, Typhir had not only beaten us to the stables, but had brought someone else along.

"Hey, Lex!" Gabriel said in a tone that was much too excited for my liking, but true to my word, I kept my thoughts to myself.

"I wasn't aware you'd be coming, as well," I said in the most neutral voice I could manage as I reached for my saddle to ready my lymere.

"Father said it would probably be best, since I've been to so many other parts of Sefaera as part of my diplomatic emissary work," he said. "If Gabe—sorry, His Grace—can't identify the creature, there's a chance I can, if it happens to just be a rare beast from our world."

"You can call me Gabe," Gabriel said with genuine excitement and a grin on his face. "It's my name."

"As long as it's okay with you and His Majesty," Lexios said, nodding to me in deference.

"He is as much able to make those decisions as I am," I said, putting a hand on Gabriel's hip and kissing the side of his head.

But Gabriel scooted away a little, giving me a look like I was being an overbearing parent. "Gabe, Big G, G-man. Whatever. My frat brothers called me Hoffstet."

It had been a long time since he'd talked about his time at Columbia, and even longer since I'd heard him use his last name at all. I, myself, didn't have a last name, and we had never discussed if Gabriel would maintain his surname or if he would, like me, simply be known by his first name and title.

I studied Gabriel for a moment as he seemed to withdraw into himself, but before I could even make an attempt to pull him back, he leaned his back against my chest and glanced up, silently letting me know he was still here with me. "But I digress..." he said.

"Gabe, then," Lexios said, and I was glad he didn't dwell on Gabriel's momentary dissociation. They were fewer and farther between than they once were, and, especially now, when he seemed so natural in Sefaera, it was easy sometimes to forget that he had left behind everything he'd ever known to be here.

"If you boys are all done fucking around, we have a creature to hunt," Ari said, already mounted, as she directed her lymere out of the stable.

"Impatient, isn't she?" Lexios said with a bit of a laugh.

He wasn't wrong, but I still wasn't ready to joke about my sister's headstrong nature with him.

"Let's go," I said, hoisting myself into my saddle as Gabriel did the same. My ever-present shadow Gryfian was right behind us, separating Gabriel and Lexios, just as I would have wanted if I'd actually given an order to do so. There was something I still just didn't trust about his intentions with my soulmate.

I hadn't paid any attention to Typhir, but he seemed just as determined to get out into the forest as my sister, because he, Liro, and the rest of the hunt were waiting with a deeply disgruntled Ari, who took off at a gallop as soon as she saw the rest of us emerge.

We rode to the edge of the forest as a group, where we stopped, and Ari turned her lymere so she could address us.

"This is a bigger group than I'd like for this kind of hunt," she said. "We're likely to spook the creature with this many lymeres thundering through the trees. I suggest we ride most of the way to the fallen griffin, then go by foot, since we can be more silent that way."

"Agreed," Typhir said, as if his opinion held any weight.

Ari gave her shoulders a little shake as if to rid herself of Typhir's presence and turned to ride off into the trees.

We rode for nearly an hour through the forest before we finally came upon a small clearing, where Ari had us stop.

"The griffin is a hundred paces that way." She pointed through the trees. "We need to spread out to find it. We'll split into three groups, one moving in each direction to make a wide circle before closing slowly in. If we don't find it, we'll need to expand our search, but I'd rather start out and work our way in rather than the other way and risk it outrunning us."

"I'll remain here with the lymeres," Gryfian said, "as sentry."

I nodded at my guard and friend, who met my eyes in what I knew to be the equivalent of a smile, but without his lips joining in, since we were in front of people we didn't trust.

"Keevan, Mayria, Dom," my sister continued. "You're all well acquainted with the woods. The three of you will go to the left. Liro, you can take our... guests... to the right." Her lip curled up as her eyes drifted in Typhir's direction, but other than that, she gave no indication that he was even there. "I'll go with His Majesty and His Grace straight ahead. Each party has a signal with them." She held up a small metal whistle hanging around her neck. "Use it if you find the thing. Let's go."

We all dismounted, tied up our mounts, and took off on foot in the direction Ari had told us. She had her bow at the ready, with an arrow nocked, and I had my sickle drawn. I looked at Gabriel, who had his daggers in his hands, crouched low as he moved silently through the underbrush.

Every time I thought I couldn't be more amazed with him, either in his growth or just who he was, he managed to surprise me. While I was certain he'd learned his technique from some movie, probably one his parents had produced, it was nonetheless effective. He was the very essence of stealth, and his energy was of pure excitement. It made my heart soar to see him happy in any circumstance, and I knew how much joy being in the woods brought him.

"So, dear soulmate of my brother," Ari whispered to Gabriel, her voice barely louder than the breeze to not scare any creatures we may come across. "What exactly is going on with you and Typhir's rotten little spawn?"

It took all of my will to not laugh. I had made a promise to Gabriel, but Ari had not. And while I would hold to my promise, unlike so many others I'd failed to keep, she was not bound as I was.

"He's not... he's not rotten," Gabriel said. "And I don't really know him yet, but I'm not gonna treat someone like shit because Lord Butthurt over here has beef with him."

"I think I preferred Prince Cockbreath..." I murmured.

"Olympio's 'beef' with Lexios has no effect on *my* issues with him." Ari turned quickly, pointing her arrow at the canopy of trees, scanning it with her eyes before lowering her weapon. "He's an arrogant little bastard who, in my opinion, has followed way too closely in his father's footsteps. There's a reason he was designated to be an emissary to other parts of Sefaera. He was a liability when he spent too much time in the palace, and the sooner he's back at work—once his Union is complete—the better, if you ask me."

"What does that entail?" Gabriel asked, clearly trying to sound casual, though to a trained ear, his disappointment was as loud as ever. "He goes away again?"

"Yes," Ari said. "For as long and far away as we can manage, since his family is too close to the throne to be—"

Suddenly, Ari lifted her hand, closed in a fist, before tapping her ear. I listened. It was quiet in this part of the woods, almost too quiet. Except for...

There. A slight rustling, almost indistinguishable, and not made by footfalls. Serpent seemed like an accurate assessment.

"Ow, fuck!" Ari cried out, her arrow loosing in the direction of the forest floor and embedding in the dirt as she fell onto her backside, gripping her leg.

"Ari!" I said, rushing to her side. "Did you get it?"

"No," she said urgently through gritted teeth. "It bit me." She pointed a few feet in front of us, where a long creature with black scales was unwinding from its coil. As it rose, its head seemed to spread out to the sides in a hooded shape, and Gabriel gasped.

"Holy shit! That's a cobra!" he said. The word was vaguely familiar to me, one from his world, but it didn't matter. We needed to contain it.

Thankfully, Ari was just as quick after sustaining her injury as she was before, and she raised her hands. Normally, the way she interacted with the shadows was by conjuring weapons made of them, but this time, she created a cage that closed instantly around the beast. It hissed and thrashed, but the shadows held firm, not allowing it to escape.

Ari, too, was making noises of distress. I looked at her leg, where the puncture marks were already swelling as they trickled blood.

Gabe dropped down beside us. "She needs help fast. Those guys are poisonous as fuck."

"Not to worry. Here," I said, reaching into my pack and producing a small vial of Perla's magical cure-all potion. I dripped some onto Ari's wound, which stopped bleeding instantly, and poured the rest into her mouth to counteract any effects of the venom.

"Thanks," Ari said, sitting up. There was still a sheen of sweat on her brow, as if the stress of the moment had rattled my normally unflappable sister. "Let's get this little bastard back to the menagerie, and Gabe can tell us more about it."

She stood and blew her whistle, which sounded like the call of an omnix—perfect for use out in the woods to not frighten the wildlife. We began to walk back toward the clearing, but after only a few minutes, Ari stopped to lean against a tree.

"What's wrong?" I asked. It wasn't like her to show any signs of weakness, even just to me and Gabriel.

"Nothing," she said, though there was a tension to her voice I couldn't place. "Just been a long day. Could use a rest. Plus, that fucking thing really hurt when it bit me."

"You probably just need a little more from Perla," I said. "We're almost back."

She nodded and forced herself to start walking again, but the pain was obvious in every move she made, her usually silent footsteps crunching on every twig and leaf.

We finally made it to the clearing, where Gryfian, true to his word, was waiting. The others trickled in within seconds, and I watched my sister take one step toward her lymere, then stumble. She turned to look at me, then at Liro, her face ashen and dripping sweat.

Fuck.

"Ari?" Liro said, moving toward her. "What's—"

Before he could finish what he was saying, Ari let out a whimper and fell to the ground, her eyes wide and staring as drool flowed freely from her lips.

Then white foam started to bubble from her mouth, and she began to shake.

Chapter Eleven
Gabriel

I had never, with my own eyes, seen something as terrifying as Ari writhing on the ground with foam bubbling across her lips. In seconds, both Ollie and Liro were at her side in an unspoken battle over who would attend to her. The seconds seemed to simultaneously inch by and were also a whirlwind.

A pair of strong hands pulled me back a few feet, and without realizing it, I clung to the grasp on my left shoulder for dear life. Lexios stood there with me, neither of us even daring to breathe as we held each other, waiting.

"We have to get her to Perla," Ollie barked at Liro like a cornered dog. "The potion didn't work. She needs something else!"

"There's no fucking time," Ari's lover snarled back at him. "If we move her, it might expedite the poison."

"Shut up, both of you."

An unlikely command echoed through the hollow as Typhir stepped forward, dropping into a crouch and producing a small vial that looked like injectable fluid from my world. That suspicion was confirmed when he proceeded to produce a syringe and needle, and began to draw up some of the liquid.

"What is that?" I shouted, worried that Typhir might be using this moment to gain advantage in eliminating the royal family.

It was only then that Liro and Ollie seemed to realize he was doing anything at all, and the two of them also laid into him with questions, Ollie jumping to his feet and drawing his sickle.

Typhir sighed and pushed past Ollie, who—to my surprise—let him pass, before driving the syringe into her arm and pushing the plunger.

"By the might of the twin moons, you vile prick," Olympio growled. "If you've done anything to her, I—"

The sound of coughing and sputtering drew everyone's attention back to Ari, who began to try and sit up, tears quickly spilling down her cheeks. Liro pulled her into him, finally winning out over Ollie as he tipped backward into a sitting position, stunned that Typhir's action had been fruitful.

"It's okay, love," Liro said softly, stroking her cheek. "It's going to be okay."

Olympio looked over at me, his face a mix of relief and lingering fear, and I felt Lexios withdraw his hands quickly.

"What was that?" I asked Typhir again.

"Adrenaline and something to counter the venom of such creatures. The Gaiadan emissary brought it with him the last time he returned. I didn't know if we might need it after Her Highness said we were likely hunting a serpent, so I brought it along."

By this point, Liro had gathered Ari up in his arms and was beginning to move for the palace.

"Stop," I said, jogging over to them. "Take your horse—lymere, I'll make sure Khoria—" I indicated to Ari's mount, "—gets back to the palace."

Liro turned to me, his brow covered in sweat, eyes filled with tears, and nodded. Olympio rushed forward to hold his sister as Liro mounted his own lymere, then they worked together to get Ari situated in Liro's embrace. I watched, heart still pounding as Liro and Ollie exchanged a knowing look, and they each nodded at each other in solidarity. Then, my soulmate gave Liro's steed, Khava, a smack on the hindquarters, sending him off with top speed.

As soon as they were out of sight, Keevan, Dom, and Mayria turned to Olympio, waiting for a command.

"What are you waiting for?" he snapped in a voice I'd only heard him use one other time—when Vassenia attacked me in the middle of a party. "Get on your moons-forsaken lymeres and follow your Master!"

I turned to get on my own lymere, but there was a *whoosh* of air behind me, followed by what felt like thick steel vines turning me and wrapping around my middle. One glance told me Ollie had turned into that shadow-demon and was carrying me higher and higher, above the trees and toward the palace faster than I'd ever traveled before, even the time I "borrowed" my dad's lime green Lambo for a joyride down the Jersey Turnpike.

I threw my arms around his neck as tightly as I could. "Ollie, I'm gonna barf," I gasped in what I could only assume was his ear in this horrifying form. "Too fast."

"Don't look down," he said in that deep, thundering voice that came with this form. "And hold on tight. We need to find Perla before Liro and Ari get there so she can look her over."

It had never before been so clear how tunnel-visioned Olympio got when he was scared. So myopic, in fact, that he wasn't noticing his clawed fingers digging into my skin, drawing blood. I hardly cared, though, as my heart thudded in my chest, waiting for the rushing to stop and to be able to confront my soulmate about his control issues.

Before I realized it had happened, we stopped, and as easily as stepping out of a pair of jeans, the King transformed back into the red-haired man I loved. He rushed forward, through our room from where he'd landed on the balcony and threw open the doors, barking orders at the guard to fetch Perla before he turned to me with a lost sort of look in his eyes.

"Maybe you should tell your mother?" I suggested, shrugging, hoping that giving him some direction would help.

He nodded, but his eyes lingered on me. He took one step in my direction, then stopped, glancing down at my body. "You're hurt," he said, his face crumpling like he was just a little boy, scared and unsure what to do. "How did you get hurt?"

Our eyes met and I could tell he knew, but the idea of making him feel bad, right before bringing to his attention my own grievances, killed me. "I think it was some of the brambles in the woods. I'm fine."

He knew I was lying. I felt his guilt radiating from him as he moved toward me slowly, like he was afraid I'd run.

"Gabriel..." he breathed, tears beginning to form in his eyes. "I'm so sorry. I didn't... I was..."

"It's fine," I said, going to his side and throwing my arms around him. "You didn't mean to."

He held me just as tightly. "Doesn't mean I didn't do it," he said, kissing my cheeks. "Perla will fix you up, just like..." He let out a single sob, then stood up a little straighter. "She's going to be okay, right? Typhir saved her. I'm not going to lose her... Right?"

For the first time since I'd known him, Olympio sank into *my* arms, collapsing against me and going to his knees. I followed him down to the floor, cradling him against my chest, all thoughts of scolding him a distant memory. "A hundred percent," I said to him. "People get bit by snakes all the time back home. With Perla's help, it will be like it never happened."

This only seemed to make him cry harder, and I rocked him against me on the marble floor.

"Why didn't it work? Perla's potion. Why didn't it save her?" he sobbed, and for the first time, I noticed his tears had a slight shimmer to them, little flecks of the same gold as his—our—blood. "Why couldn't *I* save her? And why... why *him*?"

By the love of all that was holy, I wished I had a good answer for him. There was nothing, almost nothing, more insufferable than being in debt to Typhir. But that was how Gabe Hoffstet would have thought—not His Grace, Justice of Sefaera.

"Maybe..." I said tentatively. "Maybe it's time for a new era..." I felt a jolt of white-hot rage through the bond, and I squeezed him tighter to prevent him from looking up at me. "Maybe Vassenia's... exile... was the end of the rivalry, with Typhir's insubordination during our adjournment being its death rattle." It all sounded very dramatic and nearly as poetic as some of the scripts my parents used to get. "But maybe this is proof that the kingdom will be stronger if we all work... together."

I pulled back, giving him space for what was bound to be an equally dramatic reaction.

But instead of an explosion, Ollie was staring at me thoughtfully. His tears had slowed, and he was frowning, like he was trying to work through what I'd said.

"Maybe you're right," he said in a voice that sounded as tired as I felt. "Maybe it's our fault. Mine and my family's. Maybe by constantly trying to push them out, we've been making them force their way in, instead of allowing them the space to actually be helpful." He sighed and leaned his forehead against mine. "Maybe this is why you're here. To help bring the kingdom back to the way it was supposed to be. I'll tell you what—if Ari makes it, if it's not some horrid, filthy trick on Typhir's part to make us think he saved her just for her to die, I'll give them a chance. Him *and* Lexios."

I was stunned. Something I had said had helped shape the history of a world—this world.

My world.

I pulled Olympio to me and kissed his cheek, nuzzling my face into the side of his neck. "I don't know if I really helped anything but, for what it's worth, I think you're a really brave King and an even braver brother. Ari is lucky to have you."

"And we're all lucky to have you," he said. "Me, most of all."

It was at that moment that the horns of the hunt sounded through the open window, and Ollie jumped to his feet.

"Wait," I said, grabbing his wrist. "There's something I wanted to say."

He looked at me, his eyes wide. "What is it?"

"Well," I hesitated, worried that I might be breaching the subject too soon. "You were kind of a dick to the rest of the hunt. Might be worth your time to apologize. You want people to love you, not fear you. Right?"

"I was?" he asked, utterly confused. "I didn't... I was scared. I just wanted them to..." He swallowed and nodded, kissing my forehead. "One more way I need you. To keep showing me how to be a better man."

I smiled at him softly, proud of every way I constantly saw him growing. "Good little King," I said, patting him on the head. "Now you can go tell your mother before she finds out through Typhir."

He nodded again, then said, "I'll send Perla to patch you up when she's finished checking Ari."

With a swirl of shadows, he was gone, presumably to intercept Parthenea before she found Ari.

I sighed as he left the room, feeling as though I'd been holding my breath despite the fact that I'd been speaking. Being a... whatever I was, was hard. It made me reflect on my own parents' marriage and how long they'd been together. What happened in Sefaera if a bonded pair decided they *didn't* like each other? Did they have divorce for soulmates, or were you just tied together and forced to work it out?

I walked to the bed and flopped down on it, thinking about how badly I hoped that was a question Ollie and I never had to consider.

Waiting for Ollie to come back was rough. All alone in our bed, there was nothing to distract me from my worry. I closed my eyes softly, shocked at how tired I was from the day. My brain meandered back to the adjournment, which had quickly become my happy place whenever I was stressed these days, and I thought back to the color of the water and the bioluminescent sea life that lived there.

There had been one night that Olympio and I had gotten shit-faced and dove naked into the vibrant waters, Ollie coming up with the glow spattered across his face like his freckles.

"*You look like magic,*" I'd slurred, the alcohol the most potent I'd ever consumed.

"*You* are *magic,*" he'd replied.

I felt a thump of blood pulse in my lower stomach and turned over so my back was to the doors as I ran my fingers through the gentle smattering of hair above my cock.

Ollie had pulled me close to him and kissed me while stroking me beneath the waves, which bobbed us up and down while we giggled. During the adjournment, I'd become really well acquainted with exactly what noises I made that drove him crazy, so when he began to caress me, I whimpered into his ear.

"*Olympio...*" I moaned.

I could feel my pulse in my cock now, just thinking about that night, and I hoped that Ollie would be back soon to make this day end better than it had gone so far. I realized that I'd been waiting for him to have me since our little sparring match earlier.

I took one more glance over my shoulder, to ensure that Gryfian hadn't snuck in or something, then took my throbbing length in my hand and gave it a firm tug.

Heaven.

I had never been one to end a day with a "self pleasure sesh" but right now, as the final waves of adrenaline subsided, it was so relaxing.

"*You feel so good in my hand, Gabriel,*" Olympio had moaned as I writhed in his arms, his strong legs keeping us both afloat. "*You—*"

Suddenly there was a knock on the door, and in a flurry of panic, I grabbed the silken gold sheet and wrapped it around me.

"Uh... yeah?"

The door cracked open, and I saw Gryfian's face. "Your Grace, you have—"

"It's fine, man," a voice said from outside. "Gabe is expecting me."

Lexios.

Gryfian looked at me for confirmation, and I nodded, pulling the sheet further around me. He backed out, allowing Lexios to enter before closing the door between them.

"Whoa," Lex said, grinning as he noticed my state. "You want me to come back later?"

I felt my face go red. "I was changing." I stuttered.

Lexios gave me a playfully challenging look. "Don't feel like you have to stop on my behalf," he said, turning away. "I was just checking to see if the King was around."

I knew he'd lied to Gryfian, saying I was expecting him, but to lie when he wasn't even here to see me—that sat weird.

I quickly gathered a sweatshirt and pants, easy to get on, but suddenly foreign feeling to me.

"What, uh..." Lexios said as he turned around. "What the hell do they call that?" He pointed to my sweatshirt which boldly read "Columbia."

"Oh..." I shrugged. "Clothes from my world. What's up? Why did you stop by?" I struggled to read his face past his smile, and every bad word Ollie had ever said about him came back to me. "I mean—not that I'm not happy to see you or whatever."

111

Lex laughed and crossed his arms over his chest. "Since he's not here, I assume His Majesty is gonna be busy with his sister, so I figured you might have some free time. I thought you might like to see the waterfalls I was talking about. "

"Isn't it kinda... late?" I looked out over the balcony and saw the twin moons reflected on the river.

Lex shrugged. "Could be. But I've lived here my whole life. I feel pretty good about finding my way in the moonlight."

I looked out again, contemplating my options. The stars and moons kept it pretty bright, and I had yet to have a walk across the grounds at night. "You know what," I took a deep breath. "Why the hell not?"

Lexios clapped his hands together and rubbed his palms with glee. "Fantastic. Shall we go?"

I took one last look around, then nodded and followed him out of the palace.

Chapter Twelve
Olympio

Never, in my two and a half thousand years, had my mother—with her even, calm demeanor—ever outpaced me.

Until today.

She moved like smoke in the wind through the corridors. I would have shifted into shadows to keep up, but I was worn from flying so far while carrying Gabriel. And it wasn't like getting there quicker would matter, since Ari still needed to be taken to the infirmary.

We made it there seconds before Liro burst through the doors, carrying my sister, who looked around in a daze.

"Ariadne!" my mother cried out, rushing to her side as soon as Liro deposited her into a bed, each of them taking one of her hands. I put my own on Mother's shoulder to try to calm her, but her fear was mine as well. Normally, for our line, people decided—along with our soulmates, if we had them—when they were ready to depart for whatever afterlife awaited us. Like all things with the royal family, it was not a decision made in haste, but one that involved a long, deliberate undertaking, including a trip to one of the pocket dimensions like the one Gabriel and I had our adjournment in, only instead of coming back, they would simply move on.

But with two people we loved having been taken before their time, my father because of illness and Vasileios by his own hand, I was just as anxious as my mother that we had come so close to losing Ari in an unplanned event.

"Fuck..." my sister whimpered as her eyes fluttered open, her skin still ashen and clammy. "That thing really packed a punch."

"What was it?" Liro asked, looking back and forth between Ari and me.

"A cobra, according to Gabriel. A serpent from his world." I looked at my mother. "Something long and black, with a hood made of scales."

"An asp!" she said, her face draining of color. "I lost a dear friend to one of those when I was only a girl. It took mere minutes before she was lost." Her fingers trailed over the twin scars, still with dried golden blood on them. "Thank Coricas for Perla's potion."

"Perla's potion didn't work," I admitted. "It closed the wounds, but, apparently, the foreign venom wasn't dispelled."

"How did you survive?" Mother asked Ari.

"Typhir," I said, the name still tasting bitter and foul in my mouth, having to admit he'd been the one to save my sister, no matter what Gabriel had said. "He had some kind of medicine from Gaiada that countered the effects. If he hadn't insisted on coming with us, Ari might have died out in the wilds."

"Might have preferred that to being in Typhir's debt," Ari grumbled, her voice still weak.

"Well, I wouldn't have," Mother chided her. "I never thought I'd say it, but I'm glad Typhir was there."

"That makes two of us," I said, crossing my arms and shaking my head as attendants began to swarm the area, making the bed more comfortable for my sister. Perla rushed in and checked on her pulse, temperature, and other vital signs to ensure she was, in fact, recovering, and not about to keel over.

"Can everyone stop staring at me?" Ari said. "I'm going to be fine."

"You'd better be," Liro said, kissing the back of her hand, then her forehead. "Who else is going to keep His Majesty from making stupid decisions in regards to the kingdom and his soulmate?"

I gave him a challenging look, but the moment was brief as we all looked back at Ari, who looked like she was ready to bite us, herself, for fussing over her.

It was over an hour of various tests and tinctures and ointments, but she was given the all clear. She was tired, the venom no longer killing her, but Typhir's cure could only do so much.

"You'll need more rest than usual," Perla said to Ari, breaking open a few ampoules from her bag and pouring them into a larger vial, before handing it to Ari with a pointed look. "This should help keep you *calm*."

"A sedative, Perla?" Ari sighed. "How am I supposed to hunt—?"

"You aren't," Perla interrupted. "I expect you to spend the next week recovering, and since you have never been one to follow my orders—well, I remember the year you came down with plorum-pox and fainted because you insisted on training through the illness."

"I was still in my first century," Ari retorted. "I'm not as foolhardy as I was back then."

"But still hard-headed," Liro said, earning a scathing look from his partner.

"And if you intend on remaining at rest anyway, why not use the sedative to keep you from feeling restless?" I asked.

"You're all going to make me, one way or another, aren't you?" Ari groaned and laid back on the pillows. "Fine. Give it to me."

Perla handed Ari the vial. "I knew you'd come around, Your Highness."

Ari downed the liquid in a single swallow. Her eyes began to close almost instantly, and Liro caught the vial before it could fall and shatter on the floor.

I stood at the edge of the bed, my mother and Liro finally sinking into plush chairs at either of her sides. I was about to find another to sit in, myself, when I heard someone clear their throat behind me.

"Gryfian?"

He was standing in the doorway, looking uncomfortable.

"Your Majesty. If I could have a word?"

I looked at my family, not wanting to leave my sister's side, but my mother said, "Go, darling. Ari is fine now. Your obligations lie outside of this room."

She was right, and I hated it. When there was an imminent threat to Ari's life, it was understandable that I would need to prioritize her safety. But the danger had passed, and now, if my personal guard was willing to interrupt me at this moment, it was clearly something that needed my full attention.

I touched Ari's foot gently as she slept, trying to convey, in some way, that I was glad she was alright, then turned and met Gryfian in the halls.

"What's wrong?" I asked. "I thought you were with Gabriel."

"I was," he said. Only someone who knew him as long as I did would recognize the annoyed tone in his voice. "I was... dismissed."

"Why...?" My brow furrowed, matching his expression.

"Gabriel has left the palace." Those words would have been enough to strike worry in my heart, even without what Gryfian said next. "And he's not alone."

Chapter Thirteen
Gabriel

An hour and a half later, the castle was nearly out of sight, and Lex was chatting my ear off in a way I hadn't figured he was capable of.

"So, how disappointed were you when you found out you were being forced into a soulmate bond with Olympio?"

I could hear our steps against the crunching leaves much louder than I would have expected—a surprising effect of the hollows I'd seen a million times from the balcony.

"Oh, I was devastated," I laughed. "And once I realized how our bond would be solidified, I was pissed off as hell. But it wasn't long before I realized Ollie has a depth to him he doesn't share with many. Guess I just got lucky."

Lexios chuckled. "Luck has nothing to do with it. Magic can be a bastard like that."

The sweet smell of fruit filled my senses as we passed a grove of raquin trees. "There was a time I would have agreed—but he's not all that bad." I took a deep, overly exaggerated breath. "Oh, my god, that smell could make me come in my—"

"You know most royalty take lovers, right? When you can't deal with his broody shit anymore, I'm sure loads of people would line up in droves to be with you."

I stopped and turned to him. His face was friendly, but his tone was a little tense. "Lex... I'm not—"

"I didn't mean me, idiot," he said, shoving me playfully. "Very, very taken, remember?"

"Very taken and *very* into dudes. What else am I supposed to think you're talking about?"

"I'm not saying I wouldn't be into it, but I am saying I respect Olympio enough to keep you off limits in my mind. You're a good looking man, but I'm not trying to be exiled."

This had to be why I'd gravitated to him so quickly. He just... got me. Unlike Ollie at first, who'd have died before ever understanding me if it wasn't for Ari, Lex was tapped into my sarcastic, playful vibes.

We walked a while longer in silence until we found ourselves before a teal colored waterfall. As if we got the idea at the same time, Lexios and I exchanged a glance, each inviting the other for a swim.

In a matter of seconds, our clothes were discarded and we were both waist deep. The water was incredible. Hell, if you didn't mind another man's balls contaminating the liquid, you could've had a swim and a drink at the same time. If that wasn't enough, the roar of the falls as they misted down on us was majestic.

All around me, it looked like the stars were swimming as the water reflected the sky, and it was so beautiful that I nearly missed the adonis-esque physique that Lexios was sporting.

"Whoa," I said accidentally out loud. "You work out, man?"

Lex laughed but didn't seem embarrassed. "Not so much, lately. But I find it very meditative." Then he gestured to me, giving me a quick up and down. "How about you? You look like you have an assassin's build."

Now I laughed loudly. "Sure," I snorted. "If you count lifting a goblet to my lips as a workout."

"Oh, stop," he teased, splashing me with the warm water.

"You first," I giggled, attempting to splash him twice as much.

In seconds I found him on me, my neck in a headlock and laughter rippling out of me without restraint as I tried to get the upper hand. "Unfair advantage," I shrieked. "Unfair advantage."

Lexios lifted me off my feet and tossed me across the pool, his happiness echoing my own. "Guess you better start working out harder, then," he rebutted. "At this rate, Tomos could pin you."

"Ah!" I slammed both of my fists hard in the water, sending a wave in his direction. "Fuck you, dick."

Typhir's beloved son jumped at me once more, getting my arms behind my back like a cop. "I would, but you have a stance against mistresses, apparently."

"For which I am rather grateful."

Solidifying out of the shadows at the water's edge, Olympio waded ankle deep into the pool, his eyes taking in the entire scene of me, naked and wrestling with Lexios.

Lex not only took a huge step back, but dropped to his knee in deference. "Your Majesty. Forgive me. I was jesting."

I, on the other hand, couldn't really meet Ollie's eyes, feeling like I'd done something wrong. "Ari okay?"

"Resting," he said, his eyes boring a hole in Lexios, one single eyebrow quirking up, though he held his tongue about the situation before him. "She's going to be fine, though. Turns out whatever it was that your father did, it saved her life."

Now I couldn't resist looking up, dying to see the exchange before me. Lexios looked thrilled, and I saw a smile curl the edge of his lips. "It did? That's wonderful. We all know that Sefaera needs Her Highness nearly as much as it needs its king."

"More, some might argue," my soulmate said. "She's the brains of the family, after all. Are you having fun, Gabriel? I'm glad you finally made it out here."

"I..." Our eyes met, and I tried to convey that I wasn't sure what the right answer was. "Yes?"

I *felt* the jealousy emanating from him, but I could tell he was trying to keep his promise to give Lex a chance.

"Good," he said, disguising the tension in his voice well. "Well, should I leave you to it, or do you mind if I join?"

"Join," both Lexios and I said, our eyes going to each other when we spoke in unison.

"Please," Lex said. "Remember when we used to come here as kids?"

"I do," Ollie said, pulling off the hunting leathers he still wore from earlier and hanging them over a low tree-branch. "I specifically remember one time when you thought you could dive from the clifftop. Ari was quick to point out you would get hurt if you tried, but you were damned determined to prove her wrong."

Lex looked down into the water, kicking his feet. "Well, I've never been the smartest man. No one would argue that I've made a lot of mistakes."

I hovered awkwardly between my friend and my soulmate, feeling the tension there.

"Truer words have never been spoken." Ollie paused, then dove under the water and surfaced behind me, wrapping his arms around my waist and kissing my cheek. "But I have, too. And if Gabriel can move past the ways I've wronged him... maybe it's only fair that I pass that along to others."

It wasn't an outright forgiveness, but it was close enough.

"So... what I'm hearing is that it's my turn to jump off the falls? Do something stupid to make my life here official?"

"Absolutely not," Ollie and Lexios said at the same time.

My soulmate's hands gripped me tighter, making sure I didn't pull away. Not that I could have gotten far if he'd released me and wanted to pull me back. One blink and he'd do his shadow thing and grab me off the cliff before I could jump.

I looked between them and grinned. "Okay, okay. No jumping. Sounds like I should teach you two Marco Polo instead. Much less chance of injury."

"We *could* do that..." Ollie whispered in my ear. "Or... we could go back home, and I could help you finish what I felt you start earlier..."

A shiver ran down me, and I nodded. Lexios seemed to be aware of the type of interaction we were having and had the decency to go to the shore and pull himself out, away from us. While it was far from gratuitous, my eyes momentarily were treated to a full on view of Lex's toned, athletic backside.

That is, of course, until Olympio grabbed my chin and yanked it so my eyes couldn't look anywhere but at him. He moved his face so close to mine that our noses touched as he said, "See something you like?"

I had the common sense to shake my head and could only just barely see Lexios get dressed, bow, then take his leave without further discussion. "How could I possibly like anything besides you when you're this fucking magnetic?" I breathed, every hair on my body standing on end.

"Well," he said, beginning to run his lips along my jawline, "I did have an idea at Lexios's party. Something that occurred to me. Would you like to know what it is?"

I nodded, my body electric and desperate for his touch.

"I realized that while I have had well over two thousand years to have different experiences, you have been very limited in your twenty one. If you would like... You said you wanted to have a taste of party boy Olympio. How would you like to be the star of one of my special after-parties? The kind that happens in our bed, with you, me, and a handful of the most beautiful women in Sefaera?"

I wasn't sure what I expected him to say, but it sure as fuck wasn't that. "Can I... can we do that?" I asked, truly not sure what the bond did and didn't allow.

"It's complicated," he said. "The rule was always that *you* could, but I couldn't. Whether I'm allowed to now is unclear, and something I don't want to put to the test. But I am perfectly happy to worship and pleasure you while you enjoy the softness of a woman for the first time."

Suddenly I was sweating at the prospect. I'd always known how to pull off the ol' "wham bam, thank you, ma'am" (with boys), but actually spending time, which from what I'd heard was a necessity for girls—that was foreign territory. "Sounds terrifying... When?"

"That... is a surprise," he said, finally kissing me, his hands like fire on my hips, even beneath the cool water.

Suddenly we were alone, the sound of the falls the only disturbance in the energy that radiated from any point in time and space where Ollie and I collided. A drip of water rolled off my hair and onto my nose and he bent in to lick it off. "That tickles," I giggled softly. It felt like we were back on the adjournment and no one, nothing could touch us here. "Olympio..." I breathed, pulling his face to my neck.

He buried his face there, breathing me in as his hips bucked forward into mine. "Gabriel... *my* Gabriel..." he moaned.

He walked me backward through the torrent of water rushing off the falls, the purple glow, *our* glow, lighting everything around us. I felt my back hit something solid, cold, and rusty smelling. All around us, the water sparkled like diamonds as the stars continued to reflect, and the blue and pink light of the moons made everything not affected by our bond light glow.

Ollie's hands went to my spine as his strong arms pulled me tight against him, and I looked up at his handsome face, watching the teal liquid drip off his skin.

"I don't think I could love you more," I whispered, burying my face in his neck and breathing him in like my favorite smell in the world—which, of course, he was.

"Me neither," he said, his voice thick with emotion. "Every time I think I've hit that peak, you surprise me and prove me wrong."

Chapter Fourteen
Olympio

"Lord Typhir," I said, standing in front of a room full of courtiers. "Step forward."

If he hadn't just saved my sister, the smug look on his face would have been enough cause for me to have him removed from the room. But seeing as this event was in his honor, it wouldn't look particularly good for me to throw him out on the grounds of being a bastard.

"Your Majesty," he said, giving the lowest bow he'd ever offered me. All for show, I knew, but I'd agreed to this, which meant putting up with his theatrics.

And not just for today, but for a long time—until he proved to be unworthy of it once more.

"You have done the kingdom a great service," I said, the words directed at him while my voice was for the rest of the room. "Her Highness, Princess Ariadne, Royal Sefaeran Master of the Hunt, owes you her life, and so do we. Your quick and wise actions a week ago saved her from a painful, horrible death, and for that, the crown thanks you." I held up a golden brooch shaped like a laurel with a pair of hands clasped together in a handshake in the center. "Please accept this commendation, signifying that you are a friend to the crown."

Typhir climbed the four steps up to the dais where the thrones sat and knelt before me so I could pin the brooch to the drape he wore over his shoulder. I resisted the urge to "accidentally" poke him with it. He'd saved my sister and proven he wasn't out to destroy my family like other members of *his* had been, but that didn't undo the millennia of conflict between us and our families.

I was struck with the thought of how easy it would be to draw my sickle and end him while his eyes were downcast, but I quickly tucked that thought away. If he hadn't been alive when we encountered the snake in the forest, Ari would be dead.

I finished adorning him with the commendation, and he stood, bowing to me, before turning to face the crowd.

I raised my hands, signaling to everyone that it was time for them to cheer, and they did so with a gusto that grated against every part of me that had spent my entire life hating the man I was now garnering applause for. Typhir nodded his head in a superior sort of way that nearly made me roll my eyes, but I managed to keep my restraint.

With the ceremony concluded, the crowd began to disperse. In true Sefaeran fashion, there would be an after party with almost enough blue wine to rid my mouth of the taste of presenting Typhir with such high praise—and to help me to forget that I owed him my sister's life.

At last, the only people remaining in the throne room were the royal family, Liro, Lexios, and the full Council. I'd asked them to remain behind, since, in light of yet another apparent portal breach, we needed to decide on some course of action. Ari was looking well, if still a little pale.

With the need for appearances having been reduced, I leaned into my soulmate, rubbing my nose on his cheek and kissing his neck.

"That was something," I said quietly.

"Don't worry," he whispered. "I was ready to stab him if you gave the command."

"Probably best to not turn a celebration into a public execution, even if those things might be one and the same in this case."

Gabriel giggled and kissed me, sending the bond buzzing with electric energy. But since it wasn't exactly an option to take him back to our chambers at that moment, I settled for putting an arm around his waist and holding him at my side.

"How are you feeling?" I directed at my sister.

"Been better," she said, leaning her head against our mother's shoulder like she did when we were children. "But I'm here." She glanced at Typhir, for possibly the first time in her life, with a lack of vitriol.

"And to ensure that happens to no one else," I said, "we need to discuss what happens now. Her Highness is safe, but others might not be so lucky. We need to know how Gaiadan creatures are getting in, and if there are other worlds leaking through as well."

"I might have a suggestion for that," Gabriel interjected. "If His Majesty would allow it."

I looked at Gabriel, a little surprised since he had just barely stepped into his role as Justice and was comfortable enough to not only engage, but to take the lead in such a serious matter. "By all means, Your Grace."

Gabriel paused thoughtfully. "If we could, uh... adjourn to the Council room—chambers?"

"Of course." I motioned for everyone to move to the door at the side of the hall that would lead to the room that housed the Council Chambers, which doubled as a war room in times when it was necessary.

Gabriel walked forward with confidence that I hadn't seen in him since he arrived and stood at the head of the map table which displayed all of Sefaera. Silently he looked over it, occasionally reaching out to touch certain topographical details, waiting for the room to fill before speaking.

"Oll—Your Majesty, you said that there were a series of portals that were closed when Gaiada and Sefaera could no longer function as allies, is that correct?"

"Yes," I said, moving to stand beside him and looking at the map with him. "Technically there are none left. The royal line can open new ones, but they are made for single use—not to remain as pathways. They vanish after the transition between realms is complete, like the one I brought you through."

Gabriel nodded, his face more pensive than I'd ever seen it. "Perhaps it's time we ensure that those portals truly are closed." He nodded to himself. "You, yourself, said it was rare that you made it to other parts of the kingdom. I think it's time we change that."

I turned to him, brushing a lock of his chestnut waves behind his ear, beneath the golden laurel that showed everyone, even those who didn't know him, exactly who he was. "Are you suggesting a grand tour of the kingdom to visit each of the sites of previous portals?"

"It's a good idea," Ari said, her voice still sounding tired. "You could say it's to introduce Gabe to the rest of Sefaera. No need to create panic about the possibility of a breach."

"Yeah, exactly," Gabriel grinned at Ari, like two children collaborating to pull off a prank on an authority figure. "Great idea." He turned to me. "Of course, as always, I defer to your judgment, Your Majesty."

I couldn't stop beaming. I'd always known he had the capacity for this, to be a ruler, even at his young age. But to see him truly taking on this role, of coming into his own as both Justice and Consort, nearly brought a tear to my eye.

Resisting the urge to kiss him again in such a serious moment, I chose instead to nod, knowing that the bond would carry the feelings of pride I felt to him.

"I think it's brilliant," I told him before turning to the rest of the room. "We'll need to discuss who will rule in my absence." I looked at my sister. "Ari—"

"No."

Her answer was so sudden and firm that I was momentarily frozen, staring at her, but her eyes were steady, despite the pale purple bags beneath them. She broke her gaze first, looking at Liro, who spoke for them both.

"We... In light of everything happening, and with the Princess nearly losing her life, we've decided to stop putting things off without reason. We will be taking a leave of absence from the palace for a week beginning tomorrow, and will need time upon our return to... adjust."

Gabriel looked bewildered. "Adjust to what? What's going on?"

I looked back and forth between my sister and her partner, the meaning of what Liro was saying immediately apparent to me.

"They're going to have a child," I told my soulmate.

"Oh!" he said. "In just a week? Or is it gonna be a week of... never mind."

Ari rolled her eyes, and Lexios, who had just sipped from a glass he'd poured himself from a station nearby, laughed so hard he spit out his drink.

"Delightful..." Typhir said, curling his lip in disgust at his son.

"Apologies, Father," he said, his face settling back into a neutral expression.

Liro leaned in to whisper to Gabriel, likely not wanting to embarrass him in front of the entire Council. Realization dawned on my soulmate's face as Liro reminded him how the royal family conceived children. Unlike everyone else, our bloodline conceived by the same magic that granted us soulmates and the right to rule. We would adjourn to one of the pocket dimensions for a year, where we would meditate, make love, and combine our energies to create a new life.

"Well..." I said. "You have the full support of the crown, and we will ensure that you are well cared for and your roles are covered so that you can focus on what you need to."

Liro nodded, and I turned my attention back to the matter at hand.

"In that case..." I looked around at the people gathered. My mother was the clear choice to preside as Justice, having done the job, herself, for thousands of years. But as far as who would take on my duties... I decided to buy myself some time by making an easier delegation. "Well, Gabriel and myself will be going, of course. And we will need guards and attendants, which means Gryfian will join us, as well as Tomos."

"And Lex," my soulmate said matter-of-factly. "Lexios has shown great friendship to me, and I believe he represents what the nobility of Sefaera stands for." Gabriel turned to me, and I felt something akin to a static shock as he gave me a look that told me my face was betraying my feelings about the suggestion.

"With his Union coming up, though," I said, "wouldn't it be better for him to remain here? After all, he'll be back to traveling once the Union is completed."

"If I may, Your Majesty," Typhir said in that voice of his that was condescending without even trying, putting a hand on his son's shoulder. "Might it not be prudent to have someone with you who knows the lands under your rule as well as Lord Lexios? After all, as an emissary, he spends more of his time in other parts of our world than you do and could be a rather useful guide."

The logic of the words was nearly lost on me in light of my desire to *not* be on an extended trip with my rival, even if he was making steps toward making amends.

"I will, of course, adhere to whatever my King commands of me," Lexios added. "But it would be a great honor to accompany you on this trip to not only introduce you to some of the peoples I am well familiar with, but also to protect you and Gabe—" His eyes flashed with panic, and they went to his father. "His Grace—my apologies—with my life."

And here I was again, stuck in the difficult position of deciding what was best for my soulmate and my kingdom, while those things were strictly at odds with my own desires. I looked at Gabriel, who was gazing expectantly at me, as though waiting for me to make the right choice. I knew what it was, but it was a hard one to make.

My mind flashed back to a small room in a small apartment in New York City, in Gabriel's world. To a night when he'd been drunk, and I'd been impatient and frustrated. When I'd broken the first promise I ever made him and took him away from everything he'd ever known. When I'd forced him away from his friend, as bad for him as that friend may have been, and nearly lost him before I ever truly had him.

I wouldn't do that again. Gabriel was young and sometimes still a bit naive, but if I could trust him to rule a kingdom at my side, to make decisions on behalf of that kingdom, I needed to also trust him to choose his friends and attendants.

"Very well," I said. "Then our party will consist of myself, His Grace, Lord Lexios, Gryfian, our personal attendants, and a small group of additional guards."

"And who will rule in your absence?" Typhir said in a self-satisfied way, as if he knew the only reasonable answer.

I swallowed and took a deep breath. Only one person remaining, aside from my mother, had any experience in making and enforcing policy. Typhir had led the Council for thousands of years between my father's death and my rise to the throne, and had, himself, taken on the role of Justice. Of course, his reign as Justice had been one of terror. But perhaps with the Council there to temper him and my mother presiding over the Justice hearings, he could be trusted. He did just save my sister's life, after all. Perhaps that family was truly going to become allies.

"The Council," I said before addressing Typhir directly. "And as the head of the Council, it will be your responsibility to ensure that my wishes and commands remain the law of the land. And, as a reminder, while they work together, the ruling entities are separate but equal—neither has authority over the other. Am I clear?"

Typhir gave another exaggerated bow. "Of course, Your Majesty. I am ever your faithful subject."

I fought back a sardonic laugh as I looked away from the spectacle. "Gabriel... I'm proud of you. You are everything I could have ever hoped for in a partner to rule our kingdom. Now... the party begins in only an hour, so we should probably begin to discuss logistics for the journey." I gritted my teeth and turned to Lexios. "Where do you propose we begin?"

Chapter Fifteen
Gabriel

I was five goblets deep in blue wine at Typhir's party when Lexios finally approached me. I'd noticed he'd been keeping his distance since the Justice hearing, where I'd thrown him under the bus, and I'd been eager to bug him about it. In hindsight—maybe I should have done it when I wasn't wasted.

As I reached to refill my goblet once more, I heard a smooth, deep voice from behind me.

"Don't let me stop you, but wouldn't you have more fun actually socializing?"

I sighed, sarcasm lacing the scoff I gave enthusiastically. "It's no fun to party with people who want to talk politics with me. And my only friend here has been avoiding me." I looked up to see amusement glinting in Lexios's eyes.

"I haven't been avoiding you."

"Oh, I wasn't talking about *you*," I said playfully. "Another friend of mine that has been really awkward with me for the past week."

Lex grabbed my goblet and took a drink before handing it back and shuddering. "How can you drink this stuff?"

I gazed into the goblet, wondering if it would be inappropriate to drink from it now. "Well," I said, throwing caution to the wind and chugging the remainder of it. "It helps me sleep at night. You know... blocking out the screams of my parents cooking to death in a fiery plane crash."

As I was talking, Lexios had grabbed his own goblet and taken a deep swallow, which he now choked on in a very unrefined way. I smacked him on the back a few times, hoping it would clear his airway, but all it resulted in doing was drawing attention.

"You really need to stop making a habit out of that," I teased.

"Y-you... need to stop b-being so amusing," he sputtered, still choking.

Unfortunately, the ruckus also meant pulling Ollie out of a conversation with some foreign diplomat.

"Everything alright?" he said, coming up and putting a hand on the small of my back as he looked at Lexios.

"I might have killed Typhir's son," I said with a slight grin as Lex panted, patting his chest.

"Which I might not be overly disappointed about," a snide drawl said from over my left shoulder, "seeing as he's decided to make a spectacle of himself at such a momentous occasion... again."

I turned to see Typhir looking at his son with a disgusted sneer.

"If you don't mind," he said, reaching for a goblet of wine, "I was speaking with Servenus about His Majesty's and His Grace's journey before I was expected to ensure my idiot son hadn't been attacked by the same creature that nearly killed the Princess."

He spun, his cloak fluttering behind him, and walked away just as quickly as he'd appeared.

"Dick," I muttered under my breath before I remembered who I was standing next to. "Oh... uh—sorry."

"No, no. Please. He is a dick. No one knows that better than me," Lexios assured me.

I glanced at Ollie, who was looking at Lex with an appraising look, as if he'd never considered that having Typhir as a dad might be worse than having him work for you.

"Well, at least you *have* a dad," I said, motioning back and forth between Ollie and me, trying to ease the tension with a drunken joke. "Fatherless children often grow up to be sluts."

I could feel Olympio smiling through the bond despite the fact he was slightly behind me, hand on my waist as always.

"Your Grace," Ollie said in a mockingly shocked tone. "Is that so?"

"Honestly, you should have met me two years ago, Lex. I was sucking cock for bedrooms back in—what?"

I turned to Ollie with a grin as I felt him squeeze my elbow with a death grip.

"Back in Gaiada," he said, his smile suddenly looking a lot more like a snarl. "But that Gabriel is in the past." He kissed the side of my head, his lips lingering as if the memories of before I came here could be enough to take me from him.

"Yeah, that was a wild time."

I could feel my buzz waning slightly and reached for another goblet. The more drunk I could get, the better. Being a royal was stressful, and lately, only wine could ease my mind enough to get me to sleep

"Uh..." I heard Lex say as I dipped my head into the fountain of blue wine itself.

Ollie's hands were pulling me back as quickly as I'd done it. "Gabriel," he admonished in a tone I hadn't heard him use since my first days here, when I'd caused him as much trouble as I possibly could. He grabbed my crown, which had fallen into the fountain. I felt his annoyance flare up, then fade into something more melancholy as he gave me a small, indulgent smile. "You might want to slow down. I have a surprise for you, but I refuse to let you have it if you're too drunk to enjoy it."

I looked up at him. Surprise?

"Your Majesty, if I may," Lexios began, dipping his head. "Allow me to make excuses for you while you take His Grace to the balcony for some fresh air."

Ollie gaped at him, as if he couldn't believe what was coming out of Lexios's mouth. "I... Yes, of course. Th-thank you." He stumbled on the words, which must have felt foreign speaking them to someone he used to hate.

"I don't need fresh air," I insisted as I dropped the half full goblet. "I need to dance or something. This party sucks as much dick as Typhir does."

I must have said that louder than I thought, because I heard a few people whisper around me.

The words had barely left my mouth when, suddenly, I felt a lot more sober. Ollie's hand closed around my arm, and before I knew it, he was pulling me across the ballroom to the balcony, where he led me out into the night.

He turned to look at me, and I expected him to yell. But he didn't. The hand on my arm slid down to take mine in his. He guided me over to the railing, where he pressed me into it, just like he did the first time, when he showed me the moons.

"What's wrong, Gabriel?" he breathed into my ear, his voice low, his worry carrying along the bond. "I haven't seen you like this since we left Gaiada."

He had used the bond to take the drunkenness away.

Fury flared inside me, and I gripped his wrist to take it back, glaring at him. "Don't do that."

"Why?" he said, his voice firm, but not angry. "Something is wrong. You're in pain, and I don't know why." He began to try to pull my drunkenness from me again, and we started a kind of tug of war over it.

"Stop," I whined loudly. "I thought this 'forcing me to be what you wanted' was done."

Ollie's arms remained tight around me, but not so tight I couldn't break free if I wanted to. "I'm not trying to force you to *be* anything. I'm trying to understand why my soulmate is suddenly using the tactics he once used to drown out the world, after I thought he was past all of that."

"How can I be *past* anything when I see my parents dying again and again in my sleep every night? How can I ever be *past* anything when I'm still not good enough for you? How can I ever move on if I'm facing an eternity of having to condemn people like Vassenia, only to befriend her cousin? No—there's one thing that I know helps, and that's booze. It's not like I can die from it. My organs are self regenerating now, my blood doesn't even look like my blood. I don't know who I am anymore aside from Justice of Sefaera."

Ollie released his hold on me, and I collapsed to my knees. I hadn't realized I had all of that inside me, but now that I'd let it out, the burden of having it in my mind was heavy.

Slowly, he dropped to his own knees beside me and put a hand on my shoulder. I could feel how unsure he was. "I had no idea, Gabriel. I knew you were still having the nightmares. I thought I could help you through them by siphoning away some of your panic and pain. But maybe... maybe I was just delaying this. You having to actually feel it."

"Ollie, I'm gonna feel it the rest of my damn life."

Then I made an impulsive decision, something I knew I might regret. I gripped Olympio's wrist and sent him every little thing I felt all the time. The sorrow, the agony, the hope, the lust, the fear, and the self-doubt. I watched his eyes glaze over, and a muscle in his cheek began to twitch. I thought specifically about the recurring nightmare I had about my parents burning. The looks in their eyes as they pleaded with me to save them. The thought that Ollie was there, in that world, not so far away. The anger I constantly felt wondering if he had let them die just to get me here easier.

Shadows began to unfurl from his body like wisps of smoke, and tears fell silently down his cheeks as he began to shake.

"Gabriel... I... please, stop."

"Why?" I asked, shaking as well. "I don't ever get to stop. I don't even get to die to escape. If it was up to you, I wouldn't even be allowed to have friends to help me get through it." I released his wrist and pulled away, covering my face as I wept in shame.

What was I doing? *Why* was I doing it? I loved Olympio with every fiber of my being, and I would never want to hurt him. Lately, I'd been waking up alone, covered in sweat from the nightmares that occurred after nights where I used wine to put myself to sleep. But it's not like I could ask the King of Sefaera to change his schedule. He belonged to the people and to the court and the Council. Not me.

Olympio's arms found me again, pulling me into his lap. He held me, just rocking me and whispering soothing little words over and over while I cried.

"I'm here. I'll always be here. I'm not going anywhere."

"And neither are the nightmares, Ollie. How am I supposed to face that? Face all of it and wake up every day to be a good Justice? You were so proud of me today in the meeting, but all it did was remind me how often I disappoint you."

Olympio took a deep breath, held it, and then released it. "I used to have nightmares every night about Vasileios, after he died. I would see myself goading him about having to be bonded to a soulmate, only hours before he would sever his bond and end his life. I would always wake up wondering if it was my fault. If I somehow pushed him into making the choice."

I clung to him like I was going to fall off the face of the world if I let go, feeling his vulnerability while also refusing to let down his stoic facade.

"But as the years have passed, new ones have taken root as well. Vassenia haunts me most nights now, showing her true colors over and over. They will never stop. I'm not going to lie to you about that, Gabriel. What I *can* tell you is that someday, it won't be every night. You'll have a night where the fire doesn't burn. And then another. And another. And on those days, you'll realize that you are stronger than the nightmares. That they still hurt, but the *suffering* has faded." He ran his hand through my hair and kissed my forehead. "You, my Gabriel, are stronger than I ever was. These battles inside you, you will fight them forever. But I know you will win."

Like a sigh that was held way too long, I allowed my body to fold into him completely, wishing to become one being. There was something so astoundingly intimate about someone who could truly share your feelings, and not only that, but someone whose feelings you could share *in*. Fighting your pain together.

I wiped away the last few tears that lingered on my eyelashes. "I really wish I could have met him," I said to Ollie. "The way you all talk about Vaseilios—like he died a week ago instead of a millenia—he sounds like the kind of guy everyone needs in their life."

"He was," he said, a slight smile on his face as he remembered his brother. "I still don't know if I'll ever be half the king he would have been. And on that note..." He tilted my chin so I was forced to look at him. "Don't ever think you aren't good enough for me. I only have the capacity to be a good king, a good *man*, because of you. It's *I* who doesn't deserve someone like you."

"Stop it," I said with a gentle smile, pushing his chin away playfully. "I'm nothing special."

"I have an entire kingdom that would disagree. Do I need to remind you that my people only gave me a chance after meeting you in the market for only one day? You are sunshine and goodness incarnate, my Gabriel."

I looked up at him and saw the eyes that were identical to my own looking back at me. "Kiss me?" I asked.

His lips were on mine almost before I could finish the request. They were soft, like a caress rather than a passionate burning. I returned the affection and wrapped my fingers into his sunset waves.

"I'm sorry—" said a voice from back in the ballroom. I looked up to find Lex standing there, covering his eyes. "But I wanted to warn you that my father is starting to make covert comments to people on how the king thinks he's too good for the partygoers. Wanted to give you time to make him look like an idiot." Lexios looked through his fingers, and when he realized we'd stopped kissing, he looked right at Ollie, giving a slight grin. "I'm happy to assist in any way I can."

My soulmate looked at him in surprise, which quickly shifted to gratitude. "Thank you. We'll be inside in just a moment." He turned back to me. "Do you feel up to returning to the party?"

I nodded. "Only for a bit, though. Now that I'm sober, I'm tired."

He looked thoughtful, then helped us both to our feet before looking at me in an exaggerated way. "Alright... I'll cancel the surprise, then," he said, goading me.

"Oh, yeah." I felt like a plant that had finally been watered and put in the sunlight. "I forgot. Gimme."

"It isn't something I can *give*... Just enjoy the rest of the party, and when we get back to our chambers, if you're not too tired... You'll have it."

"Oh..." I grinned. "It's a sex thing." I grabbed his hand and pressed it quickly to my junk so he could feel the semi I now sported at the promise of something that would be special enough to be considered a surprise.

His fingers gripped me gently, making it even harder to hide, before turning away and leaving me with a tent in my chiton. "I guess you'll find out later."

I grabbed his arm. "No... now..."

He licked his lips hungrily, then said, "Very well. Let's make our exit."

I gripped his hand and let him lead me through the party toward Typhir, almost as excited for the clever verbal beatdown Ollie would surely have for him as I was for my surprise.

"Lord Typhir," Ollie said, approaching a group that included the man himself. Typhir turned and looked at us, the sneer he was wearing quickly tucked away, trying to hide his insolence. "As lovely as your party is, I understand that you feel like I haven't given the appropriate amount of time to our guests. I would apologize, but I was simply giving you the spotlight, since you have been craving it for so long. Thank you again for saving my sister. Gabriel and I will be leaving now to allow you the freedom to speak as disparagingly as you wish, and to make a fool out of yourself for criticizing the person who just gave you a *very* public commendation."

I couldn't help myself. A loud, obnoxious giggle escaped me, and I squeezed Ollie's arm. If I wasn't mistaken, from behind us, I heard Lexios share in the amusement with a snort.

The people Typhir had been speaking to seemed to realize that he had made a social faux pas and began to disperse, disappearing into the crowd.

"Your Majesty," Typhir said in that sniveling voice of his. "My deepest apologies. I was merely saying—"

"Frankly, Typhir," Ollie interrupted, "I don't care. You did the crown a service, and you have been commended for it. As far as I'm concerned, we're even. However you choose to proceed with our relationship from here is up to you. If I were you, I might make better choices."

Before Typhir could reply with anything other than sputtering noises of shock, Ollie had me by the hand once more and was pulling me out a side door to reduce the spectacle of our exit.

I collapsed against him from the momentum and took the opportunity to encircle his neck with my arms, placing a kiss on his taut lips. He didn't even know it, but whenever he had a conversation with Typhir, you could literally watch his top lip disappear as he struggled to not let his feelings show.

"God. Intimacy and vulnerability are sexy. Is it weird to say I liked that?"

"Liked me losing my temper at Typhir *again*?" he said, smiling before moving his lips to the side of my jaw.

"No..." I ran my hand down his chest and leaned to bite at his exposed nipple. "Us telling each other what haunts us."

He sucked in a sharp breath, and I felt the spike of his arousal. "I liked it, too," he said, his voice barely managing to stay even. "Understanding you a little better... makes me want you even more."

I stood up straight and looked him in the eyes. "You already have me, Ollie. Always."

"Good," he said. "Just remember that when we get to our chambers." Before I could even try to figure out what he meant by that, he turned around and offered me his back. "Hop on."

I hesitated for a moment, then felt an impulse that had me up on his back in a second. It felt like a hand giving me a little shove. "Unfair," I giggled.

"Definitely," he replied. "But you don't seem to mind, so I'm not sorry."

He took off at almost a run to our chambers, his strides so even that I was barely bouncing.

I leaned down to bite his ear, my arms tightening. "When do we get to go on another adjournment? We've been here for two weeks already. Isn't that enough for a vacation?"

"Did you forget that we're leaving in just a few days?" His voice was filled with that rich laughter that was so rare for him.

"No. But it's not the same."

"I promise you, I will make time for us to have as many vacations as we possibly can."

We finally reached the doors, and Ollie pressed his hand to the panel that opened it. And for the first time, when we walked into our room, there was someone else there.

With a pair of guards on either side of our deep, in-floor bathtub, splashing playfully in the water, was a pair of women, submerged to their shoulders. One was curvy and blonde and could have passed for human if not for the delicate curving horns on her head. The other had skin the color of slate with shimmering white freckles and bright white hair that curled around her face wildly.

Ollie set me down and moved so he was now behind me and leaned into my ear. "Surprise."

I froze. What in the world was this supposed to be? "Ollie...?"

His lips moved to my neck, sending a shiver down my arms. "As much as I would have loved to make one of our little fantasies come true by fucking you on the throne—it would have certainly made the ceremony today more bearable—this one seemed a bit more realistic. Gabriel, meet Caillea and Deveira. You may have seen them at parties. They are here to fulfill something you never had the pleasure of experiencing."

"A stable, normal childhood...?"

He snorted, his fingers flexing on my waist. "If only—I might have asked for one of those, myself, if they could. No, they are here for your pleasure. All you have to do is tell them what you want—they are enthusiastic volunteers for the honor of being your first experience with females."

"Experience?" My brain was short circuiting. "Like... *experience?*"

"Yes. Like *sexual* experience."

I looked over to the girls, who were casually paying attention while not staring at me, which I couldn't have been more grateful for. I felt like a thirteen year old getting my first kiss, and I was terrified. "Ollie... are you... sure? I–I don't want you to think I'm not happy..."

"I know you are," he murmured, his lips still creating electric currents on my neck. "I can feel what you feel. But as I said at the falls, while I've had a long time to explore various delights of the flesh, you have not. And I'm going to be right here. This isn't something just for you. This is for *us*. As long as you want it."

I looked up at him, and a thick pulse of lust resonated in my chest. "What if I don't know what to do?" I whispered in distress.

"There's the beauty of it," he said, turning me so that we were facing each other. "Because this is for both of us, I will be right there the entire time, guiding you through any parts you're unsure of."

"Okay. Yeah... yeah, I'm into it. Can you like... introduce me or something?"

"That would certainly be a good first step." He took my hand. "Come with me."

He pulled me over to the bath, and the girls, who had been playing with each other's hair, looked up at us fully.

"Hello, Your Majesty... Your Grace," the one with the deep gray skin said as the other bowed her head in a gentle nod.

"Hello, Deveira," Olympio said. "I hope your mother is doing well." He turned to me and said, "Deveira's mother is Allenda, the head cook for the palace. And hello, Caillea. It's been too long."

"Over sixty years, Your Majesty," she said, winking at me. "It's a pleasure to be back in your chambers."

Olympio grinned, his hand moving around my back to grip my hip. "And one to have you both back. Thank you for coming. May we join you?"

I felt a knot in my throat that threatened to choke me out, and I watched Ollie to follow his lead.

"Please," Deveria said, and both she and Caillea moved back to make room. As they did, their bodies emerged slightly from the water, giving me a view of their breasts.

Ollie smiled at me encouragingly, then began to remove his clothes.

I felt like a skipping record as I tried to process what was happening. Still—I followed Olympio's lead and began to shed my clothes. That was until I was forced to stop by my soulmate's hand.

"Allow me," he said in a low purr.

Chills overtook me as Ollie moved behind me, removing my belt before untying my garment at the shoulders. He held the fabric up for just a breath before he let it drop, exposing my boxers—the only holdout of my human wardrobe—to the room. My nipples went hard, partially from the cold air and partially from a strange eroticism that was blooming deep in my stomach from being appraised like this.

His hands came around me, running across my chest and brushing the tight little nubs, making me whimper under my breath. He pressed against me, and I could feel he was already stiffening. He stroked my body, taking his time like he'd never felt me before, until his hands paused at the waistband of my underwear. Just when I thought he was going to take them off, he stopped and moved in front of me, kneeling down and burying his face between my legs. He inhaled deeply and moaned, his lips running along my hardening length through the fabric. His warm breath moistened my boxers as his fingers dug into my ass, forcing me closer.

The intoxicating shame I felt of being on display only heightened as I firmed against his touch, and both women watched as Deveria pulled

Caillea into her lap. A moan slipped out of me, and it took at all my willpower not to give into the urge to thrust. "Ollie..." I sighed loudly.

Instead of speaking, however, he ran a hand up my thigh, slipping into the leg of my boxers to take hold of my cock and stroke it in time with the movements of his mouth. "Mm..." he moaned against me, the vibrations making me whimper with need. A moment later, he tucked his fingers into the waistband and removed the last piece of clothing guarding me from their eyes.

Both Caillea and Deveira looked me up and down, and Deveira licked her lips when her eyes found my length. Ollie stood up and took my hand.

"Nothing to be anxious about." He rubbed his nose against my cheek in the way he always did. "It's just a bath... For now." With a gentle tug on my hand and one through the bond, he led me down the steps into the bath, which was the size of your average hot tub.

The water was perfect, like always, but I clung to Ollie like I was scared it would burn me. I wasn't even this nervous when I was with *him* the first time, but this... What if I was bad at it? What if I was so bad that I gained some sort of reputation as the consort who was shit in bed? What if they made up a nickname for me? What if—

My thoughts were interrupted when Ollie sat and pulled me down beside him. He leaned into my ear and said, "Are you alright? We can stop if you want, but I'm here to guide you if you want this."

I opened my mouth to say something that I could only hope would be funny, but my mouth was dry. "Wine?" I squeaked.

Ollie chuckled and nodded, reaching for a tray next to him, pouring four goblets. He'd really prepared for everything. He handed me one before giving one to each of the girls and took a sip of his own. "I thought maybe we could start slow. Let you explore their bodies without pressure before we move on. I'm going to have one of them sit in your lap. Is that alright?"

I was shaking—probably the least cool thing I could have done right now. Still... I nodded in consent, ready to take the next step into my own manhood.

Don't be a bitch, Gabe.

"Ladies," Olympio said in a voice that left no doubt in my mind why he'd been so popular at parties. He sounded like the smoothest guy who'd ever lived. "Would you mind joining us?" He reached out and took both of their hands, pulling Deveira into his lap and guiding Caillea to me, where she immediately turned her back and sat with her legs straddling mine.

I was hard in a fucking instant and felt my face burning as I tried to cross my legs and hide the fact that I was on such a hairpin trigger. These women were probably double my age, if not more. They would have had lovers and partners that I couldn't even dream of.

"So—" my voice cracked, and I looked around to see if there was a crevice in the bath tiles I could melt into. "How old are you girls? Er—that's not what I meant. I mean... I just..."

Caillea leaned back against me, my cock pressed between us. There was no way she didn't feel it, and a little wiggle of her hips against me told me she absolutely knew what she was doing. "I just had my hundredth year, Your Grace."

"And I'm in my third century," Deveira responded.

"Oh, okay," I replied, trying to steady my breathing. "I'm... well that's not important. You're both really lovely." I leaned into Deveira, looking up and down her arms where that constellation of white freckles dotted her flesh like a night sky on a clear evening. "I love your freckles. They're so beautiful." I glanced up at Ollie for approval... or maybe reassurance. Some kind of indicator that I was doing this right.

He gave a slight nod, and I felt a wave of approval as Deveira smiled at me from where she was straddling Ollie, facing him, while he began to massage her shoulders.

"Thank you. My family is originally from Hyxelon." Deveira said it as if that should somehow explain something.

Thankfully, Ollie was quick to clear it up. "Hyxelon is the desert region of Sefaera. Most of its inhabitants have similar complexions to the lovely Deveira."

Tentatively, I placed my hands on Caillea's hips. "Is this okay?" I asked, positively pulsing from the tiny bit of skin on skin contact.

"More than okay, Your Grace," she said, leaning her head back onto my shoulder, giving me a perfect view down.

The weight of her curvy body on my legs was divine—and I was not the kind of gay boy to use the word "divine." Everywhere I felt, there was something to squish my fingers into, and without intending it, I whimpered softly, sending a fresh wave of embarrassment through me. "Sorry..." I mumbled, biting my lip.

"For what, Your Grace?" she asked, her voice almost a moan. "Your hands feel incredible." She took them in her own then, moving them up along the curve of her waist, then to her front, pulling them up to cup her breasts.

I laughed nervously before the sensations of having her there, like this, overtook me, and I leaned back against the wall and closed my eyes. "Fuck..." I turned my head sideways and opened them again, finding Ollie staring directly at me while Deveira kissed his neck. He had a look in his eyes like he was thrilled with himself, but also protective of this experience for me.

Caillea shifted in my lap, arching her back slightly, and Ollie said, "She's giving you permission, Gabriel. You can touch. Explore. There's no pressure here. Just enjoy the sensations."

"Allow me, Your Majesty. Your Grace..."

I watched as Caillea slid off me, leaving my cock exposed for all to see, just beneath the surface of the water, and I was certainly pleased to see Olympio bite his lip as he stared. Caillea, on the other hand, dragged her hands down my chest, across my thighs and rested them on my knees as she sank to hers before me, her ample breasts sort of buoying on the water. It took me a second to realize what she was about to do, but when I did, I looked over at Ollie in desperation.

I wasn't sure if I could communicate, "*What if I bust all over her face before she even touches me?*" through the bond, but I sure as fuck was trying.

"Why don't you shift up to the ledge, Gabriel?" my soulmate suggested. "Don't make beautiful Caillea have to go diving to suck your cock."

A weird, deranged giggle burst out of me, and I scrambled to do as he suggested, bumping my knee hard and feeling a tear of pain well in my eye while I tried to maintain a look of nonchalance and cool. Caillea seemed either indifferent to my clumsiness or was doing me the courtesy of pretending she didn't see me fumble, and moved toward me in the water, slowly reaching out her hand to take my length.

What if I nut in her face? Ollie, goddamn it, hear these words in your head, for fucks' sake.

But he simply watched, moving his hand ever so slightly so that our fingers could interlace.

"Is this alright, Your Grace?" Caillea asked.

"Uh... Uh-huh..." I swallowed, but my throat was bone dry. Like every single drop of liquid in my body had gone straight to my penis.

Then Caillea moved closer and leaned in, and like I was watching it in slow motion, her mouth went toward the tip of my cock.

"Wait!" I said, stopping her by the shoulders. "What if this is over like...really fast?" I looked at Ollie. "I don't want to embarrass you."

A small smile creased his cheeks, and he shook his head. "You could never embarrass me. But if you're truly worried, maybe I'll show you something else instead."

I nodded vigorously, and Olympio stood, cock on full, delicious display, and reached down for Deveira, who took his hand. I did the same with Caillea, and she smiled at me reassuringly, allowing me to help her out of the tub.

The second Deveira was out, Ollie hoisted her onto his shoulder, growling at her playfully as she screamed in mock terror.

I looked at Caillea. "Do you want me…?"

She laughed, a sound that was like Christmas bells. "That's okay," she said. "Why don't you hold my hand instead."

There was something about the simplicity of it that relaxed me, and I took her hand and followed Ollie to where he'd dropped Deveira on the bed. Caillea's hand was warm and soft, and she smelled amazing. Not even for a moment did she make me feel weird or uncomfortable—well, not any more than the general situation was already doing, and when we reached the corner of the bed, I stopped and impulsively leaned down to kiss her.

She tasted like oulon-based liquor and the blue wine she'd sipped, and from some weird, animal instinct part of my brain, my hands went to her breasts.

Oh, holy fucking heaven.

I was so engrossed in the moment, I didn't even hear Ollie approach from behind me and begin placing kisses on my neck. Shivers ran down me, and I moaned against her lips, into her mouth.

"Come here," Ollie said, pulling me gently away from her and around to the side of the bed. I watched as he beckoned her over, then grabbed her by the hips and hoisted her onto the mattress, his arm and shoulder muscles defined as he lifted her.

From across the bed, Deveira scooted over so that she was side by side with Caillea, and I watched as they leaned in and began kissing each other.

"Now, Gabriel," Ollie said, wrapping his arms around my neck and speaking in a slow, steady tone. "The most important thing when making love to a female is to remember that it's not the same as being with another man. If you want them to actually enjoy themselves, you need to focus on foreplay. You aren't done until they are begging you to fuck them."

I swear to god, I could have come all over the place just at the thought of this, and I heard Olympio laugh softly as my eyes rolled back into my head.

"Okay," I exhaled. "So what do I do?"

"Just copy me," he said, tugging me forward and bending over Deveira, who promptly turned to look at him with a smile, playing with his hair. I watched as he kissed her, and a pang of jealousy hit me unexpectedly. That was until Caillea leaned up and wrapped her arms around my neck, pulling me into a kiss just as nice as the first one.

I allowed myself to sink into her, and the sweet tenderness of the way she touched me was like that first bite you take of a s'more—all gooey and delicious. I side-eyed Ollie to see if I was doing it right, but found that he had moved on to sucking Deveira's dark black nipples while he stroked himself.

Fuck, this was hot.

I pulled back from Caillea and assessed the incredible pair of breasts before me, so large that I could have probably sunk my whole face into them. They moved with every breath, almost fluidly, as her nipples tightened to bright pink peaks, the skin around them wrinkling slightly.

I leaned forward like Ollie had and took one tentatively between my lips. She gave a soft moan and arched her back, pressing her flesh even more into me, the soft pillows surrounding my mouth and cheeks. Immediately, I was moaning into them, beginning to tease her with my tongue as my hands grabbed as much of the ample offering I could, burying my face in her.

As Olympio kissed down Deveira's body, I did, too, to Caillea, until I found my face nicely buried in a soft thatch of hair.

"Gabriel," Ollie said in a deep voice. I looked at him and noticed wisps of his demonic powers coming off him in thick black ribbons. "Eyes on me."

I nodded and watched as he pulled Deveira's legs up to her thighs, over his shoulders and kissed from the inside of her knee to—

"Fuck," Deveira groaned loudly. "You always were good at that."

My feet stumbled forward without me commanding them to as Olympio used his powers to draw me closer, presumably to see what he was doing. I watched as his tongue darted in and out, his fingers spreading her wet flesh to reveal a pulsing nub that he was lapping at like a dog at a water bowl. The sounds he was making alone were enough to drive me insane, but the symphony of their noises intermingled, his baritone with her whimpers like dark caramel, were truly delicious.

I felt a tug on my hand and looked over to see Caillea beckoning me back to her, to which I happily obliged, following the exact pattern Ollie had just shown me. The weight of her gorgeous thighs as they draped over my shoulders was erotic, but nothing compared to the smell of her dripping pussy. A sweet, slightly salty smell that filled my senses and made me feel like I could sprout shadow wings, too, at any given moment. I felt like a *man*, like I wanted to make this body mine in a way that wouldn't be able to be washed away by a bath.

I kissed the inside of her knee, gripping her heavy thighs so that my fingers dug into the soft mass there.

For the life of me, as I was experiencing this, I couldn't imagine how this could possibly be half as good with some of the women I'd regularly seen around New York. Stick thin supermodel wannabes who looked like they'd break with the right gust of wind.

But, hey—they say there's someone for everyone, and I was certain *this kind of body* was for me, as far as women were concerned. I loved the feeling of being smothered between her thighs, the way her wetness was covering my face as I got closer to...

I breathed in the scent of her once more, not even trying to hide the groan I emitted, and I could hear Ollie call me a good boy from beside me. It didn't seem like there was any point to drawing this out longer, so I dove right in, face first, pressing my tongue between the folds of skin and finding her lovely center.

I copied what I'd seen Ollie do, and she whined, her fingers digging into the sheets as she squirmed against me. I clutched her hips harder and held her in place, tasting anything my tongue could get to, only coming up for air once in a while.

"Oh, fucking god..." I moaned into her, and without being instructed, my body took charge and I tucked not one, but two fingers into her warm opening. It was soft, and I felt her clench around me as I doubled down on licking her every glistening drop away.

"Well done, Gabriel," I heard Ollie say in my ear, his arm coming beneath me to stroke me while I devoured this goddess in front of me.

Heaven. This was *heaven*. Every sense I had was consumed with the pleasure—and it was pleasure shared with the man I loved more than I had ever loved anything.

"Ollie..." I whimpered. "Ollie, stop. I'm gonna..."

He teasingly stroked me a few more times then withdrew. "They're not begging yet," he growled. "Your job isn't complete."

He then stood and grabbed the back of my head, forcing it, without any resistance from me, back into Caillea's apex and holding me there for a moment while I resumed my tasting and licking.

I could feel my cock drip onto my foot with the tension of a water balloon ready to burst.

And right now, I was certain if I never did anything else besides this, I would be coming soon enough, either way.

Chapter Sixteen
Olympio

I could have watched Gabriel for days without tiring of seeing him absolutely devouring Caillea, moaning into her as I stroked him. I felt him pulsing, throbbing, bucking his hips against my touch.

Once both girls had climaxed, they rolled sideways, kissing each other for only a moment before they both reached out for Gabriel. I'd discussed with both Caillea and Deveira ahead of time what my limitations in this excursion would be, not knowing if the bond was still able to be broken, and if so, how far I could go without destroying the most important thing in my very long life. They knew that the focus would be on Gabriel.

He looked at me with a slight panic about what he knew was coming next, but his eyes were heavy with lust. I nodded my head, indicating he should copy me once more as I crawled over Deveira, bending down to take one of her nipples in my mouth, swirling my tongue around the hardened peak.

I heard Gabriel doing the same, and when I glanced over, he was thrusting into the sheets, and I knew it was time. I released Deveira's breasts and stood, moving closer to my soulmate and placing a hand on his back.

"Are you ready?" I asked him. "Here... let me help you."

He slid between her legs, and I felt him shaking ever so slightly. I placed a kiss on the side of his neck and reached between him and Caillea, who licked her lips in anticipation. I took hold of his cock, positioning him at her entrance.

"Please, Your Grace... I need to feel you inside me," she whimpered.

"Take her," I whispered.

Gabriel swallowed hard and nodded, then pressed his hips forward. Endowed as he was, the first push just barely managed to penetrate her with his tip. She gasped, which quickly turned into a moan, and I felt her thrust her hips up to meet him, allowing him to slide even further into her.

"Oh, fuck." Gabriel's voice was a low whine, his body's need taking over. My hand was still there, guiding him as he began to move his hips back and forth, slowly stretching her to accommodate him.

"Just like that..." I whispered, beginning to stroke my own cock in time with his movements.

"Talaea's mercy, Your Grace," Caillea groaned, her hands digging into his hips, urging him deeper and deeper.

Eventually, he was sheathed within her enough that I had to let go, and when I did, he bottomed out, not an inch of his impressive length outside of her.

The sight of Gabriel fucking her, his body taking control, was almost enough to make me come completely undone. I looked at Deveira, who took that as her cue to straddle her friend's face.

Caillea cried out almost at once, her body tensing and writhing with yet another climax. For as much as I knew Gabriel was nervous regarding his lack of experience, the lithe, graceful movements that made him naturally skilled with his daggers translated beautifully into how he moved in bed. I'd never been left wanting with him, and I could tell it was the same for Caillea, whose fingers were now gripping his shoulders, her nails making marks in the skin.

I grabbed the lubricant and moved behind Gabriel, watching his ass clench with every thrust into her. I ran my hand gently over the skin there, squeezing a delicious handful. I used his own momentum as I coated my fingers and moved to his cleft, spreading the cheeks and pressing a single digit to his opening, allowing his thrusts to force me inside.

"Oh, god..." Gabriel moaned, pausing only for a moment before picking up the pace once more.

Within seconds, I had not only one, but two fingers inside him, stretching him as he fucked himself on them while simultaneously fucking Caillea. Deveira began to cry out, "Yes! Yes!" as she came again, thanks to Caillea's gifted tongue.

Gabriel looked at me, panting. He was on the brink of a violent orgasm, but I was doing everything in my power to keep him from ending the party so soon.

"Ollie..." he whimpered.

"Yes, Gabriel?"

"I need you."

I didn't need a second request. I was throbbing, dripping with desire for him. I tapped him on the shoulder, indicating he should withdraw. He gave me a look of confusion, so I said, "Don't worry. We're not finished yet. Roll onto your back. It's Deveira's turn."

Gabriel scrambled to do as he was told, and I moved so that my knees were under his hips. Slickening my length with the lubricant, I shifted to line up with him, positioning my cock at his opening. As I did, Deveira straddled Gabriel's abdomen and began to slide herself down toward his waiting member.

"Are you ready?"

He didn't say a word but held still so that I could press forward. The second I'd breached his tight ring, Deveira had impaled herself on him, surrounding him with her wet warmth.

"Oh, fuck, Ollie!" he gasped as I entered him. I knew the intensity of what he was feeling. Having someone fill you while your cock was tightly held within someone else was a pleasure beyond words.

"Your Grace..." Deveira moaned as she began to ride him. "So big..."

She and I developed a synchronized rhythm on Gabriel, whose hands were gripping Deveira by the hips. Caillea wasn't one to be left out, however, and she laid beside my soulmate, kissing him and pulling one of his hands to her breast.

Gabriel moaned into her mouth. I knew this wouldn't last long. The stimulation of both his length and on his prostate would be enough to drive anyone over the edge, and he'd held on far longer than I expected.

"Ollie," he finally whimpered, turning his face away from Caillea to look at me around Deveira, who was riding him in earnest, seeking her own release. "Ollie... I'm close. I'm gonna come..."

"Then do it," I said.

"What about... shouldn't I pull out?" His voice was strained with the effort of holding back his orgasm.

"No need," I reminded him, my own climax rapidly approaching as I matched Deveira's pace.

"Right," he said, nodding. "Then..."

"Yes, Gabriel. Come for us."

"Yes, please, Your Grace," Deveira begged, digging her nails into his chest. "Fill me."

"Oh, fuck...!" he cried out, and I felt him tighten around me, the rapid pulsing as he emptied himself into her. "Ollie, Ollie, Ollie, Olympio..."

"My... Gabriel..." I breathed as my own orgasm ripped through me.

The intensity of the moment was so profound that none of us moved for nearly a full minute. Finally, as I began to soften, I slid out of Gabriel and reached for the damp cloths on the basin, using one to clean him up before handing him the other. He glanced at me in brief confusion, but then Deveira dismounted him, and he understood. He handed it to her, and she wiped away the remnants of his climax.

"Thank you, Your Grace," she said as Caillea pulled her into her arms. "That was... exceptional."

"Truly," Caillea added.

"Really?" Gabriel said, but then he cleared his throat, as if clearing away his insecurity, and continued. "I mean, of course. You're welcome."

We all arranged ourselves on the bed, Gabriel in my arms and the girls in each other's. My soulmate looked up at me through his eyelashes with a sleepy smile. "That was awesome," he mumbled.

"I'm glad you enjoyed yourself," I said.

And I truly meant it.

***

I struggled to my feet, barely conscious after the intensity of the night before. Gabriel was still asleep, along with Deveira and Caillea, who were curled into each other. Gabriel had been firmly wrapped around me when I'd awakened, but I'd managed to pull myself free without rousing him.

Gryfian stood just inside the doors of our chambers, a procedure put in place over a thousand years ago, since I never let anyone besides him and my soulmate see me asleep, not even Vass.

It was a paranoia instilled in me at a young age by my father. My mother had regaled us at bedtime with tales from her homeland—Gabriel's homeland—but my father had always told stories of *his* mother, who had been caught sleeping by someone she thought could be trusted. She only narrowly avoided an assassination when she woke up to a knife at her throat. She'd been gifted with the shadows as well, and they saved her life, but the message had stuck with me. Now, whenever there was anyone besides myself (and, more recently, Gabriel) in my chambers overnight, I would signal Gryfian when everyone else was asleep, and he would come stand guard until I awoke.

"Thank you," I said as he moved from his post to pour me a cup of steaming liramin tea from a pot on the table.

"I had it brought from the kitchens. I thought you might need something to help you recover after... whatever happened in here last night. And no, Your Majesty, that isn't me asking for details."

I snorted into my tea before taking a sip. "It was quite the adventure. For Gabriel, anyway." I couldn't even hide the slight edge of bitterness, despite my attempt to sound amused. I'd been ecstatic that he'd enjoyed my surprise when I went to sleep, but I'd tossed and turned all night, worried that perhaps I'd opened a Pandora's Box, as my mother would have called it, into something I wasn't prepared to face.

Gryfian raised an eyebrow and crossed his arms. "Not for you?"

"Of course," I said. "But not in the same way. It was fun, but... truth be told, it was no more than that, and it paled to what I experience with Gabriel on our own. I wanted this for him, so he could experience things he didn't have a chance to before me, but I only want him."

Gryfian gave me a look of pleased surprise, his eyebrows rising up to his hair. "The devilishly seductive and insatiable King Olympio has *truly* settled down?"

"It would seem that way," I said dryly.

"And yet, you look concerned."

I looked up into the fiery orange eyes of my guard and the only true friend, outside of my family and my soulmate, I'd ever had. "What if... What if now that Gabriel has seen what he was missing by agreeing to be with me, he isn't content like I am? What if he wants more? I would give it to him. Always. Because I want him to be happy and to not feel like he's my property. But it would kill me. Every time someone besides me got to share parts of him I treasure... I can't stand the idea of losing Gabriel, bit by bit."

Gryfian nodded thoughtfully. "I can see why you'd feel that way. You've already lived an exceptionally long life."

"You have, too," I reminded him. He was bound to me, though not in the same way Gabriel was. A thousand years earlier, Gryfian took a blood oath as my personal guard that would allow him to live as long as he remained at his post.

"True," he said. "But in all that time, you've never felt about anyone else the way you feel about His Grace."

"Not even close." I took another sip of tea, letting it burn on the way down.

"And from what I know of the soulmate bond, he feels the same things you do. Correct?"

I finally saw where he was going. "Yes," I said almost petulantly.

"Then maybe you should just tell him why you're feeling what you feel," Gryfian said, his voice as calm and measured as always, though he wore a playfully patronizing grin—the kind only he and my sister could get away with. "Instead of making him wonder why you're anxious."

"I'm not anxious," I said quickly. "I'm... worried." Gryfian stared at me, waiting for me to hear my own words and realize I said exactly what he had. "Yes, yes. I know. You're probably right. If I want him to be forthcoming with me, I should do the same."

"I believe Princess Ariadne offered you similar advice not all that long ago..."

"I really should just start running every single decision I make in a day by the two of you," I teased.

"Surely, it's nothing Your Majesty hasn't already thought of, yourself," he smirked.

"Hilarious," I sighed, taking another sip of my tea. "But ultimately, well meaning. I will speak to Gabriel at the first chance I have."

"Well, now would be a great time to start. He's waking up."

I turned and looked to see Gabriel begin to stir, stretch, then roll over toward the girls. His arms went around one, but then he seemed to realize it wasn't me, and he jumped a little, looking for me. His eyes found mine, and I saw relief there. I looked at Gryfian, who nodded and resumed his post at the door.

"Good morning," I said quietly, not wanting to wake Deveira and Caillea, and poured tea into a second cup for him. "Come here." I held out my hand, waiting for him to cross the room and take it.

Gabriel came to me, falling into my chest and kissing it before breathing me in. My arms went around him without so much as a second thought, my face burying in his hair.

"Did you sleep well?" I asked.

"Mm," he groaned against me.

I smiled, tears pricking the corners of my eyes. He'd woken up just like this—sleepy, affectionate, a little clumsy—his entire life, even as a baby. Except lately, of course, since his parents died, and he awoke each morning in a panic...

"You didn't have the nightmare," I suddenly realized.

"Oh," he replied, a smile slowly spreading across his face. "You're right. I guess I was just so... worn out." From the tips of his smile, a crimson colored his cheeks as he looked up at me through his eyelashes.

The thought that last night had allowed him to not wake up in a panic sent a small jolt of sadness through me. But if this was what he wanted, what he needed, we needed to talk about it.

"Join me on the balcony?" I asked before planting a gentle kiss on his lips.

He gripped my hand like he was scared I was going to slip away and sleepily followed me. "I'm hungry," he said with a tone that almost sounded surprised.

"Good thing there's breakfast out here," I said. It wasn't a special occasion—we always had breakfast delivered to our balcony each day. Of course, we hadn't had much time to enjoy it lately. It felt like the title of King came with a requirement that all meals had to be eaten while running from one meeting to another—usually ones where Typhir's presence did nothing for a mood already soured by hunger.

We sat down beside each other, and I immediately reached for an oulon. But I hadn't even touched it to my lips before my stomach lurched with worry once more.

"What?" Gabriel asked, his brow furrowed.

I opened my mouth to tell him it was nothing, but I thought back to what Gryfian had said. Gabriel could feel what I felt—he just didn't know why. Not telling him would only make him anxious, as well.

"Did... did you enjoy last night?" I asked as casually as I could.

My soulmate grinned a little to himself. "It was fun. Definitely worth sobering up for."

My heart sank a little as I watched him reach across the table and grab a slice of raquin—the way I'd seen him do at least a hundred times.

"Then... is that something you would like... more often? It certainly helped you get some long-needed rest."

He popped the fruit in his mouth whole, looking pensively out over the balcony. My pulse picked up just slightly as he took his time answering. What if he said yes? What if he preferred the company of women? What if he wanted a constant string of concubines and mistresses, even other men to pleasure him, because what we had wasn't enough?

But he didn't. He... shrugged.

"I dunno," he started slowly. "I guess it would be fun to do together every now and then. I mean, it felt great and girls are... really pretty. But I think after having world-melting sex with a man who waited almost twenty years to take care of you for all of eternity, could anything ever really hold a candle to that?"

He reached across my path to grab another couple slices of fruit, and my heart soared. I knew he was being one hundred percent truthful in the casual cadence of his voice, even if I hadn't felt it in every inch of my body, and knowing he felt the same way I did...

"Honestly... I think I really do prefer guys. Guess I am gay, after all." He giggled to himself, stuffing his mouth with fruit, his messy chestnut hair falling into his eyes.

I didn't care that his mouth was full of food. I leaned in and pressed my lips to his. His lips—*my* lips. Every part of him was mine as much as every part of me was his. I could continue with our foreseeable future with my guilt quelled, never again considering that I had stolen some part of self-discovery from him.

"Ollie," he laughed around his food, my hands unrelenting. "Ol!"

I heard Gryfian clear his throat, and I turned to see the two women waking. The moment had passed. I could dismiss them—politely, of course—but we only had a few hours before we would be departing on our journey.

"Until later," I said, giving him our special kiss.

"Until later."

Chapter Seventeen
Gabriel

Traveling had always made me a little anxious. I think I liked the stability of knowing my surroundings too much. When we'd go to California for a premiere, I'd grind my teeth from the moment we got into the chauffeured car in Manhattan until the moment we were in our house in Malibu.

Now, I was pacing the length of the floor in the entryway as servants loaded up a carriage that was meant to carry me, Ollie, Gryfian, Lex, and Tomos.

It was a giant work of art really, something that wouldn't have looked out of place at the Metropolitan. Big enough to carry seven or eight people and all white with ornate gold and black velvet interior. There were obvious influences from when Parthenea came to Sefaera, since most of the structure would have been perfectly at home in Ancient Greece. But there were little touches that marked it as truly Sefaeran and of the royal family. Wisps of artificial smoke unfurled from the corners, creating an illusion that it was made of solidified shadows itself, kind of like Ollie.

In front of the carriage were not lymeres like I expected. Instead, there were creatures that looked like stallions, except they were pure glimmering gold with black manes made of the same shadows that my soulmate could turn into. Finally, there was the carriage driver, who looked like my attendant Tomos, if Tomos suddenly grew two feet taller and put on about forty pounds of muscle. Red skin, horns, a forked tail, and sleek black hair. The first time I was told Ollie was a demon, it was hard to believe since he looked so... normal—which made sense since his mother was a human like me. But this guy looked like your stereotypical devil brought to life. There was no doubt the driver was all demon.

"Are you ready?"

I startled as a voice came from behind me, and I turned to see Ollie about to put a hand on my shoulder. "Shit," I chuckled, clutching my chest. "Yeah." I turned back to the carriage. "That thing is so fucking cool."

Olympio laughed and kissed my cheek. "Glad you like it. We have a few that are less ostentatious, but since we're on official business of the throne, it helps to keep up appearances. Besides, I couldn't miss the chance to show off for you."

I was about to ask him if we were going to be able to hook up in it, when two men in identical guard uniforms approached, and it didn't take me too long to realize...

"Lex?" I laughed, coughing as I tried to take in the sight before me.

Lexios was standing next to Gryfian in a nearly identical set of leather and gold armor, only where Gryf had an obsidian pin that indicated he was the personal guard of the King, Lexios was wearing a gold one.

"What is this?" I asked, looking at Ollie.

He looked at me with a question in his eyes. "I thought you'd indicated you wanted Lord Lexios to come along as your personal guard. Did I misunderstand?"

"No," I said, and I could feel my cheeks strain as I tried to resist the smile that was attempting to burst through me. "That was right."

"Good," he said, now speaking to Lex as much as to me. "I would have hated to give him any kind of power or acclaim I wasn't supposed to." I glanced at his face, thinking he was being shitty about my friend again, but his eyes were soft, and he held out a hand to Lexios. "Welcome aboard."

Lex accepted the handshake, bowing his head slightly. "Good to have your back again, old friend. Thank you for trusting me with something so important to you."

"To be honest," Ollie said seriously, "I don't. Not yet. But..." His hand gripped my side possessively. "I trust Gabriel. And if he thinks you're deserving of the position, I'm willing to entertain it."

I beamed. It wasn't the three amigos—yet. But it was a start. And I couldn't help feeling a little proud at being the catalyst for that.

"Come on," Olympio said, pulling his wary eyes from Lexios as he watched Tomos in deep discussion with the coachman. "Time to load up."

"Beg your pardon, *Your Grace*," a voice said from behind us, and we turned to find Ari, Liro, Parthenea, and, (regrettably) Typhir behind us. "Were you really going to leave without saying goodbye?"

"Of course not," Ollie said, turning to them. He smiled at Ari, who was finally looking almost like herself again. "But I thought you might have already left on your own journey."

"Not yet," Ari said, leaning against Liro. "Had to make sure you didn't get into trouble before you departed. Talaea knows you can't take care of yourself."

I couldn't help but laugh, and I reached out to Ari, pulling her against my chest and hugging her tight. "I'm sorry. I forgot I was supposed to be the thoughtful one in the relationship. I'm gonna miss you."

For once, she didn't pull away. Instead, she held me tightly and sighed. "Yeah... you too." If I didn't know better, I'd say she might have been tearing up.

"See you in a few weeks," Ollie said, also embracing his sister, who patted his back in an indulgent kind of way.

We were interrupted by a loud *thunk,* and we all turned to find Tomos dragging my trunk, which was at least twice his size.

"Tomos," I laughed, pushing my hair out of my eyes and jogging over to where he was clearly struggling. "Let me."

"Oh, thank you, Your Grace, but I can manage. It's my job, after all..."

"Nonsense—" I said, grabbing the trunk and lifting it. Tomos, however, was reluctant to let go, and he ended up dangling off the trunk like some sort of luggage tag. "*Tomos.*" I was nearly wheezing, I was laughing so hard, and I was forced to set the trunk down once more, lest I accidentally drop it.

This was already shaping up to be a really fun time. Something like a bunch of seniors going on a post-graduation road trip. Something I'd been excluded from in high school, having never once managed to make friends who weren't in it to be near my parents.

"Your job is to attend to Gabriel's needs," Olympio said with a smile at Tomos, patting him on the shoulder and taking the handle of the trunk from his hands. "This is not something he needs assistance with, and therefore, it is not part of your job. Allow us."

Ollie lifted the trunk with ease, and I nearly drooled watching his muscles flex. "You know," I said, stepping closer and leaning in to whisper. "You're making quite the spectacle."

He turned to me with a playful grin, the kind that was rare for him. "But how could I miss the chance to impress my soulmate and remind him why he's attracted to me?" he breathed back.

"Believe me," I replied with a voice that emphasized an uncomfortable nature and a subtle adjustment of my chiton below my belt. "I never need a reminder."

"Olympio," a soft voice called from behind us. We turned to see Parthenea, arms gracefully crossed on her chest, smiling at us wistfully. Her eyes went straight to her son, though, and her arms opened, clearly hoping he'd fill the void there.

He hoisted the trunk into a storage area on the back of the carriage and walked swiftly to his mother, who he hugged tightly. "We'll be back in just a few weeks. Hopefully with good news about the portals."

Meanwhile, Typhir had pulled Lexios aside, and they were having a tense, hushed conversation. I watched as Typhir indicated to the pin from his commendation and to the one his son now wore, saying something I couldn't hear with a harsh demeanor.

"Listen to me, *Your Majesty*," Parthenea said gently, drawing our attention back to her. "These people are going to treat you a certain way, and you're going to have to live up to their expectations. But don't let that change you. Don't ever forget that people respond to genuine, kind, humble people." I watched as she looked over my soulmate's shoulder straight to me, and Ollie followed her gaze. "You are so much more than their king. Show them that."

Ollie nodded and kissed her on the cheek.

"Lord Typhir," my soulmate said, turning his attention to the father and son, who both looked over at us in surprise, as if they hadn't realized they were on display.

Typhir straightened up, tugging at his clothes. "Yes, Your Majesty?" he drawled.

"This *should* go without saying," Ollie said, "but after your decision to speak ill of me at your party last night, I feel that I would be remiss to not remind you of something. Just because I am absent from the palace does *not* mean you are entitled to treat it as your own personal kingdom. You will follow the directives given to you by myself and by His Grace."

I saw a vein in Typhir's forehead pop as he dipped into a low bow. "Of course, Your Majesty. I live to serve."

"Hey."

"Oh, fuck!" I jumped, not having realized Lexios had come up next to me and put a hand on my shoulder.

"Sorry. Why don't we leave them to it?" he continued. "Have you seen the inside of the carriage?"

I shook my head, then held up a hand to indicate he should give me a moment. I rushed to Parthenea, myself, and pulled her into an enormous hug. It was impossible to explain, but Gaiadans hugged differently than Sefaerans did. When someone from our home world hugged you, it was as much an energy transference as if the bond existed in each of us, and sometimes, every once in a while, I forgot how good it felt to be on the receiving end of one of those hugs. "I'll miss you," I told her.

"And I you, Gabriel." She cupped my face and pulled me downward so she could kiss my forehead. "Take care of him. He doesn't mean to be... how he is."

The corners of my mouth twitched as I tried to resist a smile. I knew exactly what she meant. "I will. Always."

"Good boy," she said, patting me softly on the face. "Have a good trip."

With one last look, I ran happily to Lexios's side, peeking into the carriage to find a glamorous, regal looking set up, complete with a bar, like a limo. "Shit," I breathed.

"Right?" he laughed. "I suspect we will all be very drunk by the time we arrive."

I climbed inside, and he followed, sitting across from me and opening each of the shades.

"Your Grace!" Tomos's breathless voice squeaked from behind me. "Can I fetch you a drink? Or something to eat?"

"That's alright, Tomos," I said, patting the seat beside me. "Have a rest. You've been working so hard."

Tomos looked at me like I was crazy. "Oh, no, no, I couldn't. But perhaps, instead, I will stand here and read to you from one of the Justice manuals we were going through when you and His Majesty left for your... Your Grace!" He'd produced a small book from his own pack, and just as quickly, I'd snatched it away.

"It's a vacation, Tomos. Relax."

The carriage shifted a bit, and I turned to see Ollie climbing in, looking back and forth between me and Lexios. Right behind him was Gryfian, who remained near the door like a sentinel, giving my new personal guard, who wasn't paying attention, a meaningful look.

"Settling in?" Ollie asked as he sat beside me, kissing my cheek.

"This is *wild*," I said, burying my face into his neck. "Next thing you know, this place is gonna turn into a Bang Bros video."

"I'm going to assume that's something filthy, and I fully expect you to give me a full description when we are in private," he said quietly, nipping at my ear.

The temptation to mount him right here was starting to get ridiculous. "Ollie..." I whined.

"Are they always like this?" Lexios asked loudly, presumably towards Gryfian.

Gryfian, however, remained silent, like he was trying to overcompensate in front of him.

"Come on, Gryf. Relax. No one is gonna try and kill us in the carriage!"

"And I will be glad if you are right, Your Grace," he said. "But I will remain at my post all the same."

I slumped against Olympio, chuckling into his shoulder.

The first leg of the journey was so calm and quiet I actually fell asleep on Ollie and woke up with my head in his lap, him stroking my hair as he whispered quietly to Gryfian about something one of the Council members said. He hadn't noticed I was awake yet.

"Mirva said, and I have to agree, that, if there is a portal breach and not just a general weakening in the seals on the old portals, it's likely someone close to the throne that's behind it."

"I hate to say it," Lexios said, "but I wouldn't rule out my father."

It was then that Ollie looked directly at me, seemingly noticing my stirring in himself through our connection.

"Did you rest well?" he asked, brushing some of my hair off my forehead.

"Mm," I nodded, rubbing my eyes to clear them of sleep.

"Rise and shine, handsome," Lexios laughed. "Were you exhausted from walking to the carriage?"

I sat up with a start like one of those old-fashioned vampire films where they rise straight up out the coffin. "Maybe," I challenged playfully. "Maybe it was the steaming hot ass pounding I got this morning."

At this, Gryfian choked on the water he was drinking.

"Gabriel," Ollie said, though the scolding tone was diminished slightly by the laughter he tried to hide. Next to him, Tomos was engrossed deeply in the book he'd tried to read to me earlier. Or at least, he was pretending to be.

"Your Grace," Lexios started. "What you and His Majesty do or don't do is none of my business. Besides, if that was the case, the entire palace would have known."

"Or perhaps your chambers are just too far away to enjoy the ambiance Gabriel provides when he's being pleasured," Ollie said.

"I assure you," Gryf finally spoke up. "There is no location in the palace far enough."

I roared with laughter at this, grabbing for a bottle of some clear, shimmering liquor and practically ripping the top off. "Gryfian has jokes!"

"Sometimes," he said, his smooth, even tone almost making everything funnier.

"Allow me," Ollie said, gently taking the bottle from my hand as I tried to lift it to my lips. He grabbed a glass and a bottle of some kind of juice.

"Damn, Ol," I said, leaning into my human inflection. "Not very frat bro of you. The boys would be devastated. I mean, what would Alc—"

My words were cut off as Ollie forced my mouth closed using the bond. "Think of it as jungle juice," he said, handing me the cocktail, which smelled like the royal orchards in a glass.

I indicated to my mouth which may as well have been sealed with super glue, forcing him to let go of his control. "I don't know why you're so fucking salty about Alex Kessinger," I said, taking a sip before groaning gratuitously.

"Who's Alex Kessinger?" Lexios asked, looking at Ollie, whose face was going a bit red.

"An absolute miscreant and anal abscess of a person who nearly killed my soulmate in a moment of sheer stupidity. His jaw was even harder than yours was," he said, though the last part was said more playfully.

"I like to think I've developed some cranial padding against your blows after all these years, so I'd like to see some proof of that." Lexios gave him a tentative smile, then reached for a bottle of his own.

Gryfian, however, cleared his throat, eyeing my friend's drink choice meaningfully.

"My apologies," my new guard said, looking at Ollie rather than Gryf. "Should I not?"

"It would certainly be more... comforting... if our guards were at their most alert, just in case of any trouble." He frowned uncomfortably, then said, "I had planned on remaining sober as well, if it makes it any easier." It was an obvious lie, but the fact that he was doing it for Lexios made me happy.

"Well, I—" I said, emptying my glass, "—am not. Gimme." I gestured like I was grabbing for the bottle and noticed Olympio looking at me weird. "What?"

"You might want to consider pacing yourself," he said, though he didn't sound mad—just concerned. "The royal family hasn't paid a visit to Hyxelon in over a thousand years. We want to make a good impression and remind them why they continue their allegiance to the crown."

It shook me a little, like I was being scolded again. "Oh, uh... yeah. No worries." I set my glass down and turned toward the window, away from Ollie, curling into myself. Boys' trip, get fucked, I guess.

Shame washed over me as my brain spiraled over how immature I must appear to the rest of them, how unrefined. Gradually, I felt my breaths coming quicker, though I parted my lips just so in order to avoid making any noise. I knew Ollie would feel it, but I was slowly slipping into my own little world of panic and self-loathing.

And, as I predicted, he was there, wrapping his arms around me and whispering so quietly that only I could hear him.

"You did nothing wrong, Gabriel. I can't take this from you because you need to learn how to feel, and—"

"Can you please get off me," I hissed back. "I'm just gonna nap until we're there."

His hands withdrew like they were burned, and I felt his immediate sadness as he said, "As you wish."

I didn't want to hurt him. I loved him. But there was always going to be that little part of me that felt like the stupid frat boy who'd fallen into this role by mistake. Someone who would never quite fit in and never quite be refined enough for my peers.

And that, alone, continued to isolate me, even if I stood in a room full of people.

Chapter Eighteen
Olympio

The difference in the air when the carriage doors opened was like a blow to the face. Hyxelon was a dry, arid desert, and even the breeze was like standing in front of a bonfire.

I'd visited here once, when I was barely two hundred, with my parents. The Matriarch of the region at the time, the great-great-grandmother of the current Matriarch, had just taken command, and my father wanted to ensure that sentiment toward the crown remained intact with the new leadership. The heat had caught me just as off-guard then as it did now, having spent the entire journey here in a magically maintained climate within the carriage.

Gryfian stepped out first, taking his post beside the door at attention. Lexios watched, then realized he was supposed to do the same and scrambled out to mimic Gryfian's stance, though it was fairly obvious he was new to this. Tomos exited next, announcing us. As his high-pitched squeak called out our names, I leaned into Gabriel.

"Are you ready for this?" I asked, worried that whatever had gotten in his head would burden him for the rest of the day or even longer.

"I can handle myself," he grumbled, though the conviction was lacking. I watched as he gathered the few things he'd managed to busy himself with: a book, cleaning his knives, and a folded up piece of paper that now looked like an omnix—a large, graceful bird that frequented the rivers around the palace back home. "Don't worry, *Your Majesty*, neither myself nor my personal guard will make you look bad."

I reached for his wrist, gripping it gently. "I'm not worried about that," I told him, shaking my head gently. "I'm worried about *you*."

"Why?" he asked, pushing past me tersely and stepping past our guards, out into the sunlight. It was clear that he was instantly blinded, because if he'd seen the crowd that awaited us, he might not have loudly announced, "Fuck, I wish I had some Ray Bans."

I rushed out behind him, taking my spot at his side and putting my hand around his waist, hopefully to silence any further outbursts. I didn't want to have to manipulate the bond, but he needed to understand the gravity of this visit and what it could mean for the whole kingdom.

We were at the top of a massive platform, looking down into what appeared to be a grand stone amphitheater. But instead of the center being the focal point, it seemed the entire population of Hyxelon had gathered below to see us arrive.

"Welcome," the Matriarch said, stepping toward us in a flowing gown of red and blue. While the capitol of Sefaera, which bore the same name as the whole kingdom, had adjusted its fashion when my mother had arrived from Gaiada to take on aspects of her culture, Hyxelon had retained its native essence. The people were dressed in vibrant, rich shades of shimmering material that hung about them loosely, likely to protect from the nearly unbearable heat.

The Matriarch, herself, bore the features of most of the people here. Like Deveira, she had slate-colored skin and white freckles, though while Deveira had silvery white hair, the woman before me had hair the color of the desert sand—a medium, orange-toned tan.

Gabriel turned and looked at me, eyes wide, like he was all but frozen with fear. "Ollie?" he hissed, pleadingly.

"It's fine," I whispered before turning to the Matriarch. "Thank you. It is a pleasure to meet you, Vimaritama."

"Apologies, Your Majesty," she said with a bow. "Vimaritama was my mother. She passed only a year ago, and I have been serving as Matriarch ever since. My name is Matriarch Vijayantimala, but you may address me as my people do and call me Mal."

"Your people call you by a nickname?" Gabriel asked, looking at me with excited curiosity.

I knew what he was likely thinking. He had always asked to be called by "Gabe," but was far more often referred to as "Your Grace," or, in my case, "Gabriel."

"We see ourselves as one family here," she said, smiling graciously at him. "My people are truly my people, and I am theirs. But come. The Hyxelonian sun is unforgiving to foreigners. We will get you inside where it is cooler."

With a sweep of vibrant fabric, she turned and began to walk in the direction of what I remembered as the home of the Matriarch. It was significantly smaller than the palace, since they were running only a small region of Sefaera rather than the entire kingdom.

Tomos rushed after her, and I put a hand on Gabriel's back to guide him along after, his kormarrin flittering around our heads. Gryfian and Lexios brought up the rear, with a handful of other attendants and servants trailing behind.

I looked at my soulmate, who still hadn't recovered from whatever had struck him in the carriage. His eyes were empty and wouldn't meet mine, and I leaned closer to him.

"I don't know what's wrong," I said quietly to him, "and I know it's infuriating to have to keep up appearances when you're falling apart inside. No one knows that better than me. But I'm never going to let you face these things alone."

He blinked slowly, which was as good as I supposed I could expect when he was this lost in himself. My thoughts and worries plagued me the entire walk inside, where we were led to the chambers we would be occupying while here. It was cooler within the halls, though not by much. I supposed the people who lived here were so used to the heat that what was sweltering to those of us from more temperate regions was comfortable to them.

"I will leave you to get ready," Mal said with a smile. "The Grand Feast begins in an hour, Your Majesty, Your Grace. Thank you again, for gifting us with your presence."

Before I could say anything more, she turned and was gone. The attendants brought in our trunks, arranging our clothes in the wardrobe for us before shuffling back out, the door shutting between us and our guards.

Gabriel walked mechanically over to the bed and sat down, hugging himself around the middle and leaning forward.

I moved over to his side and sat beside him, but didn't put my arm around him again. Instead, I followed his gaze, which was staring unseeingly out the window to the massive dunes. A few small cyclones of sand moved between them, appearing and vanishing as easily as I could in my shadow form.

"Looks like Arizona..." he said to no one.

"What's wrong, Gabriel?" I finally asked. "I don't know how to fix it if you don't—"

"You can't fix it," he said. "Ollie... you've been immortal your whole life, which has been over a hundred times as long as mine. I was literally a kid until three years ago, and honestly, I still don't feel like a grown up most of the time. But I'm expected to run a whole fucking world with you, and sitting in a group of people who must see me as nothing more than young and stupid when I say or do the wrong thing just makes me *feel* young and stupid. Like you'd be better off finding someone older, who knows your world better, to rule it with."

I couldn't deny most what he was saying. I had fifteen hundred years to prepare for my role as king, and even with the full millennia of life I'd experienced prior to that, I still felt in over my head at times. Gabriel only had twenty one years alive to my two and a half thousand. The fact that he was able to do half of the things he could, and to do them with the grace his title would suggest, was nothing short of miraculous.

But it didn't stop me from worrying when he began to slip back into self-destructive habits like I saw him use when he felt alone during his adolescence and, worse, after his parents died. He'd always plied himself with liquor when he was drowning, and it seemed like he'd taken to those same habits since our return to Sefaera, something I'd hoped would pass, but only seemed to be increasing with each passing day.

"I can see why you'd feel that way," I said, nodding my head slowly. "I can't even imagine having had the kind of responsibility you do when I was your age. Sometimes it's easy to forget how large that gap is, because you are my perfect match in so many ways. Sometimes, your youthful vision is what helps me to see when I'm wrong, or when I've become jaded. Because you *don't* have the thousands of years of being beaten into what everyone else wanted you to be. You just get to be you, and Gabriel..." I finally reached out to touch him, placing a hand under his chin and tilting his face to look at me. He had tears in his eyes, and I wiped them away. "You are going to be the reason I am a good king. Because you see things in a way I lost the ability to long ago."

He sniffled slightly and gave me a small smile, leaning against me at last. "To be fair, if I had to deal with Typhir for thousands of years, I'd probably have a hard time seeing the bright side, too."

Finally, I put my arms around him, just holding him as he rested his head on my shoulder.

"So... What are the odds I can go by Gabe to the whole kingdom like Mal and her people?" he asked, the sly smile he wore telling me he already knew the answer, but he was going to try anyway.

"I'll run it by the king," I said before pausing slightly. "He says he'll think about it."

Gabriel gave me a playful shove, but I caught his hand and pulled him back to me for a kiss, one that quickly had me stirring beneath my chiton.

"Ollie!" he laughed, pulling back. "You can't do that! We have that big feast in like half an hour, and I'm *starving* after that long ride here."

I growled lightly, wishing I could come up with some kind of excuse to be late, but this was the first royal visit to Hyxelon in thousands of years. I highly doubted it would look good if the king was too busy fucking his soulmate to attend the feast in their honor.

"Fine," I said, kissing him one more time before standing. I walked over to the wardrobe and opened it.

"Are we gonna have to wear all our normal shit?" Gabriel asked, coming up behind me, and I grimaced at the thought.

"It's a bit hotter here than it is back home," I said, reaching for a particular garment. I held it up for Gabriel to see, and he chuckled.

"Trying to seduce the Matriarch?" he asked, touching the single pauldron, decorated with leather cut into the shape of feathers.

My choice of clothing was nearly identical to the same outfit I had rejected only a few weeks earlier in favor of something more regal. But in this climate, and considering we were going to a celebration, it seemed like an appropriate choice, with the bare chest and shorter bottom.

"Hardly," I said, setting it to the side and reaching back into the wardrobe. "In fact, I think you will be the one I need to worry about, once everyone sees you in it."

I pulled out the same garment for Gabriel, but while mine was black, his was white.

"Are you serious?" His mouth hung open as he stared at it.

"Only if you want me to be," I said, holding it out to him. "Truthfully, the only reason I haven't offered it to you before now is that I would be jealous of everyone throwing themselves at you. But I think you'd be more comfortable in lighter apparel tonight."

"More comfortable?" He gave one of his high-pitched, nervous giggles. "Ol, how can I be comfortable with my junk on display?"

I laughed with him and kissed his cheek. "Your 'junk,' substantial as it may be, will be well-covered, I assure you. Besides, with all of the work you've been putting in with your physical training, it would be a crime to deprive the farthest reaches of the kingdom of seeing your glorious body."

"Stop," he said in a long, drawn out whine, blushing. Nevertheless, he took the clothes. "How, uh... how do I put this on?"

I helped him dress, then stepped back to look at him. His build was a bit slighter than mine, though his muscles were no less defined. He looked strong in a subtle way, and the slight sheen of sweat on his chest tested my mettle once more as I debated flipping up the skirt and taking him fully into my mouth right then and there.

Gabriel played around, swishing his cape back and forth, as I changed my own outfit into the one that matched his. I had just barely buckled my shoes in place when a knock came at the door, followed by Tomos poking his head in, eyes closed.

"Apologies, Your Majesty, Gabe—er, Your Grace," he said.

"Gabe is still fine when the king is around, Tomos," my soulmate said with an indulgent smile. "And no one's naked. You can open your eyes."

Tomos did so and said, "The Matriarch has arrived to escort you to the feast."

"Thank you, Tomos," I said with a nod. "We'll be right out."

Tomos slipped out as quickly as he'd entered, and I turned to Gabriel.

"Ready?" I asked.

He smiled and kissed me. "Yeah. Let's go."

We met Mal in the hall, and she bowed graciously to us. "Your Majesty, Your Grace, you look wonderful." We thanked her, and she led us outside to a huge courtyard filled with grass, trees, and a small pond of water that was simultaneously dark blue *and* crystal clear, showing off every single creature beneath the surface.

"Wow..." Gabriel said, peering down into the pond. "What are those?" He pointed to a few of the larger ones, which looked quite like birds from Gaiada, but were water-dwellers rather than ones who could fly.

I was unfamiliar with them, which was more than a bit embarrassing, since I was Master of the Hunt for over a thousand years. But they weren't native to my part of Sefaera, so I hadn't had cause to learn about them.

Thankfully, Mal heard him and said, "Kiprums. Sweet little things. They'll probably let you pet them."

"Really?" Gabriel said, kneeling down at the water's edge and reaching his hand out. One of the kiprums swam over and allowed the top of its head to poke through the surface. My soulmate ran a couple of fingers tentatively over it, then smiled up at me. "That's so weird. It looks like feathers, but it feels sandy and smooth, like a shark."

I knelt beside him, watching as about half a dozen of the animals rushed over to allow Gabriel to pet them. He was delighted, and once he had his fill, he stood up and turned. "Whoa..."

I looked to where he was gazing and saw that hundreds of people had gathered while we were distracted and were watching us, whispering amongst themselves.

"Welcome," Mal said, holding up her arms. "Please join me in welcoming His Majesty, King Olympio, and His Grace, Justice Gabriel, to Hyxelon. It has been many centuries since we've had a visit from the capitol, and we are grateful to them for being here."

Unlike the feasts back at the palace, which were formal affairs, with only members of court attending, it seemed as though a feast in Hyxelon was a community event, with what appeared to be their entire population gathering. There was no grand table, where the guests of honor were seated at the head. Instead, it was far more casual, with one massive table that held at least a hundred different kinds of food, most of which I was as unfamiliar with as Gabriel had to have been.

Mal guided us over, handing us each a large tray.

"Please enjoy. Our Grand Feasts reflect the familial essence of our region, with every household contributing something to the table, so that there is always enough to go around. As our guests of honor, you are welcome to go first."

"Want to take different things and share?" I asked Gabriel.

"Hell, yeah," he said enthusiastically, taking a fruit that had little nodes on the skin, like it once had little needles that had been pulled off.

We made our way along the display, sampling the various dishes and building our own selections based on what we liked best, enjoying the new flavors. Even the bread here was different—flat but dense, but with a sweet, nutty flavor.

When we reached the end, I turned to see everyone else in attendance lining up for their turn, moving along the table just as we had.

"This way, Your Majesty, Your Grace," Mal said, guiding us to a small, round table without chairs, clearly intended to place your plate on and eat while standing. "Shall I fetch you a drink?"

"Definitely," Gabriel said quickly before looking at me. "Or, uh... maybe not?"

I leaned into his ear. "It's a party. Just don't get so drunk I can't dance with you once we've made our way through our food."

Music played from a small group of musicians in a tune that must have been traditionally Hyxelonian, since I didn't recognize it, but it was lively and upbeat.

Gabriel smiled at me and kissed my jaw. "Thanks, Ollie." He turned back to Mal. "Yeah, drinks would be great."

She nodded and disappeared into the crowd, returning only moments later with three large goblets. I expected the standard Sefaeran blue wine, but when I looked into the cup, it was a bright pink liquid—the same color as the strongest liquor we had at the palace, the kind we only served at special occasions, since it was from a rare fruit.

"Orenum cocktails," she said, naming the plant that the rare liquor was made from. "The plant is native to here."

She held up her glass, and the entire crowd lifted glasses of their own, letting loose a deafening cheer.

It was strange. I'd never even considered coming here, but the sentiment was so welcoming and congenial, that I wondered what else I was missing within my own kingdom. Suddenly, I was excited about this journey, about not only sharing my world with my soulmate, but about experiencing much of it as though for the first time, myself.

The rest of the feast passed in a haze of orenum cocktails and course after course of incredible food, the exposed parts of Gabriel's body glistening with sweat against mine as we danced beneath the moons, in the desert heat.

By the time we made it back to our room, we were both drenched and tipsy, tumbling onto the bed, tasting the saltiness of each other's skin as our lips trailed anywhere they could with our clothes still on.

"Wait, wait..." Gabriel gasped, pulling away.

"What's wrong?" I asked, my words slurring slightly between the effects of the liquor and the exhaustion of the long day.

"If I'm going to be screaming your name all night, I need to properly lubricate my vocal cords. Those drinks dried me out bad. Do you need some water, too?"

Fuck, I was weak to that devilish look in his eyes, when he knew he'd already well and thoroughly seduced me but wasn't satisfied until I was feral for him.

"Yes, please," I said. "I need to make sure I don't dehydrate *making* you scream my name."

He hopped out of the bed and looked around the room.

"Oh... Hang on. They don't have a pitcher in here," he said. "I'll run and get one."

Before I could remind him that we had guards and attendants who could take care of that for us, he was out the door.

I lay in the silence for a moment, then decided I'd surprise him when he got back. I stood and took off every single article of clothing I had on, then laid on top of the sheets, even the thought of any kind of covering in this heat making me sweat more. My cock was halfway to hard, and I reached down to stroke it, readying myself for when Gabriel would return. It was dark and quiet, and I closed my eyes while I waited, just needing to rest them for a moment.

"Gabriel..." I yawned as my hand moved slowly. "*My...* Gabriel..."

Chapter Nineteen
Gabriel

I turned over in bed and immediately felt Ollie's body there, warm, comforting... mine. I didn't even know where I was but I knew this body, and I happily snaked my arms around him, pulling him tighter against me.

"Good morning," he yawned, turning over. "It's nice to wake up next to you again. Well, I guess, wake up to you awake next to me."

I buried my face in his chest and allowed my weight to sink into him, the heat of the place having left his chest covered in a light dewiness. He smelled sweaty but in a delicious way. Like the way he smelled after we—

"I see you are thoroughly roused," he said playfully, lifting the thin blanket and looking below it.

"Can you blame me?" I asked him, still only half conscious. "We were dancing all night, and then you passed out and left me with the blue balls of the century."

"You could have woken me or taken care of it... if you needed to. I don't ever want you to think I have limitations on you when it comes to your own comfort."

"I know," I sighed into him. "But it's not half as fun that way."

Olympio shifted once more, and I found myself pinned, face into the pillows, my soulmate's full body weight atop me. "Is this more fun?" Ollie asked, his length pressing into my ass.

"Possibly," I replied as he began to kiss my neck. "If you want me to make an enormous mess all over the bedding."

Ollie growled and bit down on my shoulder. "I'd certainly be happy to help clean it up... with my tongue..." He began to thrust against me violently, making me laugh as the bed bounced. "What's that, Your Grace? You find this to be *amusing*?" He bit again, this time harder.

"Ow," I whined, still fighting giggles. "Ollie! Fuck me, already."

"As my soulmate commands," he said, pushing aside the thin sheets that he could possibly get tangled in, and pressing his thumb deep against my hole. "I could never bear it being said I left him wanting..."

But exactly as I heard him spit into his hand and press the tip of his cock against my opening...

"Your Grace."

Lexios's voice came from behind us, and we both froze.

"You had better have something terribly important to say, *son of Typhir*," Ollie grumbled. This time, truly frustrated, and I could only assume painfully aware of how in plain view his bare ass was.

"The Matriarch was just looking for His Grace. She has a gift for him."

"Fuck," I heard Ollie say, so quiet it was barely distinguishable from his breathing. Then he rolled off me, not covering himself, as he picked up the sheet and covered me instead. "Will that be all, Lexios?"

Without blood—so to speak—I wasn't sure if Olympio had a blood pressure. But if he did, I could practically feel an aneurysm coming.

"My apologies, Your Majesty. It was only that Gryfian had implied we were allowed to interrupt any and all activities, even those of a carnal nature, if it was something important enough."

Neither my friend or my soulmate moved a muscle, each staring the other down.

"I think that's your cue to fuck off, Lex," I said sheepishly. "Thanks for letting me know."

Lexios bowed and retreated, closing the doors behind him.

"Moons and fucking rivers," Ollie said, collapsing onto the bed once more. "Do you have any idea the struggle I just went through trying to figure out if it was worse to keep myself hard in front of him or let myself go soft?"

I had reached over to the side table for a drink of some fruit juice they'd left us for when we woke up, and with that revelation, I sprayed it out my nose all over the bed.

Ollie said nothing, just rolled over and buried his face in the pillow. "I can only hope that he didn't notice me shrivel up like it was my sister that just walked in. The last thing I need are jokes about my abilities—or inabilities."

I leaned over, the sticky juices drying quickly on me. "Poor little king," I said, rubbing his hair. "I'm sure next time you see him, you'll be hard as a rock."

Ollie scrunched up his face, and grabbed my jaw, pulling me down under him and kissing me on the cheek. "You're absolutely evil for that comment, and I assure you that you shall see punishment for it... later."

"Don't threaten me with a good time."

We both agreed that the moment had passed and went about preparing for the day, bathing—thank god—and dressing in the clothing they had left out for us. My understanding was that we were going to be traveling to the portal, accompanied by some of Hyxelon's best guards.

Once we were fed and clothed, we were escorted to the Hyxelonian version of what looked like the Council chambers, where we entered, bowed, then approached Mal who was dressed just as colorfully as the day before.

"Good day to you both. I am thrilled to be able to help you with the portal you seek. I have had my stablehands prepare some of their best mounts for you and will send three of my best escorts."

I heard doors open behind us, and in walked the most incredible thing I'd ever seen. Five guards, each riding what looked like a cross between an overgrown ostrich and a peacock, with four more of the birds trailing behind them.

"Holy shit," I said without thinking, utterly stunned into stupidity. "I mean—sorry—they're amazing."

Mal stood from her throne and walked to us. "Aren't they just?" She strode over to them and patted a few of them on the head and beak. "Wonderful creatures and friends, paraqueys. They can outrun any man and be gentle enough to protect a new baby."

"Kinda sounds like a dog," I whispered to Ollie, who nodded slightly, but mostly kept his "royal" smile plastered on his face.

"They're easy enough to ride," the Matriarch continued. "My men will be happy to assist you onto your mount if need be."

"Thank you, Mal," Olympio finally said. "Your generosity is only matched by your grace."

Mal laughed and waved her hand to brush off his flirtations. "Oh, my dear. That only those words were from the lips of a lovely woman rather than yours."

"Well, he does have a sister..."

Olympio gave me a warning side eye, and I laughed at my own joke under my breath.

Mal seemed to have either not heard me or chose to ignore my comment, because she went back to her dais and fetched a box that was as long as she was tall. Then she turned and walked over to me, presenting the box, which I took immediately, bowing to her.

"Thank you," I said, emotion welling inside me. "This is—"

"Well, open it before you thank me," she proclaimed. "Might well be a snake."

Gryfian took a step forward, hand on the handle of his sword.

"It's alright, Gryfan," Olympio said as I knelt down, placing the box on the floor and pulling the top off.

Inside was a beautiful, ornate glaive, carved from something that looked akin to desert ironwood and finished with polished...

"Is that... a diamond?" I choked, staring at a blade made from one of the largest glistening stones I'd ever seen in my life. Which was saying something, considering I'd once attended a party with Drake.

"It's a veristone," she replied. "The hardest stone known to my people."

I lifted it up and allowed the light to catch it, sending a scattering of rainbows everywhere across the room. I could have cried, it was so beautiful. "Thank you." I choked on my words from the weight of the emotion.

"I hope it serves you well. And after you've had some training with it, we'd love to welcome you back to our annual pit fight, where our best warriors compete for the honor of being the next leader of our army."

I looked up, confusion wrinkling my brow. "Only for a year? How do you ever get any order?" I thought to the military back home, who, half the time, weren't even sure who was in charge, let alone being willing to serve under different leaders every year.

"As I said, we're a family. We don't mind each taking a turn being the bearer of such a great responsibility."

I looked down at the beautiful weapon once more and suddenly felt the momentous nature of this gesture. They were including *me* in that family. Not just an outsider of their culture, but an outsider of their entire world.

"Thank you," I said softer this time. "This is... Thank you."

I stood, lifting it with me and held it out before swinging it like I would have done one of my knives or even a sword. Which was all it took for Ollie to come up from behind me and grasp the handle, barely ensuring that I didn't bisect someone.

"What His Grace means to say is he accepts his place in your halls, and it would be an honor to fight alongside your best."

"Yeah," I said grinning sheepishly. "What he said."

We all bowed to each other before Mal said, "Well, you had better be on your way. The earlier the better. In the afternoon, there are terrible dust storms."

And with that, we turned away from the Matriarch and headed for the paraqueys. Of course, Ollie was able to mount his without a second thought—same for Gryf and Lexios. I, however, made it look like the hardest thing in the world to do.

In an absolute comedy of errors, I first gripped the horn, hoisting myself with such vigor that I overshot the saddle, falling to the floor on the other side, just barely missing a puddle of what I could only assume was paraquey urine.

"Are you alright, Gabriel?" Ollie asked, looking down at me with amusement that only I would recognize.

"Uh... Yeah! Too much enthusiasm. You know me."

"Indeed, I do."

So now from the right side of the bird I attempted the same maneuver but with less power which now led me to sliding slowly down the bird as every member of my court and Mal's watched in confusion.

"Would you like some help, Your Grace?" she asked.

"No, no," I insisted. "Learning curve, am I right?"

With that, Ollie dismounted like he'd been riding a paraquey his whole life and grabbed me by the hips, hoisting me up and into the saddle. "I'm sure you'll get it next time, Your *Grace*." he said, emphasizing the word 'grace' like it was a joke.

I narrowed my eyes and stuck out my tongue. "Dick," I hissed.

He smirked and returned to his mount just as gracefully as the first time.

One of Mal's men, who was now at the front of the pack, signaled, and all of the birds turned to face him as the door attendants opened the heavy, desert wood doors and made a path for us to leave.

"Let's just hope you have an easier time staying on," Lexios said, pulling up next to me with ease. "Surely you have experience 'riding.'"

I had to cling to my reins as I choked on my spit, coughing and hacking in a very un*graceful* way. I wasn't sure if Ollie had heard Lex's joke, but I was certain he would feel the happiness ripple through me, breaking the tension I felt from having made Ollie look stupid—again.

"A bit," I said back under my breath. "I'm more proficient in cock than paraquey. Two totally different birds."

"Yes... Birds... Noted," Lexios laughed. "Who would have ever thought that 'stick up his ass, too good for everyone' Olympio would have landed a soulmate that is so damn funny. And so... Well, I just think you're good for him. He's definitely less of a prick when you're around."

I wasn't really sure if that was a compliment to me or a jab at Ollie, but I pretended to be really interested in the stitching on my saddle while I processed.

Thankfully, I didn't have to fake it for long as my soulmate dropped back in the pack to ride next to me, and of course, in turn, so did Gryfian.

"I have to be real with you guys," I said. "I never, in all my life, would have pictured spending a day like this. Snorting coke off a hooker, sure—"

"Gabriel..."

"Okay, okay." My cheeks hurt from smiling, a refreshing feeling after having spent so much time being plagued with a seemingly never-ending post-adjournment depression. "All I'm saying is—I'm happy to be here with you all. This is great, even if I'm definitely gonna have a chafed nutsack by the end of the day from this heat/saddle combo."

Ollie rolled his eyes as if he was giving up on trying to censor me. Then he paused, took a deep breath, and growled, "Race you to the front."

"You don't have to ask me twice," I said, kicking gently into the bird like it was a horse.

In a whirlwind of sand and dust and desert greens, Olympio and I burst forth from the pack, leaving Gryf and Lex to play catch up, racing forward to the front. Of course, Ollie left me behind pretty quickly, but I refused to be beaten so easily.

Leaning forward, I urged my mount onward, trying to aim for not being beaten *too* badly rather than winning. But Ollie didn't stop when he reached the front of the pack, instead breaking from the crowd and gaining a good hundred feet on everyone before halting, smiling like he'd just won the race of his life.

I slowed my paraquey, trotting up to him, adoration and a deep belly desire for him filling me. "So, you're competitive, huh? I never knew that about you."

"It's not often I'm allowed to do something like that. You're not the only one who has restrictions on them based on proper behavior. When I was Master of the Hunt, I could come and go as I pleased, but now... Well, I have other duties. But damn, if that didn't feel good."

"I can think of a few things we could compete over," I said, speaking low enough that only he would hear and getting my bird moving again. "Mainly naked wrestling..."

"I could be persuaded," Olympio said back, and I watched as his eyes scanned my body, a brief flick of his tongue crossing his bottom lip before he bit it. "What does the winner get?"

"Oh..." I crossed an arm down my body, giving my junk a small squeeze. "I'm sure you'll think of something."

"You had better stop teasing me, Your Grace. Do not think that because I choose to behave with decorum that I am above pulling you from that bird and fucking you right here."

"Mm," I cooed. "I love when you talk all royal to me."

As we left the oasis far enough behind that it wasn't even visible anymore, the entire landscape seemed to fade into the same shades of rusty orange and beige. I wasn't kidding when I said it looked like Arizona. I thought back to a trip I took with my parents to Sedona when I was in high school, scouting out locations for filming one of their blockbusters. The huge stone mesas looked a lot like the mountains here, but the main difference was the size. I'd thought we were high up on some of the peaks in Sedona, but the longer we rode through the desert without seeming to come any closer, it was clear that these mountains were easily ten or twenty times the size of the ones back in my home world.

A few hours of riding—and consequently stopping for water—later, one of Mal's escorts called out, "This way."

We turned left around a large rock grouping and a giant ruin came into view, tall, grand, ornate. It looked sort of like something you'd see in a textbook under the "Ancient Greece" section, but the carvings in it seemed to depict Sefaera.

As we got closer, Ollie and Gryfian dismounted, quickly going to the enormous archway and studying it.

I had no idea what we were meant to be looking for, so I stayed back in an attempt to avoid having too many cooks in the kitchen, so to speak.

"I can't even imagine—" Lexios said, riding up next to me. "What our clothing is going to smell like by the time we get back."

"Good thing there's a breeze, then," I laughed. "So you don't stink us all out."

"Mm..." he grinned. "I was certainly thinking of the way *I* smell, and not at all the way *His Grace* does after a long walk from the palace to the falls."

"Rude," I said, reaching out and pushing him with my foot. "I do not smell... well, much."

Lexios burst out laughing, causing Ollie to turn and look back at us with curiosity that bordered on suspicion.

"Perhaps we should join them to put his Majesty at ease. I would hate to charm his soulmate out from under him, despite the fact he never lets you have fun."

"Lex..."

He didn't respond, but rather winked at me, and when we dismounted, he gave me a playful shove. We walked up to my soulmate and his guard, and Ollie immediately pulled me into him, holding me tight, kissing my sweaty hair.

"It's definitely still defunct," he said, sounding frustrated. "Which means nothing other than the fact that this particular portal isn't the problem. However..." Olympio used his finger to point out several large, deep scratches in the stone which looked like they might have been newer—at least newer than the archway. "This is puzzling me."

"It would indicate, of course, that something large and clawed has been nearby recently, but what kind of creature would make such large markings, and more importantly, would be drawn to claw at stone?" Gryfian posed.

I traced them with my fingers, trying to rack my brain for anything from my world that could have done that. "They almost look like lion claws," I said, deep in thought. "Or maybe even teeth."

"Perhaps a chimera," Lexios added. "They would be capable of getting that large, or even—"

Lex was cut short by the sound of a scream from behind us where the escorts were watching over our paraqueys. We all turned on a hairpin and watched in horror as the sand shifted beneath them, and one of the men was sucked into the depths below.

"Don't move!" a female escort called out shrilly before screaming as an enormous head lifted from the depths of the sand, and like the fantasy film this was quickly turning into, a pair of giant, leathery, reptilian wings emerged.

"Is that…?"

Olympio thrust me behind him, his skin rippling, then breaking away like ash from a campfire, revealing the demon within him. I watched as he drew his shadow sickle from his hip, brandishing it at whatever was coming out of the ground. The shadow-Ollie roared, sending chills down my spine as always.

He was truly terrifying like this.

"Gryfian! Lexios!" he shouted in his deep, gravelly voice. "Protect our escorts. I'll protect Gabriel."

Gryf and Lex moved slowly forward to stand between the danger and our escorts as commanded. Their eyes never left the beast, which was slowly emerging even more from the sand, revealing a great horned head covered in spikes, with teeth as long as my forearm. It was the same color as the sand it had been hiding in, and by the time it was fully freed from its desert burrow, all I could see was a reptilian monster the size of a small school bus that looked straight out of a video game.

At last, with a great roar that sent a spray of sand into our faces, the beast thrashed its tail, knocking Gryfian and two of the guards aside before lunging at me and Olympio.

It was probably an idiot move. Not probably—it was an idiot move, but I took off running for my paraquey, trying to get to my new glaive to not only protect myself, but to eagerly put my new weapon to use.

"Gabriel," Olympio howled, rushing at the beast as it turned its attention to me.

"I can do this," I yelled back, flourishing the glaive like a bo staff. "Come at me, you nasty son of a —"

It was only when I felt its teeth clamp down on my arm that I realized I made a huge mistake.

The glaive handle shattered in the beast's mouth, nearly at the same time as it shattered the bones in my arm. I screamed in agony, fear now properly bubbling up inside me. "Olympio!"

I heard his roar again and tried to find him, to see why he hadn't come to me yet. That was when I saw the second monster taking flight, dive bombing my soulmate over and over. He was trapped in battle with it. There was no way he was going to make it to me in time.

This was really it this time. Stupid, stupid Gabe.

I closed my eyes as the beast retracted, likely to take its second—and final—bite of me. But by some miracle, it didn't come.

I opened my eyes, purposely avoiding looking at my mangled arm to find Lexios—son of my and my soulmate's nemesis—with his own sword driven through the creature's neck as it prepared to strike in retaliation.

"Tell my father... I'm sorry."

"*No!*" I screamed, trying and failing to get to my feet as I watched my only friend be swallowed whole by the beast, who tossed him in the air and caught him in his entirety in its mouth. "Ollie!" My voice broke. I needed my soulmate to make this right.

The creature's throat pulsed as it swallowed Lexios, the thrashing of his arms beneath the skin telling me he was still alive, though how long that would remain the case, I had no idea. I tried to move, to do whatever I could to help, to save him, but even just breathing caused my arm to throb and spurt liquid gold in torrents.

"Lex!"

I just barely managed to get to my feet when, suddenly, thick, black blood sprayed everywhere from the creature's belly, and I watched in horror and amazement as Lex cut his way through the monster, pulling its guts out behind him.

"Your Majesty!" Lexios called out to Ollie. "Assistance!"

I turned to find Gryfian and Olympio withdrawing their blades from the second attacker, and they both ran toward where Lexios was still trying to free himself, looking like the victim of an oil spill.

The shadow that was my soulmate moved so quickly, it was almost like he disappeared and reappeared at the side of the sand-dragon, which was drawing its final breaths. The massive hands grabbed Lex and dragged him the rest of the way free before setting him on the sandy ground and turning to cut the beast's throat, ensuring the attack was over.

Gryfian was instantly at my side, standing in front of me like there was still an onslaught of attackers rather than me whimpering on the ground with a shattered arm. "Are you alright, Your Grace?"

Sweat from the pain and heat dripped down my face. "Yeah. Never better. How about you?"

At this, Gryf turned and looked at me, eyebrow raised. "Just another day as the personal guard of His Majesty…"

I was stunned. "Is… is that… a joke? From you?"

He didn't reply, but I could see his expression turn into a look of satisfaction.

"Gabriel!"

I turned to see Olympio halfway through returning to his usual form. By the time he reached my side, he was my Ollie again, his violet eyes filled with worry and determination.

"Gryfian," he said quickly, holding out his hand, which the guard promptly filled with a vial of the yellow potion. "Here." Olympio pulled the stopper and held it to my lips. "Drink."

"Help Lexios," I insisted, pushing it away. "He saved me. He saved me, Ollie." I looked up at him, trying to impart the importance of what I was saying. "He could have let me die so easily."

Ollie's lips formed a thin line as he considered my words, but he quickly turned to Gryfian. "Make sure Lexios is unharmed. Give him the potion as well, if he needs it."

Gryf nodded and strode over to where my friend and guard had collapsed onto the sand, covered in a variety of slimy, pungent fluids.

"Now will you drink?" Olympio asked.

I looked up at him and saw fear in his eyes, though he was doing his best to try and hide it from me inside. I nodded, taking the drink and leaning into him as I consumed it. "That was scary as fuck," I whispered. "That was so, so stupid of me, and now I broke my gift."

I felt guilty but grateful. It was likely that because I'd had my glaive to take the initial bite, that I avoided having it severed completely.

"We'll have Mal fix it," Olympio said. "It's only the handle that broke. I'm sure they can repair it easily. Just try not to fight any more wyverns with it until you've trained with it a bit more."

He kissed my forehead as I felt the potion begin to work. I had expected it to heal the bite marks, but I was taken by surprise and agony when my arm began to shift and reconfigure the bones back into the right places.

"It will be over fast," Olympio said, holding me tightly. "It will be sore for a few days, but it will be healed."

I gritted my teeth and nodded, unsure if the droplets coming off my face were tears, sweat, or both. It took about five minutes, but once it was done, I could move my arm—a little stiffly, but still.

"I thought I had the worst of it getting swallowed," Lexios's voice said from nearby. "Never thought I'd get to see the inside of a wyvern, and I can honestly say I'd rather not repeat the experience."

I looked up at him and reached out my "good" arm to shake his hand. "Thank you," I whimpered, the pain still surging through me in pulses like lightning. "I don't really know the process for those 'commendation' things, but I'm gonna make sure you get a stack of them."

Ollie looked like he'd eaten a mouthful of sour candy. But it only lasted a second before he gave a tight nod to me and said, "Yes. Thank you, Lexios. You saved the most important thing in my life, and I owe you far more than a simple piece of gold can make up for."

Lexios studied Ollie hard, then put his hand out to my soulmate. "Call it pax," he said. "This still doesn't make up for what a little prick I was as a youth, but I hope that it can show you not all of Typhir's kin subscribe to his version of nobility."

My soulmate accepted the shake and said, "I told Gabriel that I hoped to be wrong about you. It seems I got my wish." He looked around at what remained of our party—two escorts and three paraqueys fewer than we started with—and sighed. "But we got what we came for. The portal here is not something to be concerned about. We should move on quickly, before anything else rises from the sand to kill us"

He stood, sliding out from beneath me, and gestured to Gryfian, who marched through the sand like it was cement, and the two went to speak with the remaining escorts.

I turned back to Lex, who crouched down beside me and studied my face.

"What?" I asked.

"You have scars on your face, just there," he touched where his cousin had marred me on each cheek, and his expression fell. "My family really have behaved abhorrently, haven't they?"

"Not all of your family," I replied.

The air stood still between us as I tried to figure out how to move us past this weird moment where I owed him my life, and he was still reeling over Olympio's admission.

A strange lump formed in my throat and I tried to ignore the feeling that was snaking its way through me. Something beyond friendship. Something I wasn't supposed to be able to feel for anyone besides my soulmate.

Did I have a *crush* on Lex?

"Gabriel." Olympio's voice came from behind me, and I whipped my head around faster than lightning to see him staring dead into Lexios's eyes, the warmth that had been there icing over. "It's time. You're going to ride with *me*, since we're short a mount."

Lexios stood and walked away, offering Ollie a small bow of his head as he did. I looked up at my soulmate, the tingly, fizzy feeling of a few moments earlier being replaced by guilt that made my stomach ache. "Of course," I said, smiling, trying to convince him *and* me that things were totally normal here. "That will be nice." I reached out my good arm to get help up, and he hoisted me with ease, forcing us eye to eye.

Then his lips were on mine, his arms wrapping possessively around my waist as he absolutely devoured me, the kiss going on far longer and deeper than I would have expected in front of so many people.

When he let me come up for air, he scooped me into his arms and carried me over to the paraquey. I looked up at the creature, worried about getting onto it with my arm still aching this badly.

"Allow me," Ollie said, seeming to understand my issue. In a swirl of shadows, he shifted halfway to his demon form and used his wings to lift us both onto the saddle with ease. "What's the point of having power like this if I can't use it to care for my soulmate?"

Fuck. Every word he said should have been innocuous, but jealousy was radiating off him like the heat from the sunlight overhead. He and Lexios had just finally gotten to a neutral place, one where I thought maybe they could be friends again. Now, with these new feelings that had rooted in my being like a weed, ones my soulmate could doubtlessly feel, I may have brought everything crashing back down.

Hopefully... Only between him and Lexios, and not between *us*.

Chapter Twenty
Olympio

By the time we got back to the oasis, I was barely able to keep myself upright. Between the heat and the exhaustion that came with using my demon form, not to mention the emotional toll of the day, I was ready to fall asleep immediately upon our return.

But there was no way, not a single fucking one, that I would allow that to happen after what I felt earlier.

After Mal greeted us at the gates and we filled her in on what had happened, she gracefully took her leave to deal with the families of the lost escorts. I grabbed hold of Gabriel's arm in what I hoped would appear to be an affectionate way to anyone watching. In reality, I needed him alone.

Now.

Dinner had been brought to our quarters, which I was grateful for, because I had no intention of either of us leaving this room until they dragged us back onto the carriage to leave for our next destination.

The second the door closed behind us, I was on Gabriel, pressing him into the wall and kissing down his neck.

"Ollie!" he gasped, clearly not anticipating this reaction.

"*My* Gabriel..." I growled into his skin, my hands ripping the fabric of his clothes to take him in my hand and start stroking him. "Did you think I wouldn't have felt it? That I wouldn't know Lexios was doing everything in his power to win over my soulmate, right in front of me? That I wouldn't realize exactly when you felt that attraction?"

Gabriel squirmed against me, pushing me back half-heartedly. "He wasn't—*Ollie!*—he wasn't trying to win me over. He hasn't done... Olympio!"

Finally, I pulled back enough to look him in the eyes, the ones that marked him as mine, just as much as my own marked me as his. My hand, however, continued its ministrations on his length, not relenting for even a second.

"Tell me I was wrong, then," I said, our noses touching. "Tell me your little moments alone haven't been slowly wearing you down, like the spawn of the great serpent himself."

"You're being ridiculous," Gabriel protested. "I'm bound, not dead. He's good-looking. How can you be mad at me when *you* used to fuck him?"

"*I* hadn't pledged myself to my soulmate," I reminded him. "And I have proven, I think, that I am happy to share you... within reason, and as long as we're together. And I *do not* think that someone who has made his interest in you plain as day, who keeps getting you alone, is someone I would consider within reason. There is not a single *reason* I can think of to trust him now."

With my free hand on his chest, holding him in place, I released his cock with my other and dropped to my knees, taking his semi-hard member immediately into my throat, my lips wrapping around his base.

Gabriel giggled nervously. "Ollie, he... Oh, my fucking god—" He grabbed my hair, pulling it hard as though he was still attempting to have this conversation. "He doesn't want me. I just thought he was cute. And he saved my life. More importantly—" He tugged my hair again, and yet again, I resisted. "I... I... Oh, my god... I don't want him. Fuck..." he gasped.

I felt him tremble, and his cock pulsed between my lips. I moaned around him as I grabbed his hands and removed them from my hair, pinning them at his sides. I began to slide my mouth forward and back, never fully releasing him until I freed my mouth long enough to say, "*Everyone* wants you, Gabriel. But... I think I can make sure you forget Lexios, Kessinger, and anyone else who I've ever had to experience you have feelings for." With that, I had his long, thick length in my mouth and throat once more, breathing through my nose to keep him deep.

"Olympio," he groaned loudly, trembling. "He's just my friend. Please, Ollie... Don't... Oh, fuck it."

He gave over to me, his resistance fading away as he slumped against the wall, allowing me to take him.

But this wasn't my end game, not by a long shot.

I used every single movement I knew drove him to the brink quickly, sucking, licking, and pumping my fist at his base. His moans and whimpers grew louder.

"Wings..." he breathed. "Your... wings..." His hips struggled against my grip to thrust, trying to achieve his primal needs quickly.

I looked to the side and saw what he meant. My shadows were forming around me. Not quite turning me into the demon form, but certainly reminding us both that it was there, just below the surface, always ready to fight for what was *mine.*

I pulled away once more to put my finger in my mouth, wetting it enough for what I was going to do next. Running my hand from his hip around behind him, squeezing his supple ass, before delving into the cleft, where I used my saliva-coated finger to slowly breach his hole. I slid closer and closer to the spot inside him I knew would push him over the edge.

"I'm yours... Okay? I'm yours... Olym—"

He spilled into my mouth, and I allowed it to run down my lips and chest, forcing him to watch his own essence spill out of me. He was exactly where I liked him, begging, whimpering, ready to be praised for giving me what I had milked out of him.

But I wasn't done just yet. If he was going to look at someone else—another *man*—with feelings that were meant for me, I was going to spend the rest of the night reminding him who he actually belonged to.

I stood, and he collapsed into my arms, ready for me to do what I would usually do and carry him to the bath, since we were now both covered in his fluids. Instead, I put my hand around his throat, squeezing gently, and whispered, "How dare you think that you'd be getting off that easy? If you cooperate, *maybe* I'll allow your little friendship to continue. Because as of now, the object of your new affection is in danger of me slicing his head off with my sickle."

His eyes went wide, and I spun us both, backing him up until he hit the bed, his legs buckling and forcing him onto his back.

"You're... you're joking, right?" he said, and I watched him wrinkle his nose sweetly as his hand went to scratch his chest and found itself in a deposit of cooling seed. The tenderness and innocence of the moment simply served to make me even more ravenous for his undoing.

"Are you brave enough to find out?" I said, grabbing a towel and roughly wiping away the mess. "Perhaps I can be a merciful king, given the right... motivation..."

Gabriel's cock had softened, but I knew well that, with the right stimulation, he would be ready to go again soon. And I intended to make him come so many times that he would be too spent to even consider looking at someone else for a long, long time.

"Do... not... move..." I said, the gravelly timbre of my demon voice coming through.

Using the shadows, I moved faster than Gabriel could react in order to ensure my task was completed before he could intercede. I rushed around the room, gathering the torn remnants of his clothing from earlier, ripping off long, thick strips. Then, I flipped Gabriel onto his stomach in the center of the bed and tied his limbs to each of the corners before coating my cock in lubricant and climbing on top of him, pressing my tip against his entrance.

"Say it again," I growled, the demon still coming through. "Say who you belong to."

"Olympio, this is... this is stupid..."

"I'd say Lexios will be the stupid one when I cut off his head in the morning," I said, pressing harder, feeling the ring of muscle beginning to loosen, but not breaching it yet. "But I think that may actually improve his intelligence. Now... Say it."

"No," Gabriel grumbled defiantly. "I'm not gonna be part of your stupid little dick swinging match over a crush that means nothing to me." He attempted to wriggle out from beneath me, but the bindings held him firmly in place.

"Have it your way." I allowed my body weight to take over and lowered myself onto Gabriel, feeling the slight bit of resistance before I was inside of him. "Fuck..." I gasped as he surrounded me, and I stilled inside him, breathing into his ear. "I hope you were ready to spend the rest of the night right there while I fuck anyone but me out of your mind, until your heart and your cock only respond to *me*. Now... say... it... again."

I began to move in and out of him, faster than I usually would at first, but any discomfort he felt was quickly overshadowed by the pleasure of my singular area of expertise...

Absolutely *undoing* my soulmate.

"Let me... get this straight—" he panted, hands gripping the sheets. "You're gonna teach me... a lesson... by giving me my favorite thing in the world? Fine by me."

I laughed, a low, rumbling sound that reverberated in my chest. I had never allowed so much of my inner demon to show itself, to be present, when Gabriel was in such a vulnerable state. But the rage his flippant tone stoked within me, combined with my unrelenting need to remind him just who he had pledged his eternal life to, had invited the monster to join in.

"Your wish," I said, thrusting particularly deep, drawing a gasp and a long, drawn out moan from Gabriel's perfectly pouted lips, "is my command..." I gripped his wrists, my hands halfway between flesh and shadow, and began pounding into him.

His whimpers were pulled from him in perfect ribbons of resistance, and the more I used him for my pleasure, the less controlled his noises became.

"Ollie..." he whined. "You're so deep... Oh, fuck, I'm hard again..."

"Good," I growled, reaching my arm around him to grip his cock, stroking him in time with my thrusts.

Holding back the full demon was getting more and more difficult with each passing second. I had never, ever allowed myself to assume that form while fucking someone. It was the darkest, most dangerous parts of me, and allowing it to be free was exhausting. Despite being as much "me" as the copper hair and violet eyes, the massive shadow beast with the long horns and gossamer wings was tiring. It was a pure adrenaline rush, and when it faded, I was usually left entirely spent.

But right now, the fatigue wasn't present, and I had almost achieved the full transformation, including my cock, which had swelled inside of Gabriel, making him moan louder and louder. Even Vassenia had never been fucked by me like this—by the true demon within. It was easy to see why Gaiadans had seen us as gods long ago, forming their mythologies around us—powerful, terrifying beings that lurked in the dark.

"Not so frightened now, are you?" I teased, the voice that was like the depths of a volcano purred at him.

"It's so much," he whimpered. "You're gonna split me in half..."

"If that's what it takes," I said, reaching up with the razor-sharp claws that now tipped my fingers and shredding the ties, releasing him. Then I withdrew and flipped him over, so he was forced to face me.

I saw a flicker of fear in his eyes as he searched mine for the violet he longed to see. But it wasn't there, and still I thrust deeper, harder, taking my pleasure in a form that, in that moment, felt like it would never run out of stamina, never tire, never get enough of drowning in the power that was coursing through me.

Gabriel's eyes hardened, and he pulled back, slapping me across the face. "I'm not gonna be fucked into submission, Olympio." And then, just to increase my rage further, he groaned, "Alex... Kessinger..."

"So be it."

In one single motion, I had his legs over my shoulders, and I was pressing into him once more. I placed a clawed grip firmly around his throat as I rutted into him, waiting for him to beg me for relief.

"Wait.. wait..." he said, begging. "Wait..."

In seconds, the demon was traded for the form that Gabriel loved, and I peered down at him as he pressed a palm into my chest. "Yes...? Are you ready to submit?"

Gabriel panted, his cheeks a gorgeous, lickable shade of rose and his cock dripping with traitorous desire. "If I say you own me, you and *only* you, forever, can we call this done, and we can just pretend none of that stuff after the fight ever happened? You and Lexios—"

"Wrong answer," I roared, the demon form resuming as I lifted him from the bed, transporting us both against the wall across the room in the blink of an eye. I doubled down my efforts, pumping into him twice, then withdrawing to allow him to really feel my absence before I resubmerged myself into his depths. "You *belong* to *me*. You have no need for another man's name to ever cross your lips."

I watched as the rose became a crimson, and I recognized the patterns of his breathing to indicate his next climax was moments away.

"Say my fucking name," I growled as I gripped the bottom of his face. "Again and again. Only my name."

"I'm not gonna... Oh, fuck..."

I felt the warm torrents of Gabriel's release spill down me in delicious splendor as he bit his lip so hard it bled to prevent himself from giving me what I wanted.

"Resist all you want," I said, taking his cock in my hand, milking the final drops of his orgasm from him, without letting go. I was going to make him come over and over again, until he finally broke. "Our carriage doesn't leave until midday tomorrow. We have hours and hours before then."

His face was covered in an exhausted sheen of sweat, and his body slumped against mine. But I was a monster of my word. I gripped his throat once more and quickly slid him down the wall, depositing him onto his knees and using my clawed finger to pry open his mouth. I used his exhaustion as an interlude to press as much of my engorged, demonic cock into his waiting mouth, his head going up against the wall as he attempted to accommodate its significant girth. "Perhaps this is the only way to prevent you from uttering another man's name, Gabriel... Maybe I will simply have to take you like this every time we're in the same room..."

Gabriel whimpered, exhaustion and weakness coming through, even though he couldn't speak.

"Is that what you wish, soulmate? For me to appear like this before you? Wreathed in shadows, with my demon cock ready to fill your throat at the very thought of another man?"

Gabriel looked at me pleadingly, and I pulled back, once more allowing the shadows to recede and giving him the Olympio he didn't fear. "Here's my offer, whore Justice of Sefaera. You are going to come for me again, and then, we can end this. But if I *ever* hear that name cross your lips again, this will be what it comes to. I'll decide by morning if that counts for your new 'friend' as well."

Gabriel whimpered, reaching up to wipe his swollen lips, "Ollie I can't... I can't even get hard again, let alone come one more time."

I crouched down before him so that we were eye to eye and licked the anticipatory drippings of my own seed from his cheeks. "Then I suppose we will just have to continue this until you do."

"Olympio," he whined, a pout crossing his face. "Please... please... I can't."

I put a single finger against his chest and trailed it down his body where, indeed, his cock sat flaccid, still moist from his previous climax. Gently, I took it in my hand, leaning in to press my lips to his neck, alternating pressing wet kisses to his skin with whispering my demands.

"You can, and you will," I said, my wings of shadow unfurling behind me, a reminder of what was still lurking just below the surface. "You are *mine*, and I will bring you to ruin with pleasure if that's what it takes for you to concede. I will *only* stop when I've come, and I will not allow myself to finish until I'm satisfied."

In a swirl of shadows, we were back at the bed, this time with him on his back, looking up at me, wearing the face he loved. The room around us filled with shadow and purple fragments of light from the bond, and he began to shiver as I allowed my full weight to press into him.

"You're mine... *my* Gabriel. My very, *very* good little soulmate," I cooed, switching tactics. As a seasoned strategist, I knew sometimes battles would be won with a truce rather than bloodshed. Particularly after you'd already worn down your opponent. "And you are going to do exactly as I tell you. And if—*only* if—you do as I tell you, I will allow your sordid little friendship to proceed. But that will only happen if you empty yourself for me entirely. Do you understand, *my* Gabriel?"

Now, at last, he nodded, the whispering of exhausted tears in his eyes.

I kissed down his chest and licked every inch of him on the way down, my cock pulsing with raging need as I continued to deprive myself in an effort to win this tug of war. When I reached his length, which had not yet receded, despite being softened, I used my tongue to lick from his tip to his base over and over again.

He sat up part of the way to watch what I was doing, and I looked up at him, my thoughts singular and finite.

You. Are. Mine.

I knew he would feel the sentiment within himself and indeed, as I drew another languishing lick up his shaft, I felt him stiffen. "Well done," I praised, and I pulled back slightly to appraise the sweat and come drenched visage of my soulmate as his length trembled back into action. Once I was satisfied that he would be able to follow my orders, I took his hand and wrapped it around his cock. "Stroke." He did so tenderly, slowly, which was fine... for now. I crawled forward over him, pausing only briefly to flick my tongue over a nipple, and then to bite at his neck. But I didn't stop there. I moved the rest of the way up until my knees were pressing down on his shoulders, my own length hovering over his swollen lips. "Now... Open your mouth."

Gabriel did as I commanded, and I shuddered, my wings flaring without my conscious thought to do so. There was no sight as delectable as the perfectly pink inside of my soulmate's mouth.

Well, there was one. And it was the look in his eyes as I slowly lowered my hips, feeding my hard member between his lips an inch at a time. I pulled back, pressing forward more, until I reached the resistance at the back of his throat.

"Yes, Gabriel..." I moaned. "Take me. Take me deep. Just like that..."

He whimpered again, and I watched as his eyes closed, not in exhaustion, but enjoyment.

"I am Olympio, King of Sefaera, and the mate to your soul. You belong to me, as I belong to you." I could feel every muscle below my navel contract and release with each thrust, eager for relief. But the matter had to be resolved before I could take my pleasure all the way.

"You will never speak that horrible, filthy, unworthy name again—not the name of the man who nearly took my soulmate from me with careless abandon. You will never even *think* that name again. And it will be a long, long time before I allow you to be alone with Typhir's son once more. Is that clear?"

My tone wasn't aggressive despite my message being exactly that, and my darling, sweat soaked, lust drunk Gabriel finally nodded his head in submission.

I retracted my length from his mouth, watching as drool deliciously strung from his lips, clinging to my tip. "Say it, Gabriel. Now."

"I'm yours..." he panted, and without looking, I could feel that his strokes were becoming more frantic. I couldn't deny the deep, visceral part of me that loved how desperate he was to please me now. How I had broken him down to a place where all he could think about was my voice, my commands, my pleasure.

"And...?"

"And I will never say that name again. I will never even think it."

"And you will *not* be caught alone with Lexios until I say that I will allow it—if ever." I exerted all of the power I had to prevent his climax from happening until I was satisfied.

"Olympio... please... I'm so close..."

"Say it."

"Lexios is nothing to me, and I will avoid being alone with him. Please..."

With a few rough strokes on my cock, I released the hold I had on him. Instantly, he cried out around me, his whole body pulsing with the intensity of his third and final orgasm. I felt his release coating my back, and I allowed myself to follow.

"Gabriel...!" I groaned as I came hard, the delay amplifying the sensations. "Fuck... Yes, Gabriel..."

I allowed my essence to burst free, covering Gabriel from his cheeks, down his neck, and onto his chest, marking him fully as mine. His eyes were closed, and some of my ejaculate clung to his lashes as he slowly came down, breathing heavily and whimpering.

"Water..." he begged quickly, coughing as the last ripples of our orgasms subsided. "Water..."

"Of course," I said softly, all traces of shadows gone. "Come here." I lifted him into my arms. It was still sweltering in the room, but the sweat-soaked comedown made Gabriel start to shiver. I carried him over to the bath and filled it as I poured him a glass of water before handing it to him and climbing in with him.

He shook against me, his face alternating between being pressed into my skin and sipping the water I'd given him.

"Are you alright?" I asked. I had no regrets about what had happened, but I wanted to make sure there was nothing he needed now.

He nodded, then yawned. "Do I really have to stay away from Lex?" he asked.

"Did I make my point?" I replied, stroking his face and hair.

He grumbled against my skin, another nod serving as his exhausted communication.

"Then we will see," I softly hummed. "I suppose it will all depend on how Lord Lexios proceeds from here. I could not be more grateful to him for saving you, but I'm still withholding trust until I'm satisfied with *his* behavior. Let's just call this a gentle reminder for now."

If Gabriel hadn't been half unconscious by now, the sound he made would have been one of his signature, musical giggles. But I could feel him fading, and to be honest, I wasn't far behind.

Tenderly, I washed us both, then I lifted him from the bath and carried him to our bed, laying him down before taking a step back to gaze upon the wonder that was my Gabriel.

And silently prayed to any gods that may have *actually* existed that this would be the end of that entirely.

Chapter Twenty-One
Gabriel

I had been standing for an indeterminate amount of time, eyes closed, breathing. Just breathing. The smell of the sea was exactly like it was in Aruba, a favorite vacation spot of my parents. The water was bluer than blue, and the waves looked like they were dancing. It was so unlike the waves back home, which were—of course—gravity based. Here, it looked like the water, itself, had life, like it was its own creature, and it was inviting.

We'd already met with Celaine's mother and the rest of the leaders here, in Jouraya. Each island had its own "mayor," and they'd all arrived to greet us. After another feast, we'd all gone to bed to rest up for today. The portal was on the farthest island from the mainland, only accessible by boat.

The ride here hadn't been anything special, though I did notice my capacity for breathing increase once we were out of the desert. The only thing worth noting was the extensive conversation Olympio and Lexios had while they both believed I was asleep. I *had* dozed off, but I was roused again by the sound of their hushed voices.

"Do I need to worry about you?" Ollie had asked. "I'm going to give you one—exactly one—opportunity to convince me to trust you. We both know your proclivities, and I highly doubt that you have found your true match in Celaine, lovely as she is."

There was a long silence, and I was tempted to open my eyes before—

"You have known me my entire life, so you are right to think the way you do. But I know what happened when Vassenia tried to get between you and Gabe." There was another tense pause, and I wondered what Ollie's face looked like. "You would be an idiot if you thought I don't find your soulmate enchanting—anyone would, and most do. I'd be a blasphemer if I pretended that something that apparent wasn't true. But I respect that he is yours, and yours alone. I would, instead, rather have the friendship of the crown and perhaps repair this feud that has been simmering long enough."

I heard my soulmate exhale through his nose long enough that I wondered if he was actually deflating. "What assurances do I have that you're not lying to me? That your father isn't pulling your puppet strings? I think we both know who was influencing you the last time. What makes now different than before?"

"Let me ask you a question instead. What will it take to prove my loyalty?"

"I... I don't know," Ollie replied. "You've already saved Gabriel's life and helped me out of tight spots with your father. In all honesty, I feel like you should have already earned it. But trust is hard to regain once broken. Believe me—I know that all too well. I suppose... I can try to give you the benefit of the doubt for now. And as long as you continue to be a friend to both Gabriel and me, I can try to accept that you have truly changed."

I heard their hands touch, and I assumed they must have shook on it. "He is gorgeous, though. You're a lucky, *lucky* fool."

"That, I am," Ollie said. "Though I feel fairly certain that if we don't stop giving him compliments he can hear while he's pretending to be asleep, his head will be too large to exit the carriage."

I let out a loud, exaggerated snore to try and prove otherwise. However, this only served to be detrimental rather than helpful, as I felt Olympio's fingers dig into my ribs and begin to tickle me awake.

"I have diarrhea!" I screamed, causing Ollie, Gryfian, Lexios, and Tomos to all look at me—repulsed. "Well, it got you to stop, didn't it?"

Olympio chuckled and leaned in to rub his nose on my cheek before kissing my neck. "I suppose it did. Just be careful. I remember a story from when you were a child of the boy who cried 'wolf.' Sooner or later, you'll be telling the truth about that, and I won't believe you, and everyone will be the worse for it."

I turned to face him in what was quickly becoming my favorite way to look at my soulmate—nose to nose. "Don't threaten me with a good time."

"You consider shitting yourself a... good time?" Lexios asked, one eyebrow rising all the way up into his hairline. "On second thought, you can drop me off here, Your Majesty. I would like to rescind my offer of friendship."

Ollie snorted, trying to hold back his laughter.

"Well, now that *that's* settled," Gryfian said without a hint of amusement. "Perhaps Lord Lexios could indulge us with some information to help us prepare for our arrival."

"Certainly," Lex said, clapping Gryfian on the back, which made Gryf look wholly uncomfortable.

All leading up to us being here, standing on the docks in front of a seemingly endless cerulean sea, several boats prepped and ready for us to sail out to the place where the closest portal once stood. From behind me, I could hear Ollie trying to negotiate someone to sail the boat for us with the dockmaster, who was confused why he wouldn't just sail it himself.

"While my talents are many," he said with a good-natured laugh, "sailing is not among my skills. I've always been the 'sit back and enjoy' type. Have you no one who can captain one of the ships?"

"I'll do it," I called out to him, finally opening my eyes and turning around to face him. "I know how to sail."

Ollie looked dumbfounded. "How did I not know this?" he asked, narrowing his eyes. "When did you learn?"

"The summer my parents sent me to France to stay with my great aunt Jane. I was fourteen... wait. Where were you? Weren't you, like, stalking me my whole life?"

He closed his eyes and nodded. "That would make sense. You'd gone out partying the night before, and I'd made sure you weren't ill when you went to bed by sharing in your drunkenness. It made me oversleep, and I missed getting on the plane with you. I tried to fly over the ocean, but it was too far for me to hold my demon form for that long. I spent that entire summer pacing the flat I had, terrified something would happen, and I wouldn't be able to get to you."

I stared at him trying to even imagine that he was right there, all that time. "Either way..." I said. "I will sail us. That is, if His Majesty approves."

He pulled me to him for a quick kiss and said, "I approve. Lexios can provide the navigation, I assume?"

"Actually," I said, stepping slightly closer. "I thought maybe it could be... just us..."

His eyes lit up, and he broke into the biggest smile I'd seen from him in weeks. "I would like nothing more," he said, turning back to the dockmaster. "Just the boat for us, then, and a second for our companions."

Thirty minutes later, we were casting off, and Ollie was relaxing on the deck with a map and compass in hand. The sun was glorious, beaming down on us without the scorching heat like we'd just come from, the lake effect in full force with a gentle breeze to boot. It felt like we were flying over the water, and I'd specifically promised Tomos any rare edition of book he wanted from the marketplace back home to keep Lex and

Gryfian held up for a bit at the dock before they set sail, too. Poor Gryf would be having a heart attack over the distance between him and *His Majesty*, but it was worth it to get a few minutes alone.

"Gabriel," Olympio said from behind me, wrapping his arms around my shoulders. "I can't tell you how oddly thrilling it is to see you in action, doing something I had no idea you knew how to do."

I grinned at him. "Good to know our marriage has a few surprises yet."

"Indeed."

I watched as the sails filled and swayed with the changes in direction, a graceful dance in its own right. "How long do you think we could go missing before we get in trouble?" I posed.

Olympio, who was now leaning against the mast, gave me a funny look. "Why?"

I lifted my hand and pointed behind him, and he turned to look out in the direction I had indicated. Off and slightly to the starboard side was a small island with no visible civilization and a gorgeous pale pink beach. It looked like something that would be trashed by influencers in days if it existed in my world, and I was curious to see it closer.

Olympio studied it, looking at the map, then the compass, then back at me. "I'm not really sure we should—"

"Okay," I said a little too quickly. "Fine."

I heard Olllie get to his feet once more and come up beside me. "Then again..." he crooned. "Maybe I should flex my power a little. If my soulmate wants to deviate, why shouldn't I have the power to allow it?"

I turned my face and grinned at him, pecking him on the lips before turning us toward the singular island, which couldn't have been more than a mile long.

Docking was a little more difficult without any actual dock to align with, but Olympio jumped out after I'd slowed us down and used some of his demonic strength to act as a sort of anchor until we could drop it officially.

The island could have been straight out of the Bahamas, with its pristine beaches and crystal-clear waters, if not for a few striking differences. The sand, instead of the familiar white or golden hue, was a soft, shimmering pink that glowed under the midday sun, giving the shoreline an almost dreamlike quality. Towering above the beach were palm trees, their leaves an unusual teal, swaying gently in the warm tropical breeze. The vibrant colors clearly belonged to another world, as if the island had been touched by some magical force, setting it apart from any paradise back in my world.

Almost immediately, Olympio threw himself at me, tackling me into the soft sand with a force that knocked the breath from my lungs. Before I could react, we were already tumbling, wrestling as his weight pinned me down. I tried to push him off, using every ounce of strength to twist free, but even as I flailed, grappling for some kind of leverage, I knew it was pointless. His grip was firm, his movements quick, and I could feel the futility of my efforts.

Laughter filled the air, bright and carefree, as we rolled across the beach, the warm sand clinging to our skin, and for a moment, all the world faded away except for the playful struggle and the sound of our shared joy.

Quicker than I would have liked, my muscles tired, and I gave into him, allowing him to pin me, then draw a circle on my cheek with his nose, trailing kisses down my neck.

Sending sand flying everywhere, I gave my escape one last laughter-filled attempt, then conceded by wrapping my arms around his neck and kissing him deeply.

He wrapped his own arms around my waist and rolled over so that I was laying on top of him.

"How is the sand not burning your back?" I asked, positively vibrating with happiness.

"Oh, it is," he said with a cheeky grin. "But having you here, on top of me, is more than worth it."

I scoffed and climbed to my feet, pulling off my sandals and tossing them up toward the treeline before taking off down the beach at a run. I half-expected the swirl of shadows to materialize in front of me, but instead, I heard the sound of Olympio's feet slapping on the wet sand behind me as he chased me. He caught up quickly because of the few extra inches he had on me, making his strides just slightly longer than my own.

I glanced at him beside me as he slowed to match my pace. His hair was blown back in the breeze, making it ripple in little copper waves, and he smiled in a way that was more unburdened than he'd been since our adjournment.

"Well, hello there," I said as he looked over at me, and the light sparkled off the violet in his eyes.

"Hello," he replied. "Moons and rivers, this feels amazing. Just running, feeling the sea air, sharing it with you..."

I reached out and grabbed for his hand, dragging him into the brisk water and tackling him into the waves. I understood what he meant. I, too, felt like this was the first feeling of freedom I'd had in a while, despite having much more of it than him.

We crawled our way out of the sea, laughter being drowned out by the gentle roar of the waves, and both collapsed onto the sand once more.

"I love you," I sighed happily, wrapping my arms around him and laying my head on his chest.

"Calling it love would truly be a disservice to the depth of the feelings I have for you, my Gabriel," he said back, kissing my head.

"You know, there's not too many things I really miss from my world. But I miss having the chance to take pictures of things. If my parents hadn't wanted me to go to Columbia so badly, I think I would have gone into photography."

Olympio played with my hair, eyes closed, the sun kissing him everywhere it could. "You do have quite the artistic eye," he mumbled.

"Do you think maybe someday we could go back and get one? A camera? Even a polaroid would be okay."

He frowned like he was thinking hard, staying silent for long enough that I was about to tell him never mind. "Maybe someday," he said. "Assuming we don't find a working portal. In fact, if we find a working portal, a trip to Gaiada may be necessary to close the portal from the other side. If that happens, I will do my best to ensure you have a camera to bring back here. I don't know if it will survive the trip, since the portals are a difficult journey. But we will try. I promise."

I closed my eyes and allowed myself to sink into him, mind, body, and soul.

Our soul.

I felt the familiar warmth of the bond glow and opened an eye to confirm that the purple shimmering fractals of light were indeed there. Between the warmth of the sun, the comfort of my soulmate's body, and the clean, fresh sea air, it wasn't long before I dozed off.

The air had only gotten hotter by the time we awoke, and we were perfectly dry as the sun beat down on us.

"I didn't want to wake you," Ollie's deep voice rumbled through his chest against my ear. "But you were out for nearly two hours."

I sat up and looked around. "Shit. Sorry, Ol—"

"It's fine. But we should probably go before Gryfian has heart failure over our disappearance."

I laughed and scrambled to my feet, reaching out a hand to pull Ollie up as well.

When he stood, Olympio looked around and pointed toward the treeline. "Go get your shoes," he commanded, and I ran for them like a kid fetching his backpack in kindergarten.

It took a few seconds for me to locate both of them, and by the time I ran back through the hot sand, I found Olympio furiously scribbling onto the map with a quill and...

"Ollie!" I squeaked in horror. "Is that your blood?"

I watched as several drips of gold slid off his arm and into the grains of pink. "Indeed it is," he said without looking up. "I needed to make a note, and I was devoid of ink."

I scooted closer and looked over his shoulder. But he was writing in Sefaeran and for the life of me I couldn't read it. "What does it say, you lunatic?"

"It says *Isa rune Ga vvriel*, and some directions to get back here."

"Eee-zah-run gave-reel?" I sounded out, trying to copy him.

"Eessa-roon hav-ree-elle," he corrected. "It means Gabriel's Island in Jourayan. They don't have the letter 'b' in their dialect, and the pronounce 'g' as 'h', which accounts for the change in your own name.."

A pulse went through me that had nothing to do with my heartbeat, and I was brought to tears nearly instantly from the intensity of the adoration and pride I was feeling from him within me. In seconds, the fragments of gold and purple floated around us like the rings of Saturn, glowing despite the brightness of the sun.

"You named an island after me?" I sniffed, throwing my arms around his waist.

"I did indeed. I would name the whole damn world after you, my Gabriel, because for me, the world is worthless without you in it." He grabbed my chin and kissed me sweetly, then pulled back to look in my eyes before saying, "Let's get going, captain. I am going to owe Gryfian quite a lot for this."

When we arrived where Gryfian, Lexios, Tomos, and the members of the Jourayan court who'd opted to come along for the adventure were waiting, right outside the portal ruins, Gryfian was indeed, pale with distress.

"Nice of you to join us, Your Majesty, Your Grace," he said in a tone that would have sounded neutral to anyone who didn't know him.

"Got a bit sidetracked," Ollie said, clapping a hand on his guard's shoulder. "Nothing too dangerous, I assure you. Only the slightest bit of mortal peril."

"Funny," Gryfian replied.

I could have listened to them banter for an hour, but instead I went to Tomos, who was holding Betty. "Hey girl," I said, taking her into my arms and tickling her chin. "Sorry for the trouble, Tomos."

"No trouble at all, Your Grace," Tomos replied in a voice that didn't quite match his expression.

I patted him on the head. "Two books," I hissed. "And the hold up we planned stays between us, okay?"

Tomos "sealed" his lips and nodded, smiling in earnest at sharing a secret.

"Gabriel," Ollie called from behind me, and I turned to see him beckoning, "This way."

I ran to him, Betty flying up over my head and followed him into the looming ruins. While I hoped we would find answers so we could protect our people, I was also eager to keep this tour going. There was still so much more to see.

I suppose I should have been careful what I wished for.

Chapter Twenty-Two
Olympio

The island with the portal was like something out of legend, even by Sefaeran standards. About half a mile wide, with a massive stone arch in the center, spanning most of the island. According to my research, the minerals that made up the structure sparkled with the magic infused within them.

But as we approached the looming edifice, it became immediately clear that whatever magic had existed here was long gone. The top of the archway had crumbled into a treacherous ruin at the center, the stone dull and lifeless.

"How long has it been like this?" I asked one of our Jourayan guides, Celaine's younger sister, Lirelle. The family resemblance was strong—they could have been twins, except that, while Celaine had sapphire blue hair, Lirelle's was the color of the water behind us.

"Hard to say, Your Majesty," she said, hovering behind those of us who had come from the capital. "To my knowledge, no one has been out here in over a thousand years—possibly longer, since this place is considered cursed."

"Cursed?" Gabriel said in a concerned voice. "Like... actually cursed?"

Magic was rare in his world and considered impossible, even by those who saw it with their own eyes. But since coming to Sefaera, he'd had to adjust to a myriad of things he once thought only existed in the movies his parents made.

"Uncertain. No one's ever gotten close enough since it was closed in order to check." Lirelle said, putting a hand on my shoulder and pointing toward the ruins. "There's the center, where the actual portal was once open. I can escort you, Your Majesty." She looked up at me through her long, dark lashes and smiled, her cheeks blushing.

Her beauty incited some very familiar stirrings within me, and I glanced at Gabriel to see if he noticed, but he and Lexios had moved off to the side, examining some kind of creature in the grass. Part of me was annoyed that, if he hadn't felt it, it was likely that he was experiencing the feeling on his own, since he was sitting shoulder to shoulder with his "crush."

I must have been watching them for longer than I realized, because Lirelle repeated, "Your Majesty?"

"Yes," I said, turning back to her. "We may as well do what we came here for."

It wasn't a long walk, only about ten minutes, moving at a leisurely pace. Lirelle was pleasant company, telling me about Jourayan customs and festivals.

"You're here just in time for the Moonwaking ceremony tonight. It's the biggest event of the year, celebrating the day when Coricas and Talaea are in perfect synchrony, shining their brightest as twin guardians over Sefaera."

"What does that entail?" I asked, not receiving an answer as, just then, she stumbled over a piece of broken stone. I reached out, catching her, and she fell into my arms. "Are you alright?"

"Never better, Your Majesty," she said with a giggle—one I knew all too well from having heard thousands of other women, and almost as many men, make the same sound in my presence.

And suddenly, the stirrings were back as I looked down into her eyes, pulling her back to her feet. Her hands lingered on my arms, fingers flexing slightly as they found the outline of my biceps, and she moved just a bit closer, so that she was pressed ever so slightly against me.

A hundred years ago, I would have kissed her. I would have pulled her tightly against me and drowned in her, tasting her, laying her on the ground and taking what she was clearly willing to offer—if I was so inclined.

And, in all honesty, I was feeling *deeply* inclined at that moment.

Which is why I cleared my throat, taking a deliberate step away from her and pointing to the spot surrounded by the most rubble. "You said this is where the portal was?"

Lirelle seemed momentarily stunned, but regained herself. "Yes, Your Majesty." She moved back to my side, and I leaned slightly away. She seemed to understand my body language, since she didn't make an attempt to touch me again. "But I don't sense any of the magic that once existed here."

"Neither do I," I said, bending down to examine the stones. I picked one up, turning it over in my hands, trying to tap into the magic that was a part of me, that was part of all of Sefaera, tying me to the land as its steward. "I think this answers our questions about this particular portal."

I stood and turned, finding Lirelle had moved close to me once more.

"Do we need to return so soon, Your Majesty?" she said in a sultry tone, running a finger down the center of my chest and abdomen, toward my belt.

My breath hitched, and I grabbed her wrist quickly, just in time to feel a jolt in my chest at the same time that Gabriel's voice carried to me on the wind.

"Ollie!" he cried out, the sound faint, far as we were. "Come back! Quick!"

I glanced at Lirelle, who looked downtrodden at the failure of her efforts. I knew two ways of getting to Gabriel quickly. The first, becoming one with the shadows, would only allow me to travel alone. The other, the only way I'd be able to take Lirelle with me, was to become the shadow demon and carry her.

The thought of holding her that close to me was torturous, knowing that I found her attractive, and that doing so would only be giving her at least some of what she wanted. But I needed to get back to Gabriel, and I couldn't just leave her out here to make her own way back.

"Hold on," I said, scooping her into my arms. She looked like she'd won some kind of prize and wrapped her slender fingers around my neck. She didn't even react with fear when I closed my eyes and focused, allowing the demon to burst forth, my wings immediately taking us airborne.

Ten seconds later, I landed near the rest of our party, setting her down and resuming my human-like appearance as I made my way to Gabriel's side.

"What's wrong?" I asked, putting my hand on his back.

He looked up at me with wide eyes, his finger pointing toward a small copse of trees. I didn't see what he was indicating to at first, but then I saw movement.

"What is it?" I whispered.

"Don't know," Lexios hissed, coming closer. "But... I don't think it's from here..."

"Shit." I motioned for everyone to remain still, and the group fell into immediate silence. I caught a glimpse of gold and black fur between the tall blades of grass and turned to Lirelle. "I need a net. A big one."

She nodded and said something in Jourayan, a dialect similar to my own, but interspersed with words native to the region, before the kingdom was unified. One of the guides moved swiftly and quietly to the boat they'd arrived on, pulling a woven silver fishing net free and handing it to me.

In a swirl of darkness, I shifted partially into the shadows, allowing me to move quickly, and in seconds, I'd wrapped the beast in the net. It let loose a high pitched snarl as I lifted it and pulled it from the brush.

"What is that?" Lirelle gasped as several of the other guides murmured amongst themselves, clearly dumbfounded as well.

My heart sank, and I looked at Gabriel. "Is it...?"

He nodded, moving closer before jumping back when the beast growled and tried to slash at him with massive claws. "Looks like a jaguar," he said. Everyone looked at him, the word foreign to Sefaeran ears. "They're predators that live in jungles and rainforests and stuff."

"They're Gaiadan, then?" Gryfian asked, bending down to look closer, but keeping enough distance to stay out of danger.

"Yeah." Gabriel frowned. "So this is the portal that's... I don't know, leaking or whatever?"

"No," I said. "It's completely shut down—not a trace of magic."

There was a deafening silence as we all considered the implications of a creature that shouldn't be here managing to be here, nonetheless. Where had it come from, if not the portal? Was it possible it was merely the descendant of one that had come through centuries ago? That seemed unlikely, since they would need a breeding pair to keep the line going. So, then... where had it come from?

"We should kill it," one of the guides said. "It can't be allowed to roam free and harm the ecosystem here."

"You're not gonna let them, right?" Gabriel asked me, looking a bit worried about my answer. "You're not going to kill it?"

"No, we aren't," I said, stopping the guide from reaching for a harpoon. "It's contained. We will take it with us and transport it to the capitol in a cage. We can send the attendants from the second carriage back early."

Gabriel looked at me like I was his hero and pulled me down to kiss him, which I was all too happy to do.

Because no matter what feelings Lirelle may have elicited from me, there was no one, in this world or any other, who I would rather kiss than my soulmate.

Chapter Twenty-Three
Gabriel

The nightlife in Jouraya was insane, and I almost felt bad for Ollie having to miss it, since he had to meet with the Jourayan leadership when we'd returned. I would have felt worse if my soulmate hadn't sent his watchdog with me, but I understood.

"Try this," Lexios said, handing me a small glass of some lilac liquor that smelled like grass.

"What is it?" I yelled over the sound of the drums pounding, in what I assumed must be the Jourayan version of a night club.

Lexios shrugged. "No idea." Then he held up one of his own. "*Stenamahs.*" he toasted.

I downed the drink, which felt like it was ripping my insides apart as it dropped into my belly, but had a wonderful, fruity aftertaste. "What does that mean?" I coughed.

Lexios leaned in close enough that I could smell his delicious cologne, and I wondered why Olympio never wore any. "It means, 'to our health.'"

"Oh," I said, nodding. "*Sláinte.*"

Lex gave me a look like I was crazy, then looked past me to where Gryfian was sitting with an annoyed look on his face. "Do you want one?" he asked Gryf.

"No, thank you," my soulmate's guard replied briskly, turning away from us slightly.

Lex and I gave each other amused looks before he grabbed my elbow and said, "Would you like to dance?"

I nodded, getting to my feet, and allowing him to lead me to where others who appeared our age (or my age, I supposed) were gyrating to a primal and rhythmic sound.

At first, Lexios went straight for a group of young women, and began chatting to them in a language I didn't recognize. He pointed to me and whispered something, and the air filled with their laughter. Then suddenly, three of them came over to me, two of them taking my hands to dance with me.

Holy bonerville.

The air was filled with a tepid smokiness, and it took me only a few more seconds to realize that it was laced with something hallucinogenic. It would only be a matter of time before Olympio found his way here when I started feeling that.

I looked around me and found Lexios dancing very closely in front of me, his hands all over one of the girls who appeared to be actively trying to seduce him, and a nervous giggle erupted from me as his toned ass accidentally rubbed against my junk.

I stumbled over my words as I tried to make a joke about it, and as one of the girls bumped me harder into him, he turned to look at me.

"I happen to be very fond of my head," he shouted into my ear over the music. "I'd like to keep it if possible, no matter how... tempting you looking in the moonlight."

I became very aware of the girls running their hands up and down my torso as they danced, and suddenly Lexios and I were dancing together, the world around me spinning like I hadn't experienced in a long while.

I was hard as hell, and I could hear the girls giggling and pointing, but the only consciousness I had was boiled down to a single foot of space—me and Lexios, touching.

His hands wrapped around my waist as he continued to smile in a playful, friendly way, nothing excessively lecherous and aggressive though there was no chance he didn't see and feel my arousal. And when a finale of sorts broke out on the drums, I felt him give me a slight tug so that my junk was pressed into him.

"Gabe..." he said, finally stopping. "Gabe, I can't... I want to, but I can't... this is too import—"

"Hello, Gabriel. Having fun?"

Ollie's voice was right in my ear, his fingers digging into my waist to pull me away from Lexios and against him.

I spun into him, clinging to him to get my balance as we collided. "Careful," I said, wafting some of the smoke out of his face. "It's hallucinogenic."

"Is that so?" he asked, and to my surprise, he tilted his head back and took a long, deep breath of it. "It's been a long time since I've indulged in carymnal flower."

I blinked, almost like I was trying to clear away a previous perception I had of my soulmate, and I heard a slight clunk as I turned to find Lexios having descended to the ground in a bow of deference. "Your Majesty," he said in a mock confidence that was transparent as hell. He was clearly terrified.

Ollie stared at Lexios for a long, long time, not moving even to blink. Finally, he reached down and pulled Lexios up by his hand.

"Why don't you fetch the three of us some drinks?" he said in a voice that was rough and forced. I could tell he was trying to be nice, despite what he'd just encountered.

Lexios didn't hesitate. He was gone in a second, and Olympio turned his attention back to me.

"Care to explain?" he asked. I expected some kind of anger, but for once, he seemed calm, genuinely giving me the chance. I'm sure the drugs had *something* to do with it.

"There were these girls..." My voice broke, adding to what was likely a very unconvincing performance. I flung into him. "Olympio... Olympio... Olympio..." I moaned in distress. "I swear I wasn't trying to... you know..." I gestured to my rapidly softening length, then looked up at him, desperate for his forgiveness. I wasn't sure I'd survive another night like before.

"I know," he said, kissing my hair and burying his face in it. "And while I can't speak for anyone *else*... I trust you. I know your soul, because it's my soul, too. And I know your intentions, your desires. And while I don't approve of the desire your body has discovered, I trust that you, Gabriel, know where the line exists and won't cross it. I love you. Now... let's enjoy the party, shall we? Tomorrow's journey will be a harder one."

My stomach did cartwheels as he crooned at me, and I jumped into his arms, kissing all over his face, eventually finding my lips on his. He kissed me deeply, his hand coming up to cup my jaw while his other hand supported me via my ass.

"Drinks?" Lexios's voice said from behind us, and I turned to find him looking directly at Olympio with a pleading gaze.

Ollie nodded and took one of the cocktails, then handed me one as well. "To new old friendships," he toasted, holding me tight while keeping his eyes on Lexios. "May they serve us well and restore the kingdom to its full, united power."

"To the kingdom," Lex echoed.

I looked from my friend to my soulmate and back again.

"Now Gabriel," Olympio growled in my ear. "You're going to dance with me and our friend here until you are fully tired of dancing, and then maybe... just maybe... I will allow you the satisfaction of living out your fantasies."

Was this for real? What was his game here?

But I only had moments to consider before the drink I'd just had nearly pulled me under, and I lost myself in color, sound, and Olympio.

Chapter Twenty-Four
Olympio

Leaving Jouraya was difficult—almost as difficult as it had been to return to Sefaera at the end of my adjournment with Gabriel. For an afternoon, we had the privilege of just being together, without the pressures of being royalty or from other outside influences. But once we'd rejoined the group, it was back to reality. Back to the investigation into why Gaiadan creatures were still being seen in Sefaera. Back to the worry that still plagued me in regards to Lexios and my soulmate.

Which was made nonetheless easier when Gabriel told me about a certain dream he had the night before, no doubt brought on by the exposure to the carymnal smoke.

"So," Gabriel announced loudly, causing Tomos to jump. "I had a weird dream last night."

"Did you?" I asked, squeezing his hand, which was intertwined with my own. "What was it about?" I knew it hadn't been the usual nightmares—I would have felt it.

He got a mischievous grin on his face and looked around to be sure he had the attention he desired. "Oh... just a little orgy..."

I could barely hear Lexios perk up and say, "Go on..." over the sound of me choking on my own tongue.

"Probably the hottest dream I've ever had," Gabriel said casually. "Who'd have thought Gryfian was hiding *all* that under *all* that!"

Gryfian went scarlet in the cheeks and busied himself with looking out the window.

"Anyway," he continued. "We went back to the bungalow—and I didn't remember falling asleep, so I thought it was real, right? But I dreamed we all piled into our room and... well... then we all *piled* into our room." Gabriel giggled at his own double entendre and looked back and forth between myself and Lexios. "You two going at it was like living porn, I swear to god."

Jealousy reared up inside of me like bile. Even knowing that his dream had included Lexios being with *me*, the very idea that Gabriel wanted to bring Lexios into our bedroom, the man he had a "crush" on, made it very difficult to maintain my composure. "Well, I'm glad you enjoyed the *fantasy*," I said, my tone making it clear that a fantasy was all that would ever be.

"And who would have thought Gryfian could take that much co—"

"Are we not almost there?" Gryfian said loudly, looking to me for help.

"Lexios would know better than any of us," I said, trying to change the topic. "How close are we?"

By the time I got Gabriel to stop talking about it, holding back the annoyance that was veering on disgust, the carriages had left the sunny islands far behind. The second carriage, including the jaguar I had captured, took a different route to head back to the capitol. The five of us plus our driver were now making our way through a dense forest, even denser than the Royal Forest back home. The deeper we traversed into the trees, the less light came through, until it was nearly as dark as twilight, despite being mid-day.

"Is it just me," Gabriel said, peeking through the curtains, "or does this feel, like, super creepy? Like some guy with a chainsaw is about to jump out and slaughter us."

"I have to agree," Lexios said, his hand actually on the handle of his sword, for once, as he followed Gabriel's gaze. "Prumius is my least favorite place to visit, and the eerie path to get there is only part of it."

"Why else, then?" I asked.

"I, uh..." He paused as if he was nervous. "I probably should have said something sooner, but they aren't exactly enamored with the monarchy here."

"What does that mean?" Gabriel asked.

"It means they think that the capitol does little to nothing for them," Lexios sighed. "And they feel that as long as they are self-sufficient, they should be self-governed. Half of my work here is convincing them to not rebel and demand their sovereignty."

I felt a lurch in my gut. If the Prumians were ill-feeling toward the crown, was my and Gabriel's presence here going to be more of a hindrance than a help? I wondered if perhaps we should turn around and find lodgings while Lexios came on his own, since they already knew him well, even if they didn't care for his employer—me.

I was about to make the suggestion, when a glance at Gabriel reminded me of how the people of the capitol hadn't been pleased with me until they met him. I had to hope that seeing their Justice, coming to love him the way the rest of my people did, would be enough to keep them complacent, if not content.

"We'll tread with caution," I said, looking at Gryfian, who nodded, understanding my silent command to anticipate hostility.

After another few hours of moving slowly, since the path wound through the trees in a confusing pattern, a bit of light began to filter in through the carriage curtains.

"Whoa..." Gabriel said, pulling them aside to show us all what he saw.

The trees were dense as ever, but as the forest had grown even darker, small orbs of glowing light danced between the trunks and branches, lighting the way.

"We must be getting close," Lexios said. "Those only—"

What he was about to say, we never heard, because at that moment, the carriage lurched to a stop, causing Gabriel to tumble out of his seat beside me and against Lexios, who caught him. I watched, feeling that pulse through the bond, the one of Gabriel's "crush," as he'd called it, his attraction to Lexios.

There was a beat where neither of them moved before they both whipped their heads around to look at me, and even Gryfian and Tomos wore wary expressions, as though afraid I would snap.

"Are you alright?" I asked instead, reaching for Gabriel and pulling him back onto the seat.

"Yeah, definitely," he said in a higher pitched voice than usual, running a nervous hand through his hair. "What was that? Why did we stop?"

"I don't know," I said, nodding toward Gryfian, who looked out his window.

"I believe we have company," he said dryly, pulling the curtain back even further so that we could all see.

The carriage was surrounded by dozens of people, most of whom had skin and hair that was a lovely shade of pale lilac. They all bore horns that looked like they were made of vines, complete with black and purple leaves sprouting from them. If they weren't illuminated by the glowing orbs, they would have been invisible, blending into the surroundings.

"Show yourselves!" a voice cried out, and that was when I realized they were all armed.

"Your Majesty?" Gryfian said slowly, asking me, without saying it outright, if I wanted to exit the carriage or not. After what Lexios had told us, it was understandable that he would be hesitant.

"May as well," I said, grabbing my crown from the seat beside me and placing it on my head. I looked at Lexios. "How bad is it here?"

He grimaced and said, "Let's just say, I'm not sure if them seeing the crown will help or..."

I sighed and moved toward the carriage door, allowing Gryfian to step out first, followed by a reluctant Lexios and a deeply nervous Tomos, who announced us. I watched from within, waiting to see what happened.

"His Royal Majesty, King Olympio, and His Grace, Justice Gabriel!" Tomos called out, his voice shaking.

Murmurs rippled through the crowd, but no one came any closer, and Gryfian didn't draw his weapon. Which meant no one had made a move to attack, because he would never remain unarmed if there was a threat.

"Could be worse," I said, kissing Gabriel one time before climbing out of the carriage. I pulled him along behind me and put an arm around his waist once we were before the people of Prumius, who, despite not attacking us outright, bristled and frowned.

"Uh... Hey, everyone. Nice to meet—"

One of the group, a man with the longest horns out of the group, stepped forward, his twig-like fingers wrapped around a walking stick that glowed like the orbs of light. "What is your business here?" he demanded, his eyes falling on Lexios. "You were not expected for another decade."

"This is an... unanticipated visit. We need to examine the old archway that used to be a portal. His Majesty is attempting to protect us all by ensuring that it stays closed."

The man I assumed to be the leader looked over at Gabriel and me, his lip curling. "His Majesty, is it?" he said with a contemptuous drawl. "Well, that is unfortunate, because we cannot allow it."

I titled my head to the side, unsure if I heard him correctly. He was telling me, his king, that I was not allowed to access a part of my own kingdom?

"And why is that?" I demanded, stepping forward. I heard the slight rustle and metallic scrape as Gryfian's sword was pulled partially out of its sheath.

A dozen Prumians shifted their stances, every one of them on the defensive.

"It's sacred ground," he said. "Only high priests and priestesses of Nurim may enter the temple."

"Nurim?" I repeated, looking at Lexios.

"Nurim is the Prumian deity of life," he said. "They have a rather... unique theology here."

Unique was correct. I wasn't aware that anywhere in Sefaera had gods or deities or idols outside of the twin moons, and even then, no one I knew actually believed they had any impact on our lives. It was a myth, nothing more. But here, in one of the farthest reaches of my kingdom, hidden from even the sunlight, we had encountered a society that was willing to allow our world to crumble into ruin for the sake of not disrupting their perception of reality.

We all stood in silence, staring at each other.

"As your king, I am ordering you to have a member of your clergy escort us," I said, knowing even as I spoke what the response would be.

"Even if we were to escort you, you would not be allowed inside," the Prumian leader said, his voice growing a bit louder. "You are not one of Nurim's chosen. You may not enter the temple."

"Ollie..." Gabriel gripped my arm, watching in fear as, all around us, weapons were drawn.

"Very well," I said. "We'll be on our way, then."

I could have shown my demon form, intimidated them into helping us. But if I were to do that, there was no way this wouldn't turn bloody, for both them and for my traveling party as well. Such a threat might frighten them into submission, but it could just as easily elicit an attack. Even if I managed to take out every single one of them before they could harm any of us, the last thing I needed was for word to spread about the Tyrant King Olympio either slaughtering an entire population or threatening them for defending their religious beliefs, misguided as they may be.

I guided Gabriel into the carriage first, then allowed Tomos to climb in behind him. I was next, followed by Lexios, and, finally, guarding us until we were all safely inside, came Gryfian, who closed the door behind him.

"Now what?" Gabriel said nervously. "What if this is the one that's letting all the animals through?"

"I don't know," I said, running a hand over my face, which was sweaty from the nerves the interaction had brought about. I'd faced distrust and contempt from the people back in the city around the palace my whole life, until recently. But this... this threat of violence toward their king was something I'd never even considered. "I don't know how far the magic that protects the royal family while a bonded pair is on the throne goes. My father's death was proof that it has its limits. We could try to force the issue, but I'm not willing to risk the lives of any of you without knowing for sure this portal is the issue."

There was a long silence as we all pondered the task at hand. Was the right move to give up on this one?

But then Lexios spoke, a distressed tone lacing every word.

"With deepest respect, Your Majesty," he said slowly. "I have a very, *very* bad idea."

Chapter Twenty-Five
Gabriel

I felt like Indiana fucking Jones, hiking through the woods, using our weapons to cut down vines that blocked our way.

"Not much farther," Lexios said, pointing to a break in the trees up ahead.

We'd been at this for over an hour, since we'd sent the carriage in another direction while we all slipped out, except for Tomos, who asked to remain behind. The driver knew where to meet us, but our hope was that the Prumians would see our carriage leaving and believe we were with it. Meanwhile, Lexios guided us through the woods to where he knew the portal was, even if he'd never been inside.

Finally, we emerged into a clearing where there was a huge temple made out of crumbling gray stone, rising all the way up through the canopy of trees. The whole scene contributed to the feeling of being a treasure hunter, sneaking into the forbidden tomb to find the cursed relic.

"In there," Lex said, pointing to a doorway carved into the stone, beyond which was total darkness.

A hush fell over us, and a shiver rippled down my back.

"Okay, now this feels even more like a horror movie," I said, instinctively looking over my shoulder, as if someone was right behind us. Thankfully, it was just more of these creepy-ass woods.

"Let's go, then," Ollie said before taking my hand and pressing it to his lips. "I won't let anything hurt you."

I tried to reply, but my throat had gone dry, so I just nodded.

After the entryway was a set of stairs that felt like they descended forever. Down and down and down we traipsed, and I couldn't help but think about the fact that we'd have to do them again in the other direction on the way out. Once we were down at the bottom, what felt like an hour later, Olympio, Lexios, and Gryfian looked around. Gryf pointed out two long troughs on either side of the hall which looked to be filled with oil. Ollie moved to one of them, dipping his fingers in and smelling the fluid there.

"Gryfian, light a torch," he commanded, and Gryf did immediately, handing it to my soulmate. Then Ollie dropped the torch low beside the liquid, and in a whoosh of flame, the trough lit all the way down and into another room.

Then he tossed the torch to Lex, who caught it and did the same.

"Sick," I said half under my breath, trying to hold back a grin that wouldn't stay hidden.

We progressed forward into the next room, which turned out to be exactly what we were looking for. There, in the middle, going so high up that it would have been impossible to see the top had it not had a gap letting sunlight in, was the archway. Though, unlike the last two, it was intact.

"This must be it," I exclaimed with enthusiasm. "It's not broken."

"No," Olympio said, stepping forward to place a hand on the stone. "But it is inactive. If it was being used, there would be signs of magic. This is no more than a large stone carving now."

I didn't understand. Was there more needed than the structure itself?

"I have to agree," Lex said, circling the other leg of it across the room. "No one has used this in more time than His Majesty and I have been alive."

I deflated at the information. "So, what now?" I asked. "We keep going?"

I watched as Olympio looked at Gryfian, then Gryfian looked at Lexios, not one of them looking my way.

"No," Olympio said at last. "I want to speak to my mother about the royal sentiment here. Perhaps she would have some suggestions. While the creatures popping up is urgent, separatists are even more important. Also, *someone* here has their Union in a week."

"Then we should go," Lexios said, a slight tension lacing his words. "Before they figure out our ruse."

Ollie nodded and walked to me putting a hand on my shoulder. "You're doing well," he affirmed. "Thoughtful and clever. Your parents would be proud."

I laughed. "Even without that chemistry degree."

My soulmate echoed my sentiment. "Even without it."

The walk back up was indeed exhausting, and the only thing that got me through was the banter that continually popped up between myself, Lexios and my soulmate.

"All I'm saying," I rebutted to Lex. "Was that if you helped us throw your dad off a cliff, you'd probably get a raise."

"Hilarious," he replied. "Though it might just be easier to dispose of His Majesty."

"Careful, Son of Typhir," Ollie said. "I have a memory like a garaphin."

When we finally reached the top, not a single one of us had our breath, and I was so happy to be done with the stairs that I screamed back down the abyss.

"Take that you dark fucking hole."

"I'll show you a dark fucking hole," Lex mumbled into my ear, making me choke with laughter.

I dashed forward, out of the temple and into the light—if you could call it that—of the woods.

"Guess the best man made it—"

And suddenly I was being flung to the ground, Ollie's body weight coming down on top of me.

And there was blood.

Lots of thick, *golden* blood.

Chapter Twenty-Six
Olympio

Searing pain tore through me as I pushed Gabriel out of the way and took the spear in my side.

I roared as I rolled off of him and onto my knees, the demonic voice ripping through the air and causing several of the Prumians who had surrounded us as we exited the temple to hesitate. Some of them, however, took it as a challenge and closed in.

The sound of stone on stone, metal on metal rang out through the trees, along with grunts and shouts of exertion and pain.

I watched Gabriel get to his feet, covered in my blood, and begin fighting for his life, his daggers slicing through flesh as easily as they did through the air. Gryfian was locked in battle as well, his sword cutting down foes left and right. Lexios, too, had his sword drawn, but his lack of recent training was evident as he swung his blade haphazardly, dodging more than parrying, and only barely managing to keep from being felled.

I hadn't wanted to do this, but it seemed there was no other option. I looked down at my side, liquid gold spilling from the wound and onto my hands. I had to end this before someone else got hurt or one of the Prumians took advantage of my injury to put an end to me.

With another roar, I rose to my feet, shadows swirling around me as my body swelled, growing several inches, my wings unfurling as darkness formed my long, sharp claws.

I rushed at one of them, grabbing him by the throat and lifting him into the air. He grunted with fear, all he had time to do before I flung him to the side, hearing his back snap as it impacted with a tree.

I had wanted to give them mercy, despite their treasonous behavior, and I might have even been willing to consider diplomacy... if they hadn't tried to hurt Gabriel.

I reached out for another, my claws ripping through the skin over their heart, shredding them until they were still. Their blood, lilac like their skin, spurted all over the grass and their companions.

"Gryfian!" I roared, seeing a single attacker stalk up behind Gabriel, who wasn't aware, his own attention on the enemies in front of him. I pointed, indicating for my personal guard to intercede, cutting the man down just in time to prevent my Gabriel from being harmed.

I watched one of the Prumians make a break for the treeline, trying to escape. I might have let him live, but the agonizing wound in my side served only to remind me that it was almost my soulmate, rather than me.

I flew up over his head, my wings buffeting once, twice, before I dove, tackling him to the ground. He didn't even have a chance to scream before I dug my claws into his throat, tearing the flesh and watching the lilac blood coming out of the gaping hole in torrents. But I wasn't finished. I grabbed his head and twisted hard, breaking his neck to ensure the job was well and truly done. Life faded from his eyes, and I looked up, ready to continue the slaughter, only to find that there were no Prumians remaining.

I couldn't do another second, my body completely exhausted. I let the shadows fade, returning me to my usual self, and collapsed onto the grass.

"Ollie?" Gabriel said, looking at me, his eyes wide with fear. "Shit! Gryf! He's hurt!"

They were both kneeling beside me within seconds, Gryfian tearing through his bag for something to help with my injury.

"Dammit!" he said, pulling out a small vial with just a few drops left of what had obviously been Perla's yellow potion. "We used most of it with the Wyvern attack. I don't think this will be enough, but it's worth a try." He tipped the contents into my mouth, and I swallowed down what little there was.

I felt it begin to work immediately, but stop just as quickly. I was no longer in danger of bleeding out, but the wound hadn't fully closed, and the pain was still crippling.

"We need to get him back to the carriage," Gryfian said. "Help me get him to his feet." I thought he was talking to Gabriel, but I felt a very different pair of hands lock onto my arm.

"Up you get, Your Majesty," Lexios said.

But I yanked my arm out of his grip. "Don't you fucking touch me," I snarled through the pain. "This was *your* fault. You brought us out here, and because you couldn't be trusted to protect Gabriel, I was nearly killed. You're no better than your father—worse, since he at least *saved* my sister instead of sending one of us to our potential demise."

"I didn't—" Lexios started, but Gabriel stepped between us.

"Are you serious right now?" he said with pointed anger. "This isn't his fault."

"Of course, it is," I replied through teeth that were gritted in pain. "He's always been like this—any chance to undermine me, to take away the things I care about. He wants you, Gabriel, and he was willing to lead me to my death to make it happen."

"Olympio," Lexios interjected. "I would never—"

"You don't speak!" I shouted, doubling over in agony once more. "You'll be lucky if I let you through the palace gates... traitor."

To my surprise, Gryfian put a hand on Lexios's shoulder. "Come on," he commanded, gripping it forcefully before bowing his head to me and escorting my nemesis away.

My eyes went to Gabriel, expecting him to be hurt, maybe even worried, but instead, I only found rage there.

"How dare you?" he growled at me. "You promised me."

"I promised I would give him a chance, and he took that chance and impaled it with a spear. It was almost you, Gabriel! What if it had been *you*? What if I lost you because he and his damn father are too power hungry for their own good?"

"He's not," he shouted, hauling off and kicking a large rock near him. "You stupid bastard."

I had never, in our whole time together, even after I kidnapped him, felt him this angry with me, and for a moment, it felt almost like a rip formed in the bond.

"How can you not see him for what he is?" I asked, the rift between us hurting even more than the spear had. "Why don't you understand that he's not who he pretends to be? You're too young, too naive to know how people like him can be."

"Oh, fuck you," Gabriel hissed back, stomping past me while continuing to scream at me. "Fucking wise Olympio, king of the fucking world, knows everything except how to act like a *person*." Then he stopped, spun where he stood, and dropped to his knee. "My deepest apologies, *Your Majesty*. May I have my leave?" His tone was irreverent at best, cutting at worst. He wanted to hurt me, and it worked.

"Gabriel..." I said, reaching for him from where I still remained kneeling. The adrenaline of the fight was beginning to fade, and the venom my soulmate was directing at me had taken root in my very soul. "You didn't... this isn't *your* fault. I'm sorry for—"

"My apologies, Your Majesty. Is this conversation an order? I understand, as your lowly concubine, that I serve you and only you. That my purpose is your pleasure. But if you don't mind, it's making me sick to look at your stupid face right now, and I'd like to leave."

Is that truly how he felt? That he was nothing more than something for me to use, to have at my disposal? I couldn't even begin to fathom why he could feel that way, when I thought I had always showed him just how much he meant to me, how deeply I loved him.

"You can't... leave..." I panted, the physical and emotional pain at war for which would be the one to take me down, once and for all. "There could be more. We need to stay together. We need to get to the carriage. I need... I need *you*, Gabriel."

"Gryfian!" he shouted into the woods. "Your master needs you."

And with that, Gabriel, *my* Gabriel, turned his back on me and walked away.

Gryfian took his place at my side, trying to lift me to my feet, but my body had gone slack.

"Your Majesty," my trusted guard and friend said. "We need to go."

"What have I done, Gryfian?" I said, my voice hollow. "What have I done?"

Chapter Twenty-Seven
Gabriel

The carriage was dead silent as it moved through the woods, which was unnerving since we were going through pretty thick foliage. Without his permission, I had Uno-reversed Ollie and put *him* to sleep, which, in turn, seemed to allow Gryf to relax enough to at least close his eyes—though I wasn't convinced he was actually sleeping.

"I'm sorry he spoke to you like that," I said to Lex, who was tending to some of his own wounds. "Unfortunately, as his *consort*, there's not much I can do besides refuse to speak to him or withhold sex or whatever fighting couples do." I looked at my soulmate and deflated a little inside. We had made such good progress.

"Don't worry about it," Lex said sadly, shaking his head. "I should have known it would never be that easy."

God, I wanted to pummel Ollie, and at the same time, I was desperately worried about him. I hadn't ever seen him lash out at someone like that, and after the other night, I really thought we were past this.

There was uncomfortable silence between us as I fought the desire to touch him in a comforting way. But, as I reminded myself, we had eternity to make this right. Maybe it would take a decade or a century—but I was sure that, eventually, Olympio would come around.

It took a full day to get back to the palace, and I spent most of the time reading and playing with Betty. When we arrived, I finally released the sleep effect on Olympio, and Gryfian helped him to our chambers. I didn't head for that wing of the palace, instead choosing to head out to the orchards on my lymere, Onyx.

I could feel Olympio's heart calling out to me as I sat beneath the tree we'd once cuddled under together. It was also the tree he'd once been stabbed under, the tree I'd made the decision to stay in Sefaera beneath.

I heard a few branches crack from behind me and turned, expecting to see Lexios, but instead found Liro.

"Did he send you to hunt me down?" I grumbled.

"No," he said, sitting down beside me. "I was just on my rounds, since Ari's back at home with the baby, and I saw you riding this way. Didn't know why you were all the way out here, so I figured I'd check on you."

"Avoiding his royal pain in my ass," I said without an ounce of effort to conceal how annoyed I was. "How have you put up with him this long?"

Liro snorted softly before leaning back against the tree. "Truthfully? I felt the same way for a long time. But when I became Ariadne's personal guard, and I was forced to spend more time with him by default, I realized he's just... a bit slow when it comes to personal interactions."

"Slow is right. Every time I feel like we're making progress, he shows me just how big a backslide can get from one man. Sometimes I wonder if I made the right choice staying."

As soon as I said it, I wished I could take it back. There wasn't a single day with Ollie that went by that I thought I'd have been better in my world, in Gaiada, than here. This was my home now.

"I didn't... I just feel like we need some space. Please tell me that's not a weird thing to feel."

"Your secret's safe with me," he said. "And if it's weird, then I'm weird, too. Believe me, there have been plenty of times over the years when Ari has gotten so stubborn over things that I wondered if I made a mistake blood-bonding myself to her. But... I love her. And that means, sometimes, accepting the imperfections, because the good parts are worth the less good parts."

A breeze blew through the orchard, cool against the warmth of the air, filling my senses with raquin and oulon and the dozen other fruits that grew here. The leaves rustled like little whispers, and I flashed back to that moment two years ago when my heart hadn't doubted for a moment where I wanted to be.

"*Are you happy?*" he'd asked. "*Right now. Here, like this, with me. Are you happy?*"

"*Very,*" I replied. "*Almost like I never had a perfect day 'til this one.*"

"Thanks, Liro," I sighed, reaching out my hand to take his. "You're kind of amazing, you know? You do all you do without ever getting an ounce of praise or recognition, and you always put everyone else first. I bet you're gonna be a great dad."

He shook my hand and smiled. "I have the best life I could have ever hoped for," he said. "I have the love of my perfect match, my dream job, and a family who accepts me as one of their own. I'm not saying you need to feel the same, but for me, that's more than enough of a reward for my service."

I watched as he got to his feet and looked out into the distance toward the river and mountains, past the orchards, past the falls, out to the sea. And suddenly, it hit me just how unfathomable life really was. I lived in my world, with my reality, without ever knowing these people who would come to mean so much to me existed. And now, my life was intended to be spent keeping people like Liro, and those who attacked us, and Mal and her people safe. Forever. Without prejudice and with consideration for all, even those I hadn't met yet or maybe ever would.

"I'll meet you back at the palace," I said to him as he leaned down to offer me a hand up. "Gotta meet my new niece."

"Nephew, actually." he replied with a grin. "Vasileios."

"Really?" I asked, happy that he was happy. "Congrats, man. That's amazing."

"He really is. I have a bit more to do out here before I return to check on that creature you found. What was it called again?"

"Jaguar," I said with a challenging look at him. "You're building quite the collection, young man."

He matched my laughter with his own. "All I ever dreamed of," he said before whistling. A few seconds later, a cat the size of your average beagle came trotting toward us from the treeline. "This is Tasos, my lynx."

I eyed the creature nervously, being very fucking aware how deadly it could be. "Good boy," I apprehensively chuckled as it smashed its face into my palm. "You're actually insane."

He shrugged and picked the lynx up, cuddling with it while it emitted purrs like a motorcycle engine. "You'd have to be insane to be a part of the Sefaeran royal family. The sooner you accept it, the more fun you can have with it." He set Tasos on the ground. "Tell Ari I'll be back soon."

He climbed onto his lymere, which was tied to the fence, and took off at a trot, Tasos following like a golden retriever rather than a wildcat.

I was left alone once more to really contemplate how I wanted to deal with this situation. Olympio was wrong, so wrong, to have treated Lexios like that, and I was determined now more than ever to take care of this friendship that I had forged on my own, just as me.

But I could also respect there was a long history of hurt feelings there, and I wanted my soulmate to feel like I was empathetic to that.

I couldn't have been sitting there for more than ten minutes when another pair of footsteps crunched toward me, and I looked up to find Lex standing there.

"Hey," I said with a sigh.

"Should I go?" he replied. "I don't want to make things worse for you."

"No," I grumbled. "Sit."

He did, keeping a wholly respectful distance, his back against the same tree as mine with only our shoulders touching. "Only one more week," he said without emotion, referring to his Union.

"Sure is," I confirmed to him. "Are you ready?"

He scoffed. "Can anyone ever be ready to spend the rest of your life with someone who you barely know and who you didn't choose?"

The air settled between us, and I could physically feel him realize who he'd just said that to.

"I certainly wasn't." I picked up a leaf and spun it in my fingers, thinking about how many hours I'd spent crying over having to be soulmates with Ollie. "But maybe it will turn out okay for you, too. Even with all his flaws, Olympio really is damn near perfect for me."

Lex didn't respond to that, but continued to stare straight forward.

"I overheard that he was asking for you," he mumbled. "Passed Gryfian in the hall telling one of your guards. It's why I came looking for you. I figure if I'm going to continue to prove to Olympio I'm on his side, I can't very well let my responsibility as your personal guard lapse."

More silence. An awkward tension that held so many unspoken feelings and so many things I wanted to thank Lexios for that wouldn't have come out in a way that was conducive to keeping this friendship platonic.

Because the truth was...

I loved him.

Not like Ollie—*never* like Ollie. But the love I felt for him was there, nonetheless. And I didnt think that I could say that and not be slightly compelled to want to kiss him.

It was fucking impossible to explain, even to myself. But it wasn't like I wanted to run away with him. Hell, it wasn't even a consideration of wanting to have him as a lover, as he'd once reminded me royals do. But to pretend I felt nothing—it was impossibly hard.

An impossibility that I would go to my grave fighting with, because I would rather have to ignore my feelings than ever make Olympio feel like I wasn't his to the fullest extent. Because if it came down to it, I'd rather never see Lexios again than to hurt Ollie. And I couldn't have been more thankful for the time I would have to figure out how to balance those two things.

"Help me up," I said, nudging him with my shoulder. "I have to go yell at my soulmate and also baby him for being injured."

Lex laughed and pulled me to my feet, and for a moment we were touching hands, a breath apart from each other, and it felt like the world stood still.

Then he gave me a playful shove. I laughed, and we walked over to where our lymeres waited.

Before we mounted, he turned to me and put out his hand, waiting to shake mine. I smiled and took it, a melancholy resolve hanging in the air between us.

"I'm really happy we found each other," he said. "If I hadn't met you, I think I would have spent the rest of my life being distant from everyone outside of my father. And thanks to you, I can now see what a mistake that would have been."

"No problem, man." I patted him on the back and turned away to mount Onyx. "See you tomorrow at the ceremony."

Lexios nodded, "See you then." and rode off towards the city.

I, on the other hand, headed straight for the palace. There was a man who desperately needed me, and I was finally in a place where I could be there for him.

Chapter Twenty-Eight
Olympio

I don't think I'd ever seen Ari as proud as when she walked in, holding her little one. He was still too small to walk, but he was upright and alert in her arms, his eyes meeting mine.

He was a perfect blend of his parents, with tan skin and horns like Liro's, but the copper hair and golden eyes that marked him as one of our family.

"Heard you got yourself stabbed," she said as she sat on the side of my bed.

"Ariadne," my mother said in a gently chiding way.

"What?" she said, kissing her son on the side of his head. "He did."

"Technically," I grunted, sitting up a little, "I was speared. Not stabbed. Though I'm getting a bit tired of being impaled in a general way."

Thankfully, they were followed in by Perla, who immediately got to work, mixing potions and salves for the mild infection that had set in.

"So," Ari said as Perla worked. "What did you find?"

"Other than another creature from Gaiada?" I sighed. "Nothing. None of the portals we visited have any residual magic that could be allowing leaks. There's at least five more, but we have just as much of a problem that needs immediate attention."

"What is it?" Mother asked.

"Prumius," I said. "Did you know that they hate us?"

"What do you mean, they hate us?"

"I didn't end up on the receiving end of a blade because they were welcoming." Perla took the pause in my words to pour some potion down my throat. It tingled and burned a bit, but I felt it move directly into my bloodstream and to the wound. The pain faded swiftly, and I sighed in relief.

"How would we know?" Ari said with just a hint of bitterness. "Lexios would be the one to tell us, and it's not like he stops in that often, since you essentially had him banished without saying so." I was about to argue, but she held up a hand. "I don't think you're wrong to do so. I'm just calling it like I see it."

I nodded. "Well, we may need to keep an eye on them, especially after I killed about half a dozen of them."

"Olympio!" my mother gasped.

"The spear was intended for Gabriel." Just the thought filled me with enough rage to assume my demon form and return to Prumius to finish the job. "If I hadn't pushed him out of the way, he would be dead."

"Where is he?" Ari asked, looking around the room. "I figured he'd be here, especially with you injured."

"He's angry with me." Tears began to form in my eyes. "I lashed out at Lexios after the attack. Told him it was his fault. Called him a traitor. Gabriel... Gabriel has feelings for him, and Lexios isn't exactly subtle about how he feels about Gabriel."

"Do you really think it was Lexios's fault?" Ari asked, already knowing my answer by the look on her face.

I shook my head. "The Prumians didn't want to give us access to the portal, and he found us another way in. It was easy to let my jealousy convince me that he'd done it on purpose, but Gabriel... he's never spoken to me like that. Not even back when he first came here."

"You know I'm no fan of Typhir's rotten little spawn," she said, "but don't you think doubling down on trying to put a wedge between them only makes you the bad guy? If you keep trying to convince Gabe he's no good, all you're going to do is drive them closer together." She paused as Perla finished up and bowed, leaving the room. "Here." Ari handed me the baby. "Vasileios... this is your Uncle Stupid."

My mother let out an exasperated sigh, but I actually laughed. It was amazing to me, even after all this time, how Ari's blunt insults could reach me in a way little else could.

I looked down at the little one in my arms, named for my brother. The one who should have been king. It struck me that it was the first time I'd held a baby in my whole two and a half thousand years. He was bigger than Gabriel had been at birth, but that was part of the magic that had brought this life into the world. He was, at only a few days old, the same as when Gabriel was half a year.

"Hello, Vasileios," I said quietly as he reached up and touched my face. Everything about him was soft, delicate, precious.

He hiccupped, surprising himself, then giggled. I thought that was all there was to it, but then...

"Uh oh," Ari said, sniffing the air. "That might be our cue to go."

Her meaning hit me in full, and I eagerly handed her the baby.

"Thank you for coming," I said to them.

"I'm glad you're doing alright, darling," Mother said, kissing my head.

"Yes," Ari said, already moving toward the door. "And maybe, if you get your head out of your ass, you'll be able to mend things with Gabe, since Perla doesn't have a potion for that."

"Thank you, Ari," I said, grinning slightly as they left.

Once they were gone, however, I was struck by an overwhelming sense of loneliness. It was incredible to me that, after so much of my life had been spent without Gabriel, I now felt empty even being apart from him for a minute. Every fight we had felt like the end of the world, because between those, what we had was perfect in every way.

Almost as if he'd been summoned by my sadness, Gabriel opened the door to our chambers and walked inside.

I sat up straighter, the sight of him like a salve of its own kind, one that healed my heart and soul rather than my body.

"Ollie..." he breathed.

I held out my hand, hoping beyond hope he wasn't too angry with me still to refuse me.

But he ran to my side, throwing his arms around me before seemingly remembering I was injured. "Oh... sorry."

But I held him in place. "No pain is greater than being apart from you," I told him, pulling his face to mine to kiss every inch of it—his lips, cheeks, forehead, even his eyelids. Every inch that was *mine*.

"I'm sorry," he said, looking down at me with his fingers lacing into my hair. "I was a dick."

"No..." I said, shaking my head and wrapping my arms around his waist. "*I* was. I was scared, and hurt, and angry. I know it wasn't his fault, and you were right to tell me I was wrong."

"I was?" His eyes brightened and he looked like he might cry from happiness. "Well, now I feel bad for all those things I said about you to Liro."

"I'm sure they were well-deserved," I said, extracting myself from him and standing to check on my side. Perla had patched it up without so much as a scar, but I was still covered in blood. "I should probably—"

I stumbled before I could say I needed a bath, the wound healed, though the pain and fatigue lingered. But Gabriel was there, keeping me from falling.

"Let's get you cleaned up, Your Majesty," he said with that smile that always made my heart beat just a little bit faster.

I nodded and, for once, let Gabriel care for me. He guided me to the bath, which was, as always, filled with water at the perfect temperature, and undressed me. I climbed down into the water, where Gabriel took the utmost care in washing my hair and body. It was so relaxing that, at some point, I must have fallen asleep because I woke up to Gabriel rubbing my hair with a towel.

"If you get out, sleepyhead, I can dry all of you."

I nodded and stood, but I slipped on the wet floor, once again losing my footing, and again, being caught by Gabriel. This time, however, we both tumbled to the floor.

We were completely intertwined as I looked up at him. He kissed me with a slight laugh, and I was thrilled to join him. But then everything, all of the pain and anger and sadness came rushing back...

And I began to weep.

Chapter Twenty-Nine
Gabriel

The feeling of the marble beneath my hands as I kissed him was such a contrast to the heat burning inside me that it made me shiver. Olympio's tears continued to slide down his cheeks and I leaned in to kiss each one away.

"Please, Gabriel," he begged. "Please, never leave. Please, be mine. I couldn't live if I ever lost you. I won't."

"I'm not going anywhere," I cooed at him, studying his beautiful face. "Never."

I leaned back and pulled him into a sitting position, still kissing him deeply as we scrambled to our feet. Ollie grabbed for my clothes, pulling them off of me as I tugged his towel off of him.

We moved with reckless direction around the room, tossing garments wherever they landed while we inched closer to the balcony in my desire to get my panicked soulmate some fresh air.

By the time we emerged into the night air, both of our bodies were without a scrap of clothes, and I backed Ollie into the railing he had me against a million times and pressed my body into his hard enough that, if wishes came true, we could merge into one.

"Gabriel," he crooned, pressing his lips to mine, over and over, his hands on either side of my face. "You deserve so much better than me, than the way I am. I love you, Gabriel."

"Stop," I begged softly against his neck, giving him one of our special kisses. "You're perfect. If not in general, then at least for me." I wasn't sure what came over me, but I reached around behind him, grabbing his hips and lifting him onto the balcony railing. Despite the fact that he was half a foot taller than me, I'd gained a significant amount of strength. Olympio looked at me with amazement, wrapping his legs around my waist and leaning down to continue kissing me.

I could feel him stiffen against my abdomen, and I groaned with desire. "I want you so fucking badly," I hummed against his skin.

"You have me," he breathed. "All of me. Forever."

I snaked my hand up his thigh and gripped him, relishing in the feeling of the firm softness beneath my touch. Olympio moaned, louder than he usually would, giving me the go ahead to pursue whatever I had in mind.

I dipped my head and took him into my mouth, his hands landing softly on my hair and playing with it. I was sure to keep a firm grip on him to hold him in place where he sat, but the flavor of his skin against my tongue was intoxicating.

"Fuck..." he moaned, hardening even more between my lips, spreading them wider. "Yes... Just like that..."

I moved with intentional slowness, savoring him as I administered pleasure, really drowning in the feeling of him being mine. He played with the hairs at the base of my neck and whispered sweet nothings, and I had never in my life felt more like we were our own cosmos as I did in that moment.

I pulled back and took his hand, pulling him down from the railing and turning him to hold him in my arms. His back against my chest and my length pressed between us made for a sensual daydream where we felt truly equal, and I wrapped my arms around his waist as I pressed a kiss to each freckle on his shoulders.

"Gabriel..." he breathed. "Gabriel..."

I flattened my palm against his lower belly and trailed it south, taking him into my hand and stroking him slowly, deliciously, thoughtfully.

For the first time ever, I heard him whimper, and I could finally understand why the "sweet noises" he said I made would drive him to want to claim me, to mark me, to fill me. It was like a siren's song, and I pressed my hips into him.

Ollie felt my need and put a hand behind his back to grip me, allowing me to pump into his fist as I continued my own task on him.

While it hadn't been my intention to tease either of us, the delicacy of our touches were doing just that, until the balcony was an echo chamber of whimpers, sighs, shuddering gasps and hushed pleading.

"Olympio," I breathed into his skin as I ran my tongue along the side of his neck. "My soulmate... mine..."

"Yours, Gabriel," he said, his hand moving in time with my hips, stroking me harder, faster.

I pulled my hands back from his length and gripped his hip with my left hand while sucking on the fingers of my right one. Then I dropped them to his ass and gently pressed a finger against his opening. Something I'd never done before. "Is this okay?" I asked, trying to sound controlled when I was anything but.

"More than okay," he said, his breath hitching. "I've been wanting to feel you like this for so long."

I pressed forward, and he spread his legs wider, his stance giving me an easier entry. Inside was warm, textured, tight, and I groaned as I tried to stay focused on his pleasure. With deft precision and care, I pressed a second finger inside him, pumping them in and out, the delicious sounds he made absolutely driving me feral with want.

"Fuck!" he cried out. I felt his hole tense and release as I hit the little ridge inside of him, and he came, dripping down onto our feet.

"Oh!" I exclaimed in surprise. "I... Sorry... What happened?"

Ollie turned his head so one of his eyes met mine, and he laughed, his voice still strained with the aftershocks. "I hope I don't... have to explain what an orgasm is... after all this time."

I giggled apprehensively, taking a step back, my rock hard length bouncing as I gave him space. "No, but... that was fast. Why?"

He chuckled again. "I've, uh... always had a bit of a quick release when being penetrated. I thought Vass had told you about that, not that I was too pleased when she did."

"Oh..." I remembered that conversation all at once, remembering how the confession didn't really make sense to me at the time. "Right. Sorry... we can be done."

But he pressed his body back, forcing me to remain with my fingers inside of him. "Why do we have to stop? There's more to pleasure than coming one time. I thought I'd taught you that by now."

I groaned aloud from the seductiveness in his voice, and leaned in to suckle on his neck. "You're fucking incredible, Olympio."

"All I am is only made better for having you in my life," he said, wrapping a hand around the back of my head to hold me there. He whimpered and moaned, rotating his hips forward and back, fucking himself on my fingers.

"Come to bed with me. If I'm gonna take you, I want to do this right."

"Anything you ask is yours," he said. "Lead the way, Your Grace."

I withdrew my fingers and took a napkin to wipe them off before taking his hand and leading him to our bed, kissing him as he fell down on top of it. I reached for his side table, pulling open the drawer in which he kept his jar of lubrication and held it out to him to pour some in his hands.

Olympio held them forward with his fingers cupped and stacked together, and I poured the oils into his hands. "Come closer," he commanded.

Why was I to disobey my king?

He knelt before me and grasped my length with both of his slickened hands, moving them back and forth with long, slow strokes, lubricating me for him.

"Ollie..." I groaned, throwing my head back and melting into his hands. "Oh, fuck, baby..."

"You know," he said, kissing my chest as he continued his motions, "that's the second time I've heard you call me that recently. Why?"

I stopped for a moment and looked down at him. "I dunno. I guess it's pretty common in my world—in Gaiada. Is it... okay? Should I not?"

"As long as it means I'm yours, I want you to call me whatever feels right to you. Because I am—yours, that is."

"Daddy?"

He made a face like he was trying not to react, but the wrinkling of his nose gave away his feelings. "Perhaps not that."

I laughed so hard that I got chills before leaning in to kiss him and then looked down into those gorgeous violet eyes. *My* eyes.

"I'm going to take you now, because I have never, ever wanted you as bad as I do right this second."

"I'm ready," he said, laying back on the pillows and opening his legs for me.

I climbed forward and laid my cock against him, kissing him deeply, breathing the air from his lungs into me. "You're my everything," I groaned, and I gripped the tip of my length to press into him. "I will always be yours."

Then I entered him, and the world burst into fireworks as I felt, for the first time, what being truly inside my soulmate felt like. "Oh, god, Olympio..." I grunted, dizzy with feral desire.

"Yes, Gabriel," he panted, his eyes rolling as I pressed deep. "Moons and rivers... I knew you were big, but feeling you stretch me like this... it brings it to a new level."

"I'm not... hurting you... am I?" I panted, thrusting slowly once more.

"Not... even... a little," he panted, arching his back to urge me even deeper.

I grabbed onto his ankles and gently hoisted his knees over my shoulder, scooting forward, inch by inch touching new depths inside him. "Oh, god," I whimpered. "Does it always feel this good?"

"Every damn time," he said, his eyes fluttering half-closed with pleasure.

Slowly I pulled out before sliding back in, my abdominal muscles screaming as I balanced my whole weight there, passionately fucking him with every fiber of my being.

"I love you so fucking much," I said, leaning into kiss him and forcing his knees to his chest. He wrapped his arms around my neck as he kissed me back, emotion filling his eyes as well.

When it felt as though he was truly relaxed, I began to thrust harder.

"More," he begged. "Please."

I gave him what he asked for, my own whines turning to rumbling grunts as my very breaths themselves began to take on a throaty sound.

"You feel so fucking good," I groaned. "So fucking good, baby. You take me so fucking deep."

His eyes met mine, wide with delight as I praised him the way he always did to me. He reached between us, taking his cock in his hand and stroking himself, matching my rhythm.

In that moment, we felt like one being. Like our bodies had connected in exactly the right way, and the two halves of our souls had become one at last. Ollie's wings flared out across the bed, and my own recognition of this unity, this feeling of oneness, caused the gold and purple sparkling light to not just surround us, but fill the entire, enormous chambers.

The light was so bright that it blotted out every other object around us, leaving just Olympio's radiant, handsome face in my view.

I pressed my body down harder so I was close enough to his shoulder to bite it, and he moaned in my ear as my teeth found their mark.

"Forever," I whimpered.

"Longer," he promised.

And then I was spilling into him, and he was reverberating my sentiment with his own climax, each of us taking on the feelings of the other. No matter how hard this life got, this feeling, this iconic singularity of not-aloneness, would soothe and heal all our wounds.

As soon as I was able to, I withdrew and threw my arms around him, my heart pounding with emotion for this man and for the way he saved me.

"I love you," I panted. "I love you, I love you, I love you. Only you. Always you."

He took me into his arms, kissing my head and twisting so that we were spooned together in the way we typically did. "You are the most precious being that has ever lived, my Gabriel. In this and every other world."

And with that sentiment, all was right again in our world.

Soulmates bound eternally.

**

The Union ceremony was elegant, if not heartwarming, and Lexios smiled like he was happy, whether he truly was or not. I was glad to see my friend resolving some of the loose threads in his life, even if it wasn't precisely how he would have envisioned it. There was something bittersweet in watching him take this step forward, knowing that beneath the regal surface lay more complexities than anyone else in the room could guess. Still, his poise was commendable, and I admired his ability to move through it with grace.

As I sat alone, there was a measure of discomfort that settled in my chest, a soft pressure that came from the subtle stares around the hall. I could feel their eyes on me, likely wondering why their king was not at my side.

Ollie and I had briefly discussed the matter, weighing the delicate balance between public appearances and personal boundaries. Ultimately, we agreed it would be permissible for him to stay away, given that he hadn't yet made amends with Lexios and still wasn't at full strength.

But even without Ollie, the reception was incredible. It was everything one could expect from a Sefaeran gathering, where magic blended seamlessly with sophistication.

The grand hall of the palace had been transformed into a realm of wonder, as though the very walls had come alive to celebrate the occasion. Tall, gilded pillars lined the room, their surfaces swirling with soft, enchanted lights that flickered like distant stars. The ceiling above stretched high, a dome of intricate stained glass, casting vibrant hues across the floor like the shifting colors of a sunset.

The only thing that was missing was the king, my soulmate.

Despite understanding why he would want to sort things out with Lexios in his own time, it felt raw to be here, in a public way, without him on my arm, and it wasn't long before I found myself at the fountain of blue wine.

"I should have known I would find you here," a voice said behind me.

I turned to find Lex, decked out in his finest clothes, crimson and gold and a green laurel on his head that matched his new partner's.

"Well, you know me," I chuckled, dipping a goblet into the imbibement. "Creature of habit."

Lexios reached around me for a glass of his own and nodded. "You certainly are that, aren't you?"

I smiled softly and shrugged. "You looking forward to your wedding night?" I joked, trying to make this conversation normal between us.

But the elephant in the room couldn't be ignored. "He didn't want to come?" Lex asked, looking around and sounding a little off.

I shook my head. "He's still not well," I said, sipping my drink once more to avoid the lie coming through.

"That's bullshit, and we both know it," he said, crossing his arms. "He's still angry at me. For literally nothing."

My cheeks burned with shame. I couldn't deny that it was true, no matter how much I wished I could. Olympio was a slow learner, no matter how much I adored him, and even more so, he was the kind of person that needed time to figure out how he wanted to approach things. "I'm sorry," I said for lack of any other good excuse.

Lexios shook his head and placed a hand on my shoulder. "Come with me, really fast. I want to give you something."

He turned and headed, not for the balconies as I thought he might, but rather to the small room off to the west where the drinks were being served out of.

As soon as we entered, any and all staff made themselves scarce, and I peered at Lexios in confusion when he closed the curtain, cutting us off from the rest of the party. "Is this an assassination attempt?" I asked him, only half-joking as Ollie's many warnings about Lexios came to the surface.

"Hardly," he snorted. "It would be pretty stupid of me to allow the entire party to see me bring you in here if I was about to kill you."

"Fair." I grabbed another drink, this time one of the pink orenum cocktails. Lexios pulled something from the chest of his chiton and walked toward me, looking at the ground. "What's up?" I asked, never having seen him this nervous before.

"Gabe," he said, his voice breaking. "You have been... Well, you've been the best thing that has ever happened to me." He put his hand on my shoulder and looked up into my eyes. "And I have no doubt, since His Majesty is still trying to work through his complicated feelings about me, he will be sure to send me away on a diplomatic mission as soon as he has the strength to give the command."

I wanted to argue with him, to tell him he was wrong, but he wasn't. Ollie was the love of my life, and that gave me the awareness of his strengths and weaknesses. I couldn't deny that he was petty to a fault. "I won't forget you," I said. "If that's what you're worried about."

Lexios studied me a little then said, "Put out your hand."

I did, and he placed into it a small metal cuff that looked like it had been hand hammered. "What is this?" I asked in wonder.

"I... made it. For you. Pieces of metal I've been picking up wherever we've had important moments together. I wanted you to remember that Olympio isn't the only one who cares about your happiness, even if it's in a different way."

My breath knotted in my chest as the metal caught the light of the sun from a nearby stained-glass window. "Lex..."

"You don't have to wear it. I'm not trying to get you in trouble. But I needed you to know, before it's years of separation, that I... I..."

"Lexios..." I begged, knowing exactly what he was about to say. "Please..."

"Fine," he said, softly, taking a step back and sighing. "I won't."

He looked up at me, his eyes welling with tears that I couldn't have ever imagined seeing there, and I stepped forward to hug him.

But in seconds he had also stepped forward to meet me, and his hands went to my face, cupping it on my cheeks and neck, pulling us flush against each other.

And then he was kissing me.

It felt like a ton of metal dropped out of the sky and landed on top of me as my arms, which had gone around him, froze where they were. Heat boiled up in my face as the sensation of the kiss took over my thoughts and my lips parted, allowing him to deepen it without true permission. His hands slid down my back, clutching me above my waist, and he sighed into my mouth with happiness.

"Gabriel…"

The voice was like ice in my veins.

Olympio, my soulmate, was right behind me. Right fucking there, while I was kissing the guy I told him he didn't have to worry about.

I didn't dare turn around, knowing what I would find there, and Lex, too, froze with his forehead against mine.

"Do you have *any* idea what you've done?"

I knew that I would have to face him. I would have to face this catastrophe that I hadn't wanted but hadn't rejected, either. Shame filled me, and in a far delayed reaction, I pushed Lexios away.

That was when I heard Typhir clear his throat.

"Well, Your Majesty," his slimy voice said. "It would seem that my son and your… *soulmate*… have decided to bring Sefaera to ruin."

I turned at last, and what I found there made me drop to my knees. Not only was my soulmate practically evaporating in thick ribbons of shadow, but he had pulled back the curtain which had been separating the two rooms, and a large, horrified crowd of Union guests had gathered there, watching as the son of the Council leader and their Justice shared an intimate moment, believing they were alone.

I tried to speak, but my words caught in my mouth, and I broke down into tears instead. Lexios simply stayed looking at the floor, fear radiating off him, knowing that he'd just set himself up for a repeat of his cousin's fate.

Then, the worst part hit me. It was likely that I would have to precede over the hearing that would make that determination.

I watched as Ollie turned away, dropping the curtain once more. Immediately, I scrambled to my feet, tears pouring down my face, and tore after him.

What had I just allowed to happen?
This would ruin... *everything*.

Chapter Thirty
Olympio

I stopped in the halls, bending over one of the tall vases and vomiting into it, retching over and over.

I had shown up, thinking I could repair some of what I'd broken between Gabriel and me by being a gracious guest to Lexios. By surprising Gabriel with a dance, seeing him smile in my arms, where he belonged.

Instead... I found him in the arms of that bastard, kissing my soulmate, who was kissing him back. And worse... I couldn't even deal with it in private, because the entire court of Sefaera and the leadership of Jouraya had seen it.

I had allowed so many people, Gabriel most of all, to convince me that I was wrong. That I was imagining things. That Lexios was just a friend, that he would never try to drive a wedge between Gabriel and me.

And I had never hated being right more than I did right then.

"Fuck!" I screamed, kicking a second vase and shattering it. I heard footsteps behind me, but I didn't wait to find out who it was. I allowed the shadows that had been threatening to overtake me swallow me, carrying me swiftly to my chambers, where I stood in the center of the room.

I didn't know what to do. I started to pace, but then stopped to hit a wall, splitting the skin at my knuckles and spreading my blood across the marble floor. I walked out to the balcony, but even the fresh air felt like a personal attack.

Nothing... nothing would ever be right again.

And I'd allowed it to happen, because I didn't trust my gut.

I heard a clatter in the hall, and Gryfian loudly said, "No!"

I heard another voice shouting, then some loud knocking on the door. "Olympio, open up. Let me explain."

It wasn't Gabriel at all.

In a swirl of shadows, I was across the room and throwing the door open and dragging the interloper inside.

"Traitor!" I shouted in his face, the words reaching him only one split second before my fist.

He fell to the floor, holding his jaw and looking up at me in a mix of fear and deluded determination. Nothing, not a single thing he could ever say would make this right. He had broken the only thing in my life that had been real and good.

My foot lashed out next, impacting his ribs and making him cough.

"Your Majesty!" Gryfian shouted, trying to intercede, but I wouldn't allow it.

"At your post!" I yelled back before slamming the door in his face.

Lexios was trying to get to his feet, but the second he was upright, I grabbed him by the hair and dragged him out to the balcony.

"You are a traitor," I growled, shadows forming claws at my fingertips. "You have committed treason, more than once."

He looked up at me, his mouth dropping open as the meaning of my words took root.

I hit him again, then lifted him into the air by his throat, taking twenty long, slow steps to the railing and holding Lexios over the edge.

"I told you what I would do if you crossed me. You will never, *ever* go near Gabriel again—I'm making sure of it. Any last words, you unbearable, conniving, treasonous, evil prick?"

"Stop!"

Gabriel.

I turned to look at him slowly. I didn't even know how I was supposed to look at him after what I'd seen. But I forced myself to.

His face dripped sweat, likely from having run the whole way here. He was still Gabriel, but now... I didn't even recognize him as *my* Gabriel. His eyes, the ones that marked him as mine, looked like those of a stranger. His arms, which I could still feel around me, having held someone else the way that should have only been for me. His lips, which had once belonged to me and only me, now defiled by the man whose life I literally held in my hand.

"Why?" I growled.

Gabriel had tears in his eyes, and his arms were around him like he was holding himself. "This isn't you."

"Isn't it?" I asked. "Or do you just want me to spare your *lover?*"

"You're insane," Gabriel spat, his tears finally spilling over. "Everything I ever loved about you is getting eaten away by this jealousy."

I almost laughed, it was so comical. "Tell me I didn't see it, then. Tell me you weren't kissing him."

"No..." Lexios gasped.

"No?" I said, turning back to him. "No, you weren't kissing my soulmate, after telling me you would never come between us?"

"I... I made a poor judgment... Gabriel.... Did.... nothing..."

I heard my soulmate wail and fall to his knees. "I would never betray you, Olympio."

"Then tell me what I saw, Gabriel," I demanded. "Since I clearly have no idea what you were truly doing, if not betraying me."

"I was hugging my friend," he sobbed. "I didn't have time to react before you saw us."

"It's true..." Lexios coughed, trying to pry at my fingers as his breath was restricted. "It was my fault. It was impulsive... It was... goodbye..."

"It certainly fucking was," I growled. "And since it was your fault, I fully expect Justice to pass judgment to rectify the mistake." I looked back at Gabriel again, giving Lexios a small shake to remind them both the predicament he was in. "I believe the punishment for treason is death."

Gabriel collapsed in on himself. "Please, Ollie... please... don't make me do this again..."

And then he began to shake as his eyes glazed over and his crying ceased.

"Help him," Lexios begged.

My head snapped around to him once more before pulling him back and throwing him to the balcony.

"I don't need you to tell me what he needs," I snarled, gripping his clothing at the chest and hauling his face up to mine. "You're finished."

I turned to Gabriel, craving the rush of the anger, but seeing him like this, despondent and trembling, sapped me of my rage.

"Gabriel..." I said, moving to his side, kneeling and placing a hand on his back.

My soulmate screamed and began to flail at me in terror, more terror than I'd ever seen him look at me with. "Don't hurt me," he begged. "Don't hurt me."

My heart broke. The expression had crossed my mind a thousand times for a thousand different reasons, but never before had I experienced the physical pain, the shattering, that the emotional damage could cause.

"I won't," I said quietly, my hands up in a show of surrender. "Gabriel... I won't hurt you."

He came back to me, his eyes clearing, and silent tears fell from his cheeks as he pulled his knees into his chest. "This isn't right, Ollie. This isn't how we do things. Lexios was wrong, he shouldn't have done that. But we don't punish people without a trial. That's how Typhir does it, not us. And the punishment should fit the crime." He shuddered out a breath before looking behind me at his "*friend.*" "Clearly Lord Lexios has made a grave error in judgment to think that I would ever betray my soulmate. To think that I could ever want anyone more than I want you." He looked up at me, his pupils trembling as they tried to entice me to reason. "But this isn't us. This isn't how we rule. And unless you don't want me anymore, I won't stand by as you turn into *his* father."

His words hit me like a boulder as I stared at him. Everything good about me was only there because Gabriel had dug it out of the refuse Vassenia and my own insecurities had buried it under.

But I couldn't allow this grievance to go unpunished.

"You are Justice," I said, looking once more at my fallen foe. "And if you feel he deserves a trial, I won't kill him here and now. But I will remind you, Justice, that the punishment for treason is death. Because I am not like him or his father, I will make a ruling that will allow for you to banish him, as I did with his cousin. But I would be careful about choosing that path, since we both remember what happened when we let *her* off easy.'

Gryfian entered once more. "Your Majesty?" He was waiting for a command.

With my eyes on Gabriel, I said, "Take Lexios to the dungeons. His hearing will be tomorrow, before the leadership of Jouraya leave, so that they can know their humiliation did not go unchecked."

Gryfian took Lexios by the arm, pulling out a pair of shackles and fastening them to his wrists.

"I'm sorry," he said, and I raised my head in order to tell him there was no forgiveness here. But he wasn't looking at me. He was looking at my soulmate who was looking straight back.

I nodded at Gryfian, who dragged Lexios from the room before any more could be said between them.

We were alone then, and I went to the railing, looking out over my kingdom, the one Gabriel had pledged himself to ruling at my side. I was hurt. I was angry. And the trust I once blindly had in him was broken.

"I'll see you in the morning, Gabriel," I said, turning and walking to the door of my chambers. I had no idea where I was going, but I knew I couldn't stay here, couldn't spend the night with the person who held my entire soul in his own, and who had hurt me more than anyone else ever had, even Vassenia.

And it wasn't only my own feelings. The political fallout was going to be incredible, with Gaiadan beasts showing up in Sefaera, and the Gaiadan Justice being infidelious against the king, with a member of court who was supposed to be United with another powerful figure in Sefaera.

I only hoped that we would find a way through this, because right now, I couldn't see how.

Chapter Thirty-One
Gabriel

I woke sick in the morning, feeling the effects of yesterday's events all the way down to my bones. I knew what today would hold, and I wished with every atom of my being that I could disappear into my bed or call in a sick day.

I hadn't even had time to process what happened between me and Lex. The kiss had been sudden and caught me off guard. It had been so different than I'd ever allowed myself to even consider, and I didn't even realize until later that there was no spark there. In fact, in another life, I would have said we should have done it sooner so the curiosity of the tension could have gone away a long time ago.

But it didn't matter now. I had hurt Olympio so deeply that he had turned into someone I didn't recognize, someone who hated me and everything I stood for. Now, nothing would ever be right again, and I had an eternity to look forward to with a man who would never trust me.

Attendants entered and pulled me from my bed, bathing me, dressing me, and occasionally grabbing a bowl for me to be sick in as I tried to numb myself to what I had to do here. To sentence my best friend, the only person who had been brave enough to look past Olympio's insecurities, to exile.

I moved through the morning numb, sitting at the table with my breakfast, not touching a single thing. Then, walking through the palace escorted by Gryfian and Tomos, not making eye contact as they made sure I made it to the Justice Hall.

And then I was sitting down in my seat, next to Olympio, staring down the most populated hearing I'd ever attended, and looking at dozens of eyes filled with loathing.

"I can't do this," I squeaked, trying to whisper to Olympio, who acted like I wasn't even there. "Ollie I'm gonna throw up."

Olympio lifted his hand and snapped his fingers, and Tomos rushed over with a bowl for me to be sick in.

But at that exact moment, the main doors opened and Typhir walked in, Lexios being dragged by two guards behind him. Lex's eyes were red, and it was clear he hadn't slept. Behind him was the woman he had just been joined to, Celaine. She looked angry and heartbroken, certainly not the start to a Union she had imagined.

Lexios looked up at me and Olympio, his expression begging for understanding. Understanding that I was desperate to give him. But Ollie's fingers wrapped around mine and squeezed them with forceful pressure, as if to remind me exactly who owned me.

The room went still as the proceedings began, and all eyes turned to me in waiting. I could hear my own breath echo in the silence, and I tried not to cry.

"Lexios, son of Typhir," Ollie called out from beside me. "You know why you are here, I presume?"

Lex nodded, his eyes dropping to the floor as I'd seen so many prisoners do before him.

"Very well. Let's begin." Olympio stood, taking a single step down from the dais where we were seated, so that he was closer but still above Lexios. "You are here because you have committed treason. You have used your position and title to infiltrate royal circles and have used my soulmate, His Grace, in your attempts to undermine the crown. You have embarrassed me, your Union, His Grace, and all of Sefaera with your actions. You have caused your king physical harm and brought discontent to the entire court. Have you *anything* to say in your defense?"

Lexios lifted his eyes, but made the mistake of looking at me.

"Lexios!" my soulmate snapped. "In your position, do you think it wise to look to the person you used for your own means for comfort or assistance?"

Lex looked back at the floor and began to speak. "We were friends. Just friends, only friends. Indeed, as I confessed to you many times, I found Justice Gabriel enchanting, and clearly I let my feelings take hold of my sense. But I never meant any harm to the crown. I never intended to try to take him from you."

"As if you could..." Olympio growled. "And since, as per your confession, you are unable to use logic in place of your 'feelings,' you have proven yourself to be a danger to the crown, just like your cousin."

A gasp rippled through the crowd, and, at last, Typhir stepped forward.

"Your Majesty, if I may—"

"What could you possibly have to say, Typhir?" Ollie spat. "You were banned from one hearing regarding your family because you were belligerent and disruptive. Don't make me have guards escort you out a second time."

"I have no intention of causing any sort of disturbance, Your Majesty," he said, bowing low. "In fact, I was going to agree with you, that my son has brought shame to both the crown and my family. However... Since none of his actions led to any permanent physical harm, I would only hope to argue in favor of banishment, rather than death. But I will, of course, defer to the ruling of Justice."

All eyes went to me once more, and I felt my heart break. I looked to Olympio, begging him for something, anything that would show me if I got through this, we could be okay again.

But his eyes remained guarded and cold, refusing to meet mine. "Your request will be considered," he said to Typhir. "Does anyone else have anything to say before Justice makes his ruling?"

"I would like to say something," I said, suddenly imbued with the awareness that this might be my one and only chance to reclaim the favor of my people. "You all saw what happened. I won't insult your intelligence by denying it. But it wasn't what it appeared to be. If anything, I would hope this event would serve as a cautionary tale on the harms of how much we as a people choose to fill our time with liquors and other things that can alter our decisions. Lord—Lexios was trying to bid me farewell before returning to his responsibilities as a diplomatic emissary, but because we had both partaken in too much to drink, affection and intent were skewed." I turned to Ollie specifically for the next part. "No one was trying to hurt anyone. Wires were simply crossed, and I felt... nothing." The last part was said to Lexios, who trembled where he stood.

"Nor I, Your Grace."

I searched his face for truth and as I suspected, his eyes betrayed him. Unfortunately, Olympio saw it, too.

"I believe it's time for sentencing, *Your Grace*," he said in a flat voice that couldn't hide the rage I felt from him.

"Right," I breathed. "Then... Lexios, son of Typhir. For the crime of... treason, I banish you from the capital for as long as you draw breath."

The crowd erupted, mostly the Jourayans, with applause as though they'd been watching a cage match, and I had to excuse myself at my disgust. I painstakingly pushed past Olympio and Gryfian, then sprinted down the halls, dropping my ceremonial garments behind me.

I thought about going to our room but instead, made a quick turn at the entrance and bolted through the front doors, straight for the stables where I could retrieve my lymere.

Shaking sobs ripped through me, and I couldn't help but to scream as my heart broke. It broke for me, for Lex, but most of all for what might have been—a friendship I'd been dreaming of and the love I'd been holding so close to me, now ruined in one stupid, impulsive moment.

This was my life now. A life of distrust and heartache, of loneliness and isolation.

The exact thing I'd been trying to escape when Olympio first spoke to me.

Chapter Thirty-Two
Olympio

"Fuck!"

I kicked at a plaster post as I screamed into the openness of the menagerie. I was alone with the animals, all of which startled at my outburst.

I sank to the floor against one of the glass enclosures. I'd come directly from the hearing, hoping it would help, that seeing the animals, feeding them, might be enough of a task to free my mind. But all it served to do was give my hands something to do while my mind screamed at me.

I should have helped Gabriel. I should have held his hand and told him I could *feel* that the kiss had meant nothing, that I was there for him and always would be. That even though Lexios had proven himself untrustworthy, it wasn't a reflection on Gabriel.

But instead, I'd been cold to him, made him face it alone. One more promise broken, that he wouldn't have to face the painful parts of life alone ever again. I'd been right beside him, and still, he was *alone*.

"Your Majesty."

Typhir's voice came from behind me, and I turned to see him striding through the doors of the menagerie.

"Get out," I said. "I have nothing to say to you."

"Perhaps not," he drawled. "But a conversation needs to occur, nonetheless."

"Shouldn't you be saying goodbye to your son?" I hissed.

"Already done," he said, a slight curl to his lip. "He was always useless. At least his cousin had ambition. Lexios could never see past what his cock wanted to make intelligent choices."

I snorted harshly, but guilt gnawed at me. "Was it too much?" I asked Typhir. He'd ruled with an iron fist as Justice, but he also tended to have a soft spot for his family.

"Hardly," he said. "Of course, you only addressed... half of the issue."

"What do you mean?" I could tell what he was hinting at but wanted to give him the chance to change tactics, since down this road lay nothing good for him.

"I mean, Your Majesty, that His Grace was caught with my son as much as my son was caught with him. And yet, only one party received punishment for it."

I turned to face him, walking slowly toward him, forcing him to back up until he was pressed against one of the cages.

"Be careful what you say next, Typhir," I growled, the shadows that I'd been holding back all day swirling around my finger like smoke as I pressed it into his chest. "I can only stay my hand so many times in a week."

But he looked at me wholly unbothered as he said. "If stating that a guilty party should receive the same punishment as the other involved is grounds for execution, then I would fear what other kinds of tyranny exist in King Olympio's Sefaera."

I stepped back from him and turned around, petting a meerad to try to avoid his eyes. "It's not tyranny."

"It's favoritism, Your Majesty," he said, and I turned to see him adjusting his chiton and cape, fingers brushing over the brooch I'd given him just a couple of weeks earlier. "But I suppose it's up to you how you choose to deal with your soulmate. I only hope that your people see it the way you do. Otherwise, Prumius may not be the only place where discontent exists."

"Thank you, Typhir," I said, firmly indicating the conversation was over.

He gave me a hint of a smile, as if he knew something I didn't, then turned and left.

I gave the meerad another scratch on the head before collapsing to my knees once more.

Even in my deepest rage, I'd never wanted to lose Gabriel. He was mine, and I was his. But Typhir was right about one thing: I couldn't risk rebellion, especially not because of a stupid mistake on Gabriel's part, because he trusted the wrong person.

I buried my face in my hands, seeing him kissing Lexios over and over, just like I had for the last day, every time I closed my eyes. Would this be what the kingdom thought of every time they thought of Gabriel now? Would *I*?

I looked out over the grounds of the palace and toward the forest, where I saw a lone lymere—unique in its black and white coloration, so different from the other rainbow-hued beasts.

Onyx.

Gabriel.

Where he was going, I didn't know. But I knew that I had decisions to make before he came back.

And none of them would be easy.

Chapter Thirty-Three
Gabriel

I awoke near twilight to Ollie touching my shoulder to wake me before lifting me into his arms. I'd fallen asleep in the orchard, right beneath our tree. I think there was a part of me that would hope that being there would be enough for him to find me, but I wasn't really sure.

"Ollie," I began to cry. "I'm so, so sorry. Please don't let everything be ruined."

Olympio didn't speak, but rather looked down at me calmly, carrying me back toward the palace.

"Onyx..."

"Will be retrieved later," he said, his tone low and soft. "I need to show you something."

Beautiful little blue glowing bugs surrounded us as Olympio carried me, and my heart lightened a little at how tightly his fingers gripped me. Protective, possessive, so purely Olympio.

I could tell things were still off between us, because our bond didn't sing in my chest like usual, but maybe this was a sign that he was willing to take the first step to fix what had been broken. Like he said, every day it would hurt a little less.

The fire wouldn't burn every night.

My throat was sore from crying, and I tucked my face into his neck, holding tight to him as we moved, needing to know that he was there, needing to feel him.

We approached the palace but instead of going inside, Olympio took a turn for a back set of stairs that led to a balcony we'd used a time or two to get up into the clouds. Only a time or two, though, because he knew I hated to go up there.

"What are we doing?" I asked softly, closing my eyes as he took the first jump onto a cloud.

"I told you," he said. "I want to show you something."

There was something about the tone in his voice that I didn't like, and I laced my fingers into the back of his hair. "Ollie, you're scaring me."

He jumped to another cloud then looked down at me. "There is nothing to be scared of, Gabriel. I would never drop you."

I smiled a little at his recognition of my fears and kissed some bare skin on his arm. "Well after all that, I wasn't so sure."

"I didn't kill Lexios. Why would I kill you if I was willing to let *him* live?"

It was a reasonable question, and yet, something still felt horribly wrong. "I'm sorry I disappointed you," I said, hoping my apology would spark one of his own. "Sorry that I didn't shove him away." I was painfully aware that even as I said this, I was wearing the cuff he gave me. A friendship that I would miss for a long, long time.

But he remained silent, not saying a single word as he leaped from cloud to cloud.

When we reached the final landing, the one he'd once tried to convince me was a great place to have a picnic or relax for an afternoon, I anticipated him setting me down, but he didn't. "So, what's the surprise?" I asked.

He nodded toward the mountain in the middle of the cloud, the one that he'd created a portal on top of to take us to our adjournment, where he'd brought me through to Sefaera.

"It's up there."

He continued to climb, the air growing thinner and thinner, until we reached the flat area near the peak.

Confusion filled me. Was he here to show me what would happen to me if I ever failed to heed his warnings again? And suddenly all my hopes of reconciliation vanished, panic shoving aside any confusion that had existed. "Ollie, please. You don't have to do this."

"And you didn't have to kiss Lexios," he said coldly, the bond feeling as distant and empty as it ever had, like he'd managed to put thousands of miles between us without moving an inch. "But you've proven to be a liability to my reign and an embarrassment to my family."

I struggled against his grip now, fear coursing through me. "I get it, okay? I understand I fucked up. I swear I will spend the next hundred years apologizing. This is totally unneeded. You don't have to threaten me. I will behave, I promise."

"And I might have believed you before," he said, waving his hand, creating a void of shadows that slowly began to grow into a portal. "But I saw the look between you at the hearing."

I turned to look at the void, and then back to the love of my life. "Olympio..." I said, my throat drying. "What are you doing?"

"You never really wanted to come here, anyway," he said. "I'm simply giving you what you wanted."

"No," I moaned in emotional agony. "Ollie, no. I want you, I want us, our kingdom. Don't do this..."

"Enjoy your life back *home*," he said. "I'm certain you'll find there what I couldn't give you here."

"*Olympio*," I screamed, falling to my knees. "Olympio... no. Fuck no. I'm not leaving you. I'd rather die than leave you."

"I suppose that's your choice," he said. Then, with both his hands on my shoulders, he shoved me backward.

I stumbled backward, tripping so that I landed on my hands, backing away from him slowly. "Tell me what to do," I sobbed. "Ollie... baby... Please, god, please... Tell me what to do to stop this. I love you." I got to my feet, my adrenaline going so fast my vision blurred as I tried to lunge at him and kiss him.

But he caught me by the wrists and grappled me into a vice-like hold, dragging me, kicking and screaming, to the portal.

"You've been nothing but a problem since you arrived," he growled. "And that problem needs to end... now."

"Ollie," I said, turning in his arms. "Wait." I dug my fingers into his beautiful sunset curls and gazed deep into his eyes.

My eyes.

And then he shoved me hard through the portal.

And Sefaera slipped out of my reach forever.

Chapter Thirty-Four
Olympio

I paced my chambers, the moons shining through the windows to illuminate my steps. The anxiety was overwhelming as I waited for any news—any word. Betty was curled up in my arms, seeming to realize that something was wrong by the way she whimpered instead of trilling like she did when she was happy.

Gryfian had given the order for the entire city to be searched. It had been hours, and still, Gabriel hadn't returned. I hadn't felt the bond sear with the pain that would indicate he was in danger, but it felt like he was a million miles away, his feelings only just barely discernible to me for the first time in his entire life. I couldn't even visualize where he was or figure out what direction to go to find him.

Finally, shortly before midnight, a knock came at my door, and Gryfian entered.

"Anything?" I asked frantically, setting Betty on the bed. "Has anyone seen him?"

"I'm not sure, Your Majesty, but... you have a visitor."

"A fucking visitor?" I said, incredulous that he would allow anyone other than my soulmate to come in here until he was found.

"He says it's about His Grace."

"He?" I repeated, dreading the answer. I hoped beyond hope it would be Liro.

"Lord Typhir," Gryfian said, confirming my fears.

"Have him tell you what he came to say. I can speak to him after Gabriel is found."

Gryfian sighed. "He's rather insistent that he needs to speak to you *now*."

"Fine!" I shouted, throwing my hands in the air. "It's not like there's anything I can do right now, anyway. All I can do is wonder where the fuck Gabriel went and why."

Gryfian acted like he had something he wanted to say, but instead, he nodded, then opened the door for Typhir to enter.

"Your Majesty," he said in an overly solemn voice, bowing. I had no idea what he could have to say that was so urgent, since he shouldn't even know that there was anything amiss. My orders had been clear—no one but the guards searching for him should know Gabriel was missing.

"Say what you must," I said, throwing myself haphazardly onto my chaise and waiting for him to speak.

He took his time, toying with a scroll of parchment in his hands. "Your Majesty, I... I was just at the stables, paying a visit to my lymere, when His Grace's mount returned."

"He's here?" I said, jumping back to my feet. "Where?" I looked around as if Gabriel was hiding in plain sight, ready to jump out and tell me it had all been a ruse.

"He... he wasn't with his mount, Your Majesty." Typhir had never been one to mince words or to delay things he felt to be important, so his hesitation worried me as much as anything else. "The lymere returned with only its saddle and... this."

He handed the scroll to me. The seal was broken.

"You opened this. You read it," I accused.

"Yes, Your Majesty, and I hate to be the bearer of what's inside, but you must have it."

I reached out and took the parchment, opening it so that I could read what it said.

It was Gabriel's handwriting, but the words...

Olympio,

While I am forever grateful to you for showing me your world, the events of the last few weeks have shown me that this is not the life I envisioned for myself. I was never cut out to be royalty, and I don't want to be a burden to you or your reign. I will always love you, but I need to return to my world. It's where I belong, and you belong in Sefaera, as its king. I've found a way home, and I'm taking it. Goodbye, Olympio.

—Gabe

I stared at the page, reading the words over and over, each part of the brief, blunt message hitting me like a hammer.

He was gone. Gabriel was gone. He'd found a way back to Gaiada, and he left. Left the palace. Left Sefaera.

Left *me*.

I'd always known I wasn't worthy of someone like him, but he'd never left me doubting the connection between us was real. He finally realized as much as I did that he was better off without someone as broken as me holding him back from the life he deserved.

I don't know how long I screamed for or when I even started, but when my voice finally burned out, Typhir was gone, and in his place was Gryfian, his arms around me as I lay on the floor.

"He's gone," I choked out, my voice hoarse. "He... he's gone!"

"We'll figure this out, Your Majesty," Gryfian said, though my own despair echoed in his voice, and Betty wailed from the bed as if she understood that her master had left her behind.

"No," I sobbed, though I'd already run out of tears to cry. "We won't."

And as my friend tried his best to soothe me, I truly didn't know which of us was right.

Chapter Thirty-Five
Gabe

Anguish.

Blind rage and emotional pain like I'd never felt before. If my parents' death was numb, this was a burning fire, consuming me whole, like a pack of rabid dogs tearing at my flesh.

I couldn't think or breathe, and it took me several long minutes to realize where I was.

Columbia.

Ollie had sent me to Columbia.

Fucking *Columbia*.

It was night, and the breeze was chilly. I stood, getting off my hands and knees, realizing I was across the street from fraternity row. I caught sight of my reflection in a car window as I did and wanted to collapse all over again.

I still looked like me. Shaggy hair tousled in the way that the erula water always seemed to cause it to do, the fabric of my garments still draped where they'd been placed this morning. But here... Columbia—the streets of Manhattan in general—looked more like another planet than I had ever remembered it doing before.

Then I noticed the worst part of this whole deal.

I could still feel him—my supposed soulmate.

My kidnapper.

My tormentor.

My betrayer.

Ollie's heart was pounding, but I couldn't tell for the life of me why. My mind raced with all the possibilities, and my stomach clenched in a way that had me vomiting my breakfast across the pavement outside the gated steps to the university in seconds.

He didn't want me.

He didn't believe me.

The city smelled more foul than anything I'd been exposed to in two years, and my heart thudded with homesickness. I suddenly realized how little this had ever truly felt like that—almost as if my heart knew where it belonged.

Not that it mattered now.

I sank back down onto my knees and felt the pavement dig in as the skin hit. I had no reason to live anymore. I had no one.

"Hoffstet?"

It took me a few seconds to recognize that name as meaning me, but when I did, I looked up to find someone watching me from across the street. A blond, athletic someone whose face had left my mind but whose name had never left my lips.

"Oh, my god, Gabe," Alex said, rushing to where I'd decided to allow my body to take root in the ground. "Dude. Everyone thought that creepy Ollie guy murdered you."

Ollie.

Ollie.

It had been years since anyone besides me had said it, and now it was like a knife in my brain. I tried to muster words, but I only shook my head, tears pouring from me as I realized for the first time...

This was real.

This was happening.

And I would never see my soulmate again.

"Oh... baby..." Alex cooed, crouching down beside me and putting his arms around me. "Don't cry. We can call the cops—"

"No!" I gasped. "No cops. Just... I'm not ready to... to..."

Alex nodded without me needing to explain and helped me to my feet. "You must be freezing," he said, pulling off his hoodie and slipping it on over my head. "Come on. I've got a place a few blocks over. Do you want me to call a cab?"

I tried to shake my head no, but I couldn't seem to convince my body that we were still attached to one another. "I can walk," I choked out in a monotone sigh.

We began to move, and Alex tucked his arm around my shoulders in a protective, possessive way that he'd never once bothered with before I left—when I still wanted him.

Before...

In what felt like no time at all, I found myself standing in the entryway of a gorgeous townhouse, and Alex pulled me against his chest.

"I never thought I'd see you again, man... Gabriel." The name choice hit me hard. He had never once called me Gabriel. No one had ever called me that besides my parents and Ollie. "Where the fuck have you been?"

He grabbed my chin and gently tipped it up so he could look me in the eyes, and for a moment, just a moment, I could have sworn I saw Ollie there.

And then my world crumbled in on me, and right there in Alex Kessinger's upscale townhouse, Gabriel, Justice of Sefaera, the king's consort, His Grace—

Ceased to exist.

And like Ollie's shadows themselves swept through my body with a maniacal force, I vowed that I would spend every waking moment I lived—for my now very, very long life, trying to forget the one person I would never be able to.

I looked Alex Kessinger in the eye and threw him a smile I had never in my life felt less.

"Who cares?" I coughed in an unnatural, forced cantor. "Take me to your bed."

"Promise we can talk about it tomorrow?"

"Guarantee it."

"Then you don't have to ask me twice."

BONUS CONTENT PREVIOUSLY ONLY
AVAILABLE IN THE PROUD ANTHOLOGY

Gryfian

ELEANOR ROSE
AUGUST OLIVER
CHASE ST. CLARE

Finch Benson
Publishing

"This way."

My hands shook as they guided me through the halls. I'd spent my life thus far in the city around the palace, seeing it from the outside, but never dreaming I'd enter its walls.

And certainly not for this reason.

I could tell my father wasn't pleased, but when the prince, himself, sends for you, having seen you in the market, you don't refuse.

"Why, um... Why has the prince sent for me?"

I'd asked the question no less than five times since they came to my home. My parents seemed to know something I didn't, but neither they nor the guards would answer me.

The smell of erula blossoms wafted in from the courtyard. Outside the palace, they only bloom a few weeks out of the year, and it had been months since they were in season. Here, it seemed, whatever enchantments were on the palace allowed them to share their fragrance all the time.

It took nearly an hour of walking from the gates to my destination, until, finally, I stood outside a grand pair of doors, white with gold embellishments. As the child of poor merchants, these doors alone were likely worth more than anything I'd ever touched in my life.

The guard to my left stopped at the door and gripped the handle as the one on my right mirrored the motion. I stood back as they swung them toward me, opening them into a room that was even more opulent than the doors, more than anything else I'd seen thus far.

The floor was a shimmering, pearlescent white marble that almost seemed to undulate beneath my feet. Golden gossamer curtains covered the half dozen windows that stretched to the ceiling, which stood higher than my entire house. The right wall was dominated by a golden tub set into the floor that had a layer of swirling steam sitting atop the aquamarine water. And the left...

In the center of the left wall was the largest bed I'd ever seen, massive gold posts on each corner and the same gold curtains that graced the windows. And in the center of the iridescent white comforter was...

"Your Highness," I gasped, sinking to one knee and dropping my head instantly. I hadn't expected to see Prince Olympio lounging so casually, his shining copper hair spread out on the pillows, one hand behind his neck and the other holding a deep red leather-bound tome.

And he was naked, his perfect form on full display.

I'd seen him from afar, but this, being only a couple dozen feet from him, in his own chambers, without a stitch of clothing on...

It was like staring into the sun.

My eyes remained on the glistening floor, even as I heard him slide from the bed and make his way over to me. I didn't even look up when I saw his feet just before me, his tanned, well-muscled legs stretching up toward...

I forced my eyes to remain on the floor, the gesture equal in deference and in fear for what I would see if I looked up.

"Welcome. I'm glad you came."

I'd never heard him speak before. Prince Vasileios had made speeches since His Majesty, the king died, and his voice was smooth and powerful, like deep, rich honey. Prince Olympio's voice, on the other hand, was still deep, but was rougher, like the burn of potent liquor and sounded like bottled laughter, as though he was perpetually amused. Or perhaps that was just my perception, since he was well known for his... various exploits.

"Of course, Your Highness," I said, as though I'd been given any kind of choice. "It's an honor to be in your presence."

And then he did laugh, and the sound was so genuine that I was taken aback, and my eyes shot up to find him grinning at me, extending a hand as though to help me to my feet. My eyes flicked downward for just a second to take in his nude form, causing a jolt in my chest.

"That's a matter for debate," he said. "Many would agree with you, though I believe just as many more would disagree. Come."

I placed my hand in his and stood, but as he stared into my eyes, I found myself unable to hold his gaze. I looked back down, which I regretted immediately when the prince said, "Can't take your eyes off of it?"

I hadn't been looking at his cock, but he seemed to think so.

"No, Your Highness," I stammered, looking back up at his face.

He grinned again and tugged at my hand, guiding me over to a divan, where he immediately laid back, lounging casually as he left me standing. "First... what's your name, boy?"

Hearing him call me "boy" sent a flutter of delight through me, and I stood just a little straighter. "Gryfian, Your Highness."

"And you know why you're here?" The set of his brow was almost a challenge, as though I should know, and by being here, I was taking him up on it.

"Well... um... no, Your Highness," I admitted, my palms beginning to sweat slightly as the naked prince stretched out, his eyes moving slowly, hungrily up and down my body. And suddenly, I had a vague idea why I'd been asked here.

He held up a finger and twirled it around. "Turn for me." I began to, but at a sound from him, I paused, realizing I'd done something wrong. "Slower."

I obeyed. Of course, I obeyed. Prince Olympio may have only been the Master of the Hunt, unlike his brother, the future king, but he was still my prince, and I feared what denying him might bring upon me.

Besides... I would be lying if I said I wasn't aware of how much of an honor it was to be here, and how pleased I was at the interest he was taking.

When I finished my rotation, His Highness had stood again and was only inches from me, my eyes at the level of his chin as he looked down at me.

"Beautiful."

He wrapped a hand around my waist and pulled me to him. I could feel every muscle of his body against mine, and his cock was stiffening against my hip.

And then he kissed me.

I gasped into his lips. It was hardly my first kiss, but something about being kissed by a prince, especially one as handsome as Prince Olympio, was enough to make me tremble.

His lips trailed down the sides of my neck, and I let out a whimper as his hands turned me in his arms, so my back was pressed against his chest.

"You're strong," he murmured against my skin, his fingers digging into the muscles of my arms.

"My parents... they own a shop, and I help them with lifting crates of supplies."

"I like it." His hands moved across my chest, covered by the light blue fabric of my tunic, tracing the lines on my chest and abdomen.

"Your Highness..." I breathed. "What... what is... I mean, what are we...?"

He paused, his hands no longer continuing their movements across my body.

"Have you truly no idea?"

I shook my head, and he sighed before leading me over to his bed, where he sat me down and stood before me, studying me. I knew what he saw. Tall, though not nearly as tall as he, with tanned, golden skin, olive-colored hair, and soft orange eyes above high, sculpted cheekbones. An appearance carefully put together by the best enchanter I could afford on the meager allowance I received from my parents.

I also knew what he didn't see. What no one had ever seen, and which no enchanter in the city could change. I know because I'd tried like hell to find one, to no avail.

"You, Gryfian, have been hand chosen by me to be my companion for the night. My usual companion is away on a diplomatic mission, and I'm in need of someone to warm my bed."

The implication of what he was saying finally hit me. Part of me had known all along, but hearing him state it aloud seemed to make it real.

"Your Highness... I don't... I mean, I've never..."

The words wouldn't come, but he seemed to understand. He raised an eyebrow, then gave me a single gentle nod.

"You're a virgin."

I opened my mouth, but no sound came out, and I simply nodded.

He looked long and hard at me, as though trying to figure something out. Finally, he said, "It would be my honor to be your first, but you are not compelled to do anything you are not comfortable with. If you choose to leave now, there will be no repercussions upon you. But... if you choose to stay—"

We were interrupted by the sound of raised voices and crashing sounds outside on the balcony. The prince turned, reaching for a belt hanging on the poster of the bed and pulling forth a shining black sickle.

"Stay here," he said, but before either of us could move, the balcony door burst open, and two masked demons entered, dressed head to toe in black leather, one brandishing a gold sword, and the other holding a bow, and arrow drawn back and aimed at the prince.

"Wrong prince," the one with the bow said to the other.

"Doesn't matter," the other replied. "Orders are clear. The royal line ends here."

There was something surreal about seeing the prince of Sefaera standing before a pair of assassins, fully naked, holding his sickle, and it only got stranger when he smiled.

"I don't think it does," he said.

Before I could even fathom what was happening, His Highness seemed to expand, growing taller and broader, his flesh darkening and beginning to swirl like smoke, and a pair of wings made entirely out of shadow unfurled from his back, spreading wide.

"Do it now!" the swordsman shouted to his fellow, and he released the arrow, but he was too slow.

The shadow that had been the prince moved faster than my eyes could track him, the arrow moving through empty air and ricocheting off of the solid marble wall. Suddenly, he was behind the assassins, a massive, winged creature made entirely of shadow. He grabbed the bow from the one who'd tried to shoot him and spun it so that the bowstring was pressed against the assassin's neck, slowly cutting off his ability to breathe.

The one with the sword faltered, everything happening too quickly for him. But then he turned to Prince Olympio, realizing his comrade was seconds from being garroted to death with his own bow, and he raised his sword.

And the prince wasn't looking.

As fast as I was able, I rushed across the room, grabbing the assassin by the arm, pulling it behind him sharply and at such an angle that he dropped his weapon. The clattering of the metal on marble drew the shadow-beast's attention, and its bright yellow eyes turned to me.

With a twist of the bow and an echoing crack, the archer assassin's neck broke, and then I was surrounded by shadow as the prince grabbed the one I still gripped the wrist of by the throat and lifted him off the ground. Just as quickly, I dove forward, grabbing the sword and turning, driving it through the assassin's heart.

As he went limp, I watched as the shadow beast began to shift and solidify, until Prince Olympio stood before me once more, a slight sheen of sweat glistening in the light of the fireplace. With an approving glance in my direction, he threw the body to the floor next to the other, a splatter of jade-green blood marring the pristine marble. Then, without stopping to put any clothes on, he moved resolutely to the door to his chambers.

"Your Highness, wait!" I cried out, rushing after him, the sword held before me, but he was already through the doorway.

I skidded to a stop to find him approaching two flabbergasted guards. In quick, low voices, he relayed what had happened, and one of the guards turned to leave, prepared to search the palace for other intruders and verify the safety of the other members of the royal family. The other remained still, but Prince Olympio looked at him and said, "Why are you just standing here?"

"Someone needs to guard your room, Your Highness," he answered.

To my surprise, the prince looked at me with a smile. "I think we have things under control here."

The guard looked confused but did as the prince commanded. Then, His Highness walked past me into his chambers, motioning for me to follow. I let the doors shut behind us, then bolted the lock.

When I turned around, he was on his bed, just as he was when I entered, though instead of reading, he was lounging with his hands behind his head, studying me.

"You handled that well," he said appraisingly, nodding toward the sword still in my hand.

"Oh," I said, setting it on the table near the divan. "Well, I had to learn how to fight young. When I was little, someone broke into our shop and stole everything of value. We nearly starved in the weeks after. After that, I took it upon myself to guard our livelihoods, not ever wanting to come that close to such a fate ever again."

"Well, tonight, you saved my life," he said. "And I'd like to reward you."

"I don't need anything, Your Highness," I said quickly before realizing that a gift from the prince could change my entire life.

"Very well, then. You're free to go." He gestured toward the door, but my feet were frozen to the spot. He laughed, realizing I wasn't leaving. "Come here."

My adrenaline was still running high, and my heart pounded as I did as the prince instructed. He patted the bed beside him, and, almost without a thought, I joined him on the luxurious mattress, where he wrapped his arms around me, pulling my back against his chest once more.

"Your Highness..." I said softly, not wanting to insult him. "Shouldn't we wait to make sure your family is safe?"

"Wait for what?" he said, that same tone of laughter surprising me. "Those idiots made it clear that they thought they'd found my brother, and they never made it out of this room. Certainly, others might have gotten in, but I doubt it."

His hands began to move up and down my arms and sides, sending little bumps across my skin. "You said before..."

"That you were free to go, and you are. At any point, you are welcome to tell me to stop, and I will."

I fell silent. From the moment I'd walked in here, I'd wanted him. I'd wanted everything he was offering. But I was terrified he would discover my secret, one that only my parents knew.

"Is this... my reward?" I asked.

He chuckled low in my ear, chills running down my spine. "Is it a reward to do exactly what we were going to do before we were interrupted?"

His hands drifted to my hips, the linen fabric bunching beneath his grip. I'd never had anyone touch me like this, and my body was like a live wire, writhing against him as I felt him harden against my back.

And then his hand moved between my legs, and he paused. "What's this?"

I froze, saying nothing. I knew what he'd found. The reason I'd never been intimate with anyone before. The reason I'd been worried to allow the prince to touch me.

"I..." I shuddered and started to pull away, but Prince Olympio held me tightly and dipped his fingers beneath my garment, running them along the wet slit where he'd been expecting to find a cock.

From childhood, I knew, despite being born female, it never felt right. My body never felt like mine, and I'd done everything I could to make my outsides match my insides.

"I've heard of people like you," he said, finding my throbbing bud and beginning to slowly rub circles around it, making me gasp. "I didn't even realize you weren't a born male."

"No one does," I admitted, my voice breaking as pleasure like I'd never felt coursed through me. "I found enchanters who could make sure that no one would ever know. They changed my face, my body, but they couldn't change..."

"This?" he asked as his finger slid deeper, making me gasp.

"It doesn't bother you?" I gasped, trying to hide how embarrassed I was to be enjoying it so much. "To have been expecting a male, and to instead—"

"I enjoy all kinds of bodies," he said, his lips finding my neck. "The beauty of being attracted to both males and females means I would be perfectly happy to enjoy time with you regardless of your gender and will treat you exactly as you wish to be—like the male you are."

My entire being—mind, body, and soul reacted to him like he, himself, had possessed me, and if his expert touch wasn't enough to commit me to his desires, the way he was treating me was. "Fuck..."

"That is the general idea," he said with a throaty chuckle in my ear, his fingers moving in and out of me in a steady rhythm.

Sounds left my throat that I wasn't even aware I was capable of making and each one seemed to please him immensely. "I... I don't know..." I held up my hand, hoping he understood. I wanted to touch him, too, but how did one pleasure royalty? Hell, I didn't even have experience with pleasuring non-royals.

Prince Olympio moved then, rolling me onto my back and hovering over me. "Here," he said. Then he took my hand and directed it to his fully stiffened member, closing my fingers around it and guiding me in a stroking motion.

Moons and rivers, it was heavenly. I'd never found myself fantasizing about cocks, but the way it felt in my hand was soft, yet structured and easy to maneuver. I looked up into his perfect face and felt a swell of pride as his eyes fluttered, then rolled. "Is this good?" I asked tentatively.

"Incredible," he said, beginning to thrust into my fist as his own hand picked up its pace, striking a spot inside of me that had my gasping with every breath.

Suddenly, a powerful knot formed in a place I'd never realized existed, and as if a singularity formed inside me, I was flung from an emotional, physically overwhelming cliff that left me panting, and my nails digging into the prince's flesh on his side.

"Oh..." I whimpered, the most powerful orgasm of my life rippling through me, leaving me shaking. "That... oh, gods."

"Is the first of many," he filled in the rest of the thought for me before shifting, kissing down along my body until his face was positioned between my thighs.

"Oh, you don't have to—"

"Why wouldn't I want to? You expect me to be presented with a cock unlike any I've ever sampled and expect me to not thoroughly enjoy everything it has to offer?"

Hearing him refer to the parts I was cursed with as a "cock" sent a different kind of pleasure through me, and I became keenly aware of just how lucky I was to have this be my first time.

He gave me a last reassuring look then pressed forward, his fingertips parting the crease before placing his lips firmly against where my member was throbbing. Softly, he opened his lips, and it felt like he made a small "O" shape with them before wrapping his tongue around the underside of the elongated flesh there.

"Fuck," I gasped, my hands going to the soft, sunset hair.

"Yes..." he breathed into my wet flesh.

Then slowly, with purpose, he began to bob up and down, the dexterity of his tongue giving me exactly the feeling of being sucked in a way that any born male would recognize. The groans that rumbled across my skin as he enjoyed himself only heightened the sensation, propelling him, it seemed, into even more vigorous motions.

"So... good..." I groaned.

The rising pleasure his movements brought only grew with every little bob of his head. That singularity from before began to form once more, though it seemed to take root somewhere deeper within me, pulling more of my being into it. I began to whimper, my hands gripping his hair like I would die if he stopped now, and before I even realized it was fully about to happen, I came completely undone, the previous throbbing of my cock exploding in waves of pleasure.

As the prince continued to savor me, my orgasm eventually faded out, and suddenly, it was too much. The sensations had reached a zenith that was almost painful.

A giggle rippled forth as I tried to push him away and he gave the soaked folds a few more playful licks.

"That was—"

But before I could fully elaborate what it was, the prince had grabbed hold of my bicep and flipped me onto my stomach, yanking my thighs apart and examining what he found there with a delighted groan.

"Gods, look at you," he moaned. "You're positively dripping for me." There was a slight pause then, before he said, "At the risk of sounding like an absolute idiot, which of these delicious holes are you wanting me to fill?"

I'd never be able to explain it to anyone, had I ever cared to mention it, but there was a way the prince purred that made you want to give him anything. And that was exactly what I intended to do.

"Whatever hole you want," I whimpered. "I just want you to do it."

He covered my body with his own as he reached past our heads for a jar on the nightstand, and I heard that rumbling growl in my ear.

"Seeing as my usual companion is female, and I want to treat you as the male you are, I think that makes the choice clear."

He opened the jar and began to rub a slick liquid into the crevice of my ass, prodding delicately at my rear opening. My heart raced with anticipation, my fingers now gripping his luxurious bed sheets. "I'm ready," I panted, almost with too much enthusiasm.

He spent the next several minutes using his fingers to slowly open me up for him, and before I knew it, he was pressing the tip of his glorious length into me.

"Fuck, you feel amazing," he said breathlessly as I adjusted to the size and feel of him.

The initial pain quickly gave way to yet another kind of pleasure as he began to slowly move in and out of me, the movements deliberate and controlled, like he was trying to draw the act out as long as he could.

"I'm close," he said, his thrusts becoming just a bit faster, more erratic. "Are you ready?"

"Yes, Your Highness," I gasped. I could still feel the final waves of my last orgasm, and the idea of allowing the prince's fluids to saturate me alongside my own was delicious.

His teeth sank into my shoulder as he pinned me in place and moaned loudly against my skin. The pulsing feeling inside of me was enhanced by the small, slow thrusts as he came, milking every last drop from him. It was a sensation unlike any other, and at that moment, you couldn't have convinced me that I didn't belong right here.

As the prince came down from his climax, he tumbled to the side and pulled me into his arms, kissing the sweat from my brow. It wasn't quite like lovers, but it had a gentle intimacy despite the short time we'd been acquainted. In his care and deliberate respect, even I had all but forgotten that I wasn't a born male.

Several quiet moments passed, and finally, he said, "Now, Gryfian... your reward."

I sat up to look at him, wondering what he could possibly have to offer me. "Your Highness?"

He smiled and rolled out of the bed, making his way over to the table where I'd placed the sword and walked back over to me. For a moment, fear struck me. Surely, he didn't bring me here just to fuck me and then kill me?

But instead of cutting me, he turned it to present me the handle.

"I'd like to offer you a job."

"I'm sorry?" My mouth hung open in shock.

The prince laughed and nodded down toward the sword. "Tonight, when I was attacked, you responded with bravery and haste, and a regard for my life that, truthfully, I do not believe that many of the guards currently employed in the palace would show. I would like you to be my personal assigned guard."

I shifted a bit uncomfortably. I had greatly enjoyed my time with him, and I was glad to have been lucky enough to have him be my first. But...

"You're not hiring me just because you want me to share your bed again, are you?" While not entirely opposed to the idea, since I had clearly enjoyed myself, the truth was that, romantically, I was interested in women. Not to mention, I knew well Prince Olympio's reputation, and even if there was a chance of me falling in love with him, it would only end in heartbreak.

He shrugged with that same playful smile. "It would be hard for you to guard me properly if you were in my bed instead of at your post, though I would call it an occasional perk of the job—but only if you want it. I already have a companion who shares my bed more often than not, so I'm not looking for a paramour. I'm looking for a friend. I have precious few of those, and even fewer who I would trust with my life. In one night of knowing you, you've proven that I can put that kind of trust in you." He moved the sword, clearly indicating I should take it.

"What about my family?" I asked. "Without me, they won't have enough hands to run the shop, and there will be no one there to protect them if someone else breaks in."

"Your family will be taken care of. As my personal guard, I will ensure that your family is financially secure and will personally provide security for their shop." His smile took on a gentler appearance, one more tender than anything I'd seen from him yet, and he took my hand, placing it around the handle of the sword.

I looked around the room, at the luxury I could never have imagined. When I saw Prince Olympio walking through the market that morning, I'd never dreamed I would end up here, being offered the job of a lifetime and the chance to ensure not only my family's survival, but their comfort and safety.

Finally returning his smile, I took the sword and stood.

"Your Highness... it would be my honor."

Acknowledgements

Eleanor:

This, like all my stories, would be impossible without my best friend and soulmate, Nathan. Without you, fantasy wouldn't even be in my periphery.

I'd also like to thank the FB squad. Your understanding and support is the reason we're going to the top.

Karma is the thunder
Rattling your ground
Karma's on your scent like a bounty hunter
Karma's gonna track you down
Step by step from town to town
Sweet like justice, karma is a queen
Karma takes all my friends to the summit

Also, thanks to Fi, you're my other half and I don't even care that we live such a weird fucked up reality because at least I get to do it with you.

To Chase and August, for letting me be part of telling your love story, and Erin, who lets me be my best and worst in cul-du-sac chats.

And as always, I'd like to thank all the other queer fantasy lovers who know that love is love, and the penultimate representation of that doesn't have to be reproduction. You are my people.

Chase:

August, August, August.

August:

To Eleanor,
I don't have to tell you that I wouldn't be here without you. It's because of you that my dreams are coming true day after day. You never let me slack on improvement, whether it's in my writing or as a person. You don't accept half-ass *anything*, and I may not always like the tough love you offer, but I'm forever grateful for it.

To Ashley,
Thank you so much for stepping in at the last minute to provide a second set of eyes on this book. Paragon is a much stronger story because of your help.

To Carly,
You have been such an amazing friend to me in ways that I've never experienced before in my life. Thank you for your support and love. It's mutual, I promise <3

To Mal,
You are the definition of OG superfan, and I was so happy you enjoyed your cameo in Sefaera. No one deserves to spend time with Gabe and Ollie more than you, the person who has been with us from the first portal.

To my own found family (much like Gabe's),
Nathan, Nancy, Kimmi, Rowan. Your acceptance and love have been a lifeline during times of loneliness and uncertainty. You have embraced me as one of your own, seeing the best in me even when I struggled to see it myself, and given me a safe space to be myself. I am eternally grateful for your kindness and belief in me.

Finally, to Chase,
"I only have the capacity to be a good king, a good *man*, because of you."

"I can never make up for the mistakes I made. For the lies I told or the ways I manipulated you. I wish I could regret them more than I do, because each of those mistakes still led you here, to me. But loving you the way I do, I know that I cannot stand to see you in pain because of my actions. And I will spend the rest of eternity trying to prove to you that I am better than who I was before you showed me who I could be...

Until my heart no longer beats."

About the Authors

Eleanor Rose is an emerging author in the fantasy genre, known for dynamic storytelling and the prominent inclusion of queer couples in her narratives. Her commitment to authentic representation is not just limited to her novels; she is also a vocal advocate for accurate portrayals of transgender individuals and those living with Complex Post-Traumatic Stress Disorder (CPTSD).

Eleanor's passion for travel, particularly her explorations across the diverse cultures and landscapes of Europe, greatly influences her writing. These experiences infuse her work with rich descriptions and varied perspectives, adding depth and authenticity to her narratives.

Chase Tyler Kyle St. Clare stands out as a multifaceted creative force, expertly merging his skills as a photographer and a ghostwriter for the renowned Finch Benson. His artistic vision, deeply influenced by the complexities of identity and celebrity, often finds expression in his contemplations about being or being with pop icon Troye Sivan.

In his personal life, Chase, who is openly bisexual, shares his journey with his partner, author August Oliver. Their relationship, steeped in mutual respect and creative synergy, is a testament to their shared dedication to literature and the arts.

August Oliver has carved a niche for himself in the literary world by crafting stories that embrace classic tropes with queer characters, ensuring they are represented authentically without being fetishized. His profound love for fantasy and paranormal genres has been a significant source of inspiration for his diverse and compelling characters.

When he's not immersed in the world of writing, August enjoys spending quality time with his partner, Chase. Together, they explore various interests, including traveling to new destinations, indulging in video games, and experiencing the excitement of live concerts.

Made in the USA
Columbia, SC
27 March 2025